Critical acclaim for David Baldacci's novels

'Baldacci inhabits the skin of his creations –
tripping us up with unexpected empathy and
subtle identification'
Sunday Express

'As expertly plotted as all Baldacci's work'
Sunday Times

'A plot strong enough to make
the bath go cold around you'
Independent on Sunday

'Baldacci is still peerless'
Sunday Times

'Top book! Thrill a minute, page turning stuff'
Sun

'One of the world's biggest-selling thriller writers,
Baldacci needs no introduction . . . Brilliant plotting,
heart-grabbing action and characters to die for'
Daily Mail

The Sixth Man

David Baldacci is the internationally acclaimed author of more than 20 bestselling novels. With his books published in at least 45 languages and in more than 80 countries, and with over 110 million copies in print, he is one of the world's favourite storytellers. His family foundation, the Wish You Well Foundation, a non-profit organization, works to eliminate illiteracy across America. Still a resident of his native Virginia, he invites you to visit him at www.DavidBaldacci.com, and his foundation at www.WishYouWellFoundation.org, and to look into its programme to spread books across America at www.FeedingBodyandMind.com.

Also by David Baldacci

The Camel Club series

The Camel Club
The Collectors
Stone Cold
Divine Justice
Hell's Corner

Sean King and Michelle Maxwell series

Split Second
Hour Game
Simple Genius
First Family

Shaw series

The Whole Truth
Deliver Us From Evil

Other novels

True Blue
Absolute Power
Total Control
The Winner
The Simple Truth
Saving Faith
Wish You Well
Last Man Standing
The Christmas Train
One Summer

DAVID BALDACCI

The Sixth Man

PAN BOOKS

First published 2011 by Grand Central Publishing, USA

First published in Great Britain 2011 by Macmillan
This edition published 2011 by Pan Books
an imprint of Pan Macmillan, a division of Macmillan Publishers Limited
Pan Macmillan, 20 New Wharf Road, London N1 9RR
Basingstoke and Oxford
Associated companies throughout the world
www.panmacmillan.com

ISBN 978-1-4472-5701-1

1 3 5 7 9 8 6 4 2

A CIP catalogue record for this book is available from
the British Library.

Typeset by SetSystems Ltd, Saffron Walden, Essex
Printed and bound by CPI Group (UK) Ltd, Croydon, CR0 4YY

Visit **www.panmacmillan.com** to read more about all our books
and to buy them. You will also find features, author interviews and
news of any author events, and you can sign up for e-newsletters
so that you're always first to hear about our new releases.

To David Young and Jamie Raab,
the dynamic duo of publishing and my friends

The only thing potentially worse than not being able to see the forest for the trees is not being able to see the trees because of the forest.

– Anonymous

The Sixth Man

PROLOGUE

"Make it stop!"

The man hunched over the cold metal table, his body curled tight, eyes screwed shut, his voice cracking. He sucked in each breath and let it out like it would be his last. Through headphones a fast blast of words filled his ear canals and then flooded his brain. An array of sensors was strapped into a heavy cloth harness that was buckled over his torso. He also wore a cap with electrodes attached that measured his brain waves. The room was brightly lit.

With each bite of audio and broadside of video his body clenched as though staggered by a shot delivered by the heavyweight champ.

He started weeping.

In an adjacent and darkened room a small group of stunned men watched this scene through a one-way mirror.

On the wall inside the room with the sobbing man the screen was eight feet wide and six feet tall. It seemed perfectly designed for watching NFL football. However, the digital images racing across its face were not huge men in uniform knocking brain cells out of each other. This was top-top-secret data to which very few people in the government would be privy.

Collectively, and to the experienced eye, they were remarkable in revealing the clandestine activities going on around the globe.

There were crystal clear pictures of suspicious troop movements in Korea along the Thirty-Eighth Parallel.

Satellite images of construction projects in Iran showing underground missile silos that looked like huge pencil holders carved in the dirt, along with boiling thermal silhouettes of a working nuclear reactor.

In Pakistan, high-altitude surveillance photos of the aftermath of a terrorist explosion at a market where vegetables and body parts held equal sections of the ground.

In Russia, there was real-time video of a caravan of military trucks on a mission that might push the world into another global war.

From India flowed data on a terrorist cell planning simultaneous hits on sensitive targets in an effort to promote regional unrest.

In New York City, incriminating photos of a major political leader with someone who was not his wife.

From Paris, reams of numbers and names representing financial intelligence on criminal enterprises. They moved so fast they seemed like a million columns of Sudoku delivered at hyperspeed.

From China, there was clandestine intelligence on a possible coup against the country's leadership.

From thousands of federally funded intelligence fusion centers spread across the United States flowed information on suspicious activities being carried out either by Americans or by foreigners operating domestically.

From the Five Eye allies—United States, Britain, Canada, Australia, and New Zealand—a compilation of top secret communications, all of colossal importance.

And on it poured, from all corners of the globe, delivered en masse in high definition.

If it were an Xbox or a PS3 game it would be the most exciting and difficult one ever created. But there was nothing made up about it. Here real people lived and real people died, every second of every day.

This exercise was known, in the topmost echelon of the intelligence community, as the "Wall."

The man hunched over the metal table was small and lean. His skin was light brown, his hair short and black and plastered to his small skull. His eyes were large, and red from the tears. He was thirty-one years old but looked like he had aged ten years in the last four hours.

"Please, make it stop. I can't take this. I can't *do* this."

At this comment the tallest man behind the mirror

stirred. His name was Peter Bunting. He was forty-seven years old and this was, plain and simple, his operation, his ambition, his life. He lived and breathed it. At no time did at least part of his brain think of anything else. His hair had grayed considerably over the last six months for reasons tied directly to the Wall, or more specifically, problems with the Wall.

He wore a custom-fitted jacket, shirt, and slacks. Though he had an athlete's body he had never played competitive sports and wasn't particularly coordinated. What he did have was an abundance of brains and an inexhaustible desire to succeed. He'd graduated from college at age nineteen, held a postgraduate degree from Stanford, and had been a Rhodes scholar. He had the perfect blend of strategic vision and street smarts. He was wealthy and well connected, though he was unknown to the public. He had many reasons to be happy, and merely one to be frustrated, angry even. And he was staring at it right now.

Or rather at *him*.

Bunting looked down at the electronic tablet he was holding. He had asked the man numerous questions, the answers for which could be found in the data flow. He hadn't gotten a single response. "Please tell me this is someone's screwed-up idea of a joke," he finally said. Only he knew it wasn't. People here did not kid about anything.

An older, shorter man in a wrinkled dress shirt

spread his hands in a gesture of helplessness. "The problem is he's classified as an E-Five, Mr. Bunting."

"Well, this Five ain't cutting it, obviously," shot back Bunting.

They turned to look through the glass once more as the man in the room ripped off the headphones and screamed, "I want out. Now. No one said it would be like this."

Bunting dropped his tablet on a table and slumped against the wall. The man in the room was Sohan Sharma. He had been their last, best hope to fill the position of the Analyst. Analyst with a capital A. There was only one.

"Sir?" said the youngest man in the group. He was barely thirty, but his long and unruly hair and his boyish features made him appear far younger. His Adam's apple skittered nervously up and down like an elevator stuck shuttling between floors.

Bunting rubbed his temples. "I'm listening, Avery." He paused to crunch some Tums. "Just make it important. I'm a little stressed, as I'm sure you can tell."

"Sharma *is* a true Five by every acceptable measure. It was only when he got to the Wall that he fell apart." He glanced at the bank of computer screens that was monitoring Sharma's vitals and brain functions. "His theta activity has spiked through the roof. Classic extreme information overload. It began one minute after we cranked the Wall's throughput to max."

5

"Yeah, that part I figured out for myself." Bunting motioned to Sharma, who was now on the floor weeping. "But a legit Five and this is the result we get? How is that possible?"

Avery said, "The chief problem is there's exponentially more data being thrown at the Analyst. Ten thousand hours of video. A hundred thousand reports. Four million incident registers. The daily satellite imagery collection is in the multiple terabytes, and that's *after* it's been filtered. Captured signals intelligence requiring attention are in the thousands of hours. Combat field chatter alone could fill a thousand phone books. It pours in every second of every day in ever-increasing amounts from a million different sources. Compared to the data available only twenty years ago it's like taking a thimble of water and transforming it into a million Pacific Oceans. With the last Analyst we'd been ratcheting down the data flow considerably simply out of necessity."

"So what exactly are you telling me, Avery?" Bunting asked.

The young man drew a rapid breath. The expression on his face was like a man in the water who'd just realized he might be drowning.

"We may have bumped up against the limits of the human mind."

Bunting looked around at the others. None of them would meet his eye. Electrical currents seemed to pop in the damp air thrown off from the sweat on their faces.

"There is nothing more powerful than a fully utilized, fully deployable human brain," said Bunting in a deliberately calm tone. "I wouldn't last ten seconds against the Wall because I'm using maybe eleven percent of my gray cells—that's all I can manage. But an E-Five makes Einstein's brain look like a fetus's. Not even a Cray Supercomputer comes close. It's quantum computing with flesh and bone. It can operate linearly, spatially, geometrically, in every dimension we need it to. It is the perfect analytical mechanism."

"I understand that, sir, but—"

Bunting's voice grew more strident. "That's been proven in every study we've ever done. That is the gospel upon which rests everything we do here. And more importantly, that is what our *two-point-five-billion-dollar contract* says we have to provide and that every last son of a bitch in the intelligence community depends on. I've told this to the president of the United States and every person down the power chain from him. And now you're telling me it's not true?"

Avery stood his ground. "The universe may be constantly expanding, but there are limits to everything else." He gestured to the room beyond the glass where Sharma was still weeping. "And that may be what we're looking at right now. The absolute limit."

Bunting said grimly, "If what you're saying is true, then we are screwed beyond belief. The whole civilized world is screwed. We're toast. History. Done. The bad guys win. Let's all go home and wait for

Armageddon. Hail to the Taliban and al Qaeda, the bastards. Game-set-match. They win."

"I understand your frustration, sir. But ignoring the obvious is never a good plan."

"Then get me a Six."

The young man looked stunned. "There's no such thing as a Six."

"Bullshit! That's what we thought about Two through Five."

"But still—"

"Find me a damn Six. No arguments, no excuses. Just do it, Avery."

The Adam's apple cratered. "Yes, sir."

The older man said, "What about Sharma?"

Bunting turned to look at the sobbing, failed Analyst. "Do the exit process, have him sign all the usual documents, and make clear to him that if he says one word about this to anyone he will be charged with treason and he'll spend the rest of his life in a federal prison."

Bunting left. The cascade of images finally stopped and the room grew dark.

Sohan Sharma was walked out to a waiting van. Inside were three men. After Sharma climbed in, one of the men slid an arm around Sharma's neck and another around his head. He jerked his thick arms in different directions and Sharma slumped over with a broken neck.

The van drove off with the body of the pure E-Five whose brain simply wasn't good enough anymore.

NINE MONTHS LATER

1

The small jet bumped down hard on the runway in Portland, Maine. It rose up in the air and banged down again harder. Even the pilot was probably wondering if he could keep the twenty-five-ton jet on the tarmac. Because he was trying to beat a storm in, the young aviator had made his approach at a steeper trajectory and a faster speed than the airline's manual recommended. The wind shear culled off the leading edge of the cold front had caused the jet's wings to pendulum back and forth. The copilot had warned the passengers that the landing would be bumpy and a bit more than uncomfortable.

He'd been right.

The rear carriage wheels caught and held the second time around, and the lead aircraft-grade rubber bit down a few moments later. The rapid and steep flight path in had caused more than a few of the four dozen passengers on the single-aisle jet to white-knuckle their armrests, mouth a few prayers, and even reach for the barf bags in the seatbacks. When the wheel brakes and reverse thrusters engaged and the aircraft slowed perceptibly, most of the riders exhaled in relief.

One man, however, merely woke when the plane transitioned off the runway and onto the taxiway to the small terminal. The tall, dark-haired woman sitting next to him idly stared out the window, completely unfazed by the turbulent approach and bouncy touchdown.

After they'd arrived at the gate and the pilot shut down the twin GE turbofans, Sean King and Michelle Maxwell rose and grabbed their bags from the overhead. As they threaded out through the narrow aisle along with the other deplaning passengers, a queasy-looking woman behind them said, "Boy, that sure was a rough landing."

Sean looked at her, yawned, and massaged his neck. "Was it?"

The woman looked surprised and eyed Michelle. "Is he kidding?"

She said, "When you've ridden on jump seats in the belly of a C-17 at low altitudes in the middle of a thunderstorm and doing thousand-foot vertical drops every ten seconds with four max-armored vehicles chained next to you and wondering if one was going to break loose and crash through the side of the fuselage and carry you with it, this landing was pretty uneventful."

"Why in the world did you do that?" said the wide-eyed woman.

"I ask myself that every day," replied Sean sardonically.

He and Michelle both had their clothes, toiletries, and other essentials in their carry-on bags. But they had to stop by baggage claim to pick up an eighteen-inch-long, hard-sided, locked case. It belonged to Michelle. She picked up the case and slid it into her carry-on.

Sean gave her an amused expression. "You're the queen of the smallest checked bag of all time."

"Until they let responsible people on planes with loaded guns, it'll have to do the trick. Get the rental. I'll be back in a minute."

"You licensed to carry that up here?"

"Let's hope we don't have to find out."

He blanched. "You're kidding, right?"

"Maine has an open carry law. So long as it's visible I can carry it without a permit."

"But you're putting it in a holster. That's concealed. In fact, it's concealed right now."

She flipped open her wallet and showed him a card. "Which is why I have a valid nonresident's concealed weapon's permit for the great state of Maine."

"How'd you score that? We only found out about this case a few days ago. You couldn't have gotten a permit that fast. I checked into it. It's a mountain of paperwork and a sixty-day response period."

"My dad is good friends with the governor. I made a call to him. He made a call to the governor."

"Nice."

She went to the ladies' room, entered a stall, opened the locked case, and quickly loaded her pistol. She holstered her weapon and walked to the covered parking garage adjacent to the terminal where the rental car companies were clustered. There she found Sean filling out the paperwork for the wheels they needed for the next phase of their trip. Michelle showed her operator's license as well, since she would be doing most of the driving. It wasn't that Sean minded driving, but Michelle was too much of a control freak to let him.

"Coffee," she said. "There's a place back in the terminal."

"You had that giant cup you brought on the flight."

"That was a while ago. And where we're going is a long drive from here. I need the caffeine pop."

"I slept. I can drive."

She snagged the keys from his hand. "Don't think so."

"Hey, I drove the Beast, okay?" he said, referring to the presidential limo.

She eyed the rental car tag. "Then the Ford Hybrid you reserved will be no challenge. It'll probably take me a day just to get it up to sixty. I'll spare you the pain and humiliation."

She got an extra-large black coffee. Sean bought a donut with sprinkles and sat in the passenger seat eating it. He dusted off his hands and moved the seat back as far as possible in the compact car, and still his six-foot-two-inch frame was bent uncomfortably. He finally ended up putting his feet on the dash.

Noting this, Michelle said, "Air bag pops out of there, it'll smash your feet right through the glass and amputate them when they hit the metal roof."

He glanced at her, a frown eclipsing his normally calm features. "Then don't do anything to make it pop."

"I can't control other drivers."

"Well, you insisted on being the wheelman—excuse me, wheel-person. So do the best you can to keep me safe and comfortable."

"All right, master," she snapped.

After a mile of silence Michelle said, "We sound like an old married couple."

He looked at her again. "We're not old and we're not married. Unless you really slipped something by me."

She hesitated and then just said it: "But we have slept together."

Sean started to reply but then seemed to think better of it. What came out instead seemed to be a grunt.

"It changes things," she said.

"Why does it change things?"

"It's not just business anymore. It's personal. The line has been crossed."

He sat up straight, removing his feet from the perilous reach of the air bag. "And now you regret that? You made the first move, if I recall. You got naked on me."

"I didn't say that I regretted anything, because I don't."

"Neither do I. It happened because we obviously both wanted it to happen."

"Okay. So where does that leave us?"

He sat back against his seat and stared out the window. "I'm not sure."

"Great, just what I wanted to hear."

He looked across at her, noted the tense line of muscle and bone around her jaw.

"Just because I'm unsure of where to go with all this, doesn't lessen or trivialize what happened between us. It's complicated."

"Right, complicated. That's always the case. For the *guy*."

"Okay, if it's so simple for the ladies, tell me what you think we should do."

When she didn't answer he said, "Should we run off and find a preacher and make it official?"

She shot him a glance and the front end of the Ford swerved slightly. "Are you serious? Is that what you want?"

"I'm just throwing out ideas. Since you don't seem to have any."

"Do you want to get married?"

"Do you?"

"That would really change things."

"Uh, yeah, it would."

"Maybe we should take it slow."

"Maybe we should."

She tapped the steering wheel. "Sorry for jumping on you about this."

"Forget it. And we just got Gabriel squared away with a great family. That was a big change, too. Slow is good right now. We go too fast, maybe we make a big mistake."

Gabriel was an eleven-year-old boy from Alabama that Sean and Michelle had taken temporary custody of after his mother was killed. He was currently living with a family whose dad was an FBI agent they knew. The couple was in the process of formally adopting Gabriel.

"Okay," she replied.

"And now we have a job to do. Let's focus on that."

"So that's your priority list? Business trumps personal?"

"Not necessarily. But like you said, it's a long drive. And I want to think about why we're heading to the only federal maximum security institution for the criminally insane in the country, to meet with a guy whose life is definitely on the line."

"We're going because you and his lawyer go way back."

"That part I get. Did you read up on Edgar Roy?"

Michelle nodded. "Government employee that lived

alone in rural Virginia. His life was pretty average until the police discovered the remains of six people buried in his barn. Then his life became anything but average. The evidence to me seems overwhelming."

Sean nodded. "Roy was found in his barn, shovel in hand, dirt on his pants, with the remains of six bodies buried in a hole he was apparently putting the finishing touches to."

"A little tough to dance around that in court," said Michelle.

"Too bad Roy's not a politician."

"Why?"

Sean smiled. "If he were a politician he could spin that story to say he was actually digging them out of the hole in order to save them but was too late; they were already dead. And now he's being persecuted for being a Good Samaritan."

"So he was arrested but failed a competency hearing. He was sent to Cutter's Rock." She paused. "But why Maine? Virginia didn't have the facilities for him?"

"It was a federal case for some reason. That got the FBI involved. When the competency remand comes it's wherever the Feds decide to send you. Some Fed max prison facilities have psych wards, but it was decided that Roy needed something more than that. St. Elizabeth's in D.C. was moved to make way for a new Homeland Security HQ, and its new location was not deemed secure enough. So Cutter's Rock was the only game in town."

"Why the weird name?"

"It's rocky, and a cutter is a type of ship. Maine is a seafaring state, after all."

"I forgot you were a nautical guy." She turned on the radio and the heater, and shivered. "God, it's cold for not being winter yet," she said grumpily.

"This is Maine. It can be cold any time of the year. Check the latitude."

"The things one learns in enclosed spaces over long periods of time."

"Now we *do* sound like an old married couple." He turned his vent on full blast, zipped up his windbreaker, and closed his eyes.

2

With Michelle's foot typically heavy on the gas the Ford raced along Interstate 95, past the towns of Yarmouth and Brunswick and on toward the state capital in Augusta. Once past Augusta, with the next big town coming up being Bangor, Michelle began eyeing the surroundings. There were dense evergreen trees on either side of the highway. A full moon gave the forests a silvery veneer that made Michelle think of wax paper over salad greens. They passed a warning sign for moose crossing the highway.

"Moose?" she said, glancing at Sean.

He didn't open his eyes. "Maine's state animal. You don't want to hit one. They weigh more than this Ford. And they have nasty tempers. Kill you in a heartbeat."

"How do you know? Have you ever encountered one?"

"No, but I'm a big fan of Animal Planet."

They drove on for another hour. Michelle continually scanned the area, left to right and back the other way, like a human radar. It was a habit so drilled into her that even after being out of the Secret Service all this time she couldn't shake it. But as a private investigator maybe she didn't want to shake it. Observations made you forewarned. And being forewarned was never a bad thing, particularly if someone was trying to kill you, which people often seemed to want to do to her and Sean.

"There's something wrong here," she said.

Sean opened his eyes. "Like what?" he asked, doing his own quick scan.

"We're on Interstate 95. Runs from Florida to Maine. Long stretch of asphalt. Big travel route. Pipeline of East Coast vacationers."

"Right, so?"

"So we're the only fricking car on it in either direction, and have been for at least a half hour. What, was there a nuclear war and no one told us?" Her finger hit the scan button on the radio. "I need news. I need civilization. I need to know we're not the only ones left alive."

"Will you chill? It's just isolated up here. Interstate or not. Lots of space, not lots of people. Most of the population lives near the coast, Portland, back where we came from. The rest of the state is big on land and pretty low on human beings. Hell, Aroostook County is bigger than Rhode Island and Connecticut combined. In fact, Maine is as large as all the other New England states put together. And once we get past Bangor and keep heading north, it gets even more isolated. The interstate stops near the town of Houlton. Then you take Route 1 the rest of the way up towards the northern tip of the Canadian border."

"What's up there?"

"Places like Presque Isle, Fort Kent, and Madawaska."

"And moose?"

"I suppose. Lucky we're not going there. It's really far."

"Couldn't we have flown into Bangor? They have an airport, right? Or Augusta?"

"No direct flights. Most of the available flights had two or three stops. One took us all the way south to Orlando before heading north. We could have flown out of Baltimore, but we'd have to connect through LaGuardia and that's always dicey. And we would have still had to drive to Baltimore, and 95 can be a nightmare. It's faster and more certain this way."

"You're just a fountain of useful facts. You've been to Maine much?"

"One of the former presidents I protected has a summer place up here."

"Bush Forty-One at Walker's Point?"

"You got it."

"But that's southern coastal Maine. Kennebunkport. We flew over it going into Portland."

"Beautiful area. We'd follow Bush in our chase boat. Could never keep up with him. Guy's fearless. Has over eight hundred HP spread over three Mercury outboards on a thirty-two-footer named the *Fidelity III*. Man loved to go full throttle in the open Atlantic in pretty heavy chop. I rode in the Zodiac chase boat trying to keep up with him. Only time I've ever puked on duty."

"But that area's not as isolated as this," said Michelle.

"No, lot more humanity down there." He looked at his watch. "And it's late. Most people up here probably rise at dawn to go to work. That means they're probably already in bed." He yawned. "Like I wish I was."

Michelle checked the GPS. "Around Bangor we get off the interstate and head east to the coast."

He nodded. "In between the towns of Machias and Eastport. Right on the water. Lot of back roads. Not easy to get to, which makes sense because then it's not easy to get away from if a homicidal maniac has managed to escape."

"Has anyone ever escaped from Cutter's Rock?"

"Not to my knowledge. And if they ever did, they'd have two options: the wilderness or the chilly waters of the Gulf of Maine. Neither one is too palatable. And Mainers are hardy folk. Probably not even homicidal maniacs would want to cross them."

"So we're hooking up with Bergin tonight?"

"Yep. At the inn where we're staying." Sean checked his watch. "In about two and a half hours. Then we see Roy at ten tomorrow morning."

"So how do you know Bergin again?"

"He was my law professor at UVA. Great guy. Was in private practice before he started teaching. Few years after I graduated he hung his shingle back out. Defense lawyer, obviously. Has an office in Charlottesville."

"How'd he end up repping a psycho like Edgar Roy?"

"He specializes in hopeless cases, I guess. But he's a first-rate attorney. I don't know what his connection is to Roy. I'm assuming he'll fill us in on that, too."

"And you never did elaborate on why Bergin engaged us."

"I didn't elaborate because I'm not quite sure. He called, said he was making headway in Roy's case and needed some investigation done by people he could trust in preparation for taking the case to trial."

"What sort of headway? From my reading of the case they're only waiting for him to get his mind back so they can convict him and then execute him."

"I don't profess to understand what Bergin's theory is. He didn't want to discuss it on the phone."

Michelle shrugged. "I guess we'll find out soon enough."

They left the interstate, and Michelle steered the Ford east along increasingly poor and windy surface roads. As they neared the ocean waters, the briny smell invaded the car.

"Fishy, my favorite," she said sarcastically.

"Get used to that smell. It'll be everywhere up here."

She calculated they were about thirty minutes from their destination along a particularly lonely patch of road when the silvery night was broken by another set of car lights. Only they weren't on the road. They were on the shoulder. Michelle automatically slowed as Sean rolled down his window for a better look.

"Flashers," he said. "Somebody's broken down."

"Should we pull over?"

He debated this. "I suppose. They might not even be able to get cell reception up here." He poked his head out for a better look. "It's a Buick. I doubt someone would use a Buick to lure unsuspecting motorists into a trap."

Michelle touched the gun in its holster. "I doubt we qualify as unsuspecting motorists."

She slowed the Ford and pulled in behind the other car. The hazard lights blinked off and on, off and on. In the vastness of coastal Maine it looked like a small conflagration stuck in the limbo of fits and starts.

"Somebody's in the driver's seat," noted Michelle, as she put the Ford in park. "Only person I can see."

"Then he might be worried about us. I'll get out and put the person at ease."

"I've got your back in case someone's hiding in the floorboard and they don't want to be put at ease."

He swung his long legs out and approached the car slowly from the passenger's side. His feet crunched over the sparse shoulder gravel. His breath came out as puffs of smoke in the chilled air. From somewhere

25

among the trees he heard an animal's call and briefly wondered if it was a moose. Animal Planet hadn't been clear on what a moose actually sounded like. And Sean had no interest in finding out for himself.

He called out, "Do you need any help?"

Blink, blink of the hazard lights. No response.

He looked down at his cell phone clutched in his hand. *He* had reception bars. "Are you broken down? Do you want us to call a tow truck for you?"

Nothing. He reached the car, tapped on the side window. "Hello? You okay?"

He saw the silhouette of the driver through the window. It was a man. "Sir, you okay?" The guy didn't budge.

Sean's next thought was a medical emergency. Maybe a heart attack. A marine haze had obscured the moonlight. It was so dark inside the car he couldn't make out many details. He heard a car door open and turned back to see Michelle climb out of their ride, her hand on the butt of her weapon. She glanced at him for communication.

"I think the guy's in medical distress."

She nodded and moved forward; her boots made clicks on the asphalt.

Sean eased around to the driver's side and tapped on the window. In the darkness all he could see was the man's outline. The red light from the flashers lit the interior of the car, casting the surroundings into a bright crimson before going dark again, like the car was heating up one second and going cool the next. But it didn't help Sean see inside the car. It only made it more difficult. He tapped on the glass once more.

"Sir? Are you all right?"

He tried the door. It was unlocked. He opened it. The man slumped sideways, held in the car only by his seat harness. Sean grabbed the man's shoulder and righted him as Michelle rushed forward.

"Heart attack?" she said.

Sean looked at the man's face. "No," he said firmly.

"How do you know?"

He used the light from his cell phone to illuminate the single gunshot wound between the man's pupils. There was blood and grayish brain matter all over the car's interior.

Michelle drew closer and said, "Contact wound. You can see the gun's muzzle and sight mark burned onto his skin. Don't think a moose did that."

Sean said nothing.

"Check his wallet for some ID."

"Don't have to."

"Why not?" she asked.

"Because I know him," replied Sean.

"What? Who is he?"

"Ted Bergin. My old professor and Edgar Roy's lawyer."

3

The local police showed up first. A single Washington County deputy in a dented and dusty but serviceable American-made V8 with an array of communication antennas drilled into the trunk. He came out of the cruiser with one hand on his service weapon and his gaze fastened on Sean and Michelle. He warily approached. They explained what had happened and he checked the body, muttered the word "Damn," and then hastily called in backup.

Fifteen minutes later two Maine State Police cruisers from Field Troop J slid to stops behind them. The troopers, young, tall, and lean, came out of their aquamarine cars; their crisp blue uniforms seemed to glow like colored ice even in the weak, hazy light. The crime scene was secured and a perimeter guard established. Sean and Michelle were interviewed by the troopers. One of the officers pecked the responses into the portable laptop he'd yanked from his cruiser.

When Sean told them who they were and why they were here, and, more important, who Ted Bergin was and that he represented Edgar Roy, one of the troopers walked away and used his handheld mic to presumably call in more assets. As they waited for reinforcements, Sean said, "You guys know about Edgar Roy?"

One of them replied, "Everybody around here knows about Edgar Roy."

Michelle said, "Why's that?"

The other trooper said, "FBI will be here quick as they can."

"FBI?" exclaimed Sean.

The trooper nodded. "Roy's a federal prisoner. We got clear instructions from Washington. Anything happens with him, they get called in. That's what I just did. Well, I told the lieutenant and he's calling it in."

"Where's the closest FBI Field Office?" asked Michelle.

"Boston."

"Boston? But we're in Maine."

"FBI doesn't maintain an official office in Maine. It all goes through Boston, Mass."

Sean said, "It's a long way to Boston. Do we have to stay until they get here? We're both pretty beat."

"Our lieutenant is on the way. You can talk to him about it."

Twenty minutes later the lieutenant arrived and he was not sympathetic. "Just sit tight" was all he said before turning away from them to confer with his men and look over the crime scene.

The Evidence Response Team arrived a couple of minutes later, all ready to bag and tag. Sean and

Michelle sat on the hood of their Ford and watched the process. Bergin was officially pronounced dead by what Sean assumed was a coroner or medical examiner—he couldn't recall what system Maine used. They gleaned from snatched bits of conversation among the techs and troopers that the bullet was still in the dead man's head.

"No exit wound, contact round, small-caliber gun probably," noted Michelle.

"But still deadly," replied Sean.

"Any contact wound to the head usually is. Crack the skull, soft brain tissue pulverized by the kinetic energy wave, massive hemorrhaging followed by organ shutdown. All happens in a few seconds. Dead."

"I know the process, thanks," he replied dryly.

As they sat there they could see the members of the Maine constabulary look over at them from time to time.

"Are we suspects?" asked Michelle.

"Everybody's a suspect until they're not."

Some time later the lieutenant came back over to them. "The colonel is on his way."

"And who is the colonel?" asked Michelle politely.

"Chief of the Maine State Police, ma'am."

"Okay. But we've given our statements," she said.

"So you two knew the deceased?"

"I did," answered Sean.

"And you were following him up here?"

"We weren't following him. I explained it to your troopers. We were meeting him up here."

"I'd appreciate if you could explain it to me, sir."

Okay, we are *suspects*, thought Sean.

He went through their travel steps.

"So you're saying you didn't know he was here? But you just happened to be the first ones on the scene?"

Sean said, "That's right."

The man tilted his wide-brimmed hat back. "I personally don't like coincidences."

"I don't either," said Sean. "But they sometimes happen. And there aren't a lot of homes or people around here. He was going to the same place we were, using the same road. And it's late. If any one was going to happen on him, it would probably be us."

"So not such a big coincidence after all," added Michelle.

The man didn't appear to be listening. He was looking at the bulge under her jacket. His hand went to his sidearm and he gave a low whistle, which brought five of his men instantly to his side.

He said, "Ma'am, are you carrying a weapon?"

The other officers tensed. Sean could tell in the fearful looks of the first two troopers on the scene that there would be hell to pay later for them missing such an obvious fact.

"I am," she said.

"Why didn't my men know this?"

He gave a prolonged look at the two troopers who had turned about as pale as the moon.

"They didn't ask," she replied.

The lieutenant drew his pistol. A moment later a total of six guns were pointed at Sean and Michelle. All kill shots.

"Hold on," said Sean. "She has a permit. And the gun hasn't been fired."

"Both of you put your hands on your heads, fingers interlocked. Now."

They did so.

Michelle's gun was taken and examined, and they were both searched for other weapons.

"Full load, sir," said one of the troopers to the lieutenant. "Hasn't been recently fired."

"Yeah, well, we don't know how long the man's been dead, either. And it's only one bullet. Just replace it to make a full clip. Easy enough."

"I didn't shoot him," Michelle said firmly.

"And if we did, do you think we would have hung around and called the police?" added Sean.

"Not for me to decide," said the lieutenant, who handed Michelle's gun to one of his men. "Bag and tag."

"I do have a permit to carry it," said Michelle.

"Let me see it."

She handed it to him and his gaze ran swiftly over

it before he handed it back. "Permit or not, doesn't matter if you used the weapon to shoot that man."

"The deceased has a small-caliber entry wound with no exit," said Michelle. "An intermediate range shot would have left powder grains tattooing the skin. Here the powder was obviously blown into the wound track. The muzzle end was burned into his skin. Looks to be a .22 or maybe a .32-caliber. The latter's an eight-millimeter footprint. My weapon would have left a hole nearly fifty percent bigger than that. In fact, if I'd shot him at contact range, the round would have blown through his brain *and* the headrest and probably shattered the back window and kept going for about a mile."

"I know the weapon's capabilities, ma'am," he said. "It's an H&K .45—that's what we use in the state police."

"Actually, mine is an enhanced version of the one you guys just pointed at us."

"Enhanced? How?"

"Your weapon is an older and more basic model. My H&K is more ergonomic and it's got a ten-round mag box versus your twelve because of the restyling. Textured, finger-grooved grip and back-straps let it sit lower in the hand web, translating to better control and recoil management. Then there's an extended ambidextrous slide, a universal Picatinny rail instead of the H&K proprietary USP rail for accessories that you have. And it has an O-ring polygonal barrel. It'll drop pretty much anything on two feet all in a compact twenty-eight-ounce model. And it's built right across the border in New Hampshire."

"You know a lot about guns, *ma'am?*"

"She's an aficionado," replied Sean, seeing the look of growing anger in his partner's eyes at the officer's condescending tone.

"Why?" she said. "Are girls not supposed to know about guns?"

The lieutenant abruptly grinned, took off his hat, and swiped a hand through his blond hair. "Hell, in this part of Maine pretty much everybody knows how to use a gun. My little sister's always been a better shot than me, in fact."

"There you go," said Michelle, her anger quickly receding at his frank admission. "And you can swab my hands for gunshot residue. You won't find any."

"Could've worn gloves," he pointed out.

"I could've done a lot of things. You want to do the GSR or not?" He motioned to one of the techs, who performed the test on both Michelle and Sean and did the analysis on the spot.

"Clean," he said.

"Wow, how about that," said Michelle.

The lieutenant said, "So you two are private investigators?" Sean nodded. "Bergin engaged us to help with the Edgar Roy case."

"Help with what? Man's as guilty as they come."

"Just like you said, not for us to decide," said Sean.

"You licensed in Maine?"

"We've filed the paperwork and paid the fee," said Sean. "Waiting to hear back."

"So that's a no? You're not licensed?"

"Well, we haven't done any investigative work yet. Just found out about the job. We filed as fast as we could. The jurisdictions where we're licensed have reciprocity with Maine. It's just a formality. We'll get the approval."

"People looking to be PIs need some sort of special background. What's yours? Military? Law enforcement?"

"United States Secret Service," said Sean.

The lieutenant eyed Sean and then Michelle with a new level of respect. His men did the same.

"Both of you?"

Sean nodded.

"Ever guard the president?"

"Sean did," said Michelle. "I never got to the White House before I left the Service."

"Why'd you leave?"

Sean and Michelle exchanged brief glances.

Sean said, "Had enough. Wanted to do something else."

"Fair enough."

Forty-five minutes later another car pulled up. The

35

lieutenant looked over and said, "That's Colonel Mayhew. Must've put the pedal to the metal, think he was over near Skowhegan tonight."

He hurried off to greet his commander in chief. The colonel was tall and broad shouldered. Though in his fifties, he had retained his trim figure. His eyes were calm and alert, his manner brisk and businesslike. He looked, Sean thought, like a Hollywood-inspired poster for police recruitment.

He was briefed on the situation, took a look at the body, then came over to them. After introductions Mayhew said, "When was the last time you had contact with Mr. Bergin?"

"Phone call earlier today, around five thirty p.m. A little while before we got on the plane."

"What did he say?"

"That he was going to meet us at the B-and-B where we're staying."

"And where is that?"

"Martha's Inn near Machias."

The colonel nodded approvingly. "It's comfortable, food's good."

"Nice to hear," said Michelle.

"Anything else from Bergin? E-mails? Texts?"

"Nothing. I checked before we got on the plane. And then when we landed. I tried calling him around nine o'clock but he didn't answer. It went right to voice mail and I left a message. Any idea how long he's been dead?"

The colonel ignored this. "See any other cars?"

Sean said, "None, other than Bergin's. Pretty lonely stretch of road. And we didn't see any evidence of another car having pulled up to his, although unless it leaked some fluid there probably wouldn't be leave-behind trace."

"So you have no idea where he might have been going tonight?"

"Well, I presume he was going to meet us at Martha's Inn."

"Do you know where Bergin was staying? At Martha's?"

"No, she didn't have any more rooms, apparently." Sean searched his pockets and pulled out his notebook. He flipped through some pages.

"Gray's Lodge. That's where he was staying."

"Right, know that one too. It's closer to Eastport. Not as nice as Martha's place."

"I guess you get around," said Michelle.

"I guess I do," replied the colonel impassively. He looked over at the car. "Only thing is, if Bergin were coming from the direction of Eastport, his car would have been going in the opposite direction. You were coming from the southwest. Eastport is to the north and east. And he never would have come this far. The turnoff for Martha's is five miles further on this road."

Sean looked over at the vehicle and then at the colonel. "I don't know what to tell you. That's how we found him. Car was pointed the same way as ours."

"Complicated," said the lawman.

Sean looked over as a black Escalade screeched to a stop and four people in FBI windbreakers literally leaped out. The federal cavalry from Boston had just arrived.

And it's about to get a lot more complicated, he thought.

4

The lead agent's name was Brandon Murdock. He was about Michelle's height, a couple inches under six feet and rail-thin, but his grip was surprisingly strong. His hair was thick but cut to FBI standards. His eyebrows were caterpillar-sized. His voice was deep and his manner was compact, efficient. He was briefed first by the lieutenant. He then spent a few private minutes with Colonel Mayhew, who was the highest-ranked Maine police representative on-site. He checked out the body and the car. Then he walked over to Sean and Michelle.

"Sean King and Michelle Maxwell," he said.

Something in his tone made Michelle remark, "You've heard of us?"

"Scuttlebutt from D.C. makes its way up north."

"Really?" said Sean.

"Special Agent Chuck Waters and I went to the Academy together, still keep in touch."

"He's a good guy."

"Yes he is." Murdock glanced over at the car. The chitchat was over. "So what can you tell me?"

Sean said, "Dead guy. Single GSW to the head. He

was up here repping Edgar Roy. Maybe somebody didn't like that."

Murdock nodded. "Or it could've been a random thing."

"Any money or valuables missing?" asked Michelle.

The lieutenant answered. "Not that we can tell. Wallet, watch, and phone intact."

"Probably not random, then."

"And he might've known his attacker," said Sean.

"Why do you think that?" asked Murdock quickly.

"The driver's side window."

"What about it?"

Sean motioned to the car. "You mind?"

They trooped over to the Buick.

While they all looked on, Sean pointed to the window and then to the body. "Entry head wound, lot of blood splatter. No exit wound, so all the blood was driven out of the front of his head. It would have been a gusher. The steering wheel, Bergin, dashboard, seat, and the windshield all have splatters. I even got some on my hands when I opened the car door and he slumped out." He pointed to the clear window. "But not here."

"Because it was lowered when the shot was fired," said Michelle, as Murdock nodded.

"And then the killer raised it back up because obviously Bergin couldn't," said Murdock. "Why?"

"Don't know. It was dark, so he might not have noticed that the window was clean, or else he could have smeared some blood on it to throw us off. But blood splatters have reached such a level of forensic sophistication now that the police would see right through something like that. And maybe the shooter also initiated the flashers, to make us think Bergin had broken down or stopped of his own accord. But if you pull off and lower your car window on a lonely road at this time of night? Well, that's very telling."

"You're right. That means you know the person," said Murdock. "Good observation."

Sean eyed the troopers. "Well, there could be another explanation. The person who stopped him might have been in uniform."

To a man, all the state troopers angrily stared back at him. Mayhew said indignantly, "It wasn't one of my men, I can tell you that."

The county officer said, "And I'm the only unit in this sector tonight. And I sure as hell didn't shoot the man."

"I'm not accusing anyone," said Sean.

Murdock said, "But he is right. It could have been someone in uniform."

"Only an imposter," amended Michelle.

"Hard to pull off up here," said Mayhew. "Getting the uniform, police cruiser. And they could have been seen. Big risk."

"It's still something we have to check out," said Murdock.

"How long has he been dead?" asked Sean.

Murdock glanced at one of the Maine forensic techs. The person said, "Best guess right now, about four hours. We'll have a firmer number after the post."

Sean checked his watch. "That means we missed the killer by about thirty minutes. We saw no car pass us, so whoever did it must've gone the other way or else turned off the road."

"Unless they were on foot," said Murdock, looking around at the dark countryside. "But if it was an imposter in uniform they would've been in a car. I doubt Bergin would have stopped just because he saw someone in a uniform walking down the road."

Mayhew cleared his throat. "My men did a perimeter search in all directions. Found nothing. We'll be able to do a far more thorough search in the morning."

"What's the closest road to here?" asked Sean.

"About a half mile in that direction," said the lieutenant, pointing east.

"The shooter could've walked to his car, parked there," said Murdock.

"Too risky," said Michelle. "Leaving a parked car on a road like this would invite instant suspicion. They couldn't be sure a cop wouldn't stop and check it out."

"An accomplice then," said Murdock. "Waiting in the car. The person walks through the woods to avoid anyone on the road seeing them. Gets to the car and off they go."

Sean looked over at the Washington County lawman who'd been first on the scene. "You see any other car parked like that on your patrol tonight or when you were heading here?"

The cop shook his head. "But I came from the same direction you did."

Mayhew said, "We've got cars patrolling the nearby roads looking for anyone or anything suspicious. But it's been hours now, so the person could be pretty far away. Or else holed up somewhere."

Murdock said, "I wonder where Bergin was going?"

"Well, he was supposed to be meeting us at Martha's Inn," said Sean. "But now we know he was heading in the wrong direction for that. He would have turned off for Martha's Inn before he got to this point. *If* he was coming from Eastport."

Murdock looked thoughtful. "Right, so we still don't know where he was headed. If it wasn't to meet you, then where? And with whom?"

Michelle said, "Well, maybe the answer is as simple as he was somewhere south and west of here for some reason and was driving up to Martha's Inn to meet us. That would put him on the same road and in the same direction as we were."

They all considered this. Murdock looked at the colonel. "Any thoughts on where he might've gone if that theory turns out to be correct?"

Mayhew rubbed his nose. "Not much down that way unless he was visiting someone at home."

"How about Cutter's Rock?" asked Sean.

"If he was leaving from Gray's Lodge to go to

Cutter's he wouldn't be on this road at all," said the lieutenant, as Mayhew nodded in agreement.

Mayhew added, "And Cutter's is locked down now. No visitors after dark."

Murdock turned to Sean. "Did he know anyone up here that he talked to you about?"

"The only one he talked to us about was Edgar Roy."

"Right," said Murdock. "His client."

The way he said it made Sean remark, "We understand that Roy was on a federal tag list. Anything happens remotely connected to him, you guys get called in."

Murdock's expression showed how plainly he disliked Sean knowing this. "Where did you hear that?" he snapped.

Behind him Sean could almost sense the heat rising from the face of the trooper who'd let this fact slip to him.

"I think Bergin told me when we talked a couple days ago. You guys knew all about him repping Roy, correct?"

Murdock turned away. "Okay, let's finish processing the area. I want pictures, video, every fiber, hair, blood splatter, print, DNA residue, footprint, and anything else out there. Let's roll."

Michelle turned to Sean. "I think he's lost the love for us."

"Can we go?" asked Sean, his voice rising.

44

Murdock turned back. "After we take fingerprints, DNA swabs, and impressions of your shoes."

"For exclusionary purposes, of course," said Sean.

"I let the evidence lead me wherever it goes," replied Murdock.

"They already checked my gun," said Michelle. "And we both passed a GSR test."

"I don't care," retorted Murdock.

Sean said, "We were retained by Bergin. We certainly had no reason to kill the guy."

"Well, right now we only have your word for it that you two were working for him. We'll need to check that out."

"Okay. And after you've taken your samples from us tonight?"

"You head on to where you're staying. But you are not to leave the area without my permission."

"Can you do that?" asked Michelle. "We haven't been charged with anything."

"Material witness."

"We saw nothing that you haven't seen," countered Sean.

"Don't get in a pissing contest with me over this," said Murdock. "You'll lose. I know Chuck thinks you guys are great stuff, but I always thought he made up his mind too fast. So the jury's still out as far as I'm concerned."

"So much for professional courtesy," groused Michelle.

"This is a homicide investigation. It's not a friend-
ship contest. And the only courtesy I owe is to the
dead guy over there."

He stalked off.

"I really think he's lost the love for us," said
Michelle.

"Can't blame him. We were on the scene. He
doesn't know us. And he's under pressure. A lot of it.
And he's right. It's his job to find the killer, not make
friends."

"On a pair of wings in minutes. All the way from
Boston. They got here so fast I'm thinking chopper
instead of a plane. Pretty high priority tag on Edgar
Roy."

"And I'm wondering why."

As they were getting back in their car after being
processed by a pair of field techs the lieutenant sidled
over to them. "My guy told me he was the source for
you about the FBI. Appreciate you covering for him,"
he said. "That could've really dinged his career."

"No problem," said Michelle. "What's your name?"

"Eric Dobkin."

"Well, Eric," said Sean, "it looks like the FBI is
throwing its typical eight-hundred-pound-gorilla act,
so the rest of us have to help each other out."

"Help how?"

"We find out stuff we bring it to you."

"You think that's wise? I mean they *are* the FBI."

"I think it's wise until it turns out not to be."

Michelle said, "But it's a two-way street. We help you, you help us."

"But it's a federal investigation now, ma'am."

"So the Maine State Police just turns tail and runs. Is that your motto?"

He stiffened. "No, ma'am. Our motto is—"

"*Semper Aequus*. Always Just." She added, "I looked it up."

"Also Integrity, Fairness, Compassion, and Excellence," Dobkin said. "That's our set of core values. I don't know how it works in D.C., but we stick to them up here."

"All the more reason for us to work together."

"But what's there to work on? You were retained by a guy who's now dead."

"And now we have to find out who killed him."

"Why?"

"He was a friend of mine." Sean leaned in closer to the officer. "And I don't know how *you* do things in Maine. But where I'm from, we don't abandon our friends because someone killed them."

Dobkin took a step back. "No sir."

Michelle smiled. "Then I'm sure we'll be seeing you. In the meantime." She handed him one of their business cards. "Enough phone numbers on there to find us," she added.

Michelle started the car and punched the gas, and the Ford hurtled off.

5

They both slept.

In separate rooms.

The proprietress was a seventy-three-year-old woman named Mrs. Burke who possessed an old-fashioned idea about sleeping arrangements, in which a wedding band was required for cohabitation on the premises.

Michelle slept heavily. Sean did not. After only two fitful hours tossing in the sack, he rose and stared out the window. To the north and even closer to the coast sat Eastport. The sun's rays would be tickling the town shortly, the first city in the United States to receive the morning light each day. He showered and dressed. An hour later he met a sleepy-eyed Michelle for breakfast.

Martha's Inn turned out to be cozy and quaint, and close enough to the water to walk down to the shoreline in five minutes. Meals were served in a small, pine-paneled room off the kitchen. Sean and Michelle sat in ladder-back chairs with woven straw seats and had two cups of coffee each, eggs, bacon, and piping hot biscuits pre-slathered in butter by the cook.

"Okay, I'll have to run like ten miles to burn this

goop off," said Michelle, as she poured a third cup of coffee.

He looked at her empty plate. "Nobody said you had to eat it."

"Nobody had to. It was delicious." She noted the local paper in his hands. "Nothing on Bergin, right? Happened too late."

He lay the paper aside. "Right." He tugged his sport coat closer around him. "Pretty nippy this morning. I should've brought warmer clothes."

"Didn't you check the latitude, sailor? This is Maine. It can be cold anytime."

"No messages from our friend Dobkin?"

"None on my cell. Probably too early yet. So what's the plan? Not hang around here?"

"We have an appointment to meet with Edgar Roy this morning. I plan on keeping it."

"Will they let us in without Bergin?"

"I guess we'll find out."

"You really want to do this? I mean, how well did you know Bergin?"

Sean folded his napkin and set it down on the table. He looked around the room; there was only one other occupant. A man in his forties, dressed all in tweeds, was drinking a hot cup of tea with his pinky extended at a perfectly elegant angle.

"When I resigned from the Service, I'd hit rock bottom. Bergin was the first guy who thought I had something left in the tank."

"Did you know him before? And did he know what had happened?"

"No to both questions. I just ran into him at Greenberry's, a coffee shop in Charlottesville. We started talking. He was the one who encouraged me to apply to law school. He's one of the main reasons I got my life back." He paused. "I owe him, Michelle."

"Then I guess I owe him too."

The initial approach to Cutter's Rock took them on a circuitous path toward the ocean. It was high tide, and they could see the swells slamming against the outcrops of slimy rock as they drove along. They made one hard right, then doglegged left. Another hundred feet carried them around a rise of land, and they saw the warning sign on a six-foot-wide piece of sheet metal set on long poles sunk deep into the rocky earth. It basically said that one was approaching a maximum security federal facility, and if one didn't have legitimate business there, this was the last and only chance for one to turn around and get the hell out.

Michelle pressed the gas pedal harder, hurtling them faster at their destination. Sean looked over at her. "Having fun?"

"Just working off some butterflies."

"Butterflies? What butterflies can you—" He caught himself, realizing that not that long ago Michelle had checked herself into a psych facility to work out some personal issues.

"Okay," he said, and returned his gaze ahead.

A man-made causeway consisting of asphalt bracketed by built-up and graded-solid Maine stone led them out to the federal facility. The entry gate was steel and motorized and looked strong enough to withstand a charge by a herd of Abrams tanks. The guard hut held four armed men who looked like they had never smiled in their lives. Their utility belts each contained a Glock sidearm, cuffs, telescopic head-crushing baton, Taser, pepper spray, stun grenades.

And a whistle.

Michelle looked at Sean as two guards approached them. "Bet me ten bucks that I won't ask the bigger one if he's ever blown his whistle to stop a rampaging psycho from escaping."

"If you make even one joke to those gorillas I will find a gun and shoot you."

"But if I did ask they'd be mad at me, not you," she said with a smile.

"No. They always beat up the guy. The girl never gets the speeding ticket. And thanks."

"For what?"

"Now *I* have butterflies."

The perimeter wall was locally quarried stone, twelve feet tall with a six-foot-high stainless steel cylinder riding on top. It would be impossible to get a grip on, much less climb over.

"Seen that equipment on some supermax prisons," noted Sean. "Latest whiz-bang technology in keeping the bad guys inside."

"What about suction cups?" asked Michelle, as they both stared at the metal wall topper.

"It rotates like a hamster wheel. Suction cups won't help you there. Still fall on your ass. And it's probably loaded with motion sensors."

Their car was analyzed by an AVIAN, or Advanced Vehicle Interrogation and Notification System, which used seismic sensors placed on their car to capture shock waves produced by a beating heart. An advanced signal-processing algorithm concluded in just under three seconds that there was no living person concealed in their Ford. The car was then subjected to a mobile trace handheld unit that screened for explosives and drugs. The portable unit was then run over them, and Sean and Michelle were personally searched the old-fashioned way, questioned by the guards, and had their names checked against a list. Michelle had instinctively started to explain to them about her weapon before realizing the police still had it. Then they were turned loose on a rigidly narrow path bracketed by high fences to continue their ride. Michelle let her gaze wander over the perimeter.

"Watchtowers every hundred feet," she noted. "Each manned by a pair of guards." She squinted into the sun. "One looks to be carrying an AK with an extended clip and the other a long-range sniper rifle with a mounted FLIR," she added, referring to a Forward-Looking Infrared scope bolted to the rifle. "Bet they have a CCTV subsystem, digital recording, and terabytes of data storage. And multizone intrusion and escape detection systems, microwave and infrared technology, biometric readers, high-security IT network grafted onto a fiber optics backbone, multistage uninterrupted circuits, and big-time backup power in case the lights go out."

Sean frowned. "Will you stop sounding like you're casing the place? With all the bells and whistles they obviously have here, we have to assume people are watching *and* listening."

She pulled her gaze back and saw that there were three rings of interior fencing around the two-story rebar-reinforced concrete building housing America's most wildly psychotic predators. Each fence was an eighteen-foot-high chain-link with concertina wire on top. The top six feet of each fence was angled inward at forty-five degrees, making it nearly impossible to clear. The middle fence carried a lethal electrical charge, as a big sign next to it made crystal clear. The open ground in between each fence was a minefield of razor wire and sharp spikes pointing up from the ground, and the glint of the sun told her that there were myriad trip wires strung everywhere. At night, the only time anyone would dare attempt to escape from this place, the wires would be invisible. You'd bleed to death before you ran into the middle fence, and then only to get charred for your troubles. But by then the watchtower guards would have finished you off anyway with *bang-bang* taps to the head and heart.

"That electric fence has five thousand volts and low amperage, plenty lethal enough," said Michelle in a low voice. "I'm betting there's a concrete-grade beam under it so no one can dig out." She paused. "But something is weird."

"What?"

"You put in an electric fence to save labor costs. And in the world of prison perimeter security labor costs are basically tower guards. But every single tower is still manned by two shooters."

"I guess they really don't want to take any chances."

"It's overkill, at least to my mind."

"What'd you expect? Our federal tax dollars at work."

She noted a large array of solar panels off to one side, angled just right to take in the maximum amount of sunlight.

"Well, at least they're going green," she said, pointing them out to Sean.

They passed three more gates and three more checkpoints, and endured three more electronic scans and body searches, until Michelle assumed the guards collectively knew every contour of her person better than she did. At the entrance to the building massive portals resembling blast doors on a nukeproof bunker swung back on air-powered hydraulics. Michelle said in an impressed voice, "Okay, I'm thinking this place is escape-proof."

"Let's hope."

"Do you think they know Bergin's been murdered?" she asked.

"I wouldn't bet against it."

"So they might not let us in."

"They let us come this far," replied Sean.

"Yeah, and now I'm wondering why they have."

"Little slow this morning?"

"What?"

He said nervously, "I've been wondering that ever since they cleared us through the first gate."

6

There was one more checkpoint inside the facility. A magnetometer for any stray weapons the other searches didn't reveal, another probe of their persons, an X-ray for Michelle's small bag, an ID and document check, a cross-reference on the visitor's list, an oral interview that would have done Mossad proud, and a few phone calls. After that they were told to wait in an anteroom off the reception area, if one could call it that. The windows were at least three inches thick and presumably bullet-, fist-, and footproof.

Sean tapped on one. "Feels like the windows in the Beast."

Michelle was examining the interior wall construction. She rubbed her hand up and down one section. "Don't think this is run-of-the-mill drywall. Feels like a composite. A composite made of titanium. I doubt a round from my .45 could pierce it."

"Called a buddy of mine who knew about this place," said Sean. "It's set on a rocker platform like they do the skyscrapers."

"You mean in case there's an earthquake."

"Right. Must have cost a pretty penny."

"Like you said, it's only taxpayer money. But I wonder if it's floodproof? We're pretty close to the ocean here."

"Retractable seawall. They can raise it in twenty minutes."

"You're kidding."

Sean shook his head. "What my buddy told me."

Michelle looked around the small, Spartan space. "I wonder how many visitors there are here? They don't even have any magazines. And I doubt you could find a vending machine."

"Would you want to come and visit someone here? Even if the person was family? I mean, it's a facility for the criminally insane."

"They don't call it that anymore, do they?"

"I guess not, but it is what it is. They are criminal and they are insane."

"Now look who's being judgmental. Roy hasn't even been tried."

"Okay, you got me there."

"But he's still probably a psycho," added Michelle, drawing a raised eyebrow from her partner. She said, "How many inmates—sorry, patients—here, do you reckon?"

"That's classified, apparently."

"Classified? How can that be? This isn't part of the CIA or the Pentagon."

"All I can tell you is I tried to find that out and ran

right into a stone wall. I do know that Roy is probably the most high-profile inmate they have right now."

"Until he's supplanted by an even crazier psycho."

"Excuse me?"

They turned to find a young man in a blue smock standing at the doorway. He held a small electronic pad. "Sean King and Michelle Maxwell?"

They rose together, towering over the shorter man. "That's right," said Sean.

"Here to see Edgar Roy?"

Sean was prepared to have a fight on his hands about them being able to see the man. But Blue Smock merely said, "Please follow me."

A minute later he handed them off to a woman who was far more intimidating. Nearly as tall as Michelle but considerably wider and heavier, she looked capable of holding down the nose tackle position for a Division I football team. She introduced herself as Carla Dukes, the director of Cutter's Rock. When her long fingers clamped around Michelle's in a handshake, Michelle wondered if the woman used to call herself Carl.

Her office was a fourteen-by-fourteen square. A desk with a computer, three chairs counting hers, and nothing else. No file cabinets, no pictures of family or friends, no paintings on the wall, no view outside the room, nothing personal whatsoever.

"Please sit," she said. They sat. She slid open her

drawer, retrieved a red file, and opened it on her desk. "I understand that Ted Bergin is dead."

Thanks for getting right to the point, thought Sean. *And now here comes the fight.*

He said, "That's right. The police and FBI are investigating. But we're still scheduled to meet with Edgar Roy today and we didn't want to forego that opportunity."

"The appointment was for Ted Bergin and you accompanying him."

"Well, he obviously can't be here," said Sean, his voice calm but firm.

"Of course not, but I'm not sure that in light of the circumstances—"

Michelle said, "But his defense will continue. He will be tried at some point. He is entitled to representation. And Sean is also a licensed attorney working with Ted Bergin."

Dukes eyed Sean. "Is that right? I just thought you were both investigators."

"I wear two hats," said Sean, smoothly picking up on Michelle's spur-of-the-moment tactic. "I'm a licensed PI and attorney in the Commonwealth of Virginia, where Roy will ultimately stand trial for the charges against him."

"Do you have some evidence of that?"

Sean handed her his State Bar ID. "A call to Richmond will verify it," he said.

She handed the card back. "So what exactly do you want to talk to Mr. Roy about?"

"Well, that's confidential. If I told you, it would break the attorney-client privilege. That would be malpractice on my part."

"It's a delicate situation. Mr. Roy is a special case."

"So we're finding out," interjected Michelle.

"We really need to see him," added Sean.

"The FBI called this morning," said Dukes.

"I'm sure they did," said Sean. "Was it Special Agent Murdock?"

She ignored this. "He said that the murder of Ted Bergin might have something to do with his representation of Edgar Roy."

"Do you think it does?" asked Michelle.

Dukes glanced sharply at her. "How would I know anything about that?"

"Had Bergin been to see Edgar Roy?" asked Sean.

"Of course he had. He was Roy's legal counsel."

"How often had he come? And when was the last time?"

"I don't know that offhand. I'd have to check the files."

"Could you do that?"

Her hand didn't stray to the computer keyboard. "Why? If you're working with him you should already know that information."

"He came up here separately. We were going to

meet with him last night and go over everything. But we obviously never got that chance."

"I see." Her hand still didn't venture to the keyboard.

"Did Special Agent Murdock ask for that information?"

"I'm certainly in no position to tell you whether he did or didn't."

"Okay, can we see Edgar Roy now?"

"I'm really not too certain about this. I'll have to consult with our legal counsel and get back to you."

Sean rose and sighed heavily. "Okay, I was really hoping not to have to go down that road."

"What are you talking about?" asked Dukes.

"Can you tell me where the local newspaper office is?"

She looked at him sharply. "Why?"

He checked his watch. "If we hurry, the paper can get the story in for the morning print edition of a federal government facility denying an accused access to his legal counsel. I would imagine the story could hit the AP wire as well, and then it's a safe bet to be all over the Internet a few minutes after that. Just to get the facts right, do you spell Carla with a C or a K?"

Dukes stared up at him, her lips twitching and her gaze bordering on murderous. "Do you really want to do that?"

"Do you really want to break the law?"

"What law?" she snapped.

"An accused person's Sixth Amendment right to legal counsel. That's the Constitution, by the way. And it's always bad to screw with the Constitution."

"He's right, Ms. Dukes."

Sean and Michelle turned to see Brandon Murdock in the doorway. The FBI agent smiled.

"Enjoy your *chat* with Edgar Roy," he said.

7

Sean and Michelle were escorted into a room that was blankly white. Small. One door. Three chairs, one table, all bolted to the floor. Two chairs faced the one. In front of the one was a three-inch metal ring cemented into the floor. Between the two chairs and the one was a three-foot-wide wall of four-inch poly-carbonate glass that ran from the floor to the ceiling.

And then the door opened and there he was.

Sean and Michelle had seen photos of Edgar Roy, both in the newspapers and also in a file packet Ted Bergin had sent them. Sean had even seen a segment of video on the man shortly after his arrest for the murders. Nothing prepared them for seeing the man in person.

He was six foot eight and extremely lean, like a giant number two pencil. He had a golf ball for an Adam's apple set on a long neck. His hair was dark, long, and curly, and it framed a face that was thin and not unattractive. He wore glasses. Behind the lenses were black dots for eyes, like the die cuts on a pair of dice. Sean noted the man's slender fingers. Tufts of hair stuck out from inside his ears. He was clean-shaven.

His arms and legs were shackled and he hobbled in truncated steps as the guards led him over to the chair behind the glass and locked the shackles into the floor ring. It allowed him mobility of about six inches. Two guards stood on either side of him. They were big men, with impassive faces. They were seemingly crafted from stone to guard other people. Neither one had weapons other than telescopic metal billy clubs. These could extend out four feet and deliver crushing blows.

At the doorway were two more guards. Each one gripped pump action shotguns that had been modified to hold a Taser component that could fire a twelve-gauge projectile up to a hundred feet, delivering a twenty-second pulse of energy that would lay an NFL tackle on the ground and keep him there for a long time.

Sean and Michelle turned their attention back to Edgar Roy behind the wall of bulletproof glass. His long legs stuck out straight, the heels of his prison-issued canvas loafers kissing the wall of unbreakable glass.

"Okay," said Sean, drawing his gaze from Roy and eyeing the guards. "We'll need to speak to our client alone."

None of the four guards even moved an inch. They could've been statues.

Sean said, "I'm his attorney. We need some alone time, guys."

Still no movement. Apparently the four men were immobile *and* deaf.

Sean licked his lips. "Okay, who's your supervisor?" he asked the guy holding a shotgun.

The man didn't even look at Sean.

Sean glanced at Roy. Sean wasn't even sure he was still alive because he couldn't see the rise and fall of his chest. He didn't blink, didn't twitch. His eyes just stared straight ahead, looking but apparently not registering on anything.

"Having fun yet?"

They turned to see Agent Murdock staring at them from the doorway.

"For starters, can you tell the muscle to leave the room?" said Sean, his voice rising slightly. "They don't seem to get the whole attorney–client thing."

"Last night you were just a PI. Today you're a lawyer?"

"I already showed my credentials to Ms. Dukes."

"And you authorized us to see the guy," added Michelle.

"So I did."

"Then can we see him?" asked Sean. "In a professional manner?"

Murdock smiled and then nodded at the guards. "Right outside the door, gentlemen. You hear anything out of the ordinary, you know what to do."

"The guy's manacled to the floor and there's a wall of four-inch polycarbonate glass between us," said Michelle. "I'm not sure there's much he *can* do."

"I wasn't necessarily referring to the prisoner," replied Murdock.

The door shut behind them, and Sean and Michelle were finally alone with their client.

Sean leaned forward. "Mr. Roy? I'm Sean King. This is my partner Michelle Maxwell. We're working with Ted Bergin. I know you've met with him previously."

Roy said nothing. Didn't blink, twitch, or seem to breathe.

Sean sat back, opened his briefcase, and looked at some papers. All pens, paper clips, and other sharp and potentially deadly instruments had been confiscated, although Sean supposed he could have inflicted a nasty paper cut on someone. "Ted Bergin told us that he was preparing a defense for you. Did he talk to you about what exactly that was?"

When Roy made no reaction, Michelle said, "I think we're wasting our time. In fact, I think I can hear Murdock laughing his ass off behind that steel door."

"Mr. Roy, we really need to discuss some things."

"They put him here because he's not fit for trial, Sean. I don't know what he was like when he got here, but I can't believe he's gotten any better. By the looks of things this guy might be stuck at Cutter's Rock for the rest of his life."

Sean put the papers away. "Mr. Roy? Did you know that Ted Bergin has been murdered?" He said it in a blunt, loud tone, obviously hoping to get some type of reaction from Roy.

It didn't work.

Sean looked around the small space. He leaned close to Michelle and whispered, "What are the odds this room has hidden recorders?"

"Taping an attorney's conversation with his client? Can't they get in big trouble for that?" she whispered back.

"Only if someone finds out and can prove it." He sat back up, took out his cell phone. "No bars. But I had reception right before we got here."

"Jamming?"

"That's supposed to be illegal, too. I wondered why they let me keep it. At most prisons they confiscate it from visitors."

"Because cell phones in prison are going for more money than cocaine. Heard of a guard somewhere out west making six figures a year selling Nokias and service plans at a state pen. Now he's dialing from inside the place, too."

"Look at his ankle, Michelle."

The ankle bracelet was the color of titanium. A glowing red light sat in the center of it.

Michelle said, "They use them in some of the supermaxes and on the likes of Paris Hilton and Lindsay Lohan. Throws out a wireless signal, pinpoints the person's precise location. Go outside the zone and an alarm is triggered."

Sean dropped his voice. "How many places can the guy go in here that he needs an electronic ankle bracelet?"

"Good point. Want to ask Murdock? Or maybe Carla Dukes?"

Sean glanced sharply up at Edgar Roy. Had there been some slight—

No. The eyes were still lifeless dots.

"You think he's been drugged?" asked Michelle. "His pupils look dilated."

"I don't know what to think. Without a medical exam."

"He's really tall. But skinny. Doesn't look strong enough to have killed all those people."

"He's only thirty-five. So prime of his life when he did the killings."

"*If* he did them, you mean."

"Right. If."

"But the details of the killings haven't been made public. The bodies haven't even been identified."

"Maybe they have but that info hasn't been released to the public either," he replied.

"Why wouldn't it have been?"

"Maybe this is a really special case." He rose. "Mr. Roy. Thanks for meeting with us. We'll be back."

"We will?" asked Michelle in a low voice.

When they knocked on the door it immediately opened.

"How'd it go?" asked Murdock with a smirk.

"He told us everything," said Michelle. "He's innocent. You can let him go now."

"Found some interesting things at Bergin's digs at Gray's Lodge," said Murdock, ignoring her.

"Oh, yeah, like what?" asked Sean.

"Nothing you need to know about."

"Oh, you're a real tease, Murdock," said Michelle. "Do they teach a class in that at Quantico?"

Sean added, "If it's attorney work product I do need to know about it. That's privileged."

"File some papers then. The Bureau lawyers need a good laugh. In the meantime, you're not getting the document."

"So Roy is a zombie. Can he take a pee, feed himself?"

"He's in good shape. Physically. That answer your question?"

He turned and left.

"That guy really likes us," said Michelle sarcastically. "Think he'll want to go on a date with me? I can dispose of the body pretty efficiently."

Sean wasn't paying attention to her. He was watching the guards escort Roy back to his cell. As the man passed, Sean could see that he towered over even the biggest of the four guards. Sean also noted that Roy moved under his own power, shuffling along with his manacles clanking. But in the face there was nothing.

Black dots.

Nothing.

Which was exactly what they had right now.

8

It was easier leaving Cutter's Rock than it had been entering it, but not by much. Sean finally grew so exasperated with the level of scrutiny that he snapped at the last layer of guards, "Edgar Roy is not stuffed in our damn tailpipe." He turned to Michelle. "Hit it!"

"I thought you'd never ask."

The Ford left twin black stripes on the previously pristine asphalt ribbon of Cutter Rock's entryway. Michelle even gave them a single-finger salute out the window.

As the car made the reverse trek along the causeway Michelle glanced over at her partner, who was lost in thought.

She said, "Your brain is obviously in overdrive. Want to share?"

"While you were getting probed on the way out, I had a chance to ask Duke's assistant a couple of questions. Roy eats, though not much, and does his necessary bodily function duties during the day. He's lost some weight, but he's technically healthy."

"So he can do all that, but he can't communicate with anyone?"

"There's a medical term for it the guy used, but I don't remember what it was. In any event, apparently his body is working but his mind has shut down."

"Convenient."

"Okay, Bergin is dead. Murdered. FBI is on the scene. They've covered his lodgings. All his work product is in their hands."

"So like the guy said, we file some papers in court to get it back."

"The only problem is I'm not really Roy's lawyer."

"But you *are* a lawyer. You were retained by Ted Bergin, who was Roy's counsel of record. Doesn't take a big leap to get you as his legal mouthpiece. Bergin certainly can't dispute it. So who's to know or say otherwise?"

"I haven't practiced in a while."

"Your license is still active, right?"

"Maybe."

She slowed the car. "Maybe? That doesn't quite cut it for death penalty clients, does it?"

"I might need a couple of CLE courses to make things right."

"Great. I'm sure Agent Murdock will drive you to class."

"Besides, we were retained as PIs, not lawyers. The court will go by the record in the case. I'm not on the papers as his counsel."

"All right. Stupid question, then: Was Ted Bergin a solo practitioner?"

Sean shot her a glance. "That's actually a brilliant question. And one we really need an answer to."

They got back to Martha's Inn and both headed to Sean's room. This caught the eye of the owner, whose name was not Martha but Hazel Burke. She'd lived in this part of Maine all her life, as she had told them at breakfast.

"Your room is on the other side of the hall, dear," she called up to Michelle from the bottom of the short stack of stairs. From this vantage point she could clearly see the entrance to both rooms. "That is the gentleman's room you're about to enter."

Michelle called back in a tight voice, "But I'm not going to my room. I'm actually going to the gentleman's room."

"And will you be staying long in the gentleman's room?" asked Burke, as she started to climb the steps.

Michelle looked at Sean. "I don't know. How frisky are you feeling?"

Burke had arrived on the second floor in time to hear this. "Now, dear, we are ladies here."

"Maybe *you're* a lady."

Sean cut in. "We're just going to be working on something, Mrs. Burke. A legal case."

"Oh, you're a lawyer?"

"Yes."

"You heard about that other lawyer, didn't you? That poor Mr. Bergin?"

"How did you know about that?" asked Sean quickly.

Burke wiped her hands on her apron. "Oh, well, dear, murders aren't so frequent up here that folks don't talk about them. Everybody knows, I suspect."

"Right. I guess they do."

The woman turned to Michelle. "You're not a lawyer, are you?"

"Why do you say that?" said Michelle stiffly.

"Well, dear, I don't know you, really, but you just don't seem the type to wear, you know, dressy clothes." With obvious distaste, she ran her eyes over Michelle's faded, tight jeans, dusty boots, white T-shirt, and worn leather jacket.

"You're right. I actually prefer spandex and spikes."

"That's not very nice," Burke admonished, her broad face growing pink.

"Well, I'm not a very nice person, I guess. Now if you'll excuse us."

"I'll come and check on you in about five minutes."

"I'd wait a bit longer," said Michelle.

"Why?" Burke said suspiciously.

Michelle rubbed Sean's arm. "The *gentleman* took his Cialis." She closed the door of Sean's room with a definite thud. "Okay, that lady is really starting to piss me off."

"Forget that. I'm going to call Bergin's office in Charlottesville."

"Do you think they know?"

"I don't know. They usually notify the next of kin first. But Ted's wife is dead and they never had children, at least that he ever mentioned."

Sean sat on the bed and made the call. Someone answered.

He said, "Hello, it's Sean King. Is this Hilary? I spoke to you on the phone the other day." Sean cupped his hand over the phone. "Ted's secretary."

Michelle nodded.

"Yes," said Hilary. "Aren't you supposed to be meeting with Mr. Bergin at Cutter's Rock about now?"

Sean looked grim. She didn't know. "Hilary, I'm afraid I have some bad news. I don't like doing this on the phone, but you need to know." He told her.

The woman gasped, tried to steady herself, and then dissolved into tears. "Oh my God. I can't believe it."

"Neither can I, Hilary. The FBI are investigating right now."

"The FBI?"

"It's complicated."

"How, how did he die?"

"It wasn't by natural causes, obviously."

"Who found the body?"

"I did. I mean me and my partner, Michelle."

At that moment Hilary's professional façade completely dissolved.

Sean waited patiently for her to stop sobbing. When it didn't look like she was going to cease he said, "We can talk again later, Hilary. I'm really sorry to have been the one to have to tell you."

With a massive effort she composed herself. "No, no, I'm all right. It was, it was just such a shock. I just saw him yesterday morning, before he left on his flight."

Sean had only talked to Hilary on the phone before and had never met her in person, but he could envision the woman wiping the tears and perhaps most of her makeup and mascara away with a tissue.

"What time was that?"

"His flight or when I saw him last?" To Sean it seemed she was concentrating hard on the details in order to take her mind off her boss being dead.

"Both, actually."

"Eight o'clock at the office," she answered promptly. "He had a puddle jumper from Charlottesville to Reagan National. And then a noon flight from there to Portland."

"Jet or prop?"

"One of those regional jets. United, I think."

"Same type of plane we took. Okay, they fly high and fast, so that would have put him in Maine a little after one?"

"That's right."

"Do you have his schedule? I'd like to know if he met with Edgar Roy while he was up here. And also any times in the past he might have done so."

"Well, I know he went there yesterday. He told me he had an appointment there at six o'clock. He was concerned that if his flight was delayed he wouldn't get there in time. I understand it's quite a drive from Portland."

"Yes, it is."

"And he's certainly been to see Mr. Roy in the past. I don't recall the exact dates, but I can look them up on the computer and e-mail them to you."

"That would be great. Uh, I know Ted's wife had passed away, and I don't believe they had any kids. But is there anyone that needs to be contacted? I mean any extended family?"

"He had a brother. But he passed on about three years ago now. I never heard him mention anyone else. His family was his work, I guess."

"I guess."

Michelle caught his eye and held up two fingers.

Sean nodded and said, "Hilary, did Ted have anyone else working with him? I just assumed he was solo but it suddenly occurred to me that I didn't know that for sure. I'd been out of touch with him for a couple years."

"He has an associate. A very bright young lady barely a year out of law school."

"Really? What's her name?"

"Megan Riley."

"Is she in the office now?"

"No, she's at a court hearing. She said she'd be back a bit after lunch."

"Was she working on the Roy case?"

"I know that she knew about it. Small firm and all. And she's done some research on it for Mr. Bergin, because he mentioned it to me."

"Can you have her contact me when she gets in? I really need to talk to her."

"Absolutely, I sure will." She paused. "Sean, are they going to find out who did this awful thing?"

"Well, if the FBI doesn't, we will. I promise you that."

"Thank you."

Sean put the phone down and looked at Michelle.

She said, "Well, that's good news. He had an associate."

"A first year. That's not good news. No way a judge will let her rep a capital murder case. Not one with this high a profile. Too much risk for an incompetent counsel affirmative defense on appeal."

"But you're an experienced lawyer."

"Michelle, I told you, I'm not even sure if my license is active."

"Then if I were you I'd find out."

Sean made a few calls. He clicked off the last one with a tiny smile.

"I forgot I had some carry-forward credits. I'm still

active." His smile faded. "But I haven't been in a court in a long time."

"Like riding a bike."

"No, it's really not."

"Don't worry, I'll be right there with you the whole time."

"If going to court consisted of shooting the wings off butterflies and kicking ass there'd be no one I'd rather have with me. But it doesn't."

"From what I've seen of some trial lawyers, a good ass-kicking sounds like just the ticket. So what do we do now?"

"We wait to hear from Megan Riley."

"Think she'll take the case given the fact that her boss just got murdered maybe for repping Edgar Roy?"

"Not if she's smart she won't."

"Do you really think that's why he was killed?"

"We have no evidence to support that conclusion."

"Have no worries—you sound just like a lawyer. But put away your analytical side for a sec and answer from your gut."

"Yes, I think that was why he was killed."

Michelle leaned against the wall and stared moodily out the window.

Sean said, "Okay, what are *you* thinking?"

"I'm thinking how long do we have before they target us?"

"You want to quit and hop on a plane back to Virginia?"

She looked at him. "Do you?"

"I thought I was clear on the point. I'm going to find out who killed him."

"Then I thought I was clear, too. We're a team. Where you go, I go."

"You don't think I can take care of myself?"

"No, but I can take care of you better."

9

Sean was outside taking a walk along the rocky coast when his cell phone buzzed a bit after two o'clock. Megan Riley sounded young, green, and stunned. His hopes sank. There was no way the young woman would be able to handle this.

"I can't believe that Mr. Bergin is dead," she said. He could envision her eyes filling with tears. A perfectly normal reaction under the circumstances, but he didn't need normal right now, he needed extraordinary.

"I know. It's a shock to all of us." As he spoke he watched Michelle make her way over from a rickety pier with an equally rickety fishing boat tied up to it. She reached him and sat down on a huge boulder that served as riprap to keep the ocean at bay.

"Who would do such a thing?" asked Megan.

"Well, we're working on that right now. Hilary mentioned that you had worked on the Roy case for Ted?"

She sniffled. "I did a little research for him that he asked me to do."

"Did he ever talk to you about his theories of the

81

case? What defense he was planning, steps he'd taken, conversations he'd had with Edgar Roy?"

It would have been a one-way conversation, obviously.

"He did go into some of that with me. I guess I was a sounding board for him. And I talked to him yesterday."

"What time?"

"Around six."

"What did he want?"

"Just checking on some cases I was handling."

"Did he talk to you about Edgar Roy?"

"He said he was going to meet with him. In fact, I think he was on the way there. In a car, I mean."

"Nothing else?" asked Sean.

"I called him back about nine o'clock."

"Why?"

"To go over a court hearing I had the next day. I needed his advice."

"Okay, Megan, this is really important. Did he mention that he had seen Edgar Roy last night?"

"No, he didn't talk about that."

"Did he mention to you where he might have been going late last night? I mean other than to meet with Michelle and me?"

Her voice sounded frightened. "No, he didn't say anything about it. I didn't even know he was meeting with you. I just assumed he was in for the night."

"Nothing at all, you're sure?" Sean persisted. "Just some comment he let slip?"

"There was nothing. Most of the conversation was about the court hearings I had the next day. He didn't say anything about Edgar Roy and I didn't ask."

"Why not?"

"Because if Mr. Bergin had wanted to discuss the case he would have. I've only been working for him a short while. I wasn't comfortable just injecting myself into a case I wasn't really working on. He was always very particular about client confidences."

Sean said, "Okay, let's get down to specifics. Do you know whether you're on the papers filed with the court?"

"As a matter of fact I am. Mr. Bergin said it was always good to have another attorney on the papers. Just in case something happened."

"Well, unfortunately, he was prophetic. Look, we'll need to talk to you about what Ted's theories and strategies were. And anything else that might be connected to Roy."

"Have you talked to Edgar Roy?"

"We've seen him. Talking is somewhat problematic. Can you fly up here?"

"I'm not sure. I've got some cases I'm working on and—"

"Megan, this is really important."

He heard her take a long breath. "Of course. I know it is. I . . . I can get continuances. And bring work with me. The legal community down here knows and respects Mr. Bergin. They'll understand."

"I'm sure they will. And can you bring with you whatever files Ted had on the case?"

"Absolutely."

Sean checked his watch. "You can catch a seven o'clock evening flight to Portland from Dulles. Think you can make that?"

"I think so, yes. I can get things organized here and then drive really fast."

"I'll make the reservations and e-mail you the details. We'll pick you up at the airport in Portland."

"Mr. King?"

"Just make it Sean."

"Sean, um, should I be scared?"

Sean looked over at Michelle before answering. "We'll stick to you like glue."

"I guess that means yes."

"It's never a bad thing to be scared, Megan."

"I'll see you in Portland," she said in a shaky voice.

Sean clicked off and filled Michelle in on his conversation with the young lawyer.

Michelle nodded. "So she had two conversations with the guy and Roy never came up. Obviously Bergin was playing this really close to the vest. Maybe he realized there was some danger involved here and wanted to keep Riley out of it."

"That actually sounds like Ted. Chivalrous to the last."

Michelle said, "So what do you think about Riley?"

"I think it'll be a miracle if she's actually on the plane."

"If she *weren't* scared that would be telling, too. In a bad way."

"I know. I'm sure she's smart and a good lawyer, or else Ted wouldn't have brought her on. But this is a hell of a situation to throw a baby attorney into."

"Well, we just need any info she has and what she can tell us about Bergin's discussions about the case. I don't think anyone really expects her to step into the man's shoes and try this sucker."

"Problem is, if another counsel comes in we'll find ourselves off the case."

"Not if we work hard now and make ourselves invaluable to said counsel." Michelle's expression changed. "Who was paying Bergin's bill? If Edgar Roy can't even talk, someone else had to hire Bergin."

"That's a good question. It should be in the files."

"Did Roy have money?"

"Well, he had the farm and he had a government job."

"But probably not rolling in cash."

"Probably not."

They walked back toward the inn.

The breeze off the water was chilly, and Michelle dug her hands into her jacket. "So until we leave to get Megan in Portland, what's on the agenda?"

"How about a ride over to Gray's Lodge?"

"To Bergin's room? You know Agent Murdock will have that locked down tight."

"But we might run into our friend Eric Dobkin of the Maine State Police."

"You really think he'll be our inside guy on this?"

"Never hurts to ask. And if I'm reading Murdock right, he's probably pissed off the entire Maine constabulary by now."

"We still don't know if Bergin met with Roy yesterday."

"And we also don't know where he was headed last night."

"It would be great to get a list of all his phone calls and e-mails."

"Wouldn't it?" agreed Sean.

"But Murdock has all that."

"Maybe, maybe not."

"What's that supposed to mean?"

"All we can do is try."

"Crossing the FBI? Not a smart career move," she said.

"Finesse is the key."

"Finesse is not my strong suit."

"Which is why I'll be handling that end of the equation."

"Opposites attract."

He smacked her on the arm. "Apparently so."

10

A wall of cops and Feds enveloped Gray's Lodge. Guests had been interrogated and their rooms searched. And then they'd been told to get other lodgings but not to leave the area. Posing as tourists, Sean and Michelle, by a bit of luck and deduction, happened on the lodge owners, a husband and wife in their sixties, who were visibly upset by what had happened.

"Damndest thing," said the man, a burly fellow with soft white hair and a tanned face, over a cup of coffee at a gas station within sight of the lodge. He wore a bright red flannel shirt and new jeans.

"The cops just came in and told everyone to clear out?" asked Michelle.

The wife nodded. She was slender, wiry, and looked like she could work her larger husband into the ground. "After they gave them the third degree and searched their underwear drawers. Some of our guests have been coming here for decades, too. They had nothing to do with that man dying."

"Well, those guests may never come back after this," said the husband miserably.

"And the dead man, this Bergin guy, he'd just arrived that day?" prompted Sean.

"That's right," said the husband.

"But we'd seen him before, of course," added the woman.

Sean pounced. "So he'd been up here before?"

"Twice before," said the husband.

"Did you know what for?" asked Michelle.

"Wasn't for the hunting or fishing," answered the wife.

"He was a lawyer," opined the husband.

"Any idea what he was doing up here?" asked Sean.

The husband studied him. "You folks aren't from around here."

"No, we just came up yesterday. Staying at Martha's Inn. Mrs. Burke is really nice."

Michelle stifled a snort.

"Yeah, she's a real nice gal," said the husband in a way that made his wife purse her lips.

"I've never been around a murder before," said Michelle. "Pretty eerie. But I love those true crime shows."

Sean added, "I wonder why anyone would want to kill a lawyer. He was probably just up here on vacation."

The wife started to say something, but then looked at her husband questioningly.

He said, "He wasn't here on vacation. He was Edgar Roy's lawyer."

"Edgar Roy?" Sean said blankly.

"Serial killer they got up at Cutter's Rock. Waiting to be tried. Local paper did a big story on it when they brought him here. They say he's nuts. I say he's just playacting so they won't send him back to Virginia and execute him."

"My God," said Michelle. "What'd he do?"

"Murdered a bunch of people and buried them on his farm," replied the wife, as she shuddered. "He's not a man. Wild animal, more like it."

"And this Bergin fellow was his lawyer?" said Sean. "So he had to go to this Cutter's Rock place and talk to this guy?"

"Well, I guess he had to if he was representing him," said the husband. He looked at his wife. "And the man's not been convicted yet."

"He's as guilty as sin and everyone knows it," his wife shot back.

"Well, anyway, I guess it takes all kinds to make a world. Wouldn't have figured a fellow like Bergin would be a lawyer for the likes of a person like that."

"So you got to know him?" asked Michelle eagerly. She looked at Sean and feigned naïve excitement about such serious business. "I mean this is so creepy, it's like a TV show or something."

The husband nodded. "Yeah, I guess it is. Anyway, the lodge isn't a large place. Not many guests even when we're full up. Bergin would come down for breakfast and such. We were close in age. Natural that we would talk about stuff. Interesting fellow."

Sean said, "And he just told you what he was doing up here? Thought he'd keep that confidential, being a lawyer."

"Well, not at first and not in so many words. But he asked for directions to Cutter's Rock one time, and I asked him why he was going up there. And that's when he told me what he was doing."

Michelle said excitedly, "Gosh, maybe he was going up to Cutter's Rock when he was killed?"

"No, don't think so," said the husband.

"Because he'd already been there," said the wife.

"How do you know that?" asked Sean.

The husband answered. "He told me he was heading up there right away. When he checked in he was in a hurry. His flight had been late and he needed to get up to Cutter's before visiting hours were over. In quite the rush he was."

"Okay, but maybe he never made it."

"No, he did. Because he came back here. Had a cup of coffee. I asked him how it went. He said okay, but he didn't really seem like it had gone okay."

"What time was that?" asked Sean.

The husband looked at him suspiciously. "What does it matter to you?"

The wife added, "You two ask a lot of questions."

Before Sean could say anything, Michelle spoke up. "Okay, we should have told you before." She paused and then said in a low, girlish voice brimming with awe, "We were the ones who found his body."

The couple looked at her and then Sean. He nodded. "We did," Sean said quite truthfully.

The words tumbled from Michelle's mouth. "And it was awful. But exciting at the same time. I mean nothing ever happens to us like that. I've never even seen a dead body before. And certainly not one that was murdered." She shivered. "I absolutely hate guns," she added with a completely straight face. But then her features lit up. "But it was so exciting. It's weird, huh?"

The husband said derisively, "Well, it's excitement I can do without."

"We found the body around midnight," prompted Sean. "But he must've gotten back from seeing Roy long before that."

"Oh yeah, about eight. He didn't have any dinner. Said he wasn't hungry."

"Did he talk to you before he left again?"

"No. I didn't see him leave either. I know he was here around nine. Saw his light on in his room. But I got busy after that." He looked at his wife. "You didn't see him either?"

"No. Told the police that too. I was back in the kitchen cleaning up."

Michelle said, "So it was after nine when he left. But when you talked to him after he got back from Cutter's Rock, did he mention going out again? Or where he might be going?"

"No. Nothing like that."

Sean asked, "Did Bergin get any phone calls or packages that day?"

"Phone calls, no. Most people have cells now, of course. And no messages or package at the front desk, nothing like that."

After asking a few more questions they thanked the couple and left.

Outside, Agent Murdock was waiting for them.

"Playing detective?" he said in a surly tone, nodding toward the couple through the window.

"Just having a cup of coffee. It's chilly today."

"Yeah, a cup of coffee with the owners of the lodge where your guy was staying."

"Another coincidence," said Michelle.

"Let it be your last one," replied Murdock.

"Can I have my gun back? I'm feeling kind of naked without it."

"Ballistics isn't done yet. I'll let you know. Could be a while. Paperwork gets backed up. You know how it is." He stared up at Sean. "I'm hoping I don't run into you two again. Why don't you get back to Virginia? Nothing to keep you here."

"I thought you said we were material witnesses and couldn't leave the area."

"I changed my mind. So go!"

"It's a free country," said Sean.

"Until it's not free," shot back Murdock.

After he left, Michelle headed over to the gas station attendant. "Where's the closest gun shop?"

"About two miles north of here, right on this road. Place called Fort Maine Guns."

"Nice assortment of pistols?"

"Oh yeah. You shoot?"

"Only when I have to."

11

Michelle slipped the 9mm Sig into her belt holster and let out a prolonged sigh of satisfaction.

Sean stared at her in amusement. "Smoke 'em if you got 'em."

"Why do I think having a gun up here is a really good idea?"

"Because it is."

"I'd just gotten used to the H&K, but I have to say I've always been partial to Sigs."

"You carried a Glock for a while, too."

"You know what they say: Some girls like shoes, some girls like guns."

"I've never actually heard anyone else say that."

She stuck a couple boxes of ammo in her bag and said, "Time to head to Portland to pick up the baby lawyer."

They had traveled about twenty miles when Michelle said, "Possible tail."

Sean kept his gaze straight ahead. "Where?"

"Dark sedan two hundred yards back. Lose it on the curves and pick it back up on the straights."

"Could be nothing. He could be heading where we are."

"We'll see, won't we?"

When they reached the cut over to the interstate the car kept going.

Michelle said, "Guess you were right."

"Still, good to be alert. Now if the folks at Gray's Lodge saw Bergin at around nine and he was killed around midnight, that still leaves him with nearly three hours or so to move around somewhere."

"He didn't go back to Cutter's. It's locked down after dark. So—"

The bullet broke through the passenger's side window, passed in front of both Sean and Michelle, and shattered the driver's side glass on the way out.

Sean ducked down and Michelle immediately cut the vehicle to the left. She rode the shoulder momentarily while Sean looked behind them.

"No other car?" he asked.

"No. Shot came from long range."

"Pull the car down there," he barked, pointing to the trees set off the road. "And keep down."

She banked into the soft grass and pulled the Ford farther down to a stop next to a stand of trees. They slid out of the car on their bellies, keeping the metal of the car between them and where the shot had come from. Michelle had her Sig out and was scanning the possible firing lines. Sean edged his head over the hood and then ducked back down.

"No optics signature that I can see."

Michelle eyed the broken windows. "Helluva shot with us going at speed."

"I'm taking this as a warning."

She nodded. "Anyone who could make that trigger pull could've easily killed us. I think I saw the damn round pass right in front of me, although I know that's not really possible. And auto glass these days is not the crap it used to be. To shatter *both* and keep going takes some horsepower."

Sean studied the surroundings. "Slight breeze, lots of trees, maybe some high ground where the shooter was. Sun behind him, which favored the shot. Still impressive. We're moving perpendicular to the shot at sixty miles an hour."

"Seventy," corrected Michelle. "Shooter must be a hell of a mil-dot counter. That was some fancy reticle figuring."

Sean nodded. "Military sniper?"

"Maybe. Only question is whose. If ours, it's not a pretty picture. Question is why, and the answer is pretty obvious."

"Edgar Roy," said Sean. He put his back to the front panel of the car and slid down on his butt. "Government bean counter?"

"What the file said."

"FBI watch list. Lawyer murdered. Cutter's Rock hospitality. Long-range warning shot for us."

"Doesn't add up, does it?"

"Not in the world I live in, no."

She said, "You think it's safe to get going?"

"I guess we have to chance it. But you have my permission to drive like you're auditioning for NASCAR."

No more shots hit as they raced onto the interstate.

They retraced their journey from the night before and got to Portland ten minutes before the flight from D.C. landed. They took a couple minutes to clean out the shattered safety glass, which had acted as designed, shattering into a zillion pieces but staying together as a cracked whole.

Sean waited for the deplaning passengers while Michelle went to check on another rental car.

There were thirty-nine passengers on the flight.

Megan Riley was the thirty-ninth coming through the exit gate. *She probably didn't want to get off the plane*, he thought.

She looked over at Sean expectantly. He said, "Megan?"

She nodded and headed toward him.

Michelle walked up to him at that moment and whispered, "She looks like she's about to start high school."

Riley was petite, her red hair sprawled across her shoulders and her face heavily freckled. She was struggling with a roller and a heavy litigation bag that no doubt contained Ted Bergin's old-fashioned paper files. Sean took the bag from her, shook Riley's hand, and introduced Michelle.

When they got to the Ford, Riley saw the shattered windows and the broken glass still littering the floorboards.

"My God, what happened?"

Sean looked at Michelle, who said, "Could've been worse. Only problem is there are no more rentals available. Hope you brought a heavy jacket, Megan."

"Was it an accident?" she asked.

"Not exactly," said Sean, as he opened the rear door for her.

12

"We got you a room at Martha's Inn, Megan," said Sean, as Michelle drove them back. "A couple of guests checked out."

Megan's gaze had really never left the shattered windows. She tugged her thin jacket closer around her. "Did you report this?"

Sean glanced back at her. "Not yet. But we will. Unfortunately, the police are pretty busy with other things. Bullets that missed from an unknown shooter probably rank pretty low on their priority list right about now."

"I know one FBI agent who'll probably be sorry they missed," added Michelle.

"Their priority is Mr. Bergin's murder?" said Megan.

"You can call him Ted."

"No, he'll always be Mr. Bergin to me," she said stubbornly.

Michelle asked, "Anything good in the docs you brought?"

"I'm not sure. I was in court all day yesterday and

just got back to the office when I called you back today. But I brought everything that looked relevant."

"We appreciate that," said Sean.

"So are you working with the FBI?"

Sean glanced at Michelle and said, "Sort of."

Michelle added, "What about Bergin's house in Charlottesville? Has the FBI searched it?"

"I don't know. Does it matter?"

Sean said, "If we can get there first, it might matter a lot."

"But wouldn't that be interfering in an official investigation?" Megan pointed out.

Michelle raised her eyebrows but held her tongue.

Sean turned around in the seat. "Do you have Hilary's home phone number?"

She gave it to him off her cell phone contacts list. He punched it in, waited.

"Hilary? Sean King. Quick question." He asked her about Bergin's house.

"Okay, how far away are you from it?" He paused as she answered. "Do you think you can drive over there and let us know if there's any activity? Okay, thanks a lot. We'll wait to hear from you. Oh, one more thing. Did the FBI come by the office? Nobody? All right."

He put his phone away and glanced at Michelle, who was swinging her gaze back and forth like a lighthouse beam. "See anything suspicious?"

She shrugged. "We won't see any optics sig until the round hits. End of story."

Megan must've overheard this remark because she immediately sank lower in the backseat. "Do you need me to stay up here long?"

"Maybe," said Sean.

"I have to get back at some point." Her gaze flicked to the darkness all around.

"We're all hoping to get back home at some point. Unfortunately it's too late for Ted," he added, his tone a bit harder.

She obviously noted this. "I'm not trying to chicken out. It's just that—"

Sean turned around in the seat once more. "You don't look like a coward to me at all, Megan. You got on the plane and came up here. You saw what happened to our car and didn't turn tail and run. That takes courage."

She said slowly, "Well, truthfully, I almost did run. But I do want to help."

"I know." A thought struck him. "Was Hilary at the office all day?"

"No, by the time I got back from court she'd left to look into some funeral arrangements for Mr. Bergin. But no one came by while I was there."

Sean turned back around. "I'm not sure when they'll be done with the remains."

"I still can't believe he's dead."

He turned back around and saw the tears trickling down her face. He reached over the seat and took her hand. "Megan, it's going to be okay."

"You can't promise that."

"No, I can't, but we can do everything possible to make sure it turns out that way."

She quickly wiped her face dry. "I'm cool. It's okay. No more tears."

Michelle said, "No law against grieving."

"From the looks of things up here I'm not sure we have time for that."

Sean and Michelle exchanged another glance, each visibly impressed at her insightful remark.

"So what's the first order of business?" asked Megan.

Sean answered. "We go back to Martha's Inn, make a big pot of coffee, and start going over these files."

They were an hour out when Michelle's phone rang. It was Eric Dobkin from the Maine State Police. Michelle listened and then clicked off.

"He wants to talk. Got some info for us. I know it's late, but why don't I drop you and Megan at the inn and then swing over and meet him? Save us some time to split up."

"After what happened this afternoon I'm not sure splitting up is a good idea."

"I can take care of myself."

"I know that. I was worried about me and Megan."

"I know Tae Kwon Do," said Megan. "I have my green belt."

"That's nice," said Sean, holding back a smile. "But if they go with their prior method, they won't be near enough for you to kung fu them."

"Oh."

Sean studied Michelle. "Okay, you meet with Dobkin. The legal stuff will go faster with Megan and me anyway. We can fill each other in when we're done. Where are you meeting him?"

"At his house. He gave me the address."

"Okay, but you better put on your A game all the way. Okay?"

"Only way I know how to play, Sean. Thought you would have known that by now."

13

Eric Dobkin's house was in a location that the GPS finally gave up on about a half mile away. Michelle had to call him, and he led her the rest of the way by voice instructions. When she turned a corner and saw the lights of the house up ahead, she also saw a late-model Dodge pickup truck parked in the driveway. Next to it was an old Chrysler minivan. As she peered inside the van she saw three car seats buckled in. "Wow," she said to herself. "I'm betting no one in that house is sleeping much."

The house was constructed of pine logs, the roof of cedar shakes, and the door of unadorned oak. The little flower garden around the house had long since lost its summer luster and just looked exactly what it was: dead.

She knocked.

A light tread started somewhere inside. Not Dobkin's. Perhaps his wife. Michelle stared at the structure, figuring out the interior from her observations of the exterior.

Front room. Three bedrooms set off a central hall.

Kitchen probably in the back. No garage, which in Maine seemed a little crazy. Maybe one and a half baths. It looked sturdy, each log tethered securely to its neighbor.

The door opened. The woman was short and carrying a child on her hip. The size and shape of her belly indicated she was also clearly expecting another little one. And soon.

"I'm Sally. You must be Michelle," she said in a good-natured if tired tone. "This is Adam. Our oldest. Just turned three." The little boy stared back at Michelle, one finger in his mouth.

"You have three kids?"

"How'd you know?"

"Car seats in the van."

"Good observer. Eric said you and your partner were good at what you do. Yep, three little boys." She patted her stomach. "And one in the oven. Each a year apart."

"You didn't waste any time." Michelle stepped inside. "Sorry to come by so late."

"With Eric's work hours we're all night owls. He's back in the den."

Michelle looked around. A den? There must be a room in the back that she had missed in her internal calculation.

"I'll be right back," Sally said.

She disappeared and Dobkin appeared about a minute later. He was dressed in LL Bean jeans, a white cotton shirt, and a sleeveless orange ski parka. His blond hair was still matted down from his trooper hat.

"Nippy tonight," said Michelle.

He looked at her funny. "Nippy?"

"Well, I guess by Southern standards. You really live out in the boonies."

He cracked a grin. "I'm only five miles from the stoplight. You should see where some of the other guys live. Now *that's* the boonies."

"If you say so."

"So your partner's preoccupied?"

"Trying to cover all the bases. And I appreciate you calling. I know this can't be easy. Sort of stuck in the middle."

"Come on back."

He led her past the kitchen where they could see Sally feeding Adam and what was probably the two-year-old, who looked half asleep and ready to fall right into his plate of food. The youngest child already must be in bed, she assumed.

They settled in the small den, which held an old, battered, gunmetal-gray desk, a shelf made of planks and concrete blocks, and a scarred, two-drawer oak file cabinet. A red Dell laptop sat on the desk along with a locked portable gun case, where she presumed he kept his service pistol. With three little and no doubt inquisitive kids in the house, that was a real necessity. One window looked out onto the back of the house. A rectangular blue rug did its best to soften the starkness of the wooden floor. Dobkin sat behind the desk and indicated a ladder-back chair with a faux leather seat for Michelle to take. She drew it up and plunked her butt down.

Dobkin eyed her waistline. "Fresh hardware?"

She glanced down at the revealed Sig. "When in Maine, you know. And Murdock was vague about when I could expect my weapon back."

"Heard you got over to Cutter's to see Edgar Roy."

"We did. Impressive place. No dollar spared, I take it."

"Lot of good-paying jobs. And we need every one of them."

"So homicidal psychos do have their benefits."

"Didn't get very far with him, did you?"

"Been talking to Special Agent Murdock?"

"No. My wife's friend works at Cutter's."

"So you have a direct line into the place?"

Dobkin shifted uneasily in his chair. "Wouldn't go that far."

"So how's the investigation coming?"

"FBI is being characteristically tight with developments."

"What did you want to see me about?"

"Couple of things. In addition to the phone message your partner left him, Bergin received one phone call about the time he left Gray's Lodge last night. And made one as well."

"Who called him and who did he call?" Michelle knew the answer to the first question but not the last.

"The one he received was from a Megan Riley. Virginia number."

"That's his associate." Michelle said nothing about the woman being less than an hour away at Martha's Inn. "And who did he call?"

"Cutter's Rock confirming his appointment the next morning."

"That's strange, since he was there earlier. You'd think he would have just confirmed it then."

"Maybe he's a belt-and-suspenders kind of guy. Or at least he was," amended Dobkin.

"Cutter's Rock. What do you know about it?"

"It's Federal. It's escapeproof. Really bad dudes are kept there."

She feigned a smile. "Yeah, those salient points I got. Edgar Roy looked like he was a zombie. They include drugging folks up there in their daily health planner?"

"Think that would be against the law, unless some medico ordered it."

"They have docs there, right? Who maybe will order whatever is needed?"

"I suppose, yeah. But they do some of that tele-health stuff too."

"Tele-health?"

"So they don't have to transport prisoners back and

forth. Docs can look at them via computer with health techs on-site. Look down a throat with a little camera, take vitals, stuff like that. Same with court appearances that don't require personal appearances. All done via computer hookup. Transportation scenarios are where escapes are most likely to happen."

"Edgar Roy doesn't look like he could escape even if they gave him the key to the place and bus fare."

"Don't know anything about that."

"Anything else?"

"Not really, no."

Michelle eyed him evenly. "You could've told me this on the phone."

"I like dealing face-to-face."

"Doesn't explain why you want to help us."

"You helped my men. Returning the favor."

"And a little payback to the FBI for taking over the investigation?"

"Got nothing against them. Roy is their problem."

"Any results back on the postmortem on Bergin?"

"Feds brought in their own cutter. No report yet that I know of."

"How's the colonel taking being put in the backseat in his home park?"

"He plays by the rules."

"Anything else that might throw light on why Bergin was killed?"

"Not on my end. Now how about from you?"

"We're just drifting right now."

"Heard tell your car windows aren't there anymore."

Michelle tried to hide her irritation. "Heard tell from whom?"

"True or not?"

"Okay, true."

"Where did it happen?"

She told him.

"You should've reported that."

"I'm reporting it now."

"See anything?"

"Nothing to see except a long-range rifle round passing before my eyes."

"Not many folks can make that kind of shot."

"Oh, sure there are. I bet your little sister could do it."

Dobkin grinned. "You always this casual during an investigation?"

"Helps to break the tension."

"You also have a lady with you. Who's that? Megan Riley?"

"So how long have you had a tail on us?"

"We don't. Just eyes over at Martha's."

"Mrs. Burke?"

"She's a good friend of my wife."

"Your wife has really helpful friends."

"Benefits of a small town."

"Uh-huh."

"So is it Megan Riley?"

"Yes it is."

"Feds will want to talk to her."

"I expect they will."

"And you'll let them know she's with you?"

"I'm sure Agent Murdock, with the full weight of the FBI behind him, will figure out where she is, especially if your wife can."

"I guess that's it."

"For now," amended Michelle.

"I appreciate you keeping this little arrangement between ourselves."

She rose. "One last thing."

"Yeah," he said quickly, his eyes looking over her shoulder as the sounds of a baby wailing reached them.

"Your youngest?"

He nodded. "Sam. Named after my dad. He was a state trooper too."

"Was? Retired?"

"No. Line of duty. Argument between two drunks that went really wrong."

"Sorry."

He tensed as the baby's cries picked up. "So what else? I got to help Sally," he said in a tone designed to close the conversation.

"Why was Edgar Roy on an FBI watch list? He's a suspected serial killer, granted. But still, his lawyer gets killed and an army of Fibbies jumps on a chopper from Boston in about twenty seconds?"

"I don't know anything about that."

"But you strike me as the sort who would wonder about it."

"Well, I guess you're wrong about what sort I am."

Michelle walked back to her car, conscious of the fact that Dobkin was staring at her until she was out of his sight line.

So much for helping Sally with the baby.

14

Sean flipped through the last few pages of a litigation binder and then looked over at Megan Riley, who was rubbing her eyes and sipping on a mug of now lukewarm tea. They were in Sean's room. Mrs. Burke hadn't put up any fight about another woman being in his room, so Sean concluded it was simply Michelle the lady didn't care for.

Sean had confirmation of this after the innkeeper had brought them up sandwiches, a couple slices of pie, coffee, and the tea for Megan. Before leaving the room Burke asked, "Where's your friend?"

"Running down a lead."

"Has she had supper?"

"I don't think so."

"Well, it's very late and the kitchen is closed."

"Okay. I'll let her know."

Sean put down the binder and looked at the notes he'd written on a legal pad. "How did Ted come to take this case in the first place?"

Megan sat forward in her chair and put down her mug. She picked up half of her turkey sandwich. "I'm not sure. He mentioned it in passing several weeks ago. To tell you the truth, I hadn't really focused on Edgar Roy. I mean I'd read something in the paper about what had happened, but I was busy getting my feet wet as a newbie lawyer. When Mr. Bergin told me I'd be on the legal papers too, I asked him about the case, and he spent a few minutes going over it with me. God, it was horrible. Edgar Roy must really be a wacko."

"That wacko is now your client, so keep that opinion to yourself."

She sat up straighter. "Oh, right. Sorry."

"And you said you did some research for Ted on the case?"

She swallowed a bite of sandwich and wiped a smudge of mayo off her mouth. "Right. Pretty mundane things. Jurisdictional issues. Competency grounds. That sort of thing."

"Any defense theories?"

"I'm not sure Mr. Bergin had any yet. But he seemed anxious to go to trial."

"How do you know that?"

"From things he said. He really seemed to want to move forward with it."

"Which again begs the question of how he ended up being Roy's lawyer. If the guy was incompetent he couldn't have hired Ted. And I can find nothing in the record that shows the two had a pre-existing professional relationship."

"Well, does he have any family that could have hired Mr. Bergin?"

"That was my next question. But the billing records aren't in the file."

"I think Hilary keeps those separate," said Megan.

"But there's no correspondence going out to a client. And that should be in these files."

"I thought I got everything, but I might have overlooked something."

Sean's phone rang. Ironically it was Hilary.

"I just got back from Mr. Bergin's house, Sean. There's no one there."

"No one there *now*. Could you tell if people had been there before you?"

"The place is pretty isolated, but there is a house you have to pass to get to Mr. Bergin's. I know the woman who lives there. I asked her if the police or anyone had been by and she said no. And she'd been home all day."

"Okay, Hilary, I really appreciate you doing that. Look, I'm here with Megan. Right, we had her fly up tonight. She brought the files, but there's nothing in here about who Ted's client was. It couldn't have been Roy. At least I don't think it was. And the correspondence file isn't in here. Who do you send the legal bills to?"

"There aren't any bills."

"What do you mean? He was doing this pro bono?"

"I'm not sure. I guess he might have. Or else he'd set up a different payment system."

"But he still had to be engaged by someone. He had to contact them. There has to be a legal representation engagement letter somewhere by a person authorized to act on behalf of Edgar Roy."

"Well, I don't know who that is."

"Was this typical for Ted?"

"What do you mean?"

"To hide the identity of his client from you?"

She didn't say anything for a few seconds. "This was the only time he did."

"Okay, thanks, Hilary. I'll be in touch." He put the phone down and gazed at Megan. "Looks like we have a mystery on both ends."

The door opened.

Agent Murdock stood there with his men right behind.

"Megan Riley?"

The young lawyer spilled her tea as she stood on trembling legs. "Yes?"

"FBI. You'll need to come with us." He looked over at Sean. "And be thankful your ass isn't being charged with obstruction."

"How would that be possible?"

"You know the lady is pertinent to our investigation."

"Pertinent but not a material witness. And I'm entitled to conduct my own investigation." Murdock started to say something but before he could get the words out, Sean added, "The way I see it I did you a favor. I brought her up to Maine. I'll be sure to send along a request for reimbursement of her plane ticket to the Bureau."

"Don't hold your breath," growled Murdock. "Let's go, Ms. Riley."

Megan looked imploringly at Sean, who said, "Call me when they're done. I'll come and pick you up."

"No you won't," snapped Murdock.

"You holding her against her will?"

"No."

"Then I will pick her up when she calls."

"You better watch yourself."

"I suggest you do the same, Agent Murdock."

15

Peter Bunting nervously adjusted his tie and nodded at the staffer who had come to escort him to his meeting. He'd been here on numerous occasions, but this time was different. This time he was prepared to have his ass handed to him.

He suddenly stopped and stared blankly at the man who was just now leaving the office he was about to enter.

Mason Quantrell was fifteen years older than Bunting and not quite as tall, with a bulldog chest and a jowly face. His hair was still thick and wavy, though the brown strands had turned mostly gray. His mind was far sharper than his features, his eyes roaming and intense. He was the CEO of the Mercury Group, one of the biggest players in the national security field. Revenue-wise, Mercury was well over twice the size of Bunting's company, but the E-Program platform gave Bunting greater clout in the intelligence community. Quantrell was from the old school. Spread the intelligence around. Let the worker bees do their thing and feed the government paper mill, spewing out reports no one had time to read. He was the dinosaur making billions off Uncle Sam. Quantrell had hired Bunting to work for him right out of college. And then Bunting had left to build his own empire. Two decades ago Quantrell had been the wonder boy of the private-sector clandestine world before Bunting had replaced him.

They were not friends. In some ways they were even more than competitors. And in Washington there were really no winners or losers, only survivors. And Bunting knew that Quantrell would do everything in his power to knock him off his lofty perch.

"What a coincidence seeing you here," said Quantrell.

I bet, thought Bunting.

"How's business?" asked Quantrell.

"Never better."

"Is that right? I heard otherwise."

"I don't really care what you heard, Mason."

Quantrell laughed. "Well, don't keep the lady waiting, Pete. I'm sure she has lots to tell you."

He strode down the hall, and Bunting watched him every step of the way until the aide touched his shoulder, which made him jump.

"Secretary Foster will see you now, Mr. Bunting."

He was ushered into the large corner office where the polycarbonate glass allowed in ample sunlight, but never a bullet. He sat across from the woman. She was dressed in pale blue—her favorite color, Bunting had observed. Ellen Foster was forty-five, divorced, childless, as ambitious as he was, and brilliant. That was just the way it was. The filter became incredibly picky at this level. She was also blond, slender, and attractive, and she could gallop the range from iron maiden to feminine flirt with ease. That didn't hurt, either, in this city where honey *and* vinegar were often used as aphrodisiacs.

Foster, the secretary of Homeland Security—a recent innovation prompted by 9/11—nodded at Bunting with an unreadable expression. She was an excellent tactician, he knew. She sat atop the largest security agency in the country. It had swallowed turf and budget dollars like a giant vacuum cleaner. This had caused a lot of envy from other agencies that resented the new kid on the block's heft and reach. But it was the new world, and Foster was the newest member of the Cabinet. She had the president's ear and confidence. When the person in the White House had your back, you were platinum. Foster knew this, of course. She could afford to appear cooperative and magnanimous to her competitors. For in the end, she knew she would come out on top.

Foster rose to greet him. "Peter, good to see you. Family well?"

"Yes, Secretary Foster, all well. Thank you."

She motioned to the couch and chairs set against one wall. A pot of coffee and cups were on the table there. "Let's relax a bit. This isn't a formal meeting, after all."

This gave Bunting no comfort at all. More professional executions occurred at informal meetings than did at the official ones.

They sat.

"I saw Mason Quantrell out in the hall."

"Yes, I suppose you did."

"Anything interesting going on with Mercury?"

She smiled and pushed the sugar bowl toward him. Obviously no answer to that was coming.

"He doesn't know about . . . ?" said Bunting.

"Let's focus on you, Peter."

"Okay."

He had just placed the cup to his lips when she struck.

"The vaunted E-Program has obviously crashed off the tracks."

He swallowed too large a mouthful of coffee and tried to keep his eyes from watering as the liquid burned his throat. He set the cup down, sponged his lips with his cloth napkin.

"We have issues, yes, but I wouldn't say that we've crashed."

"How would you describe it?" she asked pointedly.

"We've gone off course, but we are working hard to get back on. And I—"

She held up a finger, silencing him. Foster lifted a phone and spoke three words. "The reports, please."

Moments later an efficient-looking aide delivered the folder to her. She leisurely turned the pages as

Bunting stoically watched. He wanted to say, *You still use paper files? How quaint.* But he didn't dare.

She said, "The report quality has degraded considerably. Usable intel from the E-Program has fallen thirty-six percent. The reports are a mess. The dots are not being connected like they were. You told me the operation would not be measurably impacted. It clearly has."

"It's true that the bar has been set very high. But I—"

She broke in again. "Now, you know you have no bigger supporter than me."

He knew that was a blatant lie but automatically said, "I appreciate that very much. You've been a true asset and marvelous leader during very stressful times." Cabinet secretaries' butts were large indeed and required an inordinate amount of kissing.

She smiled for the requisite few seconds, then her expression turned dour. "There are those out there, however, who do not share my enthusiasm. Over the years the E-Program has ruffled some important feathers. Taken budget dollars and mission responsibility from other agencies. That is the Holy Grail in our world. The pie is what it is. Someone gets a bigger slice, others have to make do with a smaller one."

And DHS, thought Bunting, had taken by far the biggest slice of all.

He said, "But it's indisputable that the E-Program has been tremendously successful. It's kept this country safer than if every agency was competing with each other. That model just doesn't work anymore."

She said slowly, "I wouldn't necessarily agree with that assessment. But nevertheless it's the old question: What have you done for me today? The barbarians are at the gate. And do you realize what might happen if this all becomes public?"

"That will not happen. I can assure you."

She closed the file. "Well, I'm not assured, Peter, not at all. And neither are the other people who matter. When the CIA director learned of it I thought he was going to have a heart attack. He thinks it's a colossal time bomb waiting to explode. How do you respond to that?"

Bunting took another swallow of coffee, giving him a few more precious seconds to think.

"I believe strongly that we can turn this around," he said finally.

She looked at him with incredulity. "That's your answer? Really?"

"That's my answer," he said firmly. He was too exhausted mentally to think of any clever response. And it wouldn't have mattered anyhow. The lady's mind was obviously made up.

"Perhaps I'm not getting across to you, Peter." She paused, seeming to size up what she was about to say. "There are some who think preemptive action is necessitated by the circumstances."

Bunting licked his dry lips. He knew exactly what that meant. "I think that would be a most unwise move."

She hiked her eyebrows. "Really? So what's your recommendation? Wait until the other shoe drops? Wait until the crisis engulfs us? Is that your strategy, Peter? Should I phone the president and let him know of this?"

"I don't think we need to bother him at this stage."

"For a smart man you are acting incredibly dense today. Let me make this as clear as possible. This will not blow back to us, do you understand? If it seems like it will, preemptive action will be taken."

"I will do everything in my power to make sure that does not become necessary, Madame Secretary."

The use of her formal title by him made the woman smile in amusement.

She rose, put out her hand. He shook it. Her nails were long, he noted. They could scratch his eyes out. Probably reach through his skin and dig out his heart, too.

"Don't burn bridges, Peter. If you do, very soon you'll have nothing left to stand on."

Bunting turned and walked with as much dignity as he could muster from the office. He only had one thought in his head.

He had to go to Maine.

*

After he was gone Foster finished her coffee. A few moments later the man walked in, responding to the text message she'd just thumbed summoning him.

James Harkes stood at attention a few feet from Foster.

Six foot one, he was perhaps forty years of age, a bit of white in his short, dark hair. He wore a black two-piece suit, white shirt, and straight black tie. He looked ominously strong, his hands thick and fingers rough as barnacles. His shoulders had muscles on top of muscles, but he moved like a cat. Smooth, not an ounce of wasted energy. He was a veteran of many missions on behalf of America and her allies. He was a man who got the job done. Always.

He said nothing as she poured out another cup of coffee without offering him one.

She took a sip and finally looked up at him. "Did you hear all that?"

"Yes," said Harkes.

"What's your take on Bunting?"

"Smart, resourceful, but running out of options. The guy doesn't chase windmills, so we can't under-estimate him."

"He didn't ask about Sohan Sharma's 'accident.'"

"No, he didn't."

"Such an unpredictably violent world we live in."

"Yes it is. New orders?"

"You'll get them. When the time is right. Just stay on top of it all."

She gave an almost imperceptible nod and Harkes departed. Then she finished her coffee and went back to her important work protecting herself and her country. And strictly in that order.

16

Cutter's rock.

Close to midnight.

Visiting hours long over.

The tower guards patrolled their beats.

The concertina wire glistened in the strong moonlight.

The electrified middle fence was fully powered, ready to char anyone unfortunate enough to collide with it.

The outer gates swung open and the Yukon drove through.

No electronic checks, no vehicle sweeps. No requests for ID. No cavity probes. The Yukon raced down the road.

Next, the hydraulic blast doors on the facility hissed open. At the same time the doors of the Yukon swung open. Peter Bunting was the first one out. As his long feet touched gravel he looked around and pulled his trench coat tighter around him. His young assistant Avery was the only person with him.

Bunting's private jet had touched down at a corporate

jet park less than an hour away by car. They had come directly here.

Carla Dukes met the pair at the entrance.

"Hello, Carla," said Bunting. "What's the status?"

"He's never said a word, Mr. Bunting. He just sits there."

"Recent visitors?"

"The FBI. And those investigators, Sean King and Michelle Maxwell. And of course Mr. Bergin."

"And he never said anything to them?"

"Not a word."

Bunting nodded, somewhat reassured. He'd pulled many strings to get Carla Dukes assigned as the director of Cutter's Rock. She was loyal to him, and right now he needed her as his eyes up here. Who Edgar Roy really was had to be kept from everyone, including his lawyers and the FBI.

"Tell me about King and Maxwell."

"They're persistent, clever, and tough," she said promptly.

"Former Secret Service," said Avery. "So no surprise there."

"I don't like surprises," said Bunting. He nodded at Dukes. "Take us to him, please."

She escorted them back to the same room Sean and Michelle had been in with Edgar Roy. A minute later the man himself appeared. The guards escorted him in, set him down in the chair. He immediately extended his long legs and sat there, staring at nothing.

Bunting glanced at Dukes. "That's all, thanks. And kill the surveillance."

He waited until the video and audio equipment was shut down and then sat down in a chair near Roy, his knees almost touching the other man's legs.

"Hello, Edgar."

Nothing.

"I think you can understand me, Edgar."

Not a blink from Roy. His gaze was positioned over Bunting's shoulder.

Bunting turned to Avery. "Please tell me his brain is undamaged."

"Nothing wrong with it that they can find."

He lowered his voice. "Faking?"

Avery shrugged. "He's like the smartest person in the world. Anything is possible."

Bunting nodded and thought back to the first time Edgar Roy had gone toe-to-toe with the Wall. It had been one of the most exhilarating times of Bunting's life. It had been right up there, in fact, with the birth of his children.

Inside the room, Roy, covered with the same electronic measuring equipment as the now-deceased Sohan Sharma wore, had studied the screen. Bunting noted that when the screen sometimes divided into two sets of images Roy looked at one set with his right eye and the other with his left. That was unusual but not unheard of for people with Roy's intellectual ability.

Bunting had glanced at Avery, who was working the information flow in front of a bank of computers. "Status?"

"Normal."

"You mean normal but heightened."

"No, there's no change," said Avery.

"On my command send the Wall to full power. We have to know if this guy can cut it sooner rather than later. We're running out of time and options."

"Got it."

Bunting had spoken into the headset he wore. The first questions would just be warm-ups, nothing too taxing.

"Edgar, please provide me with the logistical data you just observed from the Pakistani border, beginning with US Special Forces movements and the reactionary tactics taken by the Taliban on the fourteenth of last month."

Five seconds later over his headset Bunting heard an exact replication of this data.

He turned to Avery. "Status?"

"No bump at all. Smooth and level."

Bunting had turned back to look through the one-way glass. "Edgar, you just observed the encryption code for the relay link for DOD's satellite platform over the Indian Ocean. Please provide me with every other number of that code up to the first five hundred digits."

The numbers came at him almost immediately in rapid succession.

Bunting's gaze was locked on his tablet where the correct digits were set forth. When the last number had rolled off Roy's tongue, Bunting drew a deep breath. A perfect match.

"Theta status?" he barked at Avery.

"No change."

"Full power on the data flow."

Avery cranked it and the Wall flow accelerated markedly. Bunting had muttered, "Okay, Edgar, let's see if you can play in the big leagues."

He had asked four more questions of Roy, all memorization tests, each quantitatively harder than the last one. Roy had aced all four effortlessly.

"He's very relaxed," said Avery, his voice cracking with excitement. "His theta activity actually went down."

Relaxed, Bunting had thought. *The man is relaxed and his theta went down and the Wall is at full throttle.*

Bunting tried to keep his growing euphoria in check. Memorization was one thing, analysis was quite another.

"Edgar, you observed ten minutes ago both the military and geopolitical conditions on the ground in Afghanistan's Anbar province. I want you to contrast that with the political situation in Kabul, factoring in the known current allegiances of the tribal and political heads in both sectors. Then, provide me your best analysis of what strategic steps the American military should take to solidify its holdings in Anbar and then expand that into neighboring regions over the next six months, while at the same time enhancing our control over the capital both militarily and politically."

Bunting had had four rock-solid scenarios on his tablet screen, the result of a hundred top analysts from four different agencies poring over this same data for weeks, instead of minutes. Any one of these four replies would have been more than acceptable. This was the real test. The man who would occupy this position was not called the Memorizer. He was called the Analyst. You earned your money by taking facts and turning them into something valuable, as an alchemist could purportedly turn iron into gold.

Fifteen seconds passed and then it had come.

However, Edgar Roy had not given one of the four responses he was expecting, indeed, hoping for. What he did provide made Bunting's jaw drop nearly to the device he was holding. Not one person Bunting had ever talked to at the Pentagon, the State Department, or even the CIA had come up with such a revolutionary strategy. And this man had, after bare seconds of thinking about it.

Bunting had looked at the men gathered around him who had heard this feedback as well. They too were all gaping. Bunting had gazed back at Roy, who just sat there as though he were watching a moderately entertaining movie instead of spearheading the American intelligence juggernaut.

Peter Bunting had not been born with the proverbial silver spoon in his mouth. He had grown up as an army brat; the family had moved each time his father's duties and rank had changed. His old man was career-enlisted, had bled for his country, and he instilled a pride in his son to do the same. Bad eyesight had killed any chance Bunting had to join up, but he'd found another way to serve. Another way to defend his country.

Bunting had been ecstatic on discovering that Edgar Roy was the greatest Analyst he likely would ever find. What had followed was six months of the best intelligence output the United States had ever had.

And now?

He stared at the six-foot-eight zombie sitting across from him.

God help us all.

He turned to Avery. "How is the investigation going on the death of Edgar's lawyer?"

"Slowly. Special Agent Murdock is in charge."

"And where does that leave Edgar?"

"Bergin has a young associate, Megan Riley. And of course King and Maxwell."

"Right—persistent, clever, and tough. They discovered Bergin's body, didn't they?"

"Yes."

"I had my head handed to me today by that bitch Foster. And I passed Mason Quantrell leaving a meeting with her. I know she timed it so I would run into him."

"Why do you think that?" asked Avery.

"It's obvious. She wanted me to know that she's picked Quantrell as my successor. They've been looking for any reason to pull the plug on me and let Quantrell's Mercury Group leap to the top of the pecking order. And they think they've found it."

"But why would they want to do that? The E-Program has been incredibly successful. Quantrell's approach was same-old same-old and a disaster."

"They have short memories in Washington. And in order for the E-Program to do its thing, they all have to share their information with us. Most of them want their little fiefdoms right back where they've always been, so they've got built-in support from all the alphabet agencies that matter."

Bunting focused on Roy again. "Edgar, your country needs you. Do you understand that? We can make this all work out okay for you. But we need your cooperation. Do you get that?"

Black dots. Nothing else.

Bunting persisted. "I believe that you can understand me. And I need you to think very carefully how you want this all to turn out, okay? We have a window of opportunity. But that window can't remain open forever."

A face of stone looked back at him.

After a few more attempts Bunting sighed, rose, and left. As he and Avery walked down the hall Avery said, "Sir, what if he did kill those people?"

"I've got over three hundred million *people* to protect. And I need Edgar Roy to do it."

17

Michelle sat across from Sean in his bedroom. They'd filled each other in on events.

"Megan's probably scared to death," said Michelle.

"She's got guts. As they were leaving, she told Murdock that she knew her rights and that he couldn't push her around."

"Good for her."

"But then she started to tear up and got the hiccups. I think Murdock might have sensed that as a sign of weakness."

"Right," said Michelle in a disappointed tone. "So what now?"

"We struck out with Roy. We can't really investigate Ted's murder because Murdock won't let us near anything."

"So we investigate something else pertinent to the matter? Like is Edgar Roy guilty or not?"

Sean nodded. "And also why does a guy like him garner so much attention from the Feds? Granted he might be a serial killer, but there, unfortunately, are lots of serial killers. They don't warrant late-night chopper rides and this kind of full-court press."

"I think we need to look at what he was actually doing at the government."

"Ted told me he worked at the IRS."

"So we head back to Virginia?"

"We need to take care of Megan first. And we need to find out who retained Ted Bergin."

"Seems like an attorney would check in with the paying client when he's about to talk to the defendant."

"Dobkin told you he only talked to Megan and Cutter's. What about e-mails?"

"Dobkin didn't mention any. A guy Bergin's age might not be into smartphone e-mailing anyway."

"Maybe not. But you're right. He must be in contact with the client in some way."

"Do you remember from the media reports whether Roy had family? If so, they might be the ones who hired Bergin."

He said, "I recall reading that his parents were dead. I don't remember the mention of any siblings. We'll have to run it down some other way." He opened his notepad and began scribbling. "Okay, Bergin's investigation is closed off for now. We track down Roy's background, the client, and then we need to get to the obvious point."

"Namely, did Roy kill those people?" replied Michelle. "That's what it comes down to. Which means we have to poke our nose into that investigation, too."

"We were always going to do that anyway," he pointed out. "But under discovery laws the prosecution has to provide the defense with all the evidence."

"Can we poke around at the crime scene, too?"

"I think it would be malpractice if we didn't."

"Do you think Roy is faking it? I've seen guys do that zombie routine before when I was a cop. Especially if they're staring at the death penalty."

"If he is, he's damn good at it."

"Maybe he is drugged up."

"I don't know what purpose is served by the government keeping an accused killer drugged up so he can't stand trial."

"Okay, when do you want to leave for Virginia?"

"I told Megan to call me when the Feds were done with her."

"Considering Murdock will try to screw us at every turn, it might be a while before she surfaces. Can we afford to wait for that?"

He looked at her. "What do you have in mind?"

"How do you know I have anything in mind?"

"We're an old married couple, remember? Or at least we act like one."

"Don't start finishing my sentences. You could get badly hurt."

"So?" he said expectantly.

"So maybe I head to Virginia and start looking into the murders down there and Roy's connection to the Feds while you stay up here, wait for them to kick Megan loose. And maybe you go back to Cutter's Rock again, this time with Megan, and dig up what you can on Bergin's murder. Then we rendezvous and compare notes in the near future."

He smiled. "What about you taking care of me?"

"So put on your big-boy pants and suck it up."

"So we divide and conquer."

"Or cut our strength in half." She handed him her gun. "You better keep this."

"I don't have a permit."

"Better they arrest you for not having a permit than my identifying your body because you didn't have a gun."

"I get the point. But what about you?"

"Don't worry. I'll stop by my apartment and grab a spare."

"How many guns do you have?"

"Neither one more nor one less than I need."

He took the gun.

18

Sean drove through the night and dropped Michelle off at the airport in Bangor, where she boarded a seven a.m. flight. After switching to another plane in Philadelphia, she reached Virginia a few minutes before noon. She'd slept soundly on both flights and felt recharged when she touched down at Dulles Airport. She picked up her Toyota from the parking garage, drove home, packed another bag, grabbed a spare pistol, and drove to the office. She checked messages and mail, packed a few more things, looked up some addresses, made some calls, and headed to Charlottesville. She got to town around four that afternoon and drove directly to Ted Bergin's law office, which was located in a business complex near the Boar's Head Inn and Resort.

It was on the first floor of a clapboard-sided building painted white with green shutters and a black door. It had a simple arrangement: reception area, two offices, a conference room, and a small kitchen and workspace area in the back. As was her habit, Michelle scouted out and noted the rear exit on the other side of the building.

The Sixth Man

Michelle was greeted by a woman in her sixties wearing a pale-blue blouse with a ruffled collar, black skirt, and black heels. Her hair was bottle blond and starting to thin from one perm too many. She had puffy eyes and reddened cheeks. Michelle assumed this was Hilary Cunningham and was proven right when the woman introduced herself. After offering condolences about her unfortunate boss, Michelle asked to look around Bergin's office.

"We need to track down who the client is," she explained.

Hilary led her to Bergin's office and then left her alone, murmuring something about burial arrangements. From the utterly devastated look on the woman's face Michelle wondered if their relationship had been something more than employer and employee. If so, that might be another lead they would have to run down. Bergin's death might not stem from his representation of Edgar Roy at all. He had been Sean's friend and law professor, but the truth was the two had not seen each other much over the last few years. There could be secrets in Bergin's past that might explain his death, even all the way up in Maine.

Michelle closed the door to the office and sat down behind the man's old-fashioned partners desk, running her fingers across the faded leather inlay. As she gazed around the room it seemed everything in here was old-fashioned. And solid. She closed her eyes and cast her mind back to the dead man in the car.

The diminished body. The saggy face. The hole in the head.

And the rolled-down window that had been rolled back up by the killer.

A killer Bergin might have known. If true, that could possibly cut the suspect list down substantially.

She rifled through Bergin's desk and files. There were several litigation bags parked in a corner of the room but they were empty. No address book. There was no computer on his desk. She slipped back out to the front room and asked Hilary about that.

"Megan and I use computers, obviously, but he never cared to. Pen and paper and a Dictaphone were good enough for him."

"And his calendar?"

"I kept an appointment calendar on the computer for him and would print out a copy every week. He also had a Daily Planner he carried with him."

Michelle nodded. And that Daily Planner would now be in the hands of Agent Murdock. Along with the rest of Bergin's papers.

"Do you know if he ever e-mailed or texted from his cell phone?"

"I seriously doubt he knew how. He preferred talking on the phone."

Michelle went back to his office and noted the jar of pens and pencils and stacks of legal pads on the desk.

Definitely old-fashioned. But then there's nothing wrong with that.

She turned her attention to the wooden file cabinets, the closet, a trench coat that was hanging on a wall peg, and lastly a small oak credenza.

After an hour of searching she came away with nothing helpful.

She spent another hour questioning Hilary. He had not confided much to her about the Roy case, and Michelle could tell this had somewhat irked the lady.

"He's usually very open about his cases," Hilary said. "We worked together, after all."

"And you do the billing?"

"Absolutely. Which made it strange why he never mentioned to me who had retained him to work for Edgar Roy. How were we to be paid, after all? I mentioned to Sean that Mr. Bergin might have taken the case pro bono, but the more I thought about it the less likely I think that is."

"Why?"

"He has a small practice. He's made a good income over the years, but a case like this requires a lot of time and expenses. It would have taxed his resources too much."

"Well, it's a high-profile case. Maybe he was doing it for the notoriety."

Hilary made a face. "Mr. Bergin was not into notoriety. He was a very well-respected lawyer."

"Well, maybe the client made it a condition of the retainer that he couldn't tell anyone. Do you have bank records? There might be a deposit in there that didn't go through you."

Hilary clicked some keys on her computer. "We maintain an account with a local bank. All funds from the practice go in there. I have online access, so let me check."

She looked at various screens and then shook her head. "I made every one of these deposits going back six months."

"Might have been cash."

"No, there are no cash deposits listed."

"Did he keep another account?"

Hilary looked offended by even the suggestion. "If he did, he never told me about it."

"And there's obviously no retainer agreement in the files for the Roy case?"

"No. I already checked that."

"But if Edgar Roy didn't hire him, and from what I've seen of the man it's highly doubtful he had the capacity to do so, someone with a power of attorney or something like that had to do it. You can't just appoint yourself as someone's lawyer. A court has to do that and only under certain conditions." She stared at Hilary. "Are you sure that wasn't the case here?"

"No. If the court had done so there would be a record of that in the file. Mr. Bergin has served as a public defender assisting indigent clients, but not in this case. And I don't believe Mr. Roy was indigent. He had a job and a home."

"Yeah, he's just comatose. I'm not sure in this instance which one is worse."

"I can't speak to that."

"Maybe a family member retained Bergin? Roy's parents are dead. Any siblings? Sean couldn't remember the media mentioning any."

"I really didn't get into that with Mr. Bergin," said Hilary demurely.

"But weren't you curious when he started representing the man? No retainer agreement? No payments?"

Hilary looked uncomfortable at this query. "I must admit that I thought it unusual. But I would never have questioned Mr. Bergin over a professional matter."

"But it was also a business matter. A retainer agreement and getting paid for services is important, too. He's running a business, after all, and you're part of that business."

"Again, I never questioned it. Mr. Bergin certainly would know what he was doing. And it was his practice after all. I . . . I was just his employee."

Michelle studied the woman. *But you wanted to be more. Okay, I get that.*

"He never let anything slip about who might have hired him? The financial arrangement?"

"No."

"So the client never came here?"

"Well, I'm not here 24/7, but no one like that, no, at least while I was present."

"So there were no clients in from the time he started representing Edgar Roy?"

Hilary looked confused. "I don't understand."

"If it was a new person you wouldn't necessarily know why they were here until they met with Bergin."

"Oh, right, I see what you mean. Well, with new clients they typically make an inquiry by phone. I would ask them their personal information and what the matter related to. Mr. Bergin doesn't do all aspects of law so I wouldn't want people wasting their time coming here."

"You serve as a filter."

"Exactly. Then they make an appointment if he can do what they need. And if they come to an understanding I would provide them with a retainer agreement."

"The same day they're here?"

"Sometimes. Or if it was out of the ordinary and Mr. Bergin had to revise the standard document, it might be sent out a few days later to the client's address. Mr. Bergin was a stickler for that. No work was done until the retainer was signed."

"Except in the case of Edgar Roy, apparently."

"Apparently," sniffed Hilary.

"Anyone call here asking for Bergin you didn't recognize?"

"Well, we get a lot of calls. Most of the people I know, of course. Some I don't. But nothing like that sticks out in my mind."

"Did anyone come in to meet with Bergin around the time he started representing Roy, anyone who you didn't send out a retainer agreement for?"

"Not that I can remember, no."

"But like you said, you're not here 24/7. He could have met with the person during nonbusiness hours. Or they could have called in when you weren't here."

"Certainly. He could come and go whenever he wanted."

"What can you tell me about Megan Riley?"

"She came to work here just over two months ago. Mr. Bergin had been saying for a long time that he needed to get an associate. That he wouldn't be practicing forever. And the workload was pretty substantial. There was more than enough for a second attorney. And, of course, he was representing Mr. Roy by that time, and it was demanding a lot of his attention. He needed some help."

"Did he have a lot of applicants for the job?"

"Several. But Megan and he had chemistry, right from the beginning. You could see that."

"You like Megan?"

"She's very nice and works very hard. Now, she's not very experienced, so she makes some mistakes, but that's to be expected. Mr. Bergin was being a fine mentor to her, smoothing out some of the wrinkles." She paused.

"What?" asked Michelle.

"Mr. Bergin and his wife never had any children. I

think he looked on Megan as the daughter or even granddaughter he never had. That was probably another reason he brought her on. The other applicants were older."

"That makes sense. Bergin apparently talked to her on the day he . . . on the day it happened. Did she mention that to you?"

"No. But if it was after hours she probably wouldn't have. She went straight to court the next day, and I didn't get in touch with her until she called afterward. That's when I passed along Sean's message."

"Megan said she brought up all the files on Roy. Do you think she might have left anything behind here?"

"I can check if you want."

"Please."

Twenty minutes later Hilary held up a small file that contained only two pieces of paper. "This was stuck in accidentally with another client file. That's most likely why she missed it."

Michelle took the file, opened it, and stared down at the writing on the paper.

It was from the FBI. It was a request for information from Ted Bergin on his representation of Edgar Roy. As Michelle saw who'd signed the letter, she gave a start.

Special Agent Brandon Murdock.

19

Sean had gotten back to the inn and literally fallen into his bed. He'd gotten up in time for a late lunch. There had been no call from Megan. He'd finally phoned her but it had gone directly to voice mail. Then he'd worked through the legal files twice more but found nothing of value. The case was very undeveloped, and Sean could not determine what Bergin had been planning in the way of a defense. But then again the case wasn't that old. He was probably still feeling his way. And it didn't help matters that Edgar Roy wasn't of much assistance.

Now it was dusk, and he pulled the rental with the shot-out windows to the shoulder of the road and got out. The police and Feds had finished their work here and gone; their yellow barrier tape and warning signs had gone with them.

He started his investigation by standing where the car had sat. He envisioned Bergin driving along late at night. What would make him pull off the road in the first place? Was it someone in distress? Had someone flagged him down and claimed some sort of

149

emergency? Bergin was a smart man, but someone of his generation in particular might have been more apt to pull over and help.

Yet Bergin was in his seventies, alone, no weapon. By all logic he should have just kept on driving. If whoever had killed him had faked an emergency to try and get him to pull off, he could have simply continued on and called 911 on his cell phone. He didn't have to stop and roll down his window just so he could take a fatal round to the head.

So unless he knew the person he should've kept going, but he didn't. Now Sean considered another possibility.

He might have been meeting someone and that person killed him. He studied the gravel shoulder and cast his mind back to that night. They had not seen traces of another car. But he had to admit he hadn't looked all that closely before the police showed up. But if another car had been parked here there would likely be some evidence of that. Evidence the police and the FBI would have.

He looked toward the woods. The troopers had done a preliminary perimeter search, a down-and-dirty one with a fuller one to follow at first light. Had they found anything? If they had, either Dobkin didn't know about it or else the FBI was keeping the Maine State Police in the dark, too.

If a meeting, who with and why here?

Bergin might have been a gentle, caring man, but

he was no fool. If there had been the slightest chance of an ambush the man would not have come here. Had it something to do with Edgar Roy? It had to, he concluded. The only reason Bergin was in Maine was because of his client.

And if the meeting had something to do with Edgar Roy, there might be a limited number of suspects. Sean wondered if that list began and ended at Cutter's Rock.

He tensed as a car's headlights cut through the gloomy dusk. At first he thought it was just a passing motorist, but the car slowed and then pulled in behind his Ford.

Eric Dobkin was not in uniform, and the vehicle he stepped out of was a Dodge pickup, not a Maine State Police cruiser. His shoes made clicking sounds against the asphalt as he came to stand next to Sean. He had on worn jeans, a University of Maine pullover, and a Red Sox ball cap. He looked like a high school senior on the prowl after a football game.

"What are you doing out here?" asked Dobkin, his hands in the pockets of his pullover.

"I thought it would be obvious. Checking out the scene of the crime."

"And?"

"And it's not doing me much good, frankly."

"You really think he might have known the person?"

Sean looked past Dobkin, into the stretch of dark

woods. Though they were miles from the ocean the briny smell seemed to overwhelm him, drift into every pore, like the stench of cigarette smoke in a bar.

"Just an educated guess, based on that window. And the fact that he'd pull over on a lonely road late at night. Odds are he wouldn't have for a stranger."

"Maybe somebody suckered him. Faked a car being broke down. That's what got you to stop."

"Yeah, but there were two of us and my partner had a gun."

"I know your theory about a cop pulling him over sounds plausible, but I don't think that's possible. This is an isolated area, but everybody knows everybody else. Some stranger running around in a police cruiser would've been noticed."

"I think you're right. And if they wanted Ted dead, they really didn't need to go to that much trouble." Sean paused, studying the face of the other man. "You guys totally off the case?"

"Not totally. FBI's running it, of course, but they have to use us for some stuff."

"Find anything of interest here?"

"Nothing really. I would've told your partner if we had."

"What if he were meeting someone?" asked Sean. "That would account for him both pulling off the road and lowering his window. Was there any trace evidence of another car?"

"No wheel impressions. But that's easily gotten

around. Pull your car back on the road and go back and sweep the gravel. Who would he have been meeting with?"

"I was hoping you'd have some idea of that."

"Didn't know the man. You did, though."

The last comment was said in a more accusatory tone than Sean thought the other man probably intended.

"I mean if he were meeting with someone they were probably from around here," said Sean. "And since that doesn't include a lot of people, I thought you might have at least a guess. Maybe somebody at Cutter's Rock? You must know some of the folks who work there."

"I do know some of the folks."

"I'm listening."

"I'm not sure I have anything to tell you."

"Can't or won't?"

"All the same to me."

"You spoke with my partner."

"Right. Where is she, by the way?"

"Checking some other things out."

"Murdock will be all over your ass if you get near his investigation."

"It won't be the first time we've rubbed the official machine the wrong way."

"Just giving you my two cents."

"So why'd you stop here then if you've got nothing to tell me?"

"Man was killed. Like to know who did it."

"That's what I want, too."

Dobkin scuffed the road with his shoe. "Got a chain of command. You're not in it. Got a family. Can't throw my career in the toilet. Not for nothing. Sorry."

"Okay, I get that. I appreciate what you've done." Sean headed back toward his car.

"Any idea who took a shot at you?"

Sean turned back around. "No, other than it wasn't the first time they'd fired a rifle. That fact was pretty clear."

"I'll look into that."

"Okay."

"Why didn't you notify the police? Somebody tried to kill you."

"No, they were warning us off. Different thing."

"I'll still look into it."

"Suit yourself."

"You don't seem to be taking this too seriously."

"I take it very seriously. I just doubt you're going to find anything."

"We're pretty good at our job," Dobkin said stiffly.

"I'm sure you are. But something tells me the other side is pretty good at its job, too."

The two men stared at each other and seemed to reach a silent meeting of the minds.

Dobkin finally pointed at the Ford. "If I were you I'd get those windows covered over. Supposed to rain tomorrow."

The Sixth Man

Sean watched him drive off and then he steered the Ford back to Martha's Inn, his coat buttoned all the way up against the damp chill coming through the open windows.

20

Michelle flashed her light around as she walked toward the back of the house. She'd had some dinner, reported back to Sean, and mulled over what she'd found thus far. She'd waited until it was well after dark before heading to Bergin's house. She wasn't breaking and entering, but the nighttime suited her better for these types of activities.

Ted Bergin had lived in an eighteenth-century farmhouse that he had restored about five years ago, just in time for his wife of forty years to die in a freak car accident. Sean had provided Michelle with this nugget of information, and it had served to deepen her empathy for the man and make her want to find his killer all the more.

The house was about eight miles from his office. The location was rural and isolated, with rolling green hills serving as a picturesque backdrop. She wondered what would happen to the place now. Maybe in his will he had left the property to Hilary Cunningham for years of faithful service.

The woman had given her a key to the house. She

explained that Bergin had kept a spare at the office in the case of an emergency.

Well, I guess this qualifies as such.

Michelle opted for the rear door, because she liked to avoid entering anyplace through the front entrance. Or at least she did ever since she'd nearly gotten herself ripped in half when thirty rounds from a machine gun clip had blasted through the front door of a home in Fairfax, Virginia, that she had been standing in front of a second before.

She eased the door open and peered in, flashing her trusty Maglite around.

Kitchen, she easily concluded after the beam bounced off the refrigerator and then a stainless steel dishwasher. Michelle closed the door behind her and advanced into the space.

The house was not large and the rooms were not numerous, so after an hour she had pretty much covered the basics. Unless she was committed to tearing up floors and ripping open plaster walls, she wasn't going to find anything of significance. Ted Bergin had been a man of tidy habits who had opted for quality over quantity. His possessions were relatively few but of excellent craftsmanship. She found a deer rifle and a shotgun locked behind the barred glass of a cabinet hung on the wall in what looked to be the lawyer's library/home office. Boxes of ammo were housed in a drawer built into the lower part of the cabinet.

She'd found a shotgun vest, fishing tackle, and other

sporting gear in a mudroom and concluded that Bergin had been an avid outdoorsman. Maybe if he'd retired from the practice he would still be alive and enjoying his golden years. Well, there was no maybe about it—he would have.

In a photo album she discovered a number of pictures of Mrs. Bergin. Several showed the woman in her twenties and thirties. She was pretty, with a coy smile that had probably garnered the attention of many young men. There were other photos where the lady's hair had turned white and the skin had wrinkled. But even later in life there had been true warmth and even mischievousness in her expression. Michelle wondered why they had never had children. Maybe they couldn't. And were of a generation that didn't have the availability of fertility clinics and surrogate wombs, although they could have adopted.

She put the album down and considered what to do next.

Michelle wondered why the police or FBI had not been here yet. Perhaps they were confining their investigation to Maine, which seemed shortsighted since the man's murder in Maine might be tied to something in Virginia not connected to Roy. And if his killing was tied to his representation of Roy, relevant evidence could certainly be down here as well. And there was the letter from Brandon Murdock. He, too, apparently wanted to know who Bergin's client was. Yet something must have been filed with the court. Though maybe it was filed under seal. That might be a way to keep it from becoming part of the public record.

But it would seem that the FBI would be able to get past any sealed document.

She decided to go back to Bergin's library one more time, just in case she might have missed something. She sat at his desk, which was ornately carved wood with the gravitas of a judicial bench, and turned on the green lawyer's lamp. No computer here. A few files. Some legal pads with scribbles on them. His answering machine held no messages. The mailbox outside had been empty. That did strike her as odd, since mail should have been delivered since he'd been in Maine. Unless he'd had it cut off until after his return.

She slapped her forehead.

Jesus, I'm really losing it.

Ted Bergin hadn't driven up to Maine; he'd flown. There was a single-car garage addition to the farmhouse. It was off the kitchen. She entered the garage and studied the sturdy Honda four-door. It was about ten years old but in good shape. She spent thirty minutes going over every cubic foot of it. Among the many things the Secret Service had taught her how to do quite thoroughly was search a car. However, that was usually to check for bombs. She had a feeling whatever was eluding her was far more subtle.

She sat in the passenger seat and thought about it. If Bergin didn't use a computer and he wanted to keep the information about his client secret, where would it be if not at his office, on his person, or at his house? Unless he had memorized names, phone numbers, and addresses he probably would have written it down somewhere, in order to keep it handy. He was a pen and paper man, after all.

Michelle's gaze finally fixed on the glove box. She had already been through it once and found the usual things. A spare pen, state inspection pink slip, car registration, and the Honda's pristine operating manual.

Her fingers closed around the manual. She skipped to the back, where there were blank pages for one to fill in maintenance records. Michelle had never known anyone to actually do that, but—

There it was, smack in the middle of the blank pages.

Kelly Paul. Home and cell phones and a mailing address that would put Paul somewhere west of here, near the West Virginia border—if Michelle remembered correctly the location of the town Bergin had written down. This had to be it. The client. Unless Kelly Paul happened to be a Honda salesman. Michelle really didn't think that was the case.

She ripped the page out, slid it into her pocket, got out of the car, and closed the door.

And froze.

She was no longer the only person in the house.

21

Sean King parked his rental on a side road and walked toward the causeway. He'd gone back to the inn after running into Dobkin. But he'd grown restless, and there still had been no word from Megan. He wondered how many waves it would cause if he made a stink about the Bureau keeping the lawyer under wraps, perhaps against her will. He'd concluded that if she didn't appear by morning he would have to take some sort of action.

He'd checked in with Michelle. She'd told him about her finding the letter from Murdock at Bergin's office. Other than that, she didn't seem to be making much progress. She'd told him she was planning to go to Bergin's house later tonight. He hoped she would have better luck there.

He stared in the direction of it. Across the causeway was Cutter's Rock. It was dark enough that he could actually see some of the lights of the facility from where he was standing. The Atlantic Ocean lapped against the rocky shore, waves pounding hard enough to lift sprays of saltwater onto the road. He buttoned up his jacket. A vehicle was pulling down the causeway. Sean stepped back out of the way as it turned toward him and ducked down behind some boulders lining the shore. As the car passed, he lifted his head slightly above the rock.

Carla Dukes. There was no mistaking the lady with her big, blocky shoulders. Sean checked his watch. Nine o'clock. The woman was pulling very long hours. Maybe Cutter's was just that sort of place.

He ducked down again when another car passed. A lot of traffic for this time of night in such an isolated place. He'd raised his head just in time to see the driver. He'd had on his interior light, glancing down at something.

Sean ran to his car, fired it up, and spun onto the road. He sped up, caught sight of the car's taillights, and then fell back a bit.

Although he was nervous about being spotted, Sean managed to keep the other car within sight, losing it only briefly on turns before it came back into his sight line on the straightaway. They finally turned off the main road, away from the ocean, and headed inland for about two miles. Another set of turns, and Sean was growing more nervous. There was no way the guy could not have spotted him. The three cars slowed. Dukes turned into a small subdivision of newly built cookie-cutter homes. Probably built, Sean assumed, to house the personnel at Cutter's Rock and spark a whole series of downstream employment. Now all the country needed were more murderers to put away and the economy would simply boom.

Dukes pulled into the driveway of the third house on the right.

Sean was surprised when the tail car turned down the same road, passed Dukes's house, and turned left at the next block. Did the guy live here, too? Was he just driving home and not tailing Dukes?

Sean parked his car, got out, and started walking. He turned up his collar both because of the cold and also to help hide his face. Dukes's house was a small, vinyl-sided two-story with a minuscule front porch. There was also a two-car garage that Dukes had pulled into. Sean watched the garage door crank down on its chain track.

About fifteen seconds later the lights came on inside the house. Probably the kitchen, thought Sean, since most floor plans followed that design.

Sean kept walking, turned left at the next block, and looked for the other car. The street was dark, no lights except for meager ones coming from the occasional house. People here were apparently early to bed. Sean could see his breath and not much else. His gaze swiveled from side to side. The houses here had garages, too, and if the guy had pulled into one, Sean had lost him. He mentally kicked himself. What he should have done was keep driving after he knew where Dukes lived until he reached the next block and then wait there to see what house the other car had turned into. It was a mental error leading to a tactical mistake that a man like Sean King deemed personally unforgivable.

He had drawn near to a dirty, heavy-duty Ford F250 workhorse of a truck parked on the street in front of a two-story identical twin of Dukes's house when it happened.

The car he'd been looking for had been hidden by the mammoth truck. It pulled out hard and fast, its engine whining with the effort, and bore down on him. Sean threw himself into the bed of the truck. He landed on top of some tools and a coil of heavy chain that jabbed hard into his ribs and stomach. When he looked over the edge of the truck's bed, the only thing he saw were the winking lights of the car before it turned back onto the lead-in road. A few seconds later the car and its driver were gone. Sean drew a short breath and pulled himself up. He felt around his rib cage where the tools and chain had impacted.

The lights in the house snapped on. Sean clambered out of the truck as the front door of the house opened and a man was framed there in the light. He had on boxers and a white T-shirt and his feet were bare. In his hand was a rifle.

"What the hell's going on?" the man bellowed, as Sean came into view. The man edged the rifle muzzle in his direction. "What are you doing to my truck?"

A dog started barking from somewhere.

"I'm out looking for my dog," Sean said, pressing

one hand against his side where he felt something wet. "It's a white lab, named Roscoe. I was here visiting Mrs. Dukes on the other block and he jumped out of my car. I've been looking for him for over an hour. I thought he might have jumped in the back of your truck. I've got a truck just like this and he rides in the back. I've had that dog for eight years. I . . . I don't know what I'm going to do."

The gun barrel lowered as a woman in a pullover sweater and leggings joined the man at the door. The man said, "Our old mutt just died. Like losing a kid. You want me to help you look for him?"

"I appreciate that, but old Roscoe never did like strangers." Sean pulled out a piece of paper and wrote something on it. "Here's my phone number. I'll leave it in the back of your truck. You see Roscoe, you can call me."

"Okay, will do."

Sean put the piece of paper in the truck bed and pinned it there using a can of paint that was in the truck.

"Thanks, and good night. Sorry to disturb you."

"No problem. Hope you find him."

Thank God for dog lovers.

He walked on, got in his car, and drove back to Martha's Inn. He limped up to his room. He'd banged his leg jumping into the truck. He took off his shirt and examined the bloody puncture wound in his side. That had also come from landing on a pile of tools and chains in the back of the truck. As he cleaned himself up, Sean wondered whether he had just encountered Ted Bergin's killer.

He gingerly lowered himself into bed after downing a couple of Advils. He was going to be stiff tomorrow. He mentally chastised himself for not getting the license plate number of the car. But as he thought about it, he never remembered seeing it clearly.

He picked up the phone and called Eric Dobkin. The man was now on duty, riding in his state cruiser. He was about fifteen miles from Martha's Inn. When Sean explained to him what happened, Dobkin thanked him, said they'd get a BOLO out on the car and driver, and clicked off.

Next he called Michelle's cell phone. There was no answer. That was unusual. She almost always answered her phone. He phoned again, left a message asking her to call him. Hundreds of miles away, he felt helpless. What if she was in trouble?

He lay back against the pillow, trying to make sense of everything that had happened thus far but finding no answers.

22

Michelle ducked down behind Bergin's sedan, her hand on the butt of her pistol. She'd felt the vibration of the phone in her pocket but didn't have time to answer. She crab-walked to the rear of the car and tried the garage door. It was locked. She found the locking mechanism, turned it, and pulled upward. The door was heavy, but she was strong. Leverage wasn't the problem. It was the sound. The running track and pulleys of the door must not have been lubricated in ages. Lifting it only a few inches caused a screech that hammered in Michelle's ears.

She had just given away her position to whoever was in the house and gotten nothing in return for her troubles. She set the door back down and hustled to the front of the car. The door into the house was right there, only she had a feeling that walking through it right now would not be good for her health.

It might be the cops. It might be the FBI. If so, why didn't they announce their presence? If they think I'm a burglar, they might not. And if I announce myself and it's not the cops? Classic Catch-22.

She looked around the twelve-by-twelve box she was trapped in. Neither door was an option. That left the small square of window that opened out onto the side yard, away from the front door. She snagged a can of WD40 from the worktable, undid the window clasp, sprayed the track with the lubricant, slid up the window, thankfully with virtually no noise, and hoisted herself up and through, landing on her backside in the grass. She was up in an instant, her gun out, her nerves calm, her eyes and ears alert. She came around the side of the garage and surveyed the area. Only her Toyota was visible. In any event she would have heard another car pull up, so she now assumed it was not the cops or the FBI. They tended to make lots of noise when no hostages were in play.

Whoever was here had left his vehicle somewhere else and come on foot. That was clandestine. That smacked of nefarious purpose. That indicated a direct threat to her safety.

She hit the ground as soon as she heard the slide on the pistol being racked back. The round struck to her right, plowing into the dirt and covering her with grass and particles of compressed earth. She rolled to her left, fired twice in the middle of the maneuver and in the direction of the shot aimed at her. She did a half crouch, glimpsed a figure from across the yard, fired again, and threw herself behind a tree next to the garage.

Had she heard a scream? Did her round strike home?

She'd seen a figure, fired right at it. No more than twenty meters. Even under these conditions she should have—

Her back to the tree bark, Michelle gripped her pistol with both hands and listened. To have nearly hit her, the shooter couldn't have been in front of the house. He had to be off to the right side. Perhaps across the gravel drive, in the woods on the other side. It had been a pistol; she knew that from the sound of the shot and the earlier rack of the slide. If the shooter was across the street, that was a good thing for her. At that range and at night, a direct hit from a pistol would be beyond lucky.

She did a pivot, keeping her body behind the tree trunk. She couldn't rule out the possibility that the shooter had night-vision equipment. Or that there was only one shooter. If there were a pair of them the other one might be outflanking her right now, trying to capture her in a pincers maneuver.

Her gaze darted to the far end of the garage. She saw nothing but drilled 911 on her phone and spoke quietly into it, relaying her dilemma and location to the dispatcher. She had no idea how long it would take the police to get here, but she had to assume it would not be quick.

You're going to have to get yourself out of this, Michelle.

She dropped to her belly and started to scoot backward. She alternated her gaze forward and aft, looking for an attack on both fronts. She reached the woods and stood, keeping behind a massive oak that fronted the edge of the grass. She looked for movement while trying to keep as still as possible. She kept her profile sideways to reduce her target signature.

She looked at her truck parked in the driveway. There was a lot of open ground to get there. With night-vision gear she'd be dead after two steps, pistol or not. This could be a waiting game, and maybe she should be content to do that with the police hopefully on the way.

Twenty minutes went by and nothing happened.

Sirens.

The cop car pulled up a minute later, its tires crunching into the gravel as it slid to a stop.

Two county cops emerged from their ride, guns drawn, in half crouches, peering around.

Michelle called out, "I'm Michelle Maxwell. I'm the one who called this in. There was a shooter in the front yard. I fired at someone. I think I might have hit the person."

The cops peered in her direction. One of them yelled out, "I don't see anyone. I want you to come out with your hands visible." He added, "Are you armed?"

"I just said, I shot at the person shooting at me, so yeah, I'm armed."

"Throw your weapon out and then come out, hands visible."

"And if the shooter is still out there?"

"Like I said, I don't see anyone. They must have already taken off."

Michelle tossed her gun, moved out from behind the cover of the tree, and came forward. One of the cops hustled forward, marked her weapon with his foot while his partner covered Michelle.

"I'm a private investigator, here with permission."

"Let me see some ID."

Michelle showed him her ID and her gun permit.

"I was in the garage when I heard someone in the house. I slid out the window and took gunfire over there." She pointed to the spot. "If you hit the grass with your light, you'll see where the round—"

"Joe, you better get over here," said the other cop. He was standing near Michelle's truck.

"What is it?"

"Just get over here."

Joe motioned Michelle to go ahead of him and they hustled over to where the other officer was standing.

They reached the spot and looked down.

The body was on its face, hands out wide, one shoe off. A bloody patch was dead center of the back where a bullet had gone in.

The other cop knelt down and turned the body slightly, while his partner focused his light on the corpse. There was no exit wound in the front. The round was still in her.

Michelle gasped when she saw who it was.

Hilary Cunningham, Ted Bergin's secretary.

Joe shone the light at Michelle's face making her look away. "Do you know her?"

Michelle nodded as she stared down in disbelief. In a halting voice she said, "She was the woman who gave me the keys to this house. She worked for the owner."

"Well, lady, it looks like you just killed her."

23

The phone buzzed.

He slept on.

It buzzed again.

He stirred.

It tickled his pocket one more time.

He woke. "Hello?" Sean said in a sleepy voice.

"It's me," said Michelle. "And I'm in a shitload of trouble."

Sean sat up in the bed and automatically checked his watch. He had fallen asleep in his clothes. It was one in the morning.

"What happened?"

Ten minutes later he knew as much as Michelle did as she succinctly recounted the past events.

"Okay, don't say anything else to them. I'm on my way."

"On your way how?"

Sean stopped halfway off the bed. "What?"

"No flights for six hours."

"I'll drive."

"That'll get you here about the same time as the

morning flight and that's if you drive straight through. Which means you'll be a zombie or else you'll be dead after running off the road and hitting a tree. Or a moose. I'll be okay for tonight. Just get down here with your brain intact and let's figure this out."

"Wait a minute, are they holding you?"

"I'm not local. I have a car. A woman is dead. I was the only living person on the scene. They have my gun. Which is the second weapon I've had confiscated by the cops, so yeah, they're holding me."

"Was it your slug that killed her?"

"They don't know yet. They haven't done the post. But it wouldn't surprise me if it were. I fired in that direction at someone."

"Do you think Hilary was firing at you?"

"There was no gun found on her person. All I know is a round came within six inches of landing in my head instead of the dirt."

"Well, the slug will confirm your story."

"Let's hope they find it."

"Isn't it in the dirt?"

"I think it might be. But it also might have hit a stone buried in the grass and ricocheted off. I didn't hang around to find out."

"Okay. I'll take the same flight you did to D.C. and then drive over to Charlottesville. I should be there around three." He paused. "Do the cops really think you killed her intentionally?"

"I think the fact that I called it in, and they

confirmed the call came from my cell, has made them less suspicious, but it still looks bad."

"Okay, just sit tight until I get there."

"Not much else I can do. Any news from Megan?"

"No."

"Anything exciting happen to you while I was gone?"

Sean hesitated, debating whether to tell her. "Nothing that can't keep."

"Oh, bring the gun I bought up in Maine."

"Fine. Let's just hope this one isn't confiscated, too."

Sean clicked off, called the airline, bought a ticket, packed his bag, retrieved Michelle's gun case from her room, and then called Megan's cell phone. It again went right to voice mail. The FBI was definitely keeping her under wraps. In the message Sean didn't tell her why he was heading back to Virginia, only that he would be in touch.

He also left a note for Mrs. Burke and headed out. He cranked the heater up and drove as fast as he could with the wind rushing through the shattered windows. He got to Bangor at about five in the morning. He prayed that when he went to check Michelle's gun and ammo, they would not scrutinize his permit to carry a weapon, since he didn't have one that was valid in Maine.

It was early, the airport folks were tired, and they didn't even raise an eyebrow when he showed them his Virginia concealed weapon's permit. Maine was the Vacation State, after all, and Americans did love to vacation with their weapons. And it also probably helped that he was checking the gun with no way to get to it during the flight.

He had coffee and stepped onto the plane at six thirty. He catnapped for the short flight. The connection in Philly did not go smoothly, and he had to scream at several airline personnel before they stuck him in the rear of a turboprop outbound to Reagan National. By some miracle Michelle's gun found him at baggage claim, and he cabbed it home, packed his things, and was on the road to Charlottesville in a one-way rental about forty-five minutes behind schedule.

He exceeded the speed limit the whole trip and reached the county lockup a little before four. He announced that he was Michelle's lawyer and wanted to see his client. Twenty minutes after that he was seated across from her.

"You look okay," he said.

"You, on the other hand, look like crap."

"Thanks. I've just been traveling all day to get to you."

"You misunderstood. I greatly appreciate the effort. I'm just too used to your Cary Grant-like dapperness. But it's also nice to know that you're actually human like the rest of us."

"I've seen the arrest report. I've also talked to one

of the officers who was on the scene with you last night."

"How'd you manage that?"

"I overheard him talking about it in the hallway and snagged him for a quick down and dirty. They've processed the scene, although he wouldn't tell me the results. For what it's worth I don't believe he thinks you're guilty."

"Let's hope everybody else agrees with him. I still can't believe she's dead. I was just talking to her yesterday."

"I'm meeting with the prosecutor next. I think I can get this all explained. And then get you out of here."

"What if they think I'm a flight risk?"

"I'll take care of it. I used to practice law around here. I know the folks."

"Sounds like a plan," she said doubtfully.

"I had some fun last night, too." He explained to her about Carla Dukes and his run-in with the man following her.

"What is going on up there?" she said in an exasperated tone.

"More than we initially thought, that's for damn sure."

An hour later Michelle was free to leave. She picked up her truck and followed Sean to the Boar's Head, where they ate some dinner.

"So how'd you bust me out?" she asked.

"I basically vouched for you. So if you run my ass is fried."

"I'll try to hang around this hemisphere."

"I explained everything about Bergin's death in Maine and our investigation to the prosecutor. He's a reasonable guy who knew Bergin well. He agreed that it's highly unlikely you had anything to do with plotting Hilary's death. I told him we were doing our best to find out who killed him and part of that investigation led us here. He's definitely on our side on that."

"Okay."

"But the strange thing is that he didn't know Bergin had been murdered. Someone is keeping a tight rein on the media, that's for sure."

"FBI has the muscle to do that," she said.

Sean nodded. "That's what I'm thinking, too. And I presume Hilary didn't go blaring it around. And Megan left to come to Maine right after she found out."

"Guess it'll come as a shock to a lot of people then. And now with Hilary dead, too."

"And the letter you found in Bergin's files? Agent Murdock asking for information about his client? That's pretty unusual."

"Oh my God, I didn't tell you the best part." Michelle plunged her hand in her pocket and pulled out the page from the car warranty booklet. She explained to Sean where she'd found it. "Guess if he ever went out to visit her, he'd drive. So the car was a logical place to keep the address."

"Kelly Paul. Okay." He checked his watch, pulled out his phone, and pecked in the number while Michelle dug into her fish and chips.

"Kelly Paul, please?" said Sean. He paused. "Right, this is Sean King. I'm working with Ted Bergin on the Edgar Roy case. Hello?"

He put the phone down.

Michelle swallowed a bite of breaded halibut. "Hung up on you?"

He nodded. "Guess she is the client."

"So it is a woman?"

"Sure sounded like one. She asked who it was. I told her, and click."

"Do you think she knows Bergin is dead?"

"No way to tell." He studied the paper. "If I'm remembering correctly this address is about four hours from here in Southwest Virginia."

Michelle drank down her iced tea. "Let me get a big coffee and we'll hit the road."

"Hold on. It's probably not smart for you to leave the area right now. The police will want to talk to you again at the very least."

"Then you're not going either. We split up and each of us almost gets killed."

"Okay, you've got a point. Hang on." He punched in a number on his phone.

"Phil, Sean King. Look, do you have time to talk tonight face-to-face? Say around eight? Great, thanks."

He clicked off and motioned to the waitress for the check.

"What are you going to do?" asked Michelle.

"Throw myself on the mercy of the prosecutor's office to spring you from the confines of Charlottes-ville. And if that doesn't work, I'll mortgage everything I have to post bail."

"I thought you only had to put up ten percent."

"Right now, ten percent of just about anything would tax my personal finances. Private investigation is a feast-or-famine business. And I'm not even sure we're going to get our travel expenses reimbursed now."

"And if that doesn't work?"

"I'll stuff you in a bag and sneak you out. One way or another we're going to see Kelly Paul."

"Think she has all the answers?"

"Actually, just *one* answer would be a nice change of pace right now."

24

When Sean left the meeting with the prosecutor he was smiling.

Michelle, who was waiting for him in her truck, looked at him inquiringly. "I take it the meeting went well?"

"He's pigeonholing the arrest for now. No court hearing. No bail. You're free to go, in my company."

"You must have done some sell job."

"Well, that and the fact that the cops found the slug that almost hit you."

"Nice. What was it?"

"Remington .45 ACP full metal jacket."

"Not the round that killed Bergin then. An FMJ at contact range would have blown right through his skull."

"And it wasn't the guy I spotted in Maine. He couldn't be in two places at once."

"They haven't done the post on Hilary yet, right?"

"Not yet. But I think when they do, they'll find a .45 round in her."

A half hour later they were heading toward the

home of Kelly Paul in Michelle's Land Cruiser after Sean turned in his rental. They rode Interstate 64 over to 81 and took that south. Hours later, about thirty minutes before they would have crossed over into Tennessee, they exited the highway, drove west for a few miles, and passed through several one-traffic-light towns. Ten minutes after leaving the last such hamlet, Michelle slowed the truck and looked around before glancing at her GPS screen.

Sean looked at his watch and yawned. "Nearly two in the morning. If I don't get eight hours of sleep soon my head is going to disintegrate."

"I slept fine in jail."

"No surprise there. I've seen your bed. The one in jail is probably softer."

"I never heard you complain when you were *in* my bed."

"Other priorities at the time."

"How do you want to do this? The GPS says she's down that road coming up on the left. All I see here are fields. You think she lives on a farm?"

Sean gazed out the window. "Well, that's a corn-field over there." He pointed to the right. He glanced to the left. "Not sure what that is. But it's definitely a farm of some sort. I can't even see a house."

As they pulled closer Michelle spotted the mailbox. She hit her high beams. "Nothing on the mailbox, but this must be the place."

"Kelly Paul and Edgar Roy. What's the connection?"

"Well, she might be family. Paul might be her married name."

"Or maybe there's no family tie," replied Sean.

"But like you said, there has to be something there. Otherwise how could Bergin rep Edgar Roy just based on this Kelly Paul person saying to do it? Wouldn't there have to be like a power of attorney or something?"

"Ideally, yes. But apparently Roy lost his mind *after* he was arrested. So presumably he couldn't sign off on a POA after he became incompetent."

"We don't know exactly when he zonked out. He was arrested. There must have been court proceedings. Bail, competency hearing, his being sent to Maine."

Sean nodded. "You're right. He might have hired Bergin before he went silent. But if so, why all the secrecy about the client? Why no billing or correspondence record? And then there's Murdock's letter and Bergin writing Kelly Paul's name in his car warranty book."

"So do we sit out here all night or go knock on her door?"

"Knocking on someone's door at this hour in this place might result in buckshot wounds to our person. I say we pull off the road, stretch out, and get some sleep. I definitely could use it."

"We should take turns being on watch."

"Watching for what? Cows?"

"Sean, we were both almost killed yesterday. Let's be prudent."

"Okay, you're right."

She said, "I'll take the first watch. I'll wake you in two hours."

Sean tilted his seat back and closed his eyes, and a few minutes later his soft snore wafted through the truck's interior. Michelle glanced over at him, reached in the backseat, pulled out a blanket from the floorboard, and placed it over him. She stared back out the front window, alternating this with glances in the side mirrors to check on anyone creeping up on them from the rear. Her hand dropped to the butt of her gun and stayed there.

Sean yawned, stretched, and blinked himself fully awake. Sunlight stared back at him. He jolted up and looked over at Michelle. She was tapping a tune on the steering wheel and sipping on a bottle of G2.

"Why didn't you wake me up?" He checked his watch. It was nearly eight.

"You were sleeping like a baby. I didn't have the heart."

He noted the blanket she'd put over him. "Okay, your drastically heightened sensitivity factor is really creeping me out."

"I got plenty of sleep in jail. I'm fresh and now you are too."

"Okay, now that makes more sense."

His stomach grumbled.

"Want me to run over and pick some corn?" she said with a smile.

"No, but do you have a power bar in that pile of crap in the back? I'm afraid to put my hand in there."

She reached back, snagged one, and tossed it to him. "Chocolate fudge. Twenty grams of protein. Knock yourself out."

"Any activity from Kelly Paul?"

"No cars in or out and no sightings of any humans, though I did see a black bear and what I think was a beaver."

Sean rolled down the window and sucked in the clean, chilly air. "My bladder is telling me I need to do something."

Michelle pointed to a spot across the road. "I already did my business."

He was back in a few minutes. "I think it's time we had our face-to-face with Kelly Paul."

Michelle started the Land Cruiser. "Okay, but let's hope there's some coffee in the house." She turned down the gravel road. "What if Paul won't talk to us?"

"Then I think we have to insist. We came all this way, after all."

"And we tell Paul about Bergin?"

"If Kelly Paul hired Bergin, then his death might

make her more likely to help us. How all of this connects to what happened in Maine I don't know. But I have to believe that unless Bergin had some dark secret in his past, his death and his secretary's death are connected to Roy. And that means Paul is connected too."

"Despite what you said earlier I could have been the one to kill Hilary Cunningham."

"Is that the real reason you didn't sleep last night?"

"She was an innocent old lady, Sean. And now she's dead."

"If you did it you sure as hell didn't mean to do it. Someone was shooting at you. You shot back. That's instinctual. I would've done the same thing."

"She's still dead. What do they tell her kids or grandkids? 'I'm sorry, she's dead because she was accidentally shot'? Come on."

"Life is not fair any way you cut it, Michelle. You know that and I know that. We've lived that stuff too often to recognize it any other way."

"That can't stop me from feeling guilty. From feeling like a piece of shit."

"You're right, it can't. But keep this in mind. Somebody brought Hilary Cunningham to that house against her will in all likelihood. And if you did shoot her I don't believe it was accidental, at least on their side."

"What, you mean they wanted me to shoot her?"

"Yes."

"Why?"

"Hilary might have known something that certain people didn't want to get out. And if you shoot her then the police are all over us. That puts us out of commission, or so they think."

"If that's the case these are some pretty sick people we're up against."

"We're always up against psychos, Michelle. It's what we do. But I want these sons of bitches more than I've wanted anybody else."

25

The house was a white single-story clapboard with a black shingle roof in need of replacement. The porch was wide and inviting, with a couple of beat-up-looking rockers moving slightly to and fro in the breeze. The sun was coming up to the left of the house, but the reach of a monster oak blanketed it in shadows.

The front drive was more dirt than gravel. The lawn was cut short, there were a few flowers in pots, and a rooster strutted in front of the Toyota as Michelle braked to a stop. The bird cocked its head in their direction, rustled its feathers, gave the pair a withering one-eyed gaze, and crowed as they got out of the Land Cruiser.

The edge of a chicken coop could be seen sticking out from behind the rear of the house. Beyond the coop a red barn rose up about a hundred feet from the house and at an angle to it. A clothesline hung in the right side yard, and the few garments strung on it lifted lazily with the dull movement of air.

"Okay," said Michelle. "Five gets you ten that a fireplug of a woman in either bib overalls or a cotton print dress and work boots is going to answer the door smelling of chickenshit. And she's going to be holding a shotgun pointed right at our guts."

"I'll take that bet," said Sean with an air of confidence.

Michelle shot him a glance before gazing up at the house. Somehow the woman had materialized on the porch seemingly without making a sound. Michelle, who had perfect vision and hearing, hadn't seen or heard anything.

"You must be Sean King. I've been expecting you," said the woman. Her voice was deep but still remained feminine. It was an assured voice.

When Michelle's boots hit the top step of the porch she did something she almost never had to do with another woman. She had to look up. The lady must have been at least six feet tall in bare feet. She was lean without an ounce of fat on her frame. And even though she wasn't exactly young anymore, she had retained the physique and the graceful movements of a formidable athlete.

They had to be related. Same eyes, same nose, obviously the height factor. The only differences from Edgar Roy were the color of the hair and the eyes. Her hair was light brown and the eyes were green instead of black dots. The green was less intimidating.

And obviously she could talk.

Sean put out his hand. "We're sorry for coming by so early, Ms. Paul," he said.

Her long fingers enveloped his hand and then she

waved his apology off. "This isn't early, at least in these parts. I saw your truck out there at five this morning. I would've gotten you to come in for some breakfast, but you were sleeping and the lady here was doing her business in the woods."

Michelle looked at Kelly Paul with a mixture of admiration and astonishment. "I'm Michelle Maxwell." She shook hands with Paul and came away respectful of the woman's grip.

"Would you like some breakfast now?" she asked them. "I've got eggs, bacon, grits, biscuits, and good, hot coffee."

Michelle and Sean glanced at each other.

Paul smiled. "I'll take your famished looks as a yes. Come on in."

The interior didn't have a homey feel to it. It was minimally furnished, but was clean with simple lines one would have expected from the exterior. She led them down the hall and into the kitchen that was sturdily and plainly built out with old appliances. There was a fireplace set against one wall that looked as old as the house. Another fireplace was in the front room.

"Have you lived here long?" asked Sean.

"By local standards, no. It's a typical little farmhouse. But that's what I wanted."

"So where did you move from?" asked Sean.

She reached out a hand and flicked on the coffeepot, then pulled a bowl and skillet from the cupboard.

When she didn't answer, Sean said, "You said you were expecting us?"

"You called me last night. I recognized your voice when you spoke outside just now."

"But I didn't speak to you before you said I must be Sean King."

Paul turned around and pointed a long-handled wooden spoon at Michelle. "But you spoke to your partner here. I've got excellent hearing."

"How'd you know we'd come to visit you? Or that we even knew where you lived?"

"Coffee will be ready in just a minute. Can you pull down some plates and cups from the cupboard right there, Michelle?" She pointed to her left. "You can just set them on the kitchen table right here. I've eaten but I will have coffee. Thank you very much."

While Michelle got the dishes, Paul tended to the eggs and bacon sizzling in another pan. Grits simmered in a closed pot, and Sean could smell the biscuits rising in the oven.

"Got a Smithfield ham in the refrigerator. I can fry that up too if you'd like. Nothing better than a salt-cured Smithfield."

"The bacon will be fine," Sean said.

When it was ready Paul filled their plates with food and apologized that the grits were instant. "Otherwise, it would be a while, I'm afraid."

She sat down across from them with her cup of

coffee and watched with what looked like sincere pleasure as they ate.

Sean glanced at her every few seconds. Kelly Paul had on khaki pants, a worn denim shirt, a light blue jean jacket, and beige Crocs that seemed too small for her long feet. Her hair was shoulder length and tied back in a ponytail. Her face was fair and relatively unlined. He estimated the woman to be in her early forties or perhaps even younger.

When they had eaten their fill and she had topped off their coffee cups, they all sat back, looking expectant.

She said, "Bellies full, let's get to it. Of course I knew you'd come to see me after I hung up on you. As to how you'd know where I lived, I assumed that former Secret Service agents would be able to find that out. I expect that's why Teddy Bergin hired you."

"Teddy?"

"My pet name for him."

"So you knew Bergin before all this?"

"He was my godfather. And one of my mom's best friends." Paul studied their reaction to this revelation and then said, "I want you to find out who killed him."

"So you know he's dead?" said Michelle. "How?"

Paul tapped the table with her long index finger. "Does it matter?"

"We'd like to know," said Sean.

"Hilary phoned me."

Sean looked angry. "She said she had no idea who the client was."

"That's because I made her promise me she wouldn't tell."

"Why?"

"I had my reasons. Same ones that made Teddy keep everything under seal with the court."

"What's your relationship to Edgar Roy? Are you his sister? You have the same height, same features."

"Half sister. Same mother, different father. Mother was over six feet. Funny thing is, both our fathers were shorter than she was. Guess we got her height genes."

"Is Paul your married name?" asked Sean.

"I hope not, since I've never been married. Paul was my father's surname."

"But you obviously know Edgar Roy?"

"Yes, although I'm eleven years older than he is."

"You're forty-six?" said Sean.

"Yes."

"You look a lot younger than that," said Michelle.

She smiled. "It's not from pious living, I can tell you that."

Sean returned the smile. "I guess a lot of people could make that concession, including me. But then again I think I look every day of my age and then some."

Paul continued. "Our mother divorced my father when I was nine. She married Edgar's father, and they had him shortly afterward."

"So you two were together as a family for how long?"

"Until I left for college."

"And your mother and stepfather are dead?"

"My stepfather died about the time I left. Our mother passed on seven years ago. Cancer."

"What happened to your stepfather?" asked Sean.

"He had an accident."

"What sort of accident?"

"The sort where he stopped breathing."

"And your father?"

"He and my mother divorced when I was a little girl. Haven't heard from him since. Probably why she divorced him in the first place. Not the most caring man in the world."

Sean said, "How did you get permission to hire a lawyer to represent your brother?"

"Eddie is a brilliant person. It wasn't that he could sort of remember everything he ever saw, read, or heard. He could recall it precisely right down to the date and time he'd experienced it. And he could take pieces of any puzzle you gave him and spit out the solution in no time. He operated on a different plane than the rest of us." She paused. "Do you know what an eidetic memory is?"

"Like a photographic one?" said Sean.

"Pretty much. Mozart had one. Tesla too. Someone with an eidetic memory can, for instance, recite pi's decimal places to over one hundred thousand. All from memory. It's a genetic thing coupled with a little freak-of-nature occurrence. It's like the wiring in the brain is simply better than everyone else's. You can't learn to be eidetic—you either are or you aren't."

"And your brother obviously had an eidetic memory?"

"Actually something more than that. He never forgot anything, but beyond that, like I said, he could see how all the pieces of any puzzle went together. 'This fact affecting that fact' sort of thing. No matter how disparate or seemingly unrelated. Sort of like looking at an anagram once and knowing exactly what it's really saying. Most people use about ten percent of their brain. Eddie is probably up around ninety to ninety-five percent."

"Pretty impressive," said Michelle.

"He could have achieved greatness in any number of fields."

"I sense a *but* coming," prompted Sean.

"But he didn't have a lick of common sense. Never did, never will. And if something didn't interest him he ignored it, regardless of the consequences. Years ago, after he forgot to pay his bills, renew his driver's license, and even pay his taxes, I got a power of attorney from him. I couldn't do everything for him, but I tried my best."

"If you did all that, how could you remain in the shadows of his life? The press didn't even mention that he had a half sister after he was arrested."

"I'd been gone for a long time. And I'd never come back home for long. And I had a different last name. But much of the help I provided him could be done long-distance."

"But still."

"And I'm a private person."

"Is that why you moved here?" asked Michelle.

"Partly." She sipped her coffee.

"Hilary is dead, too," said Sean suddenly. "Did you know that?"

26

For the first time Kelly Paul did not appear to be in control. She set the coffee cup down, raised a hand to her eyes, and then put it back down. "When?"

The tone was one of curiosity mixed with anger. Sean thought he might have also gleaned a hint of regret.

"Last night, outside of Bergin's house."

"How?"

Michelle glanced at Sean, who said, "She was set up and shot." He leaned forward. "Do you have any idea what's going on here, Ms. Paul?"

Paul wrested herself from whatever she was thinking. Clearing her throat, she said, "You need to understand that my brother didn't kill those people. He was framed."

"Why? By whom?"

"If I knew that I wouldn't need you. But I would say that whoever did it is particularly powerful and well connected."

"Why would people like that be targeting your brother?"

197

"Well, that's the sixty-four-thousand-dollar question now, isn't it?"

"And you're saying you don't even have an idea?"

"I'm not really saying anything. You're the investigators."

"So you knew Bergin had hired us?"

"I suggested it. He told me he knew you, Sean. I'd read about some of the work you'd done. I said we needed a pair like you on the job because it wouldn't be simple."

"When was the last time you saw or spoke to your brother?" asked Sean.

"You mean before he stopped talking at all?"

"How did you know that? That your brother had stopped talking?"

"Teddy told me. And the last time I spoke with my brother was by phone a week before he was arrested."

"What did he say?"

"Nothing of great importance. Certainly not that he suspected six bodies were buried at the family farm."

"How long had the place been in your family?"

"My mother and stepfather bought it when they got married. After our mother died, she left it to both of us. I was living abroad and so I told Eddie to take it."

"Even after he started working for the government he lived with his mother?"

"Yes. He was at the local IRS office in Charlottesville, although I know he had responsibilities that would take him to Washington fairly regularly. Edgar really had no ambition to move into his own place. He liked the farm. It was quiet, isolated."

"And he obviously lived there alone after your mother died."

"He had no alternative. I was out of the country."

"Where were you living abroad?" asked Sean. "And what were you doing?"

Paul, who had been staring at a spot on the wall about a foot above Sean's head, now swung her gaze directly in his direction. "I wasn't aware that I was the subject of your investigation. And yet the truly personal inquiries seemed all aimed in my general vicinity."

"I like to be thorough."

"A grand attribute. Just point it in the direction of my brother's case."

Sean took this snub in stride. And he did note that her vocabulary and tone had subtly changed. "We've read the police file on the bodies discovered at the farm."

"Six of them. All men. All white. All under the age of forty. And all as yet unidentified."

"As I understand it nothing has come back on fingerprints or DNA."

"Quite remarkable. On the TV police shows every-one's in the database and it only takes a few seconds to find them." Paul smiled and took a long sip of coffee.

"I could see one or two or maybe even three not being in the system. But all six?"

"I think you and Michelle need to go there and look around."

"You're officially retaining us?"

"I thought I already had."

"With Bergin dead, it gets complicated. His associate, Megan Riley, is on the papers. She's willing but really green. I'm not sure the court will allow her to continue in a solo capacity."

"You're a lawyer," said Paul bluntly.

"You checked me out?"

"Of course I did. I'd be a fool if I hadn't. You can cocounsel with Riley."

"I'm not in practice anymore."

"I think you might want to reconsider that. You can wear two hats. Detective and lawyer."

"I'll think about it," said Sean. "Right now the FBI have Megan Riley holed up somewhere in Maine emptying out her brain cells."

Paul appraised him with a shrewd look. "You think your green lawyer can hold up against the Bureau?"

"I don't know," said Sean, giving her a curious glance.

"Brandon Murdock?" said Paul.

"How do you know that?"

"Teddy told me he was trying to break through the wall of legal confidentiality to find out who the client was. Teddy said it would eventually have to come out, but he'd managed to hold the fellow off so far."

"The FBI usually gets its way."

"Not disputing it. But let's make them work a little harder. I'm no lawyer but I'd say finding out who killed all those people and Teddy and now Hilary takes precedence over trying to discover who's paying for Eddie's defense."

"So you're assuming that all the deaths are connected?" said Michelle. "The six bodies and Bergin and his secretary. Killed by the same person?"

"Teddy Bergin didn't have an enemy to his name. And why kill Hilary except for something she knew? And that right there proves Eddie is innocent. There was no way he got out of Cutter's Rock to kill either one of them."

Sean considered this. "That's true. If they are connected."

"The proof is out there. All you have to do is find it."

"I'll draw up a retainer agreement and have you sign it."

"More than happy to."

"Anything else we need to know?"

"I believe you've got plenty to think about."

As they rose to go she added, "I doubt it would be smart to leave poor Megan with the FBI too long. You might want to make some noises about unlawful detainment or something like that, just to get the Bureau's blood going. Mention something about calling up a TV

201

station or newspaper reporter. They just love that stuff down at the Hoover building. Makes their butts get all tight and squirmy."

Sean looked at her strangely. "You have a lot of experience with the FBI?"

"Oh, more than you'll probably ever know, Mr. King."

27

Peter Bunting sat in his office in Manhattan. He enjoyed living in New York. He had an office in downtown D.C. and his company had a facility in northern Virginia, but New York was unique. The energy here was visceral. As he walked to work each day from his Fifth Avenue brownstone he knew he was where he belonged.

He stretched out a kink in his neck and studied the file on his desk. It appeared on an electronic tablet. No paper was kept here. Everything of importance was locked in impenetrable server farms far away from here. Cloud computing was king in Peter Bunting's world.

He had studied the career paths of Sean King and Michelle Maxwell and came away reasonably impressed. They both appeared to be hardworking, clever, and practical-minded. But he concluded that some of their success had also been due to luck coming along at just the right moment. And luck was not something one could count on happening all the time. How that might benefit or hurt him he wasn't sure.

He thumbed a button and the screen changed along with the subject area.

Edgar Roy.

His main problem.

What to do about his E-Six was consuming an inordinate amount of his time. And yet the matter was of paramount importance to him. Even though he had set up some stopgap measures he was unacceptably behind schedule. And Secretary Foster was right: the quality of the analysis had diminished. The status quo could not be sustained. He could lose everything he'd worked for.

Ellen Foster and her ilk were unforgiving. They would cut him off without a second thought. They might be plotting against him right now. No, there was no "might" about it; they *were* plotting against him. And Mason Quantrell was probably helping to orchestrate the entire scheme. The worlds of public and private sector had meshed into a single organism in the national security field. Players from both sides hopped back and forth with increasing frequency. It was now nearly impossible to tell where the government side ended and the for-profit machines began.

When he had first decided to make the intelligence field the place where he would make his mark, the arena was a disaster. Too many agencies with too many people writing too many reports, often about the same thing, that no one had time to read anyway. Too many eyeballs watching the wrong things. And, most critical, no one wanted to share information for fear of losing budget dollars or hard-won turf. DHS didn't talk to CIA. DIA didn't interface with the FBI. NSA was its own country. The other alphabet agencies did their own thing. No one, not one person, knew it all, didn't come close to knowing it all. And when one didn't know it all, one made mistakes, enormous ones; the sort where lots of people died.

That was how Bunting had commenced building his grand plan. Combining the basic tenet of the entrepreneur and the motivation of a patriot wanting to protect his country, he had seen a national security need and filled it. Once the concept had been tested and approved, the E-Program had been expanded and upgraded every year. It was no academic exercise. In that Mt. Everest of information collected every day by America and its allies, there could be one or two pieces of data located far apart in the gathering baskets of the intelligence community that might very well prevent another 9/11.

The successes of the E-Program had been early and often. Some could argue quite persuasively that the world was basically in a shitty state. But Bunting was one of the few who knew that things could be far worse. How close the United States and its allies had drawn to the precipice. How narrowly they had avoided events that would have resulted in greater devastation than when those jumbo jets had slammed into those buildings. In six months alone Edgar Roy's analysis had prevented at least five major attacks on both private and military targets around the world. And a host of lesser but still potentially deadly incidents had been broken up because the man could stare at the Wall and get it to reveal its secrets like no other analyst in history. And the results of his strategic conclusions could be felt around the world in a thousand different ways.

But it all came down to finding that one right person. That was always the challenge. The average career of the Analyst was only three years. After that even the mightiest of minds had had enough. And then they were given golden retirement packages and put out to pasture, like stud horses—only, unfortunately, without the possibility of siring their replacements.

The phone rang. He licked his lips and tried to remain calm. It was a scheduled call. It was the primary reason he was in the office today. He lifted the receiver.

"Yes? Yes, I'll hold."

A moment later the man's voice came on. Bunting drew a shallow breath and answered. "Mr. President, thank you for making time for me, sir."

The conversation was swift. It had been pretimed for five minutes. And it was only because Peter Bunting was such an important player in the intelligence community that the current occupant of 1600 Pennsylvania Avenue had bothered to call at all.

"It's been my pleasure and honor to serve my

country, sir," said Bunting. "And I give you my word that all of our goals will be met, on time. Yes, sir, thank you, sir."

The men then got down to the details.

As the phone timer clicked to five minutes, he said good-bye, set the receiver down, and looked up at his assistant.

She said, "I guess you really know you've made it when the president calls you."

"You'd think that would be the case, wouldn't you?"

"It's not?"

"Actually it only means you have a longer way to fall."

After she left he put his feet up on his desk and interlaced his fingers behind his neck. Bunting personally knew hundreds of intelligence analysts, smart people from the best schools who operated in specialties. People in this field could devote their entire careers to a certain quadrant of airspace over the Middle East, dutifully studying the relatively same satellite imagery until their hair changed from brown to white and their skin sagged toward retirement. Specialists, good, sound people for their little sliver of the plot. But that was all they knew, their incremental slice of the intelligence rainbow. And that was hardly good enough.

But Edgar Roy's specialty was omniscience.

He was tasked to know everything. And the man had!

Bunting never expected to find another Edgar Roy, a genetic freak to end all genetic freaks. A perfect memory and an astonishing ability to see how all pieces came together. He wished that the man could live forever.

His phone buzzed. He looked annoyed but answered. "What?" He hesitated. "All right, send him in."

It was Avery. The young man had finally gotten his hair cut, but he had never learned how to dress properly. He looked like he had just woken up at his frat house after a keg party. But he was smart. Not an E-class mind but certainly useful.

"I see you're back from Maine."

"Just this morning. I wanted to tell you that I followed Carla Dukes home two nights ago. I wanted to speak with her about some issues."

"Okay. Did you?"

"No, because I noticed someone following me."

Bunting sat up straighter. "What? Who?"

"I didn't get a good look at him because it was dark. I nearly ran over him while I was trying to get away." He paused. "But I think it was that investigator, Sean King."

"Sean King? What was he doing there?"

"Apparently following Dukes and/or me."

"Did he see you?"

"Not clearly, I'm sure of that."

"Did he get your license plate number?"

"Probably, but I switched the plates out with a pair of fake ones. They'll lead nowhere."

"I'm impressed, Avery."

"Thank you, sir. I just thought you should know."

"Is that all?"

Avery looked nervous. "Actually, no. The Wall backup is bordering on cataclysmic."

"That I already know. I'm recalling a pair of E-Fives to duty. And after I got blindsided by Foster I arranged a phone call with the president to reassure him. I just finished it. That will give us some time. If Foster tries to go over me now she'll look pretty stupid."

"But that won't last."

"Of course it won't last."

"But if Edgar Roy is proven innocent and we get him back on the job, all of our problems go away."

Bunting rose, went over to the window, and looked out, his hands stuffed into his trouser pockets. "That's not necessarily true."

"Why?"

He whirled around. "Do you really think the US government will let Edgar actually go to trial?"

Avery said slowly, "But what's the alternative?"

Bunting turned back around and watched a flock of birds heading south for the winter.

I wish I could fly, he thought. *I wish I could get the hell out of here*.

"What do you think, Avery?" he said over his shoulder.

"They'll kill him?"

Bunting sat back down and switched topics. "So King was in Maine two nights ago following you. What about Maxwell?"

"She wasn't with him."

"And what have their movements been since?"

Avery took a small step back. "Surveillance was lost for a bit but it has now been regained."

Bunting rose out of his seat once more. "Lost for how long?"

"A few hours."

Bunting snapped his fingers. "More precise than that, Avery."

"Eight hours and four minutes. But now they're headed, at least it seems, to Edgar Roy's farm."

"Did it occur to you that when we lost sight of them they might have been going somewhere that could have been highly enlightening?"

"Yes, sir, but I wasn't in charge of that task."

"Fine. I am now making it your task to ensure that surveillance is not lost again." He refocused. "The six bodies at the farm?"

"Yes?"

"Not one ID made? Strange, isn't it?" Bunting's expression signaled that it was far more than strange; it was impossible.

"Yes, you would think they would be on some database somewhere."

"And there's something else."

"Sir?"

"The number."

"Number?"

"Of bodies. Now go do your job."

Avery looked very confused as he closed the door behind him.

Bunting sat back in his chair, swiveled around, and stared out the window.

Six bodies. Not four, not five, but six.

Ordinarily, Bunting was a man who embraced numbers. He loved statistics, analysis, conclusions based on solid building blocks of data. But the number six was starting to haunt him. He didn't like it at all.

Six bodies. The E-Six Program.

That hit very close to home.

Someone was really playing with him.

28

The trip to Edgar Roy's home took a number of hours. Michelle drove, as usual, while Sean stared moodily out the window.

"Are you curious about what Kelly Paul did while she was out of the country?" he asked.

"Of course I am. But she has a point about focusing on the investigation into her brother. He's the one facing the death sentence. Not her."

He didn't seem to hear this. "And she never said how her stepfather died."

"Easy enough to check, but that seems a little far afield, Sean."

He turned to look at her. "Unless it's all connected."

"You're talking a long time period, then."

He looked back out the window. "Why would a woman like that move to a ramshackle house in the middle of nowhere? She's not farming. And her country accent was a bit too well done."

"Well, she did grow up in Virginia. And they do have accents down here," drawled Michelle.

"Lot of questions," said Sean absently.

"What do you think about her advice with the Bureau?"

"It was good actually. Riley is a lawyer for the defense. You just can't detain her indefinitely. In fact . . ."

He took out his cell phone and punched in a number. "Still no answer. Okay, let's do this the hard way."

He keyed in another number. "Agent Murdock? Sean King here. What? Yeah, we took your advice and went home. But we're coming back. But that's not why I'm calling. You're holding the defense counsel in a case you're investigating. That breaks about a dozen ethical and other laws I can think of off the top of my head. I either hear from her in five minutes that she's free and on her way to Martha's Inn, or the next time you see me it'll be on CNN talking about Bureau overreach." Sean paused as the other man said something. "Yeah, well, try me. And you now have four minutes."

He clicked off.

Michelle glanced at him. "And what did he say?"

"Basic blustery bullshit." He looked at his watch. Ten seconds past the deadline Sean's phone buzzed.

"Hello, Megan, how are you doing?" He paused. "Excellent. I thought Agent Murdock would see it my way. We're down in Virginia but we'll be heading back up very soon. Go to Martha's Inn and stay there. No visitors. Do nothing. And if Murdock comes near you again, call me."

He clicked off and put the phone in his pocket.

"What have they been asking her?"

"She didn't say. From the background noise I think she was in a Bucar getting a ride back to the inn."

"Do you think they told her about Hilary?"

"No, at least she didn't mention it."

"Wait till she finds out I was the one who probably shot her."

"Michelle, you don't know if it was you, so stop driving yourself crazy about it."

"Easy for you to say."

He started to make a retort but then stopped and patted her arm. "Actually, it *is* easy for me to say. I'm sorry."

"So when are we heading back up to Maine?"

"As soon as we check out Roy's farm and talk to the local authorities."

"Doubt they'll be much help."

"No, I think they will."

"Why?"

"Up to this point it seems everyone believed that Roy was guilty. Now, with Bergin and Hilary dead, something Roy could not have been involved in, it might make people take a second look. And cops are no different."

"Who do we deal with on the federal side in Virginia? Not Murdock?"

"I know the RA in Charlottesville," Sean said, referring to the Resident FBI Agent. "He's a good guy. Owes me a favor, in fact."

"Lots of people seem to owe you. What's his debt?"

"I wrote a recommendation letter for his daughter to get into UVA Law."

"That's all?"

"Well, I got him tickets to the Skins–Cowboys game in D.C. He's originally from Dallas."

"Now that is valuable."

The FBI agent was suitably cooperative. And he told them something that was particularly intriguing.

"I know Brandon Murdock. He's a good guy. But I don't know why he would be involved in something like this."

"Why's that?" asked Sean.

"He doesn't work VICAP," the man said, referring to the Bureau's Violent Crime Apprehension Program, which also dealt with serial killers.

"What does he do?"

"Went to D.C. a while back."

"So, Hoover, WFO?" asked Michelle, referring to the FBI headquarters and the Bureau's Washington Field Office, respectively.

"No." He looked doubtful. "I shouldn't be talking about this with you, Sean."

"Come on, Barry. I'm not going to go blab it. You know me."

"And he got you the Cowboy tickets," Michelle reminded him.

The man grinned wryly. "Okay, Murdock is with the counterterrorism unit. Really specialized stuff." He pointed a finger at Sean. "And I expect tickets for this. And better seats."

"I'll see what I can do."

Next, Sean and Michelle spent time with the local prosecutor, who had heard about Hilary Cunningham's death.

"You're right, Sean," the prosecutor had said. "This thing is really starting to stink."

They were given copies of the file on the Roy case and then drove out to the farm. It was isolated, with one dirt road in and out, the Blue Ridge Mountains as a backdrop, and not another house, car, or even stray cow in sight. Michelle pulled her Land Cruiser to a dusty stop in front of the one-story, wood-planked house, and they stepped out.

Though the crime scene had long since been released, strands of yellow police tape still hung down from the front porch posts. Twenty yards west of the house was a two-story barn painted dark green with a cedar shake roof. In the back they could see a chicken coop and a small split-rail corral that looked far too small for horses.

"Pigsty," noted Michelle, as she glanced at it.

"Thanks for the insight," said Sean. "I thought they might have been breeding really small horses."

"Bodies in the barn."

"Six of them. All men. All white. All John Does as of now."

They found the front door locked, but a minute later it was unlocked due to Michelle's delicate manipulations of the deadbolt.

The house had a simple floor plan, and it didn't take them long to make their way through it. Michelle picked out one of the books from a wall shelf full of them. She looked at the spine. "The only word I recognize in this title is *the*."

"Well, you're not a genius."

"Thanks for reminding me."

"No pictures of family. No testimonials from work. No college degrees. Nothing to show the guy even lives here."

"Except for the books."

"Right, except for them."

"Well, this was his parents' house. Maybe he just has his stuff somewhere else."

"No, Paul told us their parents bought the place after they got married and before their son was born. This is the only home Roy has ever known." He looked around some more. "I suppose if he had a computer the cops took it."

"Good bet."

They headed to the barn. The doors were unlocked. They opened them and went in. The space was big and mostly empty. There was a hayloft reached by a wooden ladder, some workbenches, and an assortment of rusty tools hanging on pegs on the walls. An old John Deere tractor was parked at the far end of the ground floor.

Michelle studied a patch of the dirt floor that had been dug up on the left side of the barn to a level of about five feet.

"I'm guessing the burial ground was here?"

Sean nodded and walked a perimeter around the turned-up soil.

"How'd they know to look here?" she asked.

"File says an anonymous tip was called in to the police."

"That's really convenient. Anybody try to run down this tipster?"

"They probably tried. But it also probably would have led nowhere. Throwaway phone card. Untraceable. That's standard operating procedure for homicidal maniacs these days if the tipster was actually the murderer."

She circled the site carefully, studying it like an archaeological dig. "None identified as of yet. Were their faces disfigured or their prints burned off somehow?"

"Don't think so. They're just not in any database, apparently. It happens."

"Kelly Paul seems convinced of her brother's innocence."

"Half brother," Sean reminded her.

"Still a sibling."

"I find her more interesting than her brother in some respects. And I noted there were no pictures of her in Roy's house, and no pictures of him in her house."

"Some families aren't that close."

"Granted, but still, they seem to be really close right now."

"Well, to be fair, we've never even heard the brother say anything. And she was equal parts loquacious and stingy with details."

"Regarding details about her personal history, which was my point earlier."

Michelle looked around. "Okay, we've seen the burial grounds. Now what?"

Sean examined some old tools on the workbench. "Let's assume he was framed. How do you get six bodies in here, bury them, and no one knows?"

"First of all, the place is in the middle of nowhere. Second, Roy wasn't here all the time. He worked outside the house and also spent time in D.C. Or at least so we were told."

"So, easy enough to plant the evidence. Then the question is why?"

"Meaning if he was an unimportant cog in the nation's mighty tax collection machine, why go to all the trouble?"

"There are two possible answers to that. Either it's something in his personal history that we don't know

219

yet. A personal grudge of significant importance to justify six bodies. Or—"

"Or he wasn't just an unimportant cog. He was a lot more. Other things being equal, I'm leaning in that direction. Like his sister says, he had uncommon intellectual gifts. That would be important to certain people, or agencies."

"That and the time spent in D.C. make me lean the same way. Plus the fact that the FBI is all over this with unusual interest." He dusted off his hands. "Okay, let's make the rounds of the ME, and the office where Roy worked."

When they came out of the barn an SUV pulled into the front yard and two men in suits got out.

One of them said, "Can I ask what you're doing here?"

Sean gazed at him. "Right after you tell me who the hell you are."

The men flashed badges. Quickly.

"Didn't quite catch the name of the agency on your commission," said Sean. "Want to try that again, slower?"

The creds didn't come back out, but the men's guns did. "We're federal officers and you need to get off this property right now."

Sean and Michelle showed their IDs, explained what they were doing there, and Sean's earlier conversations with the local police force and the county prosecutor.

One of the men shook his head. "I don't really care. Get out. Now."

"We're investigating this case for the defense. We have the right to be here."

"All the same, you're going to have to leave."

"How'd you know we were here?" asked Michelle, as they headed to her truck.

"Excuse me?" said one of the men.

"There's nobody around here. We didn't pass one car getting here. How'd you know we were here?"

In response the man opened the door to Michelle's truck and motioned for her to get in.

Sean and Michelle sped off down the dirt road, billowing dust behind them and into the faces of the two Feds.

"They couldn't have known we were there, Sean. And those badges looked like the real deal even if I couldn't see what agency they were actually with. They looked like Feds."

He nodded. "We're being tailed. I wonder for how long."

"I swear there was no one following us when we went to see Kelly Paul. There's no way I could've missed that. There was no cover. Absolutely none."

"That's the rub. There's no cover here, either, and they still showed up."

Michelle gazed out the window. "Satellite?"

"We're up against the Feds here. Why not?"

"Buying satellite time is a tough step even for the Bureau."

Sean considered this. "Those guys weren't with the FBI. They want you to know who they are. They would've shoved their creds right in our faces and kept them there."

"Damn, what have we got ourselves into?"

Sean didn't answer her because he had nothing to say.

29

"He was an exceptional worker. Smart as a whip. No—smarter, actually. It was really something. Almost not human, I'd guess you could say."

Sean and Michelle were in Leon Russell's office at the IRS in Charlottesville. Russell was short and wide, with thick white hair. He wore a short-sleeved shirt with a T-shirt underneath and suspenders. His fingers were stained with nicotine, and he twitched a lot, as though the absence of a cigarette in his hand was messing with his mind.

"That's what we heard too," said Sean. "What were his duties here?"

"He was the troubleshooter. Anything out of the ordinary that no one else could figure out, we went to Edgar."

"What sort of person was he?" asked Michelle.

"Kept to himself. We'd sometimes go out for a beer after work. Edgar never joined us. He'd head home to his farm. I think he liked to read."

"Did you ever go out to the farm?"

"Only once, when I was interviewing him for the job."

"How'd you come to know about him?"

"Friend of a friend. At his college. I keep contacts everywhere. People with exceptional talent I get a heads-up on. Edgar really stood out. He'd been out of school for a while, doing what I'm not sure. But I called him up and he came in for an interview. Impressed the hell out of me. I had one of those old Rubik's Cubes on my desk. He picked it up while he was talking to me, and kept messing it up and then solving it over and over, just like that. I've never been able to do it once. It was like he could see every combination in his mind. Bet the guy could've been a hell of a chess player."

"I didn't realize the IRS went all out for that kind of talent," said Sean. "It's not like you can compete with the salaries on Wall Street."

"Edgar had no desire to go there. Don't get me wrong. He probably could've come up with some derivative algorithm that would've made him billions. Or designed some software in Silicon Valley that would have made him equally rich."

"But no interest?"

"He had his farm, his books, his numbers."

"Numbers?" asked Michelle.

"Yeah. Guy loved numbers, what he could make them do. And he loved complexities. He could take a ton of different sections of the tax code—income, gift, estate, corporate, partnerships, carried interests, capital gains—and visualize how they all worked together. Did it for fun. For *fun!* Do you realize how remarkable that is? The tax code is a freaking nightmare. Even I don't understand all of it. Not even close, in fact. No one does. Well, except for Edgar. Every page and every section and every word. Probably the only one in the country who did."

"Pretty unique," said Michelle.

"Oh, yeah. Made our little office stand out, I can tell you that. Other places wanted to snag him. I mean in the IRS system. They tried, but he was content. He didn't want to move. Thank God for me. The performance bonuses I got because of that guy, well, let's just say my retirement will be a lot better because of him."

"I understand that he went to D.C. a lot," said Sean. "Is that because he was the only one in the country who understood it all?"

Russell's amiable expression changed. "Who told you he went to D.C. a lot?"

"Is that not true?"

"Depends on how you define *a lot*."

"How would you define it?" asked Michelle.

"Once a week."

"Okay, did Roy meet that standard or not?"

"I'd have to check my files."

"Is the office here that big?"

"It's bigger than it looks."

Sean switched gears. "So he was working here when he was arrested?"

Russell leaned back and studied them both, his hands resting on his belly. Over his shoulder was a shelf full of thick white binders with sleep-inducing titles on the spines.

"And you *say* you're representing Edgar's interests?"

"That's right. We were hired by his counsel, Ted Bergin."

"Who I now understand is dead."

"That's right. He was murdered up in Maine near where Roy is being held."

"So you're technically no longer representing Edgar, then?" Russell smiled at what he obviously thought was a key and winning point in the debate.

"Actually, we are. Bergin's law firm was representing him, and there's another lawyer there who's taken the case over. So the connection still holds."

Russell, who did not seem to be listening to this, spread his hands. "I don't know what to tell you."

"Well, I was hoping you could *tell* me if Roy was working here when he was arrested." He paused. "Or is the office too big to determine that?"

"I don't need to tell you anything. You're not the police."

"By not telling us things you're actually telling us a lot," pointed out Michelle.

Sean added, "I'm sure the police have been by to

question you. Why don't you just tell us what you told them?"

"Why don't you just ask them yourself? I've already told you enough. And I've got work to do."

"It's always nice to hear it from the horse's mouth," said Michelle. "I hope you recognize your role in the proceedings."

"I don't appreciate your tone."

Sean sat forward. "Do you think he's guilty?"

The man shrugged. "Probably."

"Why?"

"These genius types. They've all got dark sides. Think too much. Not like the rest of us. So, yeah, he probably did it. Let's face it, any guy who knows every reg of the tax code has to be some sort of a wacko."

"Well, let's hope you don't get called for jury duty," snapped Michelle. This drew a scowl from Russell.

Sean said, "Did you notice anything in Roy's behavior that would have indicated he might have been a serial killer?"

Russell gave a fake yawn and said in a clearly uninterested tone, "And what sort of behavior would I have been looking for?"

Michelle pounced. "Oh, I don't know, maybe a human head or two in the jellybean bowl on his desk. Subtle things like that, you freaking moron."

A minute later they were being escorted out of the building by a security guard who looked about as tough as the accountants in the building. When he reached out to put a hand on Michelle's back to urge her along, she snarled, "Touch me and die."

The man jerked his hand back so fast he winced, as though he'd pulled a muscle.

Outside Sean sighed. "I love your interrogation approach, Michelle. So subtle, so sophisticated."

"Almost makes you want to be wearing a badge again," said Michelle. "That way they can't kick you out before you get your answers, even if you're a smart-ass. And that idiot was going to tell us nothing useful."

"You're right. He was stonewalling. Must be a good reason."

"And Roy was most definitely not working for the IRS when he was arrested. Otherwise the guy would have just told us so. He's hiding something. He tells us a lie, it comes back to bite him. He tells us nothing, nothing sticks to him later."

They were about to get in Michelle's SUV when the woman approached.

She was timid-looking, with straight light-blond hair and glasses that fronted pretty blue eyes.

"Excuse me?" she said cautiously.

They turned to look at her.

"I understand you were here asking questions about Edgar?"

Sean said, "Did you know him?"

"We worked in the same cubicle zone. I'm Judy, Judy Stevens."

"We were asking questions, although answers from your boss were hard to come by."

"Mr. Russell doesn't like to say anything that might come back to, you know . . ."

"Bite him in the ass?" suggested Michelle.

A smile crept to Judy's face and her cheeks reddened slightly. "Yes."

"But you don't have that issue?" Sean asked.

"I just want the truth to come out."

"And what do you think is the truth?"

"All I know is Edgar stopped working here over seven months before this nightmare happened. Before that he was here for eight years."

"Where did he go?"

"Nobody really knows. He just didn't come to work one day. I asked Mr. Russell but he told me it was none of my business."

"Okay. Did you hear from Edgar?"

Judy lowered her gaze. "Edgar and I were friends. He . . . he was a nice person. Just very shy."

"So did you hear from him?" Sean asked her again.

"He called me one night. Just out of the blue. I asked him what was going on, why he was no longer coming to work. He told me that he had another job, but he couldn't say what it was."

"Did he say why he couldn't tell you?"

"Just that it was very sensitive. That was the word he used. Sensitive."

"Did you hear from him again?"

"No. And from the way he was talking it seemed to me that his calling me was . . . was . . ."

"A risk on his part?" prompted Michelle.

Judy lifted her gaze. "Yes, exactly. A risk on his part."

Michelle said, "Then he must really think a lot of you for him to take that chance."

Judy's face flushed with pleasure. "I thought a lot of him."

Sean appraised her. "So you don't think he killed all those people?"

"No. I knew Edgar. Well, I knew him as well as anyone did, I guess. He's not a killer. He wouldn't know how. It just wasn't in his psyche. Even though he was so big, he was actually a very gentle man. If he accidentally stepped on a cricket it would make him sad."

Sean handed her his card. "You think of anything, please contact us."

She clutched the card. "Have you seen Edgar? I mean up in that . . . place?"

"We have."

"How is he?"

"Not that good."

"Could you tell him that Judy says hello? And that I believe in his innocence," she added in a firm tone.

"I will."

They climbed in Michelle's SUV and started off.

She said, "Okay, Edgar's got at least one person rooting for him."

"Make that two. His half sister."

"Right."

"So he just stops coming to work one day. His IRS boss clams up. Nobody is told anything. And he takes a risk and calls his friend and tells her he has a new job and that it's sensitive."

She scowled. "And Murdock is counterterrorism. So it's got to be national security, you know, spy stuff. And you know how much I hate spy stuff."

"What, you mean the double and triple backstabbing and multiple agendas for every scenario?"

"More or less, yeah."

"So if he's wrapped up with the spies? Why?"

"Because of his mental prowess, probably."

Sean shrugged. "I don't know what else he has to offer other than his height. And I doubt the CIA or any of the other spy mills have a basketball team. So he's in with the spies and then this happens. His new employer must be having a cow."

"Accounts for all the guys with guns in black suits, satellites, and Bureau involvement."

"I'd like to look at the medical examiner's report."

Michelle grimaced. "Let's hope the locals are a bit more cooperative than that IRS clown. I'm expecting to get audited any day now."

30

Two hours later Sean had a copy of the ME's report and other forensic details.

"Let's hope this gives us something to go on," said Michelle.

"You'd think if there was some smoking gun in here the police would've already acted on it. This case has been going nowhere. And I don't think it's just because Edgar Roy is sitting in a federal nuthouse."

"Strings are definitely being pulled," replied Michelle. "This sucker is being executive-lagged big time."

"Which goes to show the forces behind the scenes."

"Yeah, scary forces."

"Let's grab something to eat and see if we find anything in this report."

Over sandwiches and coffee Sean read the report and discussed parts of it with Michelle.

"No surprises. The bodies were in various states of decay. ME calculated that one of the bodies had been dead about a year. The others between four and six months."

"That means he killed six times in less than a year."

"We've seen serial killers more active than that. Besides, burial messes up the time of death some. Could be longer or shorter than that. If the bodies had been left aboveground at least we'd have fly larvae evidence. That's pretty accurate. But even in the ground there are some helpful things. Bugs in the dirt too, I mean."

Michelle put down her tuna sandwich. "Nice meal conversation. Really sparks the old appetite."

He slid the report back in his briefcase and looked around the small restaurant. In a low tone he said, "Your two o'clock, guy in the sweatshirt and jean jacket trying real hard to look like a student. He' s—"

"I know. I scoped him about ten minutes ago. He's got a pistol bump under his jacket and a bud in his left ear."

"FBI?"

"One of the alphabets, most likely. But what do we do about it?"

"Don't let on that we suspect."

Michelle picked up her sandwich again. "That just brought my appetite back."

"Well, this might just take it away again."

She stopped with the tuna special halfway to her mouth.

Sean said, "Spotted something in the ME report that puzzled me."

"I can hardly stand the anticipation."

"What kind of dirt was in the barn on Roy's property?"

"This is Virginia. So red clay. Why?"

"The findings indicated that each of the bodies showed evidence of dirt present that was different from that found in the barn."

Michelle put her sandwich down again. "But that would only be possible if—"

"Excuse me?"

They both looked up to see the man in the jean jacket standing next to their table.

"Yeah," said Sean, who looked annoyed at having allowed the guy to come right up to the table without him noticing.

"I was wondering if you two could step outside with me?"

"And why would we want to do that?" asked Michelle, whose right hand had snaked toward her own weapon and her left hand had curled into a fist.

"Let's do this the easy way."

"Let's not do this any way at all," she shot back.

The man reached inside his jacket, which was his first mistake.

Michelle swiveled, and her left leg shot out and caught him right in the gut. He was propelled back and hit the table against the wall.

His second mistake was coming at her again.

Before he could strike, Michelle had tagged him on the chin with a powerful swing kick that lifted him off his feet and put him on his back, out cold on the worn, yellowed linoleum.

Sean stood, looking down in shock at the man.

The few other patrons in the deli, mostly older folks, sat frozen in their chairs at the sudden violence.

Michelle looked at them and said, "Little misunderstanding. Someone will be in to get him shortly. Just return to your meals and, what the hell, order some dessert." She pointed at the fallen man. "It's on him." She turned back to Sean and hissed, "I suggest we get out of here before a strike team interrupts our coffee."

He threw some cash down on the table for the meal and said, "If he is a Fed we are in deep shit."

"Look, he never flashed a badge. For all we knew he was going for his gun." She edged his jacket open with the toe of her boot and the weapon was revealed.

"But still," said Sean.

"Cross that bridge when we get to it. Personally, I'm a little tired of being pushed around by the badge-and-baton community. And patience has never been my virtue."

"How is it that you actually passed the Secret Service entry psychological exam?"

"Easy. Lots of Diet Coke and a ton of chocolate."

They left the deli by the rear door, circled around, and spied another car with another man in it. Michelle edged into her truck from the passenger side followed by Sean. She fired it up and had backed out before the driver in the sedan could react.

As Sean looked in the side mirror he said, "Driver

doesn't know what to do. Follow us or, okay, there he goes inside to check out what happened to his buddy."

Michelle hit the road and sped up. The car didn't follow them. He said, "Two minutes from now there'll be a BOLO out on us for attacking a Fed."

"If he is a Fed."

"Come on, the guy was screaming it."

"Do we ditch these wheels and get another?"

"They'll have markers in the system in five minutes. Our credit cards and driver's licenses will pop up."

"Then call Murdock, tell him what happened."

"Are you out of your—" Sean's face froze. "That is actually a brilliant idea."

"Thank you. Cut him off at the pass and tell him some armed guy came at us. Wanted to warn him that something was up. When he says why the hell did we attack a Fed, we can plead ignorance."

Sean was already punching in the number. He spent two minutes on the phone and did not let the FBI agent get a word in edgewise until the end. But whatever Murdock said did not sit well with Sean, by the look on his face.

"Yeah, I can give you a description. And the plate number." He did so. He talked a bit more, answered two more questions and clicked off. "Unless he's a world-class liar, Murdock knew nothing about it."

"Then the guy is not FBI?"

"So it's another alphabet agency."

"What about the BOLO?"

"CIA doesn't use them. They go systemwide, the spooks have to explain stuff to the cops they don't like to explain."

Sean's phone chirped and he looked at the text. Smiling, he looked over at Michelle. "Want some really good news?"

"That would be a really big yes."

"This text is from my friendly local prosecutor. The kill round on Hilary Cunningham did not match your weapon."

"Then I didn't shoot her?" The relief on Michelle's face was overwhelming.

"No, you didn't. Which means someone else killed her either there or somewhere else and brought her body there in order to frame you."

"Maybe just like Edgar Roy?"

"Maybe."

"But they had to know the police would get the ballistics run."

"I didn't say they wanted to have you convicted of the crime. Just screw things up for you for a while. Mess with your head."

"Okay, on that point they succeeded. So what did ballistics show? Was it another round from the .45 that almost hit me?"

"No. Nine-by-nineteen-millimeter Parabellum jacketed hollow-point."

"If you seek peace, prepare for war," said Michelle. He looked at her curiously. "The word *parabellum* is derived from a Latin saying that means: 'If you wish for peace, prepare for war.' That was the motto of the German weapons manufacturer that made the Parabellum round based on Georg Luger's design. It's also called the nine-millimeter Luger, as distinguished from the Browning round, for example."

"You are a positive treasure trove of ballistic jewels."

"The nine-millimeter Luger is also the most popular military cartridge in the world and is used by the majority of the police forces in the US. Who was the manufacturer and what was the load?"

Sean looked at his phone screen again. "Double Tap. Gold Dot JHP load. Hundred and fifteen grain."

"Okay, that has a one-stop rating of over ninety percent and a penetration factor in excess of thirteen inches. Not in the league of a .44 or .357 Magnum load, but still plenty powerful. It can definitely deliver hydrostatic shock wounds."

"Meaning?"

"Meaning a hit to the chest can cause the target's brain to hemorrhage."

"So it obviously wasn't the round used to kill Bergin."

Michelle shook her head. "No way. That ordnance would've gone through the skull at contact range. It never would've stayed in the head."

"That's interesting. Then the odds are whoever killed Bergin didn't murder Hilary Cunningham."

"That's right. So what now?" she asked.

"I say we go back to Maine."

"Plane?"

Sean shook his head. "Stop and get a big cup of coffee. We're driving."

"Can I get my gun back from the local cops before we go?"

"With my blessing."

Michelle floored it.

31

Twelve hours later, they were in Boston, where they stayed overnight at a hotel. They hadn't gone all the way to Machias, Maine, because even Michelle's mega-caffeine pop had worn off and she'd slid into the backseat for some shut-eye after seven hours of piloting. After five hours at the wheel of the Land Cruiser, Sean's eyes had begun to close once too often. After a few hours' deep sleep and an early start the next morning, they pulled into the parking lot of Martha's Inn in the early afternoon.

Megan Riley met them outside the front door. "Agent Murdock is an asshole," she snapped.

"Well, that's one way of putting it," said Sean.

"A nicer way than I would have," added Michelle.

"What did the FBI want to know?" he asked.

"Everything. But I told them zip. I'm Roy's legal counsel. They can't bully me around even though they tried."

"Good for you," said Michelle.

"I called Murdock, sort of read him the riot act," added Sean.

240

"I know. He was not happy about that. That's why he let me go. The jerk."

"And we found out who the client is," said Michelle.

"Who?"

Sean answered, "Roy's half sister, Kelly Paul. She's an interesting lady. Haven't quite figured her out yet. But she's a force to be reckoned with." He stopped talking and led Megan over to a bench under a tree in front of the inn. "Sit."

"Why?" She looked up at him with a fearful expression.

"We've got some bad news. Another death."

They both could see Megan grip the seat of the bench so tightly her fingers turned white. "Who?"

"Hilary Cunningham."

Megan managed not to cry. At least for a few seconds. Then she bent forward and started to sob into her hands.

Sean looked desperately at Michelle, who muttered, "Sorry, not good with this stuff."

Sean sat down next to the woman and patted her back awkwardly. "I'm very sorry, Megan."

Finally the young woman sat up, wiped her face dry with the sleeve of her jacket, and said, "How?"

"She was shot. And her body was left at Bergin's home." He glanced at Michelle, who said, "I was there when it happened."

Megan looked up at Michelle. "Why would anyone want to kill Hilary? She was just a nice old lady."

Sean answered. "She worked for Bergin. Bergin represented Roy. That seems to be enough in this case for certain people."

Megan caught a breath. "So that means, what, I'm next?"

"We're not going to let anything happen to you," said Michelle.

She sat down on the other side of the young lawyer.

"Maybe I should have stayed with the FBI," said Megan, her voice barely above a whisper.

"Is that what you want?" asked Sean.

"Not really, no." Her voice grew firmer. "What I really want is to find out who did this."

"That's what we want too."

"So where do we go from here?"

"To see your client."

"But you said he doesn't talk."

"You still have to see him. I'll make the arrangements."

Sean and Michelle showered, changed their clothes, and ate. After getting clearance from Carla Dukes at Cutter's Rock, they drove to the facility. If possible, the security was even tighter. Finally, Michelle had had enough when one guard was too enthusiastic in his search of her.

"You cop one more feel on my ass, you're going to

have to learn to live with prosthetic hands," she snapped.

He stepped back, stared at the ceiling, and motioned that they could proceed.

They waited in the little room. Edgar Roy was brought in. His appearance and demeanor remained unchanged. When Megan saw him she gasped and then sat in her chair, enthralled. When the guards had left and the door had clanged behind them, Megan remained silent. Finally, Sean said, "Uh, do you want to try and ask him some questions?"

Megan started, her face reddened. She opened her briefcase and meekly tapped on the glass wall separating them.

"Mr. Roy, I'm Megan Riley." She pressed one of her business cards against the glass. Her face flushed again as Roy just sat there staring at the ceiling. She slowly withdrew the card and put it back in her pocket.

"Mr. Roy, I'm representing you in your legal case. You are being charged with multiple counts of murder. Do you understand that?"

Nothing.

She stared at Sean, who nodded encouragingly at her while Michelle gave him an incredulous look.

Megan said to Roy, "We have to prepare your defense and we need your full cooperation in order to do that."

The ceiling, however, still captured Roy's full attention.

Sean said, "Mr. Roy, another person connected with your case has been murdered. Hilary Cunningham worked for Ted Bergin. She was shot and her body left at his house."

This also prompted no reaction from Roy.

Sean abruptly got up and moved around the glass so he was standing right next to the man. Michelle immediately rose and joined him.

"Do you think this is wise?" she whispered.

"I don't know, but I figure we have nothing to lose."

"Except a body part if he really is a psycho."

"That's why I have you, for protection."

He leaned down so close to Roy that he could smell the man's breath. At least, Sean thought, he was still breathing. That was more than could be said for Bergin or Hilary, or the six guys in the barn.

"We met the client," he whispered. His voice sank even lower. The only one who could hear him now was Roy. "Your sister, Kelly Paul?"

Sean leaned back, studying the other man. Then he hunched forward again, his cheek nearly touching Roy's ear. "And Judy Stevens sends her best. And she believes in your innocence. She asked me to tell you that."

Sean scrutinized the other man's features again. Silence lingered for a few beats.

Megan started to say something, but Sean stopped her. "I think that's enough for today."

"But he hasn't said anything," exclaimed Megan.

Sean looked at Michelle in a way that indicated he didn't necessarily agree with this statement.

As they walked down the hall, Sean slowed his pace as Brandon Murdock approached.

Michelle said, "What, does the Bureau have a satellite office at Cutter's Rock now?"

"I thought you'd have something better to do with your time than talk to a wall." He glanced at Megan. "You know, you really should think about who your friends are here. The wrong alliances can get you in trouble."

"I'm Edgar Roy's lawyer. That's the only alliance I'm concerned with," replied Megan.

"You're his lawyer for *now*."

"What's that supposed to mean?" asked Sean.

"Just that things change."

"Come on, Murdock, you're among friends. What's so special about Roy? Why do you care about the guy so much?"

"Six bodies."

"Jeffery Dahmer had a lot more than that and I didn't see the Bureau flying around the country stirring up trouble."

"Every case is its own kingdom."

Michelle smirked. "So now you're a poet?"

"You folks have a productive day." Murdock walked off.

★

At the inn, after Megan went to her room, Sean and Michelle sat in the small front parlor.

"When I mentioned Kelly Paul's name to Roy?"

"I didn't know you did. I couldn't hear what you said."

"That was intentional in case they were recording. But when I did say the name, I got a reaction. It wasn't much, but there was a slight jerk of the head, a tiny widening of the eyes."

"You really think he understood you?"

"I really do. And that's not all. The same thing happened when I mentioned Judy Stevens."

"So he is faking? Why would he do that? To keep from going to trial? That's a long shot. He can't be a zombie forever."

"I'm not sure it's just to keep from going to trial."

"What other motivation would he have?"

"If we answer that question, we answer pretty much everything."

32

Edgar Roy sat in his cell. He had assumed the usual position. Long legs splayed out, his back at a comfortable angle against the metal chair that was bolted to the floor. He fixed his gaze on the far end of the ceiling. It was six inches to the right of the back wall and four inches from the wall perpendicular to that. Roy imagined that spot to represent a crossroads of sorts. There was actual comfort for him in that tiny piece of concrete.

Over his shoulder a camera recessed into the wall behind a protective transparent shield watched his every move, not that there were any moves. A listening device embedded in the wall recorded everything he said, not that he had said anything since coming here.

Lesser minds might not have been able to pull this off, at least over a long period of time. But one thing Roy had always been good at was losing himself within his mind. For him, his brain was a very interesting place to be lost. He could entertain himself endlessly with memories, puzzles, and assorted contemplations.

He'd begun thinking about his earliest recollections

going forward in exact chronological order. His first memory had been at eighteen months. His mother had spanked him for closing the door on the cat. He remembered exactly what she had said, the shriek of the cat, the cat's name—Charlie—the song being played on the radio when it had happened. Colors, smells, sounds. Everything. It had always been that way for him. Other people complained that they couldn't remember where they had been yesterday, or that long-ago memories just wouldn't come to mind anymore. Roy had the opposite problem. He had never been able to forget anything, no matter how trivial, no matter if he wanted to forget it or not. It was there. It was all there.

I can never forget anything.

Over the years he had come to terms with this ability. He had learned to compartmentalize it all in discrete places in his mind, which seemed to have limitless space, able to elasticize when he needed it to, like putting in another USB memory stick or a zip drive. He could recall it instantly if need be, but he didn't have to think about it until he wanted to.

He had never sought notoriety for this special ability. Indeed, growing up he'd always been considered a freak because of the way his mind worked. Consequently, he'd tried to hide his special talents rather than flout them. Then, conversely, people who knew of his gifts had always called him an underachiever.

It was easy to label someone, he felt, until you walked in his shoes. But no one could ever truly walk in his shoes.

Since the camera was behind him he was able to move his eyes and alight on a different spot on the ceiling. He forgot about being eighteen months old, about the spanking and the shrieking cat.

His sister.

And Judy Stevens.

They were the only friends he had.

But they had not forgotten him. They were perhaps working on the outside to help him. These people who had come to visit him. Sean King and Michelle Maxwell. And the young woman, Megan Riley. His lawyer was dead. His secretary murdered. That was what they had said. Roy actually remembered everything they had said, everything they had worn, every body tic made, every pause, every bit of eye contact. The tall woman was skeptical. The short woman was nervous and naïve. The man seemed solid. Maybe they were there to help him. But he had long ago given up on trusting anyone completely.

His mind turned to that awful day. On a whim he'd stepped into the barn. Smells from his childhood had come bolting at him from all directions. He'd looked up at the old hayloft. And more memories had come back to him. He'd walked around the bottom level of the barn, running his hand along the old John Deere tractor parked in one corner, its tires rotted. The old tool bench, the oat bins, the rusty license plates he and his sister had collected and tacked to one wall.

When he'd come to the patch of earth alongside one wall of the barn he'd stopped. The hay here had been moved aside and the dirt was freshly turned over, though he didn't know why. He'd knelt next to this section and picked up a clod of dirt, squeezed it, and let it drizzle out between his fingers. Good Virginia clay with its sweet, nauseating smell.

He'd noticed a shovel resting against one wall, picked it up, and shoved the digging end into the disturbed earth. He dug away until he stopped and dropped the shovel. Revealed in the dirt was something not even his mind would have predicted.

It was a human face. Or rather what was left of it.

He'd turned to run back to the house to call the police when he heard the sounds.

Sirens. Lots of them.

By the time he got to the door of the barn the police cruisers were skidding to a stop in front of the house. Men in uniforms with guns were leaping from their rides. They saw Edgar, pointed their guns, and ran toward him.

Roy had instinctively stepped back into the barn. It was a mistake to do so, of course, but he wasn't thinking clearly.

The police had cornered him there.

"I didn't do this," he'd cried out, glancing sideways at what he now knew was a burial site.

The uniforms had followed his gaze to the disturbed dirt. They'd crept to the edge of it, and their jaws tightened when they saw what was down there. The rotted face looking back at them. Then they'd stared down at Roy's dirty pants, the shovel lying on the ground. The clay on his hands. They'd drawn in closer.

One uniform had barked, "You're under arrest."

Another had spoken into his portable mic. "Tip paid off. We got him. Red-handed."

As Roy had looked at the man and heard what he said, his perfect mind completely shut down.

After he'd been arrested and charged, the only thing Roy could possibly think of to do was withdraw into his mind. He did this when he was afraid, when the world stopped making sense for him. Now he was afraid, and the world had stopped making sense.

They had tried to get him to talk. An army of psychologists and psychiatrists had been employed to evaluate his condition and determine whether he was faking or not. Yet they had never encountered someone with a mind like his. Nothing they asked, no ploy they used against him, had worked. He could hear them, see them, but it was as though an invisible buffer had been placed between him and the outside world. It was like experiencing it all through a wall of water. The army of shrinks had finally given up.

After that, his next stop had been Cutter's Rock.

Roy knew the exact parameters of his cell. He'd memorized the routines of all the guards. He knew when they ate their breakfast, lunch, and dinner. He knew the latitude and longitude of Cutter's Rock. And he knew that Carla Dukes was Peter Bunting's inside person. This was from two overheard pieces of conversation, innocuous to anyone who lacked stellar observational and analytical abilities. After all that time grappling with the Wall, Roy's skills were honed razor sharp.

And he knew that Bunting would do anything in his power to get him back. So he could scale the Wall again and again. To help keep the country safe.

Edgar Roy had no problem helping to keep his country safe. But nothing was ever that simple. He knew there were sixteen American intelligence agencies. They employed well over one million people, of which a third were independent contractors. There were nearly two thousand companies that worked in the intelligence field. And officially over a hundred billion dollars was spent on intelligence matters, though the exact number was classified and was actually far larger. It was a huge universe, and Edgar Roy found himself at the very center of it. He was, literally, the man who made sense out of what otherwise would be a colossal mass of ever-growing, incomprehensible data. It was like ocean waves, relentless, pounding, but bristling with importance for those who could divine its depths. It sounded poetic, but what he did was actually immensely practical.

It was a lot riding on his slender shoulders. And if he stopped and thought too much about it, he would have been paralyzed. The conclusions that he drew, the pronouncements that he made, the analyses that he helped produce were used to make polices that had global impact. People lived and people died. Countries were invaded or not. Bombs dropped or not. Deals were struck or allies jettisoned. The world shook according to Edgar Roy.

To the average citizen it would have seemed totally far-fetched: one person basically telling American intelligence what to do. But the dirty secret of intelligence was that there was simply too much damn intelligence for anyone to make sense of. And it was so interconnected that unless one had all the pieces it was impossible to make informed comprehensive judgments. It was a gigantic global puzzle. But if you had only part of the puzzle you would be doomed to failure.

He had initially been fascinated by the Wall. It was a living, breathing organism to him, one that spoke a foreign language that he had to learn. After several months, though, that fascination and interest had somewhat faded. While the subject matter was complex and challenging even to him, once he had seen the results of his input, the reality of what he was doing had come crashing down on him like a bunker-busting bomb.

I'm not cut out to play God.

33

The next morning Sean and Michelle and Megan had breakfast, not at Martha's Inn but at a restaurant a quarter of a mile away. After they'd filled up on eggs and toast and coffee, Sean said, "We think Carla Dukes is a plant."

"What makes you say that?" asked Megan.

"Her office was bare. No personal items. She doesn't intend on staying long. Like Mark Twain and Halley's Comet, I think she came in with Edgar Roy and she'll go out with him."

Megan said, "It really seems like people have it in for Edgar Roy."

"The question is why?" said Sean. "You said Bergin spoke with you about him."

"Just about some spot research, nothing substantive. You said you met the client, Roy's sister, Kelly Paul. What was her story?"

"She wants to help her brother. She has a POA for him and retained Bergin to rep him. Bergin was her godfather."

Megan finished her coffee. "So we have a client

who won't talk. The FBI won't tell us anything. Mr. Bergin and Hilary are dead with no leads."

"We need to find out what Roy was really doing," said Sean.

"What do you mean?"

"An IRS geek turned alleged serial killer does not generate this much federal excitement," explained Michelle. "We talked with his boss at the IRS. He wouldn't tell us anything, which actually told us a lot."

Sean added, "And he had a friend who worked there. She said Roy stopped working there months before he was arrested. He called her once and said he was working on something sensitive, but he couldn't say any more."

"So you think Roy was involved in something else? Maybe something criminal?"

"No, maybe something having to do with intelligence work."

"I thought you might get there," said the voice.

She was standing near their table. When Sean looked up he wondered how the woman was able to move so silently.

Kelly Paul took off her large sunglasses and said, "May I join you?"

She had on black jeans, a woolen vest, and a thick corduroy jacket over that. Heavy boots with fur toppings were on her feet. She looked ready for a long winter's stay in coastal Maine.

Sean scooted over and Paul slid in next to him.

"Megan Riley, this is Kelly Paul. Our client," he added awkwardly.

The women shook hands.

"Understand the FBI was giving you the third degree," said Paul. "Hope they didn't leave any permanent wounds."

Before Megan could answer, Sean said, "What are you doing up here?"

"Perfectly logical question," replied Paul.

"Could I have an answer?" said Sean, when it seemed apparent she was not going to provide one.

"Figured taking in the lay of the land myself was a good proposition."

"But it'll come with the cost of your anonymity," pointed out Michelle.

Paul got the attention of their waitress and ordered a cup of tea. She remained silent until it arrived and she took a sip. She set the cup down and took a moment to pat her lips dry. "My anonymity died the moment you two visited me, I'm afraid."

"No one followed us to your place," said Michelle.

"No one you could *see*," said Paul, and she took another sip of tea.

"Meaning what exactly?" said Sean.

Paul looked around. "Not here. Let's take this discussion somewhere else."

They paid the bill and climbed into Michelle's truck. Paul looked around the interior. "Have you swept this for bugs?"

Michelle, Sean, and Megan stared at her.

"Bugs?" said Michelle. "No, we haven't."

Paul slipped a device out of her bag and turned it on. She passed it around the interior of the vehicle and then studied the readout on the small electronic screen.

"Okay, we're good to go." She put the device away and sat back to find the others still staring at her.

"Care to start explaining?" said Sean.

Paul shrugged. "Self-evident, don't you think?"

"What is?"

"What we're up against here."

"And what exactly is that?" asked Michelle.

"Everybody," replied Paul.

"Can we start from page one?" said Sean. "I think we all need that right now."

"My brother is not simply an IRS agent with six bodies in his barn."

"Yeah, we'd gotten that far by ourselves," said Michelle.

"So what exactly is your brother?" asked Sean.

"I'm not convinced you all are ready for the answer."

"I think we're ready for the answers," said Sean. "In fact, we're so ready that I don't think I'm going to let you out of this vehicle until you tell us."

Before any of them could react, Paul had placed a knife against Megan's right carotid. "That would be an unfortunate action on your part, Mr. King, it really would be."

"Put that away," said Sean. "You don't have to go there."

Paul put the knife away and patted Megan on the arm. "Sorry I had to do that."

The young woman looked like she might throw up her breakfast.

"Just take deep breaths and the shock nausea will pass right on by," Paul added kindly.

"Why did you do that?" asked Sean.

"Ground rules have to be set. My loyalties do not lie with any of you, at least not completely."

"Where *do* they lie?" asked Michelle.

"Mainly with my poor brother, who's rotting at Cutter's Rock."

"Mainly?" said Sean. "Which means there's something else. Or someone else?"

"In my business there is always something else, Mr. King."

"And that business being what? Intelligence?"

She looked out the car window and said nothing.

"Okay," said Sean. "I'm done trying to work with you. Get out. We'll move on our own without you. But if we find something out that hurts your brother, so be it. The chips fall where they will."

"In many significant ways my brother *is* American intelligence."

Sean shook his head. "That's impossible. The field is way too large."

"Your intuition is endearing. But the fact is the

American intelligence system was broken. Too many cooks in the kitchen such that no one really knew anything. With the E-Program that weakness was rectified."

"E-Program?" said Michelle. "Does the E stand for *eidetic*?"

Paul smiled. "The E actually stands for *Ecclesiastes*."

"As in the Bible?" said Sean.

"A book of the Hebrew Bible, yes."

"What's the connection?" asked Michelle.

"One underlying philosophy in Ecclesiastes is that the individual can find truth by using his powers of observation and reason instead of blindly following tradition. You acquire wisdom and focus that wisdom to figure out the world on your own. It was a radical concept back then, but it really fits the E-Program concept well."

"So your brother is this guy?" asked Sean. "The analyst?"

"There are six people in the United States classified as 'super-users.' By federal law they're supposed to know everything. But they had no special mental gifts. They'd stick a retired admiral in a room with nary a pen or piece of paper and then run past him all this intelligence for eight hours until he either passed out or wet himself. It met the letter of the law that super-users be kept up-to-date on things, but it hardly passed the spirit of that law."

"Why is that so important?" asked Sean.

"We are in an information-overloaded society. Most people receive more information from just their smartphones in a week than their grandparents received in their entire lives. On the government and, most critically, the military end, it gets a lot trickier. From PFC cubicle warriors staring at hundreds of TV screens at top secret installations to four-stars muddling over their handhelds at the Pentagon. From a first-year clandestine analyst at Langley staring at a zillion satellite images to the national security advisor trying to make sense of reports stacked ceiling high on his desk, they're all trying to take in more than is humanly possible. Do you know why air force pilots call their data screens 'drool buckets'? There's so much information on there they almost turn into zombies staring at it. You can train people to use technology better or focus more effectively, but you can't upgrade someone's neurological capacity. You have what you were born with."

"And that's where this E-Program came in?" asked Michelle.

"My brother is the latest in a short line of peculiar geniuses that have sought to fill that role. He is the ultimate multitasker who also has perfect attention to detail. His neurological pipe is immense. He can see it all and make sense of it."

"And who exactly is behind the E-Program?" asked Sean. "The government?"

"Somewhat."

"That's all you can tell us?"

"For now."

"And who do you work for?"

"I don't work for anyone. I work *with* certain others. Of my choosing."

Sean said, "Isn't it a coincidence that your brother is working in intelligence too?"

"No coincidence about it. I encouraged Eddie to work in the field. I thought it would be a challenge for him, and I also thought he would be a terrific asset."

She opened the car door.

"Wait," exclaimed Sean. "You can't leave now."

"I'll be in touch. For now, just do your best to stay alive. It will become harder as time goes by."

"One last question," said Sean.

Paul paused at the door.

Sean said, "Is your brother innocent like you said you believed? Or did he kill those people?"

At first Sean didn't think she was going to answer the question.

"I stand by what I said, but at the end of the day only Eddie can definitively answer that."

"If he did kill those people, his life is over. He won't be going back to this E-Program."

"In some ways my brother's life was over a long time ago, Mr. King."

34

Peter Bunting sat down at the head of the table and looked around at the faces staring back at him. He was surrounded not by policy wonks who lived in the world of the hypothetical but by people who were deadly serious about national threats. Bunting both admired and feared these folks. He admired them for their public service. He feared them because he knew they routinely ordered the killing of other humans without losing a minute's sleep over it.

This particular briefing, while perfunctory, was being handled by Bunting because of the high level of people present and also because of the extenuating circumstances, chief of which was Edgar Roy's current situation. He didn't send in the lackeys when he had a Cabinet secretary, various directors of intelligence, and four-stars seated at a table with china coffee cups in front of them. They expected him, and they were paying a lot of taxpayer money for the privilege.

There was one person there who should not have been, but Bunting could do nothing except register his

262

official complaint before tersely being told to carry on with his report.

Mason Quantrell sat next to Ellen Foster, his hands in his lap, and his whole focus on Bunting. The only time Bunting stumbled during his presentation was when Quantrell had smiled at a statement of his and then whispered something in Foster's ear. She had smiled, too.

Bunting handled the ensuing questions, most of them penetrating and complex, with precision. He had become an expert at reading the poker faces of these men and women. They seemed, if not exactly pleased, then at least satisfied. Which meant he was relieved. He had been in meetings that had not gone nearly so well. Then Quantrell cleared his throat. All heads had turned to the Mercury CEO. Now Bunting suspected the entire meeting had been carefully choreographed.

"Yes, Mason?" asked Bunting, whose grip on his laser pointer tightened. He had a sudden impulse to aim it at Quantrell's eyes.

"You've told us a lot today, Pete."

"That's usually the point of a presentation such as this," Bunting replied, trying to keep his voice even and calm.

Quantrell didn't appear to hear him. "But what you haven't told us is how you can continue to expect a single analyst to keep up with all the data being generated. While it's true you've had some success—"

"I would modify that to say we've had enormous success, but please, carry on, Mason."

"Some success," repeated Quantrell. "But the reality is that by relying solely on one analyst we've weakened our national security considerably, possibly irreversibly."

"I disagree."

"But I don't disagree."

All heads turned, but only slightly, for this comment had come from Ellen Foster.

Bunting studied the woman who had become his most potent adversary. Yet as she was also the head of the largest federal security agency, he had no choice but to be respectful to the woman.

"Madame Secretary?"

"How do you rate your performance today, Peter?" she asked.

She wore a black dress, black stockings, and black heels with minimal jewelry. Bunting noticed, and not for the first time, that she was a very attractive woman. Nice skin, slim figure, but with curves where men usually wanted them. Foster had an impressive résumé both in the field and the boardroom, and possessed even more impressive political connections. The divorced head of DHS was low-key by nature, but every once in a while her picture would appear at some society event, where she was on the arm of an acceptably high-ranked gentleman.

She had a home in the upper-brackets region of

D.C. and a vacation place on Nantucket, where she would go to unwind with her security detail tagging along. Her ex-husband, a New York-based private equity fund manager, had amassed an enormous fortune using other people's money while paying an income tax rate lower than that of his secretary. She had gotten half of his net worth in the divorce and could do what she pleased. And what she pleased was to run the nation's security platform and apparently make Peter Bunting's life a hell on earth.

"It seems as though everyone was satisfied with my report." He eyed Quantrell and then his gaze flitted back to her. "Well, almost everyone."

"You're joking, right, Peter?" she said.

"If you have some definitive examples I can certainly discuss them with you."

"What's to discuss? The analysis you delivered today was total crap and everyone in the room knows it. Other than you, apparently."

Bunting gazed once more at the people around the table. Not a sympathetic face in the bunch. "I answered every question and every follow-up question. I didn't get a standing ovation, but I left nothing hanging, either."

Foster leaned forward. "In your contract renewal you've asked for an increase of twenty-three percent based on a variety of factors."

Bunting shot a glance at Quantrell, who was shaking his head and making clucking sounds.

"Madame Secretary, with all due respect, one of my main competitors is sitting in this room. That information was delivered in confidence to—"

"I'm sure we can rely on Mr. Quantrell's professionalism."

Bunting wanted to say, *What professionalism? He's a slimeball and you know it.* But instead he said, "Every single cost increase is justifiable. My people spent months cranking the numbers. And they worked with the government side on all of it, so there're no surprises in there."

"While we in Washington have the reputation of being a blank check with a rubber stamp, some of us do like to get what we pay for."

Though nearly a foot taller than the woman, Bunting now somehow felt much smaller than Foster. "I think we bring considerable value to the table."

"Frankly, I gave you a chance, Peter. You blew it."

"I spoke with the president," Bunting said hastily and then instantly regretted it.

She compressed her lips. "Yes, I know. Neat little end-around. But all it bought you was a little time. Nothing more."

Foster looked around the room. "I think that concludes the meeting. Mr. Quantrell, if you would join me in my office, I have some important matters I'd like to discuss."

She left the room with Mason Quantrell following.

As the room cleared Bunting stood there for a few

moments staring down at the useless briefing book in his hand. When he finally did leave no one looked at him as he passed little conversation groups in the hall. Foster had done her work well, it seemed.

He waited outside her office until she came out with Quantrell.

"May I have a word, Madame Secretary?" Bunting asked.

She gazed at him in mild surprise. "I have a full schedule."

"Please, just a minute."

Quantrell looked amused. "I'll talk to you later, Ellen." He slapped Bunting on the shoulder. "Cheer up, Pete. You can always come back to work for Mercury. I understand we need a geek in the IT Department."

Quantrell walked off and Bunting turned to Foster.

"Well?" she said. "Make it quick."

He drew closer. "Please don't do it."

"Do what?"

"The preemptive action."

"Good God, Bunting," she hissed. "You're talking about this out in the damn hallway? Have you lost your mind?"

"Just give me a little more time."

She looked him up and down and then closed her office door in his face.

★

On the drive back to the airport, Bunting noted the inconspicuous building set at the end of a strip mall. And the brick structure that backed up to a suburban neighborhood. Then there was a building that looked like it was made of all glass but that in reality had not one window in the place. These were all footprints of intelligence gathering. They were stuck like splinters into pieces of the outside world and most of the people passing by them had not the remotest idea what went on inside of them.

Intelligence work was dirty and at times deadly. Whether your adversary was killed quick with a bullet or slow with an enhanced interrogation session, or was anonymously obliterated by a drone strike launched from thousands of feet up, he was still dead. Like Edgar Roy might be soon. Dead.

Bunting settled back in his seat and let out a long sigh. Right now the two-point-five-billion-dollar contract didn't seem nearly worth it.

35

"Do we shadow Carla Dukes? Do we go see Edgar Roy again? Do we try to bust Murdock's chops somehow? Do we dig into Kelly Paul's background and see what turns up? Do we investigate Bergin's and Hilary's murders? Do we keep going after the six bodies in Edgar Roy's barn?"

Michelle fell silent and looked expectantly at Sean as they walked along the oceanfront near Martha's Inn.

"Or do we do *all* of that? And if so, how?" he replied. "There's only the two of us."

"We multitask well."

"Nobody multitasks that well."

"But we have to do something."

"The six bodies can cut two ways. Either someone knew that he was the Analyst for the government and framed him. Or he killed those people and the government is trying to keep what Roy actually did from the public."

"But you don't think he did it, do you?"

"No, though I don't have any solid reasons to back that up."

"So the people framing him must be enemies of this country. They know what he does and they're trying to stop him? But why not just kill him? He lived alone on that farm. It would've been easy."

"Well he must have had security, so it might not have been that easy. But maybe they wanted to do more than simply deprive America of its brilliant analyst."

"Like what?"

"I don't know," Sean admitted.

"Who do you think shot out our car windows?"

"Either our side or the other side."

"That's what I was thinking."

"Lot of dangerous folks out there."

"Exactly." Michelle took his arm. "Come on."

"Where are we going?"

"You'll see."

Ninety minutes later Sean was walking out of Fort Maine Guns with a new Sig 9mm.

"I haven't fired a pistol in a while."

"Which is why we're going there next." She pointed to a door in a building adjacent to Fort Maine with a sign outside that said Shooting Range.

An hour later Sean studied his results.

"Not bad," Michelle said. "Total score of ninety percent. Your kill zone shots were right where they need to be."

He glanced at her targets. The holes were huge

because the bullets had all congregated in the same spot.

"What was your score?"

"A bit better than yours. But just a bit."

"Liar."

When they got back to the inn Megan was hard at work at the round table in the parlor, with papers and files strewn around.

She looked up when they walked in the room.

"What are you doing?" asked Sean.

"Working on some motion papers."

"Regarding what?"

"Ms. Paul's information was very intriguing. I want to know whatever the government knows about Edgar Roy's background. And what he actually does for them."

Michelle said, "But if he is working in intelligence they won't tell us anything. They'll just bury it under national security mumbo-jumbo."

"That's right. But if we can get that on the record it may be enough to raise reasonable doubt in a jury's mind. It's certainly critical evidence. And in order to try to get that evidence we have to pull the government's chain. Hard."

"But the guy may never go to trial," pointed out Michelle.

Sean said, "But if he does, some of the forensics help us. The different dirt, for instance, found on the bodies. It's possible the bodies were brought from somewhere else and dumped in Roy's barn."

"Well, that could be all the exculpatory evidence we need," said Megan hopefully.

"Unless they argue Roy killed them somewhere else, hid the bodies for a while there, and then dug them up and brought them to Virginia."

"And buried them in his own barn so someone could find them and arrest him?" said Megan incredulously. "For such a smart guy that's pretty dumb."

Sean said, "And then there's the mysterious caller that conveniently tipped the police off about the bodies in the first place. Who is that person and how did he know about the bodies? Maybe the tipster killed the people and set Roy up."

"We still have to prove that," noted Michelle.

"No, proof of guilt is the government's job. We just have to raise it as a way to get reasonable doubt in a jury's mind," responded Sean.

Michelle said, "Murdock will be really pissed off when he sees the filings."

"Let him be." He looked at Megan. "You cool with that?"

She smiled. "The FBI doesn't scare me anymore."

Sean and Michelle headed up to his room. "There are a lot of roads we could go down, but I want to focus on Carla Dukes."

"She's probably an FBI agent."

"I don't think so."

"Why?"

"You and I have dealt with lots of FBI agents. She's no spring chicken, so if she were with the Bureau she'd have been with them for years now. She doesn't have the walk or the talk of an FBI vet. And an FBI agent would have anticipated we'd pull the media card to get in to see Roy and would've had an answer for it. She didn't."

"But still, to her we're the enemy," replied Michelle.

"Enemies can still reach common ground."

She cocked her head. "You mean we find some leverage with her?"

"Exactly."

"It'll have to be some damn heavy-duty stuff."

"Yes it will," said Sean.

"Do you have any in mind?"

"Yes I do."

"When do we do it?"

"Tonight of course."

36

Carla Dukes pulled her car into her garage around nine o'clock. She unlocked the door that led into the kitchen, put her bag down, and stood in front of the alarm code pad, her finger poised to hit the appropriate buttons. It took her a moment to realize that there was no high-pitched squeal from the alarm system telling her that she had to disarm it before the delay ran out.

That was because the alarm wasn't on.

She whirled around.

Sean stood there, the butt of his gun visible at the waist.

"What the hell are you doing here?" Dukes demanded.

"I need to talk to you."

"You broke into my house."

"No I didn't. The door was open."

"Bullshit. I lock everything up before I leave and then arm the system."

"You must've forgotten. As you can see, the alarm system is off."

"Then you turned it off."

"I said, you said."

"You're in my house. I'm calling the police." She eyed his gun. He looked at where she was looking. "It's a Beretta nine mil. Standard issue for the FBI, ironically enough."

She slid her cell phone from her purse. "Good, why don't we call them to come over and collect it and you?"

Before she could hit even one button, Sean said, "Would Agent Murdock want to know you're working for someone else?"

"All right. I am with the FBI. And therefore I can arrest you right now. But instead I'll give you five seconds to get the hell out of here."

Sean didn't move. He just looked at her, a tight smile edging across his features. "Just so you understand, Carla, the next minute or so will determine whether you end up in a federal prison or not."

"What are you talking about?"

"You just made a big mistake."

"I'm warning you."

"You're not FBI. You're not even close to being FBI. So if anybody's going to call the Feds I think that'll be me." He took out his phone and poised his finger over the numbers. She watched him dumbly. "But maybe you want to talk first," he said.

"Maybe," she said nervously.

Sean reached out and slipped the cell phone from her hand, and set it down on the kitchen counter.

"I think you want the FBI to believe you're working with them. You're certainly going through the motions. You have Murdock convinced. But he didn't put you into play at Cutter's Rock."

"Look, I told you I'm with the FBI."

"Then show me your creds."

"I'm undercover. I don't carry them."

"Where's your Beretta?"

"In my bedroom."

Sean shook his head. "SOP for FBI undercover is to get into the part. Your office is barren. Not even one fake family picture on your desk." He pointed to his gun. "And FYI, the FBI doesn't use the Beretta. They carry either Glocks or Sigs."

Dukes said nothing.

"So someone else put you at Cutter's. Which means your loyalties lie elsewhere. The FBI really frowns on being played for chumps."

"I was assigned to work at Cutter's Rock. I have a long career in federal correctional institutions."

"It doesn't matter. You're here temporarily. You haven't even bothered to move into your office. And this place is a rental. With a six-month lease."

"You've been spying on me?" she said.

"I'm an investigator. I spent a productive afternoon digging up stuff on you. And I'm not the only one."

Dukes paled at this statement. "What do you mean?"

"I mean there are lots of people interested in you,

Carla. You didn't think you could just waltz right into this, play both sides, and think no one would notice? That kind of naïveté could get you killed."

"These are not people to play around with."

"Believe me, I get that message loud and clear."

"Then you know I can tell you nothing. Please leave. Now."

"I'll just subpoena you for the court case."

"What court case?"

"Edgar Roy? Six bodies? Don't tell me you've forgotten."

"What does that have to do with me?"

"Edgar Roy is the only reason you're at Cutter's Rock, Carla. And since I represent Roy it's my ethical duty to try to have him exonerated. In order to do that, I have to muddy the waters. It's called reasonable doubt."

"You're a fool."

"Are you any less of one?"

"Get out."

"By the way, Murdock already knows the truth about you."

"That's impossi—" She caught herself too late.

"Say what you will about the FBI, they do tend to get the right answer."

"I need you to leave. Now."

He turned to the door. "One more thing—the Bureau has a tap on your phone and your e-mail."

"Why warn me about that?"

"In the hopes that you come to your senses and want to make a deal with me instead of them." He let that sink in. "Carla? Are you getting any of this?"

"I'll . . . I'll think about it."

"Fine. Just don't take too long."

Sean walked down the street and climbed into the Land Cruiser he had earlier parked there. He started the engine and sped off. After he was out of sight of Dukes's house, Michelle, who'd been hiding in the back of the truck, climbed into the passenger seat.

"Everything go okay?" asked Sean.

"Easy. She should watch the garage door come all the way down before she goes in the house. I was able to sneak in behind her."

Sean checked his watch. "Okay, I spooked her about her phone and e-mail. Now she has only one avenue of communication."

"Face-to-face. But if she believes she can't communicate via phone or e-mail how will Dukes arrange a meeting?"

"Coded text, probably. Innocuous on its face, it'll set up a time at a prearranged place." He stared down at the electronic tracking device cradled in her hand. "What's the range on that?"

"Couple of miles. Plenty for our purposes, even in the great wilds of Maine."

"Where'd you put the bug?"

"On the underside of the rear windshield wiper mechanism. Nobody ever looks there. Then I just climbed out the garage window. I'm actually getting good at that."

"So now we wait," said Sean.

"I don't think it'll be for long." She eyed the device more closely. "Looks like she's already on the move. Boy, you really did scare her."

"I had my lawyer hat on. We naturally scare the crap out of everybody."

37

After landing at LaGuardia and being driven into the city Peter Bunting did not go home to his lovely, socially active wife and his three privileged and accomplished children at their luxurious Fifth Avenue brownstone across from Central Park.

Nor did he return to his office. He had somewhere else to go because he was focused on keeping Edgar Roy alive.

And probably me, too.

He walked fifteen blocks to a rundown six-story building well off the famous boulevards of Manhattan. He took care to avoid being followed, going into lobbies of buildings and exiting by different ways. In the lower level of the six-story building was a pizzeria. In the upper levels were offices for small businesses. On the very top level were two rooms. He took the stairs and knocked.

The man ushered him in and closed the door behind him. Bunting moved through into the next room. The man followed him and closed the door to this room too. He motioned for Bunting to sit on a chair set next to a small table.

Bunting did so, unbuttoning his suit jacket and trying to get comfortable in a chair that was not designed for comfort. The man remained standing.

James Harkes was dressed, as always, in a black two-piece suit, starched white shirt, black straight tie. He would be anonymous among the millions of other men in this city.

"Thank you for meeting with me so quickly," Bunting began. "You know that I'm tasked to take care of you, Mr. Bunting," said Harkes.

"You've done a good job so far."

"So far."

"The six bodies at the farm? I believe that Roy was framed."

"And who would want to do that?"

Bunting hesitated before answering. "You're joking, right?"

"I don't normally employ humor in my job."

"I meant there are obviously those who would have a problem with the program."

"But why frame Roy? Either kill him or coopt him. That's what I would do."

Bunting didn't look confident as he said, "But we can't use him either. That weakens us."

"But he may be free one day. Better for our enemies to kill him. Then he can't come back to work ever."

Bunting studied him closely. "Foster is talking about

taking preemptive action with Edgar Roy. Do you know about that?"

Harkes said nothing.

"Harkes, did you take preemptive action with the lawyer, Ted Bergin?"

Harkes remained silent.

"Why kill him?"

Harkes's gaze remained fixed on Bunting but he still said nothing.

"Who is authorizing this? Because I'm sure as hell not."

"I don't do anything without the *requisite* approval."

"Who is it? Foster?"

"I'll be in touch."

"Harkes, once you go down that road, there's no going back."

"If there's nothing else, sir?" Harkes opened the door for Bunting to pass through.

"Please don't do this, Harkes. Edgar Roy is one of a kind. He doesn't deserve this. He's innocent. I know that he is."

"Take care, Mr. Bunting."

Once he reached the street Bunting started to walk back to his office but then veered away at the last moment. He went inside a bar, found a seat, and had a Bombay Sapphire and tonic. He checked e-mails, made a few phone calls, all routine, just to get his mind off the mess of Edgar Roy. He was caught right in the middle. People were getting killed and there was nothing he could do about it.

Lost in his own problems, he didn't notice the tall woman who had come in after him. She settled into a chair at a table in the back of the bar, ordered an Arnold Palmer, and watched him closely without ever seeming to.

Kelly Paul patiently waited for Peter Bunting to finish drowning his worries in good gin.

38

"She's stopping," said Sean, as he stared down at the miniature screen. "Slow down a bit when you come around the next turn."

Michelle decelerated as they hit the curve. About five hundred yards up ahead they could see the tail-lights of Dukes's car wink out.

"Lonely place," said Michelle.

"What else would it be for a meeting like this?"

"We need to get closer."

"On foot. Come on."

A low stone wall provided cover and also allowed them to draw near enough to see who Carla Dukes was meeting in a small clearing that had an old picnic table and rusty charcoal grill.

He was shorter than she was, young and thin.

She walked up and down in front of the man, talking animatedly while he stood still, watching her and nodding from time to time. They could see all this, but they couldn't hear what was being said.

Sean pulled out his camera, which he'd taken from the truck, and snapped some pictures of the pair. He studied the screen and then showed Michelle. "Recognize him?" he said quietly.

She studied the face. "No. Young and geeky. Not my idea of some super-duper spy."

"They come in all shapes and sizes these days. In fact the ones that don't actually look like spies are the most valuable."

"Then this guy is golden."

When Dukes drove off, they didn't pick up the tail again. They followed the man instead. He was the next link in the puzzle chain. And he might just lead them where they needed to go. Since they didn't have a tracking device on his car they had to stay closer than Michelle would have liked, but the man made no sign that he knew he was being followed.

Several hours later it was apparent where the man was going.

"Bangor," said Sean, and Michelle nodded.

"Do you think he lives there?" she said.

Sean looked up ahead. "No. His car looks like every other airport rental."

"Then he's going to fly out of Bangor."

"I think so, yeah."

A bit later they were proved right as the car they were following pulled into the airport on the outskirts of Bangor.

On the way Sean and Michelle had already made their plans. She parked and Sean climbed out of the truck.

He said, "Get back to Martha's Inn and keep a lookout over Megan. I don't want her ending up like Bergin or Hilary."

"Call me when you know where you're going."

"Will do." He pulled his pistol out of his holster and handed it to her. "Take this."

"You might need it."

"I don't have a case for it to take on the plane. And me getting stopped by the cops and losing this guy won't help us."

He turned and started off.

"Sean?"

He turned around. "Yeah?"

"Don't die!"

He smiled. "I'll do my best."

Only when he was out of sight did Michelle put the Toyota in gear and drive off. But she was clearly not happy about separating from him again.

39

During her drive back to Machias, Michelle had gotten a call from Sean at the airport. The man was on a six a.m. flight to Dulles Airport in northern Virginia with a connection in New York City. Sean had booked a ticket on the same flight.

"I caught a glimpse of his tickets. He's in the third row on both legs. I snagged a seat in the back on both flights. The first is a Delta, the second a United. I'll call you when we get in a little before noon."

"Did you see the name on the ticket?"

"Unfortunately, no."

He'd clicked off and Michelle had continued her drive. Around four in the morning she pulled into the dark parking lot of Martha's Inn. Guests had a key that opened the outer door. She stopped in the kitchen and got a snack, then headed up the stairs. She stopped on the second landing when she saw a light on in Megan's room. She knocked on the door. "Megan?"

The door opened a crack and Michelle eyed her. "Anything wrong?" she asked.

"I heard you drive up. I thought we could talk."

"Okay." Michelle parked herself in a chair by a small pine bureau. "What's up?" she asked.

Megan was in green surgical scrubs, which she obviously used as pajamas. "Where were you guys? You just disappeared after we spoke this afternoon."

"We had some sleuthing to do."

"I thought you said you were going to protect me, but all you do is go off and I don't hear anything until you come back."

"Look, Megan, you have a point, but we're doing the best we can with the limited resources we have. In fact, Sean is running down a lead now, but he sent me back here to keep an eye on you."

"A lead where?"

"D.C., apparently."

Megan sat on the edge of the bed. "I'm sorry. I know you all are doing the best you can. It's just . . ."

"Scary?"

"I didn't really intend to do any criminal defense work when I came to work for Mr. Bergin. This case just got dropped in my lap."

"But Sean is a terrific lawyer and he's done lots of criminal cases."

"But he's not here right now. I'm trying to draft these motions but it's not easy."

"Well, I'm afraid I can't help you there."

"Murdock came by to see me again."

"What the hell did he want?"

"He seemed particularly interested in what you and Sean were up to."

"I bet."

"It seems with every step we take we get farther away from the truth."

Michelle said, "But then one little piece falls into place and it's off to the races."

"You can't count on that happening."

"We try to make our own luck."

"I guess."

"Get some sleep. And how about we grab some breakfast around nine? We can talk more then. But right now I need some sleep."

"Okay, but I'm going to lock my door and then slide the bureau against it."

"Not a bad idea, actually."

Michelle left the room and headed to her own. She yawned and stretched some kinks out, and then became fully awake. There was someone moving downstairs. At first she thought it might be Mrs. Burke, but the elderly landlady undoubtedly would have turned on a light in her own inn. Michelle crouched low and slipped over to the staircase, her pistol out. She focused on the movements downstairs.

It actually took a lot of energy to tread quietly. One had to hold his position, shift, and balance at optimal points.

Young. Fit. Trained.

Definitely not Mrs. Burke.

"Maxwell? Is that you?"

"Dobkin?"

"If you have your gun out, put it away. I don't want to get shot accidentally."

"Then stop breaking into places in the middle of the night."

"I have a key. And I'm the police. I'm allowed."

She holstered her weapon and came down the steps.

"Over here."

He stepped in front of a window where the moon-light was coming through. Eric Dobkin was in uniform and looked anxious.

"Where's your partner?" he said. "Upstairs?"

"No, he went out of town. What's up?"

"Have you heard?"

"Heard what?"

"They found Carla Dukes dead about an hour ago in her home."

40

The pilot easily handled the swirling winds off the East River, and the plane touched down on the runway at LaGuardia right on time. Sean was one of the last passengers off but picked up his pace once he left the jetway and entered the airport. The man he was tailing was up ahead, walking at a leisurely pace. Sean slowed but kept him in sight. The flight attendant on the Bangor-to-New York leg had announced the number of their next gate, and the connecting passengers headed to it. They reached it; the flight was not yet up on the marquee because they had a three-hour layover before the short hop to Virginia.

Sean grabbed some coffee and an egg sandwich. He remembered something, reached in his pocket, and turned his phone on. He immediately saw that Michelle had called numerous times. He quickly phoned her.

When she heard his voice she said, "Thank God. I tried calling you before, but it wouldn't go through. Lots to fill you in on."

"Don't tell me—someone else is dead," he said in a joking tone.

"How the hell did you know that?"

Sean's face fell. "What? I wasn't being serious. Who is it?"

"Carla Dukes. Dobkin came by the inn a little while after I got back and told me."

"In the middle of the night? Why would he do that?" Sean said suspiciously.

"I'm not sure. Maybe he thinks he still owes us for covering for his guys with Murdock. Whatever the case, she's dead and they have no leads. The FBI is handling it."

Sean sipped his coffee and bit off a chunk of his sandwich. There had been no food service on either flight. He wasn't sure when he had eaten last but it had been a while. The grease and fatty calories felt spectacular going down. "Did you tell Dobkin about what we saw last night?"

"What, are you drunk? Of course I didn't. Not without talking to you first."

Sean frowned. "I don't want to get hit with an obstruction charge, but I'm also not ready to commit us to anything."

"So we say nothing for now?"

"Right. Nothing."

"If Dukes was killed because she talked to the guy you're following, things might get really hairy really fast."

"But if I can crack who he's with, we might just take a giant leap forward."

"You also might end up getting yourself killed."

"I'll be careful. You watch out for yourself and Megan."

"How are you going to follow him once you get into D.C.?"

Sean glanced across at a gift shop located a little down the concourse from his gate. "I think I see an answer. I'll call you when I run this guy to his base."

He clicked off, checked to make sure the fellow was still sitting and working on his laptop, and walked quickly to the gift shop. It took him a couple of minutes but he finally saw what he needed.

A toy fireman's hat. And a small bottle of glue. He ducked into the bathroom, grabbed an empty stall, opened the box, and pried the piece of gold plastic off the front of the hat. He opened the glue, pulled out his private investigator's credentials and, using the glue, he attached the plastic piece inside a leaf of his ID. He slipped it back in his pocket, discarded the box, the hat, and the glue in the trash can, washed his hands and face, and stepped back out.

The flight to Dulles Airport was on a Canadian Regional twin-engine jet operated by United Express. Sean got on ahead of the man he was following. He settled in the back in an aisle seat and opened a newspaper someone had left in the seat pocket. He alternated between reading the paper and eyeing his target as the man took off his jacket, folded it quite deliberately, placed it in the overhead bin, and sat down. He had his phone out and was talking to someone, but there was no way for Sean to hear any part of the conversation. When the jet door closed and the flight attendants made their announcements about electronic devices, the man turned off his phone. A minute later the jet pushed back and the man gripped his armrest as they began to taxi to the runway.

Nervous flyer, thought Sean.

They lifted off into the airspace over New York City. They turned south, accelerating on the climb out, and once they hit their cruising altitude the onboard computer punched the throttles forward and they were soon soaring along at nearly 550 miles per hour.

Thirty minutes later they began their descent into Dulles through quite a bit of cloud cover. They raced along, fighting a decent headwind and changing altitudes. Sean watched the man's right hand tighten on the armrest with every little interruption of the relatively smooth flight path.

The guy would never have cut it in the Secret Service, thought Sean.

They landed and taxied to the gate. The passengers deplaned and headed to the main terminal. They had come in through Terminal B, so they didn't need to use the people movers that transported passengers to and from the more distant terminals.

Sean followed the guy down moving walkways and up and down escalators until they came out into the main terminal. When the guy headed to the baggage claim Sean knew what to expect next. The guy had had no baggage. He must be meeting his driver.

And so here comes the dicey part.

As they approached the baggage area, the limo drivers were lined up holding white placards with names written on them. Sean tensed when the man he was following pointed at one of the drivers. Sean eyed the sign the burly driver held.

Mr. Avery?

Sean followed them through the airport and out the exit. He eyed the Dulles Flyer taxi lines. Pretty full. He watched as Avery and the driver headed to the area across from the terminal where the car services routinely parked.

Sean made his move.

He butted in front of the people waiting in line for taxis. When they complained and an airport employee whose job it was to get folks in and out of cabs approached, Sean pulled his ID and flashed his gold plastic badge and identification card. He did so quickly but confidently, giving none of them time to focus on it.

"FBI. I need to commandeer this taxi. I've got a suspect under surveillance."

The people in line backed off when they glimpsed the badge, and the airport employee even held the door open for him.

"Go get him," he told Sean.

Feeling a little guilty, Sean managed a smile. "I will."

The cab headed off and Sean gave the driver instructions. They exited the airport and pulled in behind the Lincoln Town Car. He wrote down the license plate number just in case he might need it later. They drove along the Dulles Toll Road, which was also known as Silicon Valley East because of the large number of tech companies headquartered along it. There were also numerous defense contractors and companies working in the intelligence field located here, Sean knew. Several former Secret Service agents he'd worked with now made far more money on the private side toiling away at some of these for-profit outfits.

The car ahead turned off at an exit and proceeded west. The cab followed. When the Town Car pulled into an office complex, Sean told the taxi driver to stop. He got out and handed a twenty to the man, who refused to accept it.

"Just keep us safe," the guy said before driving off.

A little embarrassed, Sean put the cash away and looked at the office building. He quickly discovered that it didn't belong to simply one company. It housed a number of firms. That was problematic, but he had to keep going. You typically got only one true break on any case, and this might be it.

He watched as the Town Car driver headed off. Sean watched Avery walk into the building. He reached the lobby at about the time the elevator arrived to take Avery up. A quick glance allowed Sean to see that Avery was the only one in the car. There was a security guard in the lobby behind a marble console, and he glanced at Sean.

"Visitors sign in over here, sir."

Sean walked over and pulled out his wallet. He dropped it and took his time picking it back up and pushing some cards back into place in their respective slots. When he stood and turned he saw that the elevator carrying Avery had stopped on the sixth floor.

Then the car began to descend. Avery must've gotten off.

He turned to the guard.

"You may not believe this, but I'm from out of town and I'm a little lost."

"It happens," said the guard, though he didn't look pleased by Sean's confession.

"I'm looking for the Kryton Corporation. They're supposed to be somewhere around here, but I think my secretary got the damn address wrong."

The guard frowned. "Kryton? Never heard of them. I know they're not in this building."

"They're on the sixth floor. That I do know."

The guard was shaking his head. "Only company on the sixth floor here is BIC Corp."

"BIC. Doesn't sound anything like Kryton."

"No, it sure doesn't," said the guard firmly.

"Kryton's in the intelligence field. Government contractor."

"So is just about every company in this area. All looking for Uncle Sam's last dollar. That is to say, my last dollar as a taxpayer."

Sean grinned. "I hear you loud and clear. Well, thanks." He turned to leave but then said, "BIC. Is that like the pen?"

"No, Bunting International Corp."

"Bunting? Wasn't he a baseball player and then a senator?"

"That's Jim Bunning you're thinking of. From Kentucky. Retired now."

Sensing the guard's patience was coming to an end and his suspicions were heightening, he said, "Well, I better get going or I'm going to miss my meeting." He pulled out his phone. "But right now I'm going to give my secretary hell."

"Have a nice day, sir."

Sean walked out the door and called Michelle. "We finally got a break," he said triumphantly.

41

"When?" asked Peter Bunting, his voice shaky.

He sat behind his large desk holding the phone receiver to his ear. He had just been told that Carla Dukes had been murdered in her home.

"Do the police have any leads? Any suspects?"

The person answered.

"All right. But the minute you hear anything I need to know."

Carla Dukes had been his handpicked person to take over the director's slot at Cutter's. They went a long way back. They hadn't been close friends, but they had been professional colleagues. She was good at what she did. And Bunting had respected her. He'd also unwittingly led the woman to her death.

Instead of taking the long walk to the pizza building he decided to phone.

James Harkes picked up on the second ring.

"What the hell is going on?" Bunting said.

"I'm not sure what you mean."

"Carla Dukes was murdered last night."

Harkes said nothing. All Bunting could hear was the man's breathing. Regular, calm.

"Did you hear what I said?"

"My hearing is excellent, Mr. Bunting."

"She was my operative. I put her at Cutter's for a specific reason."

"Understood."

"Understood? What does that mean? If it was understood, why did you have her killed?"

"You need to calm down, Mr. Bunting. You're not making any sense. I would have had no reason to kill Ms. Dukes."

Bunting had no way to know if Harkes was telling the truth or not, but something told him the man was lying.

"Not only is a good person dead, I have no eyes at Cutter's now. Roy is up there with no coverage."

"I wouldn't worry about that, sir. We have the situation in hand."

"How?"

"You'll just have to trust me on that."

"Are you insane? I don't trust anyone, Harkes. Particularly people who won't answer my questions."

"If you have any other concerns just let me know." Harkes clicked off.

Bunting slowly put the phone down, rose and went to the window, and stared down at the street. His mind was literally catapulting forward to one devastating scenario after another.

Why would anyone have wanted Dukes dead? She was the director of Cutter's, but it wasn't like she had any real power. If Harkes had killed her, why?

He sat down and called Avery, who had just flown in to the D.C. office. Bunting knew he had met with Dukes last night. It had been a last-minute thing, prompted by a frantic text to Avery, who had gone back up to Maine only the day before. Dukes had wanted to meet with Bunting, but since Avery was already on the ground in Maine and Dukes had wanted to meet immediately, Avery had gone instead.

"Avery, Carla Dukes is dead, murdered, not too long after she met with you."

Avery said, "I know, I just heard it on the news." His voice was shaky.

"What did she want to meet about? When she texted me that she wanted to meet, she didn't say why. That's when I texted her back to contact you directly."

"Sean King had approached her at her home."

"King? About what?"

"He said he knew she was working with someone other than the FBI. That the Bureau wouldn't be happy when they found that out. He really shook her up."

"How the hell did he know about that?"

"No clue."

Bunting thought quickly. "It must've been guess-work on his part."

"But she was frightened. He gave her an ultimatum of sorts."

"What did he want?"

"Us, I guess."

"How good is our wall?"

"No one at Cutter's Rock will talk to him."

"But they suspect someone else is involved." Bunting had a sudden, terrible thought. "Did King meet
with her right before she came to see you?"

"Yes. She was upset. Sent me a coded message and
in it she said King had told her the FBI had tapped her
phones and e-mails."

"And you met with her where?"

"The rendezvous point we had designated previously. It's a little picnic area really off the beaten
path, even for Maine."

"So King put the fear of God into Carla with the
result that she got spooked and went running to you.
Was Michelle Maxwell with King when he met with
Carla?"

"She said he was alone."

"Shit!"

"What is it?"

"They played us."

"What? How?"

"While King was busy scaring the crap out of Carla,
Maxwell was doing something else, maybe placing a
tracking device on Carla's car. Then King bullshitted
her about the FBI tapping her phone and e-mails. The
result was that the only way to safely communicate
with us was face-to-face."

"They followed Dukes to the meeting?"

"Of course they did. And then they saw you there."
Bunting felt a dull ache in his head. "And then they
followed *you*. They're probably standing outside your
office as we speak."

"Oh shit."

Bunting rubbed his temples. "Did you notice anyone that looked like Sean King on your flights?"

"No, but I really wasn't paying attention."

Bunting nervously tapped the top of his desk. "Did
you cab it from the airport?"

"No, I had a driver meet me at the airport."

Bunting ground his teeth together. "So they have
your name now, too. Okay, they followed you to the
office and have no doubt discovered that you work for
BIC. From BIC it's only a Google search to Peter
Bunting."

"But, sir—"

Bunting hung up on him and paced his large office,
nervous energy feeding his system like liquefied rocks
of crack.

He calmed himself, sat back down. He had to think.
Even if King had connected the dots to BIC, he had
no proof of any wrongdoing because there was none.
But that wasn't the point. Revealing to the public
what Edgar Roy really was could be catastrophic.

And now Bunting had no one he could really trust.
Except myself, apparently.

Right now that was small comfort.

303

42

Kelly Paul sat at her desk in her hotel room in New York and looked around the small, comfortable space. How many such rooms had she inhabited over the last twenty years? She wouldn't sound clichéd and say *too many*. Actually, the number had been just about right.

She didn't doodle with the hotel-supplied pen and paper because she might inadvertently leave behind some clue that might one day lead back to her. Her bag was packed, her traveling documents in order. She carried no weapon with her but had ready access to any she might need only five minutes from here.

She had learned of Carla Dukes's death at six thirty a.m. She didn't spend much time wondering who had killed the woman. The answer to that question was important. But not as important as the matters she was focusing on presently.

By now Peter Bunting had to know about the woman's death, too. His inside source at Cutter's Rock had allowed him to take certain liberties in seeing her brother. Well, Paul had her own sources, and they had told her that the prisoner's condition had not changed.

Keep it that way, Eddie, keep it that way. For now. Don't let them get to you.

She glanced down at her cell phone, hesitated, and then picked it up. She punched in the number. It rang twice.

"Hello?"

"Mr. King, it's Kelly Paul."

"I was hoping to hear from you. Do you know about Carla Dukes?"

"I heard."

"Theories?"

"Several. That's beside the point right now. Where are you?"

"Where are *you*?"

"East Coast."

"Me too. I've had an interesting search on the Web this afternoon."

"About what subject?" she asked.

"BIC, stands for Bunting International Corporation. Peter Bunting is the president of it. Heard of him?"

"Should I?"

"That's why I'm asking you."

"What did you find?" Paul wanted to know.

"BIC is based in New York, but it has facilities in the D.C. area because it's a government contractor. Sells intelligence services. Talked to some of my buddies on the inside. They say the BIC government contract is worth a gazillion dollars but they don't know exactly what the company does for it.

Apparently no one who will talk to me does. Highly classified."

"Some do know what he does. Otherwise Uncle Sam wouldn't cut that check."

"So you do know about him?"

"I'd say it's time we met."

"Where?"

"I'm in New York."

"I can come up there."

Paul said, "Up? So you're in D.C.?"

"When?"

"As soon as possible."

"Do you have anything to tell me?" Sean asked.

"I wouldn't waste your time otherwise. How did you get onto BIC?"

He said, "Just good old-fashioned detective work."

"I think you rolled Dukes, somehow she got scared, and she led you to them. And the price she paid for being weak and stupid was her life."

"Do you really think that's why she was killed?" he asked.

"Not really, no. But I don't want to speculate right now. Can you be in New York by this evening?"

"I can catch the next Acela. Be there by six."

"There's a little French restaurant on Eighty-Fifth." She gave him the address. "Say seven o'clock?"

"See you then."

She clicked off and set the phone back down on the desk. She rose and went to the window, pulled back the heavy drapes, and eyed Central Park across the street. The leaves were turning, the crowds were thinning, and the overcoats were getting heavier. The rain had started, just a drizzle, but the darkening skies promised more foul weather later. It was in this sort of weather that the city was at its most grimy. The black and dirt and filth were revealed in all their abundance.

But that's my world too. Black, grimy, and full of filth.

Paul slipped on her raincoat, put up her hood, and set out on a stroll. She crossed Fifty-Ninth Street and passed down the line of horse-drawn carriages. She patted one horse on the snout and eyed the driver. They were all Irishmen. It was an old law, or an older tradition, Paul couldn't exactly remember which.

"Hello, Shaunnie." The man's full name was Tom O'Shaunnessy, but she had always called him Shaunnie.

He continued to clean out some trash from his carriage and didn't look at her. "Haven't seen you for a while."

"Haven't been around for a while."

"Heard you retired."

"I unretired."

He glanced at her with interest. "You can do that?"

"Is Kenny in the same spot?"

Shaunnie refilled the bucket of oats. "Where else would Kenny be?"

"All I needed to know."

"So you're back working?" he asked.

"For now."

"You should have stayed retired, Kelly."

"Why?"

"Live longer."

"We all have to die sometime, Shaunnie. The lucky ones get to pick the time."

"I don't think I'm in that group."

"You're Irish, you have to be."

"What about you?"

"I'm not that Irish," said Paul.

The rain picked up as she eased her way through the park. She kept to the walking paths until she drew near to her destination. She had on waterproof boots that raised her considerable height another two inches. The old man was hunkered down on a bench behind a large rock outcrop. On sunny days people would drape over the stone, improving their tans. On this rain-drenched day, it was deserted.

Kenny sat with his back to her. At the sound of her approach, he turned. He was dressed only a notch above a street person. This was by design—less attention that way. His face and hands were clean, however, and his eyes were clear. He pulled his crumpled hat down farther on his head and studied her.

"Heard you were in town."

She sat down next to him. He was small and seemed smaller still with her tall frame beside him.

"News travels uncomfortably fast these days."

"Not that fast. Shaunnie called me on the cell just now. What do you need?"

"Two."

"The usual?"

"Always worked for me."

"How's your trigger finger?"

"A bit stiff, actually. Maybe early arthritis."

"I'll factor that in. When?"

"Two hours. Here."

He rose. "See you in two hours."

She offered him cash.

"Later," he said. "I trust you."

"Don't trust anybody, Kenny. Not in this business."

She slowly made her way back to her hotel. The rain was coming down harder, but Paul was lost in thought and didn't seem to notice. She had walked through many such rains in many different parts of the world. It seemed to help her think, her mind clearing even as the clouds above thickened. Light from darkness. Somehow.

Bunting. King. Her brother. The next move. It was all building. And when the pressure spiked it would burst out like a freed rocket. And that precise moment would decide the winners and the losers. It always did.

She hoped she was up to it, one more time.

43

The train pulled out of Union Station in D.C. and accelerated on its way to New York. Sean sat back in his comfortable business class seat. At the rate they were racking up travel costs on this case, he might have to declare personal bankruptcy at the end of the month when his credit card bill came due.

A hundred and sixty minutes later the train pulled into New York's Penn Station. Before leaving Virginia, Sean had gone to his apartment and packed a bag to bring back with him. He rolled it out of the station, grabbed a cab, and drove off. The weather was wet and chilly, and he was glad of his long trench coat and umbrella. With evening traffic the cab pulled to the curb on Eighty-Fifth Street at one minute past seven. He paid the cabbie and rolled his bag into the restaurant, which turned out to be small, quaint, and full of French-speaking waitresses and patrons.

In the back corner, behind a load-bearing wall that jutted out into the seating space like a wedge, he found Kelly Paul, her back to the mirrored wall. He took off his coat, rolled his bag into a sliver of corner next to the table, and sat down. Neither said anything for a few seconds. Finally, Paul spoke.

"Bad weather."

"That time of year."

"I wasn't speaking of the rain."

He settled back in his chair, stretched his long legs a bit. There wasn't much room under the table for two tall people.

"Okay. Yeah, the weather sucks too."

"How is Michelle?"

"Hanging tough, like always."

"And Megan?"

"Frustrated. Can't say I blame her."

Paul glanced at her menu and said, "The scallops are very nice."

Sean put down his menu. "Works for me."

"Do you have a gun?"

He expressed surprise at the question. "No. I flew back into D.C. Didn't want any problems at the airport."

"You'll have far worse problems if you need a weapon and don't have one." She patted her bag. "I have one here for you. Glock. I prefer the Twenty-One model."

"The big bore .45? As American as apple pie or as close as an Austrian gun manufacturer can come to it."

"I've always liked the thirteen-round mag. For me thirteen is a lucky number."

"You needed thirteen shots?"

"Only if the other side had twelve. Do you want it?"

They exchanged a long stare.

"Yes."

"After dinner, then."

"BIC?"

She put down her menu. "Peter Bunting is an extremely well-respected player in the intelligence field. He started his own company at age twenty-six. He's now forty-seven and has made a fortune selling to Uncle Sam. He owns homes here in New York and also in New Jersey. He's married and has three children; the oldest is sixteen. His wife plays the social circuit well, has substantial charity involvement and part ownership in a trendy restaurant. The kids are by all accounts no more pampered and privileged than others of their ilk. From what I've heard they're actually quite a nice family."

"And he owns the E-Program platform you talked about?"

"It was his invention. Brilliant and ahead of its time."

"Which means he owns your brother."

"Peter Bunting also has a lot to lose. That makes him vulnerable."

"Do you think he framed your brother?"

"No. His best asset is sitting in a cell. I understand that Bunting's last briefing in D.C. was a disaster. He

312

has every incentive to get his Analyst back as soon as possible. And there's something else."

"What?"

"There are some serious players who don't like Bunting or the E-Program."

"Who are these serious players?"

"You've probably heard of Ellen Foster."

Sean blanched. "The secretary of Homeland Security? Why wouldn't she like the E-Program? You said it was a brilliant idea."

"Intelligence agencies don't like to share. The E-Program forces them to. And Bunting runs the show. A show that used to be theirs. Feathers get ruffled. Word is Foster is leading the pack in bringing the hammer down on Bunting. She has the full backing of CIA, DIA, NSA, and so on."

"And then do what?"

"Turn the clock back to where everybody did their own thing."

"So you think they might have set up your brother? To discredit and knock out the E-Program? That's highly unlikely, isn't it? I mean they're putting their country at risk every second your brother isn't doing his job."

"National security trumps a lot. It can trample civil rights. It can denude personal liberties. But it cannot and never will triumph over political gamesmanship."

"Do you really believe that?"

She took a sip of wine. "I've actually lived it, Sean."

He stared at her for a long time before speaking. "Okay, then tell me, are we a match for these guys?"

"David beat Goliath in the Valley of Elah."

"But is our slingshot big enough?"

"I suppose we'll find out."

He sighed and tapped the table. "Comforting. So what about Bunting?"

"He'll have figured out by now how you got on to him."

"You think?"

"He's a very smart man. Otherwise he would not have achieved what he has. However, he's also a very nervous man right now. I've been following him around town. He's met with several people, one of whom I find very intriguing."

"Why?"

"When you see a rich spy king leave his usual haunts of upscale Manhattan to enter a ragged six-story walk-up with a pizza parlor in the lobby, you know something is off."

"Who did he meet with there?"

"His name is James Harkes. A man that even I would find intimidating. And while I know you don't really know me, that's saying a lot."

"You actually know this Harkes guy?"

"By reputation only. But it's an impressive one."

"Is he Bunting's fail-safe?"

"More his guardian angel. For now. But he plays to

more than one master. That's the reason I gave you the gun. It must have occurred to you that because Bunting knows you're on to him, Harkes may be unleashed against you and Michelle."

Sean said, "I understand."

"And that doesn't take into account other assets that Foster and her allies could deploy."

"Pretty overwhelming assets, I would imagine."

Paul leaned forward and moved the olive oil bottle out of the way so she could hold Sean's hand.

"What's that for?" he said in a puzzled tone.

"I am not an overly affectionate person. I wanted to see if your skin was clammy and whether your hand was trembling."

"And?"

"And I'm impressed because neither physiological reaction is occurring. I know you guarded the president, had an outstanding career until you made one mistake that destroyed it all for you. I know about Maxwell, too. She's a bulldozer who can shoot the pants off most of the premier snipers in the military."

"And I haven't met the man she can't put down."

Paul let his hand go and sat back. "Well, that might change. Soon."

"Are we on the same team now? Because everything you just said about us could just as well apply to you."

"I don't think they know I'm on to them yet, but I can't guarantee that."

"So, a team?"

"I'll think about it."

"We don't have a lot of time."

"I never said we did."

"Why did you want me to come up to New York? All of this could be said over the phone."

"This couldn't." She slid a package over to him. "The Glock, as promised."

"Is that all?"

"No. One more thing. Would you like to see where Peter Bunting lives?"

Sean looked at her in surprise. "Why?"

"Why not?"

44

Edgar Roy had known something was wrong because the routine at Cutter's Rock had changed. Every morning since he'd been here Carla Dukes had made her rounds. Cutter's Rock could hold two hundred and fourteen prisoners, but currently only fifty inmates were being held here. Roy knew this by observation and deduction. He knew it by listening to the sounds of meal trays being delivered to cells. He knew it by hearing and distinguishing between forty-nine voices emanating from those cells. He knew it by overhearing the bed check calls from the guards.

And Carla Dukes had made a point of walking past each of these cells at precisely four minutes past eight each morning and four minutes past four each afternoon. It was now six p.m. and Roy had not seen the woman at all today.

Yet he had heard a lot. Whispers among guards. Carla Dukes was dead. She'd been shot in her home. No one knew who had done it.

Roy was lying on his bed staring at the ceiling. Dukes's murder had interrupted the chronology of each memory he'd ever had. He wished ill of no one, really, and at some level he was sorry she had been killed. She had been brought here to keep an eye on him. She didn't want to be here. And thus she blamed him for her dilemma.

He sensed the presence near his cell door. He didn't look. He smelled the air. Edgar Roy didn't simply have a nearly unique level of intellectual ability. He had senses heightened to an astonishing degree. It was all a case of special hardwiring in his brain.

It wasn't a guard. He had processed and organized the smells and sounds of all the guards. There were a few support personnel who were allowed in the cell area, but it was none of them either. He had smelled this person before. He had also logged in his rhythm of breathing and his singular way of walking.
It was Agent Murdock of the FBI.

"Hello, Edgar," he said.

Roy remained on his bed, even as he heard another man approach. A guard this time. It was the short one: wide hips, burly chest, thick neck. Name tag said Tarkington. He smoked and drank. Roy didn't need heightened senses to know that. Too may breath mints, far too much mouthwash.

The electronically controlled door slid back. Footsteps.

Murdock said, "Look at me, Edgar. I know you can if you want to."

Roy remained where he was. He closed his eyes

and let the darkness in his head settle him into a place this man could not reach. Another sound. The rub of shoe soles on cement. Murdock's bottom settled into the chair bolted to the floor.

"Okay, Edgar. You don't have to look at me. I'll talk and you listen."

Murdock paused and then when he heard the next sound, Roy realized why. The guard walked away. Murdock wanted privacy. Then there was a nearly imperceptible cessation of powered machinery. Roy knew what it was. The video camera built into the wall had just been turned off. He expected the audio feed had as well.

Murdock said, "We can finally have a private conversation. I think it's time."

Roy didn't move. He kept his eyes closed, forcing himself to sink into memories. His parents were fighting. They often did. For university professors existing in worlds of genteel theoretical tinkering they were unusually combative. And his father drank. And when he was in the bottle he was no longer genteel.

His next image was of his sister coming into the room. Already tall and strong, she had gotten between the two and separated them, forcing them into at least a temporary truce. Then she had picked Roy up and taken him to his room. Read books to him. Soothed him, because his parents fighting like that had always terrified him. His sister had understood his predicament. She knew what he was enduring, both in the outside world and, more subtly, within the complex confines of his mind.

"Edgar. We really need to end this," said Murdock in a low, comforting tone. "Time is running out. I know it. You know it."

Roy moved up to age five in his chronology. His birthday. No guests—his parents didn't do such things. His sister, now sixteen, had already grown to her full height. She towered over her stepfather.

Roy was already five feet tall and weighed over a hundred pounds. Some mornings he would lie in bed and could actually feel his bones, tendons, and ligaments lengthening.

There was a small cake, five candles, and another argument. This one had turned violent, with a kitchen knife involved. His mother had been cut. And then Roy had watched in amazement as his sister had disarmed her stepfather, placed him in a hammerlock, and forced him out of the house. She had wanted to call the police, but their mother had begged her not to do it.

Roy tensed a bit as he heard the squeak of feet against the cement. Murdock was on the move. He was standing over him. A subtle prod in the back.

"Edgar, I need your full and undivided attention."

Roy didn't move.

"I know that you know Carla Dukes is dead."

Another jab in the back, harder still.

"We got the slug out. It's the same gun that killed Tom Bergin. Same killer."

Age six. His beloved sister was preparing to go off to college. She was a tremendous athlete, basketball, volleyball, and crew. An academic star, she had given the valedictory address at commencement, a feat she would repeat in college. Roy was stunned by her ability, her absolute will to win, no matter the odds against her.

He had waved at her from the door of the old farmhouse as she put her things away in the car she'd bought with her own money working odd jobs. She had come back and hugged him. He had taken in her scent, a smell he could conjure up perfectly right this minute lying in his prison cell.

"Kel," he had said. "I'll miss you."

"I'll be back, Eddie. A lot," she had told him. Then she had given him something. He had held it in his hand. It was a piece of metal on a chain.

She had said, "That's the medal of Saint Michael, the Archangel."

Roy had repeated this back to her, something he unconsciously did whenever someone gave him new information. It always made her smile. But this time she didn't. Her look remained serious.

"He's the protector of children. He is the leader of good versus evil, Eddie. In Hebrew *Michael* means 'Who is like God?' And the answer to that is no one is like God. Saint Michael represents humility in the face of God. Okay?"

He had repeated this back to her word for word, including her inflections. "Okay."

"He is an archangel. He is the supreme enemy of Satan and of all fallen angels."

She had said this last part while looking directly at her stepfather, who had glanced the other way, his face reddening.

Then she was gone.

A half hour passed and there was another argument and Roy had been at the center of it. It began with a slap. His father was drunk. The next blow was harder, knocking him out of his chair. His mother had tried to intervene, but this time his father would not be denied. She finally fell unconscious to the floor under his battering.

His father had turned to him, made him pull down his pants. Six-year-old Eddie was crying. He didn't want to do this, but he did because he was terrified. His trousers fell to the floor of the kitchen. His father's voice was low, soft, a singsong tone in his inebriated stupor. Roy had felt the man's hands on his privates. Smelled the alcohol on his cheek. The man—Roy could no longer refer to him as his father—pressed against him.

Then he had been ripped backward off his son. There was a crash. Roy had pulled his pants back up and turned. He was knocked head over heels against the wall as the two struggled and slammed into him. His sister had come back. She was fighting her stepfather with the ferocity of a lioness. They crashed around the room. She was taller, younger, the same weight as her opponent, but he was still a man. He fought hard. She hit him in the face with her fist. He rose back up and she kicked him in the stomach. He went back down but the alcohol and the fury at having been discovered doing vile things to his son seemed to energize him. He grabbed a knife off the kitchen counter, rushed at her. She pivoted.

With all his prodigious mental skills, this was the one memory Roy had never been able to draw on at will.

She pivoted.

That was all he could recall about those few seconds of his life. Age six.

She pivoted.

And then it was a blank. The only memory gap he had ever had in his life.

When the blank ended his father was lying on the floor, blood dripping from his chest. The knife stuck out from his body; his sister standing over the man and breathing hard. Roy had never seen anyone die until that moment. His father gave a little gurgle, his body stiffened and then relaxed, and his eyes grew completely still. They seemed to be staring solely at him.

She had rushed to hold him, make sure he was okay. He had rubbed the medal, the medal of Saint Michael that was around his neck.

Saint Michael, the protector of children. Satan's nightmare. The soul of redemption.

And then the memory faded. And then it was gone.

"Edgar?" said Murdock sharply.

They had taken his Saint Michael's medal when he had come here. It was the first time he had been without it since that day years ago. Roy felt an enormous hole in his heart without it. He didn't know if he would ever get it back.

"Edgar? I know. I found out about the E-Program. We need to talk. This changes everything. There are people we need to go after. Something is really wrong."

But the FBI agent could not break through. Not now. Not ever. Eventually there was the squeak of shoe soles on cement. The door slid open and closed. The smells, the sounds of the man receded.

Saint Michael protect us.

45

"That's it," said Kelly Paul.

She and Sean were standing outside a block of four-story brownstones on Fifth Avenue up in the East Seventies.

"Which one specifically?" he asked, as they stood there on the sidewalk opposite, a tree canopy shielding them from the rain.

She pointed to the largest one that had moldings and pediments and columns handcrafted by skilled workmen from over a century ago. "Nine thousand square feet. A lovely treetop view of the park from the front windows. And the inside is as splendid as the outside."

"Have you been inside it?"

"Once."

"How?"

"I never reveal my sources."

"Is he there now?"

"Yes."

"Describe him."

"I can do better." She pulled out a photo and showed it to him.

"He looks arrogant."

"He is. But no more so than others in his position. He's also paranoid, which makes him careful. Sometimes too careful, which can be exploited."

"Why did you bring me here, really?"

"For this."

She took his arm and drew him further back into the shadows. A few minutes later five people came out of the brownstone; all were carrying large, open umbrellas. Bunting, his wife, and their three children: two girls and a boy. The kids wore two-hundred-dollar sweaters and equally expensive shoes. Their heads had never seen the inside of a barbershop, only a salon. The wife was beautiful, refined, tall, slender, and exquisitely dressed, her hair and makeup at the level of a black-tie event. Bunting had on a tweed jacket, pressed jeans, thousand-dollar Crocs boots, and a swagger.

They were the epitome of the American Dream, displayed on the illustrious cement of New York's high-dollar area.

"The family?"

Paul nodded. "And their guards."

Sean turned his head to see the two men appear from the shadows and trail the Buntings.

"One is a former SEAL. The other is ex-DEA. Both are contractors working for a sub of BIC. He has two other men in his security detail. Sometimes they run four on, particularly when traveling abroad. Other times they rotate two on and off. Like now."

"How did you know they would be coming out tonight?"

"They do this four times a week at roughly the same time. I believe the wife insists. Bunting doesn't like it. He doesn't like routines as a general rule, but he likes to keep the peace at home, too. He actually loves his wife and family very much."

"How do you know that?"

"Sources again, Sean."

As they watched, Bunting reached into his pocket and pulled out his phone to receive a call. He stopped walking and motioned to his wife that he would catch up. Sean noted that one guard stayed with Bunting.

Paul said, "He seems to have gotten an interesting call just now."

They watched as Bunting walked in a tight circle while his guard stood by patiently. He was gesticulating and obviously not happy. He clicked off and immediately made another call. This took less than five minutes. Then he put the phone away and jogged onward to catch up with his family.

"So where do they go on these jaunts?" asked Sean.

"They'll go ten blocks, enter the park, make their way back, exit in the Sixties, turn north, and head back here. They talk, the kids can be kids, normal."

"Because they're not? Normal?"

"Bunting certainly isn't. He exists in this world, but he doesn't really live in it. If he had his preference he'd live only in his world. But of course he can't, so he makes certain concessions. But I can tell you that even though he's out now with his family and talking about school and grades and the next charity event Mrs. Bunting has planned, his mind is really working on what to do about my brother."

"How much does his wife know about what he does?"

"Let's just say she is not intellectually curious about that. She plays the good wife. She's smart, ambitious to a certain degree, good with the kids. Exactly how her husband generates the money necessary to keep the brownstone and vacation house, private school tuition and all the rest going, she doesn't really care."

"You've really done an exacting study of the Buntings."

"Once I knew my brother would be working for him, I thought it was my duty."

"Did you want him to work there?"

"I thought I did. I was wrong, of course. Eddie was just fine right where he was. But I just wouldn't let myself see it. Misguided loyalty. Putting country over family. It's not a mistake I would repeat."

"You feel guilt for this, then?"

"Yes."

Sean stared at her, obviously more than a little surprised. It was a frank admission for someone who so clearly gave little away. He had just assumed that she would do what she often did, answer a question with a question. Sensing she might be receptive to opening up more now he said, "Can I ask something?"

"Certainly."

"Are we going to follow them?"

"They are being followed. Just not by us."

"You have help?"

"I have acquaintances that assist me from time to time," she answered.

"Another question?"

She started walking in the direction opposite the Buntings and he followed, rolling his travel bag behind him.

He took her silence as acquiescence. "You talked about the E-Program before, but what is the recruitment like?"

"You never even get asked to come in unless you're the best of the best based on your track record. A lot of preliminary testing that all ordinary people would fail, but that all potential E applicants pass with flying colors. Then the testing becomes more and more rigorous. People start to fall away at these intervals. Eventually it comes down to the Wall. Only about three percent make it that far."

She had stepped inside one of the entrances to Central Park. They slowly made their way along one of the walkways. Sean remained silent until they had gone well into the park.

"The Wall?"

She nodded. "That's what they call it. It's the monster through which all intelligence flows. The Wall is like going from high school football straight to being MVP of the NFL. Very, very few make it."

She stopped and sat down on a bench.

"How do you know all this? From your brother?"

She shook her head. "He would have, but I didn't let Eddie talk to me about it. He could have gotten into trouble."

"So, your inside sources again."

She stared off into the darkness, the gloom dispelled only by the path lights overhead. The rain had picked up, and Sean could feel a chill seeping into his bones.

"No," she finally said.

"So how then?"

"Peter Bunting recruited me for the program seven years ago."

46

Michelle Maxwell had been busy up in Maine while her sidekick was traipsing between D.C. and New York. She'd met with Eric Dobkin and gone over what the Maine State Police knew about Carla Dukes's death. The most telling piece had been that an expedited autopsy had been done and the slug removed from the woman's brain. It was a .32-caliber and had been matched to the slug found in Ted Bergin. There was no forced entry in Dukes's home, so she might have let the person in. That could mean that Dukes and Bergin had known the same killer. Yet how could that be? They had both only recently come to the area and, so far as anyone knew, didn't even know each other.

Was the killer a cop? Or an FBI agent?

That's what Michelle was thinking now, even more strongly than before. And if that was true, it was beyond troubling.

She had also gone over to Cutter's Rock to see from a distance if anything unusual was going on. She had set up her observation post on a high point that allowed her to see the compound almost in its entirety.

On the surface everything seemed normal. Guards were at their posts. Gates were closed. Patrols were ongoing. The fence was no doubt electrified. She was there for an hour and saw only one visitor go in and out the whole time.

But that one visitor had been Brandon Murdock. Had he gone to see Edgar Roy? That would hardly be legal, since Roy was represented by counsel now and was in no shape to be questioned or to waive any of his rights. Or maybe Murdock had gone to search Dukes's office? To see if any incriminating evidence had been left behind. Evidence that might lead to Murdock, perhaps, if he was involved in this some-how?

As Michelle had been about to leave her post, she noticed something unusual. She'd done one more sweep of the surrounding countryside, and her optics picked up on another pair of artificial eyes at a position about a half mile distant from where she was. She focused her binoculars on this spot, but all she could see was the sunlight reflecting off the scope.

Was someone else running surveillance on the federal facility?

She gauged the location of this observer, jumped in her truck, and headed there as fast as possible. However, by the time she pulled down the road, ditched her truck, and made her way forward stealthily through the woods, whoever had been there was gone. She checked the road for recent marks but found none.

They could have come on foot and left on foot. She checked for this, too, but found nothing helpful.

She drove back to the inn full of questions.

A little before dinnertime she walked down the steps at Martha's Inn and found the landlady, Mrs. Burke, in the foyer gazing at her disapprovingly.

"You keep very irregular hours, young lady," said Burke. "And you never eat meals on time. I don't like that. It's extra work for me."

Michelle gazed down at the woman, a look of annoyance on her face. "Since when have I asked you to make me a special meal?"

"The point is I have to be ready to make the meal in case you request it."

"Who says?"

"It's a courtesy of our inn."

"Well, thanks, but you don't have to do it. So problem solved." Michelle headed past her to the front door.

"Where are you going now?" Burke asked.

"Uh, that would be out your front door and then into my truck."

"I meant where are you going in your truck?"

"That would be none of your business."

"Are you Southern girls always so rude?"

"Who says I'm from the South?"

"Please, I can tell from your accent."

"Okay, I'm not trying to be rude. But I am an investigator looking into a series of murders. So when

I say it's none of your business, it's just a polite way of telling you that it's none of your business."

Burke glanced down at Michelle's waist. "Do you have to wear that thing around here?"

Michelle looked at her holstered pistol revealed through the opening in her coat. "Two people up here are dead. I would think you'd like someone with a gun around. Just in case the killer shows up here."

Burke gasped and took a step back. "Why in the world would they do that? You're just trying to scare an old woman. That's not very nice."

Since Burke did indeed look very frightened, Michelle sighed and said, "Maybe I was trying to scare you, but just because you got under my skin."

"That was not my intent."

"Sure it was," she shot back.

At first Michelle thought Burke was going to launch into a tirade, but the old woman instead sat down in a chair, wrapping her sweater more tightly around her and said, "You're right. It was."

Michelle relaxed a notch. "Why?"

"You remind me a lot of my daughter. Well, when she was younger. Fiery, independent, her way or no way at all."

"Okay."

"We had our differences. We had our words."

"Moms and daughters often do."

"Are you close to your mother?"

Michelle hesitated. "I . . . was."

Burke looked confused. "You were . . . Oh, yes, oh, I see, I'm sorry. Was it recent?"

"Recent enough, yeah."

A few moments of silence lapsed. "So what happened to your daughter?" asked Michelle.

"She left to go to college. I just assumed she'd come back here. But she never did."

"Where is she now?"

"Hawaii."

"Long way away."

"About as long as you can get and still be in America. I'm sure that was intentional on her part."

"Do you ever see her?"

"No. It's been decades now. It amazes me when I think about it. All those years. The time goes by so fast. She sends me pictures. I have three grandchildren. Before my husband died we had planned to fly out there and break the ice. But then he passed and . . . Well."

"I think you should still go."

She shook her head vigorously. "I think I would be too afraid. When my husband was alive he was the buffer. I could make the trip with him. But alone, no."

"And not see your grandkids?"

"They don't even know me."

"But they will if you go out there."

"I think it's just too late." She stood. "Well, you be careful out there. And I'll leave some food for you in the fridge. And I'll put on the coffee. You just have to turn it on."

"I appreciate that."

"And I'll keep an eye on your young friend. She seems very withdrawn. Scared, even."

"She's under a lot of pressure."

"When will Mr. King be back?"

"I'm not sure."

"He's very handsome."

Michelle looked away. "Yes, I guess he is."

"Are you two an item?"

Michelle did her best not to smile at this quaint term. "Maybe we are."

"Then you should get married."

"It's complicated."

"No, it's only the people who make it complicated. Do you want to marry him?"

This question caught Michelle off guard. "What? I . . . I haven't thought about it, really."

Burke scrutinized her so closely that Michelle found her face growing warm.

"I see," said Burke skeptically. "Well, good night."

"Good night. And for what it's worth, I think you should go see your daughter."

"Why?"

"I didn't get to see my mom again. I'll always regret that. You have to take your chances when you have them."

"Thank you, Michelle. I appreciate the advice."

Michelle hurried outside, her thoughts now unfocused. A phone call was about to change all that.

"Hello?"

"Maxwell?"

"Who is this?"

"Murdock."

"What's up?"

"We need to meet."

"Why?"

"About this case."

"What about it?"

"Things you and your partner need to know. Things that I've found out."

"Why are you suddenly playing nice?"

"Because I don't know if I can trust anyone on my side."

"That's a hell of a statement coming from an FBI agent."

"It's a hell of a situation."

"Where and when?"

"Ten o'clock. I'll give you directions."

She took down the information, started to walk to her truck but stopped.

This was all a little too fishy.

She pulled out her phone, called Sean. It didn't go through.

"Crap!" She thought for a few moments and then called another number.

"Dobkin," said the voice.

"Eric, it's Michelle Maxwell. How would you like to provide me with a little backup tonight?"

47

"They recruited you?" exclaimed Sean.

Kelly Paul nodded. "Not to be the Analyst. I was smart, but my mental acuity did not come close to the level required."

"What then?"

"They wanted me to run the program."

"They? You mean Peter Bunting?"

She rose. "How about some coffee? I know a place close by where we can talk in private."

It wasn't a café or restaurant. It was a one-bedroom apartment three blocks off the park on a normal-looking residential street where little kids probably played on the sidewalk during good weather.

The inside was no more than what one needed to survive. It had a door with locks, a window, a kitchen, a bed, a TV, and a toilet. No paintings, no drapes, no plants; there was the original gray carpeting, eggshell white walls. A few pieces of furniture.

Paul made the coffee and brought two cups with sugar and cream into the living room. The decision to seek shelter had been a good one. The rain now lashed the window, and there were rumbles of thunder and flashes of lightning.

Sean looked around the space while he sipped the hot coffee. "This yours?"

"Not just mine, no."

"Shared facilities?"

"Everyone's budget has been cut."

"Must be nice to actually have a budget."

She eyed him over the rim of her cup. "You would think."

"We were talking about your recruitment. Bunting wanted to hire you?"

"Understand that the E Program even seven years ago was not what it is today. It came on line two years after 9/11. Since then it's grown immeasurably both in fiscal appropriation and operational scope. Its budget is in the billions, and there's not one intelligence arena it does not serve. That alone makes it totally unique. Well, my brother's intellectual gifts made it even more special."

"And he wanted you to run it. I'm sure you were more than capable, but wasn't it his job to do that?"

"Bunting was expanding his business back then. He wanted to delegate. I'd had a very successful career. And to those in the field my successes were well known. I attracted his attention. We were contemporaries. Our philosophical identities weren't so different. It would have made me a great deal of money and taken me out of what had become a very dangerous occupation. And it would free him up to pursue other business opportunities. On paper it seemed perfect."

"On paper," said Sean. "But not in practice?"

She put her cup down. "I came very close to accepting. For a number of reasons. Eddie was with the IRS by then. He seemed happy and challenged. Well, to the extent anything can actually challenge him. But our mother had just died."

"And he'd be all alone?"

"Yes. I wasn't sure that he could cut it all by himself. This job would allow me to spend more time with him, become more of a presence in his life."

"So what happened? It seemed perfect."

"At the end I couldn't do it. I wasn't prepared for what would amount to a desk job. I'd also gotten used to being my own boss, running my own show. Bunting had the rep of being a micromanager. I wasn't ready for that."

"And maybe you weren't ready to be a caretaker for your brother either."

"Maybe I wasn't," she admitted. "In retrospect it was astonishingly selfish of me. I put my career wants over my brother's needs. I guess maybe I'd always done that."

"You wouldn't be the first person."

"Small comfort." She hesitated. "I had been his protector when he was young."

"Against his father?" asked Sean quietly.

Paul rose and walked to the window, looked out at the stormy night.

She said, "He was just a little boy. Couldn't take care of himself."

"But you did."

"I did what was right."

"Your stepfather's death?"

She turned to look at him. "I have probably more regrets than most. That is not one of them."

"So you recommended your brother for the program years later?"

Paul seemed relieved by the change in the direction of the conversation. She sat back down. "There was no one to touch him in the very skill sets the program required. He was so good they designated him an E-Six, the first ever." There was sisterly pride in her voice.

"And Bunting and you?"

"What about it?"

"You and your brother were both vetted for positions with the E-Program. Bunting must know you two are related."

"So? I seriously doubt Bunting thinks I framed my own brother for murder."

"But he may think you're working from behind the scenes to help him."

"Well, I am. But again, I don't think Bunting will perceive that as a threat. If Eddie is cleared Bunting gets him back."

"At Cutter's your brother just stares at the ceiling, never says a word, never moves a muscle. Is he pretending?"

"Yes and no. It's hard to explain. Eddie can lose himself in his mind like few others. He did that as a child, too."

"Because of his father?"

"Sometimes."

"So now your brother has withdrawn into his own mind as a form of protection?"

"He's afraid."

"Well, if they convict him for those murders they can execute him. And what's more dangerous than facing lethal injection?"

"Yes, but at least lethal injection is painless. The people we're up against won't be that generous. I can guarantee you that."

48

The place Murdock wanted to meet at turned out to be a post office building set two miles off the main cut-through between Eastport and Machias. It was one-story, all brick and glass with an asphalt parking lot. In front of the building an American flag flapped in the breeze atop a thirty-foot stainless steel pole.

There was one car in the parking lot, next to the mailbox drop-off.

Even from a distance Michelle could see the man in the driver's seat. As her headlights hit the car, she saw the government plates. And she saw the man stir in the front seat. She pulled up beside the car, killed her engine and lights, and got out.

She looked around, studying the topography. The building was on one acre of cleared land with some grass, poured concrete sidewalks and curbs, and good old American-made asphalt to park your wheels on. Besides that there was nothing but wilderness.

She wondered what position Dobkin had taken up. He had several to choose from. She would have posted to the left of the building right near the tree line. That provided for decent cover and optimal sight lines.

"Thanks for coming," Murdock said, as he got out of his ride and joined her.

"You made it sound important."

"It is."

She leaned against her truck and folded her arms. "One preliminary question."

Murdock frowned. "What?"

"Sean and I have pretty much been on your shit list from the moment you met us. Now, you want to work together?"

Murdock drew out a stick of gum and popped it in his mouth. "I flew off the handle. I tend to do that more than I probably should."

"We've all been there."

"This case is giving me ulcers."

"You're not alone on that."

"Every time I think I'm close something else happens."

"And something tells me none of us have really been close to solving this."

"You're probably right," admitted Murdock.

"So your change in tactics? You said you couldn't trust your own side?"

"Let's just say I'm getting paranoid from the chatter on my own end. And you can also put it down to wanting to get results. I've got my boss screaming at me every five minutes. If I waste any more time fighting with you and King and don't solve this thing, it won't matter. I'll be cradled around a cubicle buried in some Bureau outpost and wondering where the hell my career went."

"Sean was right about you and national security, wasn't he?"

"Not that I like to broadcast that, but yeah, I am Counterterrorism unit."

"So national security and Edgar Roy. The connection?"

"All I can tell you is that when he was arrested and got sent up here the FBI received an order from very high up to put a tag on him. He was a special person of interest and we were to keep a close eye on him. There, I said it. Now what can you tell me?"

"We have some things in play, but nothing definitive."

"Care to share?"

"No. You called me. You said you had some things to tell me. I'm listening. If you wanted this to be a two-way I wouldn't be here."

"Okay, okay, fair enough." He spit out the gum. "I went to see Edgar Roy today."

"Why's that?"

"Just to talk to him."

"And did he talk back?"

"Not so much, no."

"Not so much?"

"Okay, nothing, nada. Guy never made a sound."

"So?"

"So I never expected him to. He's a genius. So smart, in fact, that he's a very valuable asset of the federal government."

"Is that right?"

He cocked his head. "Why do I think I'm preaching to the choir?"

"On the contrary. This is fascinating stuff."

He stepped closer. "Okay, let's cut to the chase. I did some hard digging. Called in a few favors and finally hit the mother lode. I know what Roy was doing for Uncle Sam. And I also found out that there are persons in D.C. who might have reason to wish Mr. Roy harm."

"Who?"

Murdock drew closer. Only a few inches separated the two. "You ever heard of the E-Pro—"

Michelle felt like she'd been slapped. She tasted the liquid that had appeared on her face and then spit it out. The pain in her arm was mildly annoying. When Murdock fell into her two seconds later, she realized what was happening. She gripped him by the shoulders and jerked both of them behind her truck. The next shot hit twenty feet behind where she had been standing. It cracked the asphalt, sending pieces spiraling off into the grass. One shard hit the mailbox and left a deep gouge in the blue-painted metal. If she hadn't moved, Michelle's brain matter would have collided with the mailbox instead of the asphalt.

More gunfire opened up, different from the two rifle shots. Dobkin.

Murdock was lying on top of Michelle.

"Murdock? Agent Murdock!"

She rolled him off her, checked his pulse. There was none. She looked at his face. Glassy eyes. Mouth slightly parted, blood trickling out. He looked surprised. She saw the hole in his shirt, stained red. She turned him over. Entrance wound midspine. Kill shot. She looked down at herself. Blood on her face. His blood.

She looked further down at her arm.

My blood.

The round had exited his chest and found her arm. She slipped off her jacket, rolled up her sleeve. It was only a nick. Something scrunched underfoot. She picked it up. It was the misshapen rifle round. She placed it in her jacket pocket.

She pulled out her gun and her phone. She hit 911, relayed what had happened.

Someone was still firing out there. Pistol. She was pretty sure it was the reports of Eric Dobkin's H&K .45. Then the shots stopped.

She phoned his cell. Four rings and she was thinking maybe something was wrong, or he was dead too, when he picked up.

"You okay?" Dobkin said immediately.

"I am. Murdock's dead."

"Thought so when I saw the round hit."

"Did you see the shooter?"

"No, but I worked back the trajectory and fired that way. Eight shots and then I moved in. I called in backup."

"So did I."

"There's no one around that I can see."

"Escaped through the woods again. Enough with the damned trees already."

"Is Murdock really dead? You're sure?"

She looked down at the still body. "Yeah, he really is. No chance. Shooter knew what he was doing."

"And you're sure you're okay?"

"Nothing that a Band-Aid won't fix. If I were you I'd watch myself out there until help arrives. I know we were pretty exposed here, but it was still a fair shot. He could be far away and still nail you. Keep your head down."

"Okay. Did he tell you anything?"

"Unfortunately nothing I didn't already know. But he couldn't have known that." She hesitated, the words not forming the way she wanted. "He was trying to do the right thing."

She clicked off and slumped next to the dead man. Counterintuitively, with a long-range rifle round the farther the bullet traveled the more damage it could actually do to the target when it hit. She took the fired round out of her pocket and studied it. Then she gauged the size of the hole in Murdock's back. From that she reverse-engineered the flight length of the bullet.

The shot had come from over five hundred yards.

She hadn't cared very much for Murdock, but he was a Fed. She had been a Fed. There was an unspoken bond there. When you killed a Fed you took a little bit of the soul from all other Feds. It could not be tolerated. It could not be left to pass without consequences, severe consequences.

She ripped off part of her shirtsleeve and wound it around her wound, neatly stopping the minimal blood flow. Her injury seemed grossly lame in the face of the mortal wound suffered by Murdock.

She opened her car door, snagged a bottle of water, and used it to wipe the blood off her face.

His blood.

She gargled, spit out more of it from her mouth, tried not to think how much of it she had inadvertently swallowed, how salty it tasted.

Finished, she looked down at Murdock again. She knew she shouldn't do it, screwing with a crime scene, but she reached over and lifted out his wallet. Flipped it open.

Three kids. Three little tow-headed boys and a woman who looked like any mother with an overworked and always gone FBI agent husband and three little balls of energy: tired.

Michelle put the wallet back, leaned against the running board. She tried not to, but she just couldn't help it.

She covered her eyes but the tears still trickled out.

49

"What else can we do here?" asked Sean, as they sat in the small apartment.

"Not clear," said Paul.

"Bunting had no incentive to frame your brother."

"No. But that's not the same for Bergin or Dukes," she replied. "Bergin's death delays the trial. Dukes might've screwed up somehow and made the wrong people nervous."

"Granted, those are motives to kill. Although with your brother unfit to stand trial, killing his defense lawyer probably wasn't absolutely necessary."

"If it was even fifty percent necessary they would do it. And they might have been afraid Bergin would find something out."

"Bergin was my friend," said Sean.

"He was my friend, too. I'm sorry I ever got him involved in this."

Sean's phone rang. He answered. "Michelle. What? What's wrong? Slow down. Okay, okay. Murdock?" He listened in silence for about sixty seconds. "I'm on my way. Be there as soon as I can."

He clicked off and looked at Paul.

She said, "Murdock's dead, isn't he?"

"How did you know?"

"I wondered who Bunting was talking to so animatedly back there."

"You think he ordered the hit on Murdock while we were watching him? While he was out walking with his wife and kids?"

"I didn't say that. But Bunting is never off the clock, Sean. So you're going back to Maine?"

"I have to. And Michelle told me something else."

"What?"

"She went to do a recon on Cutter's."

"And?"

"And she swears someone else was watching the place too, just like she was."

Paul's nostrils flared. She seemed to be searching the air for a scent to go after. "I think I'll join you up in Maine. Just give me a few minutes to pack."

Five minutes later she was ready to go.

They cabbed to a car-rental place, got a four-door Chevy, and headed north out of Manhattan. At this time of night the traffic was fairly light, even for the city that never sleeps. They reached Boston in the wee hours and checked into a motel on the outskirts of the city because neither one of them could keep their eyes open. They got up at eight the next morning after four hours of sleep. That afternoon, several cups of coffee and two fast-food meals later, they pulled into Machias.

They had phoned when they got close and Michelle met them outside of the inn.

When Sean saw the bandage around her arm he gaped. "Did you get shot too?"

"Not really."

"How could you not really be shot?"

"It was the slug that killed Murdock. It's a scratch."

Sean hugged her and Michelle felt his arms trembling.

She said softly, "I'm okay, Sean, really." But she squeezed him tightly back.

"We're not splitting up again. Every time we do something bad happens."

Michelle looked up at Kelly Paul. "I didn't expect to see you."

"I didn't expect to be here."

They went inside where Mrs. Burke had clearly been fussing over Michelle. She checked her bandage and brought her another cup of coffee before leaving them alone. Megan was sitting in the front parlor, a cup of tea cradled in her lap.

"People keep dying," Megan said in a faraway voice.

They all looked at her but said nothing.

Megan turned to Paul. "You're not going to pull a knife on me again, are you?"

"Not unless you give me reason to, no."

Megan shuddered and fell silent.

"Tell us everything you remember about last night, Michelle," said Sean.

She did, interrupted only by questions posed by Sean or Paul.

"So Murdock knew or had discovered the existence of the E-Program?" said Sean.

"Well, he got cut off by the shot, but I think so. And he talked about certain people in D.C. who might have a reason to want to harm Edgar Roy."

"By framing him?" asked Sean.

"Well, considering he could get the death penalty if convicted, yeah."

Sean looked at Megan. "What's the status on the case?"

"I've been drafting motions but I need you to look them over."

"Okay. Have you heard anything from the prosecutor on the case? Any notice from the court?"

Megan shook her head. "There's no one left at Mr. Bergin's office. But I've been checking e-mail and voice messages. The case is technically in legal limbo because of Roy's mental condition. But the court ordered periodic evaluations done on him to see if he's mentally competent to stand trial. One of those is coming up soon."

Sean glanced at Paul. "How would you like to see your brother?"

She turned to him. "When?" she said slowly.

"How about now?"

50

Because he had absolutely zero other options, Bunting made the trek once more, going from rich, busy Manhattan, to poor, just as busy Manhattan. He looked up and saw the sign: Pizza, $1 a Slice.

If only he were here for pepperoni and cheese. Right now he was so angry he could barely contain himself. He wanted to hit something. Or someone.

He walked up the six flights. He was in good shape, worked out regularly at his members-only club, but for some reason he felt winded and sweaty when he reached the top.

He knocked.

The door opened.

James Harkes stood there, dressed exactly as before. As Bunting was ushered in he wondered if the man's entire wardrobe consisted of the same color suit, shirt, and tie, namely black, white, black.

The men sat at the same small table. A little fan buzzed and oscillated on a side table. It was the only airflow in the place, other than the men's breathing.

Bunting could feel the heat rising from the pizza ovens six floors below.

"Murdock!" began Bunting.

"What about him?"

"He's dead, but I know you already knew that."

Harkes said nothing. He just sat there, large hands resting on his flat stomach.

"He's dead, Harkes," Bunting said again.

"I heard you the first time, Mr. Bunting."

"When we talked last night and you said you'd discovered that Murdock had stumbled onto the E-Program's existence, I didn't say to kill him."

Harkes leaned forward just a bit. "You're assuming certain actions on my part."

"Did you kill him?"

"I'm here to protect you, Mr. Bunting."

"But he's a damned FBI agent. You had him murdered."

"Your words, not mine."

"Christ, are you really going to play semantics now?"

"I have a few other things to take care of. Is there anything else I can do for you?"

"Yeah, you can stop killing people. You have just made a complicated situation nearly impossible."

"I wouldn't characterize it that way."

"Well, I *would*."

"Maxwell knows now. And King."

"About Edgar Roy being the Analyst?"

"Yes," said Harkes.

"How could they?"

"Outside source."

"Who?"

"Kelly Paul."

Bunting stared at him.

"Kelly Paul," Harkes said again. "I know that you know her."

"How is she involved?"

"She's Edgar Roy's half sister." Harkes studied him. "But then you knew that."

"Is that where King and Maxwell went when we lost track of them?"

"Possibly."

Bunting pointed a finger at Harkes. "Listen very carefully. You are not to go near Kelly Paul. Or Sean King. Or Michelle Maxwell. Do you understand me?"

"I'm afraid you're not grasping the seriousness of the situation."

"So what the hell is the plan? Kill everybody?"

"Plans are ever evolving," said Harkes with maddening calm.

"Why would Paul be working to harm her brother? That's preposterous."

"You're assuming that Paul is still working for us. She's been off the grid for a while. She could be freelancing for our enemies."

"I don't believe that. Kelly Paul is as patriotic as anyone I've ever met."

"That is a dangerous perspective for someone in your position to have."

"What perspective?" snapped Bunting.

"That someone can't be corrupted."

"*I* can't be. I would never do anything to harm my country."

"That's a nice speech. But if the right inducement came along even you could be turned."

"Never."

"You're missing the point."

"If anybody else ends up dead, it's over for you, Harkes. You have my word."

"You have a good day, Mr. Bunting."

Harkes opened the door, and Bunting stormed through it.

51

Two hours later Bunting was seated in a comfy leather chair on the company jet as it taxied toward takeoff. It was a Gulfstream G550. It could fly from London to Singapore on a single tank of gas. It had an office, a bed, TVs, Wi-Fi, state-of-the-art avionics, a full bar, seating for fourteen, two pilots, and two flight attendants. It could hit nearly 600 miles an hour and fly at a max ceiling of 51,000 feet. It had cost Bunting's company, BIC, over $50 million new, and millions more per year in maintenance and operating costs.

The flight from New York to Dulles, Virginia, would take less than half an hour in the air. He sat back as the G550 executed its climb out over the friendly if crowded Manhattan skies, banked smoothly south, and headed to D.C. Before Bunting could even settle into work, the pilot announced their descent into Dulles. Twenty minutes later they were on the ground. They taxied to a private part of the airport, and the retractable steps housed on the G550 came down. He stepped off and into the waiting limo, which sped away as soon as his rear end hit the seat.

It really was the only way to travel, even if it did cost $50 million and change. But right now he wasn't thinking about his lofty and privileged ability to move around. He was thinking about the possibility of losing everything he'd worked for. His meeting with Harkes had troubled him greatly. He really felt things slipping out of control.

Once they left the airport Bunting ran into the world of the peasant commuter and got bogged down in traffic on the toll road. It took him far longer to go six miles by car than it had over two hundred miles through the air. But he finally made it.

The building he entered seemed ordinary. Passersby would not give it a second look. It was not the office building that Sean had followed Avery to. That was located several miles from here. This place was the most important facility in Bunting's empire. This was where the Wall was located. He entered the building and sped through interior security portals, before taking an elevator down and then walking along a corridor.

It had taken him years, millions of dollars, and many an anxious moment before he had convinced the American security community to move into the twenty-first century and embrace his vision for what intelligence collection and analysis could actually become. When it had finally happened, the floodgates had opened and billions of dollars of government money had flowed into his coffers. It was the greatest triumph of his life. And what many took for granted was the fact that aside from the money, the E-Program worked. It had foreseen and stopped countless terrorist attacks on American soil and against US interests overseas. It had allowed CIA, DHS, DIA, Geospatial, NSA, and a host of the lesser-known intelligence agencies to rack up success after success. The FBI, armed with leads provided by the E-Program, had set up and sprung sting upon sting, bagging criminals and terrorists, and gathering valuable intelligence used to stop future heinous acts.

The Wall was the focal point. The Wall was Bunting's masterstroke. While teams of traditional analysts, so enmeshed in the trees that they had no comprehension a forest even existed, had no reasonable chance to successfully ferret out the true threat, one person, the right person sitting in a chair and taking up the challenge of the Wall, had led them to the promised land. The Wall would give up its well-hidden secrets to just the right person. And the rewards were immense, and also immediate.

The program had worked well for years. And then the snag had come. The information that required analysis had bested the most superior minds he could find. The E-Program had finally shown a chink in the armor. Opponents like Ellen Foster at DHS and Mason Quantrell in the private sector had started circling like the vultures they were.

And then Bunting had found Edgar Roy. Even against the high benchmarks of the E-Program Roy had stood out. Time and again he had picked up on things that even powerful supercomputers together with a hundred thousand toiling and lesser analysts had missed. Bunting was convinced that if Edgar Roy had been staring at the Wall prior to September 11, 2001, that day would have simply been like any other, and utterly forgettable.

He entered the room, far below the basement level of the facility. He nodded to people who worked there. They nodded back and then quickly looked away, perhaps sensing his nervous detachment. Even though Foster had made it clear that his last chance had passed, Bunting had arranged one more attempt to salvage the program. Results so far had not been good.

He entered the control room and nodded at Avery, who sat, as he usually did, in front of the computer banks that operated not only the Wall but also the feedback from the Analyst. There were three in the room today to check the goings-on at the Wall: two women and a man, all longtime analysts at BIC.

As Bunting settled into his seat and opened his electronic tablet he noted that two of them were perfectly capable E-Fives and the other a top-level E-Four. Indeed, the E-Fives had been the best he had seen until Edgar Roy had entered his life and sent the possibilities quite into the stratosphere.

But now things had changed. As Avery had correctly pointed out previously, the information flow grew exponentially, outpacing the abilities of minds that a year ago could have handled it. Roy could handle it. But he didn't have Edgar Roy anymore.

Bunting looked through the glass. The three Es were doing their best, but he could see that the throughput on the Wall data had been throttled back sixty percent. At this rate the conclusions reached would be worthless before the folks even memorialized their findings and sent their reports on up the chain. It simply wasn't going to cut it.

He let this exercise go on for another five minutes and then looked despondently at Avery and flicked a finger across his neck.

Avery immediately spoke into the headset he wore. "Thank you all. We will be shutting the Wall down in five, four, three, two, one."

He hit some keys and the screen became dark.

Bunting nearly fell into a chair and sat there staring at the floor. Foster was right. It was over. He was over. They'd probably kill him. And Roy next.

A man opened the control room door. "Mr. Bunting?"

He looked up.

"Secretary Foster wants to see you ASAP."

Oh, God.

52

Sean thought it would be a problem getting into Cutter's Rock, especially after the murder of Carla Dukes. However, her absence seemed to have lessened the hurdles necessary for them to see the prisoner, even with Kelly Paul in tow.

Thus, the mighty gates had opened, the guards did their search, and very soon after that they were waiting in the visitor's room for Edgar Roy.

Megan stood by the glass wall, Michelle beside her. Sean was watching the door. Kelly Paul paced, her gaze on the floor. Sean thought he knew what she was thinking. And she was probably right. Roy might react to seeing her and blow his cover of insanity.

The door opened and in came Edgar Roy. He was dressed the same, looked the same, smelled the same. He towered over the guards and over Sean and Michelle. Towered most of all over the petite Megan.

Sean heard it first, a long, low whistle that sounded like some tune Sean couldn't place at the moment. He turned to find its source. Kelly Paul was against the wall, her face turned away from her brother. Sean whipped back around to Roy. The whistle had come right when Roy had been looking down, so his eyes could not be seen. Sean thought he noted the slightest flinch in Roy's shoulder. They seated him behind the glass, locked him down to the floor ring. The guards slammed the door shut on the way out. Roy sat there, legs splayed out, face to the ceiling. Eyes fixed on that damn spot. As always.

Except for that flinch, thought Sean.

The whistled tune came again. Once again Sean turned. This time so did Michelle.

Kelly Paul was now facing her brother.

"Hello, Eddie, it's good to see you," she said, her voice calm, her smile genuine.

She walked toward him, curved around the glass wall, and stood in front of him. She did not bend down. In fact she seemed to be standing as tall as she could. Her hands came up to her chest.

Sean's gaze flitted around the room and then, behind him, he saw it and wondered why he hadn't before. A slight imperfection in the wall, up high. The camera lens was pointed right at the wall of glass, the chair. The prisoner. But now Paul was blocking its view of her brother.

Sean moved forward, skirted the glass wall, and came around to stand facing Paul. Now he understood why she had stood as tall as possible. The message she was holding was aligned perfectly with her brother's angle of sight. She had written it in large block letters with a pencil.

I KNOW. E. BUNTING. FRAMED. SUSPI-CIONS?

Roy made no visible reaction to this, but as Sean glanced down at him, he could see that his eyes had finally come to life and that the tiniest fraction of a smile tugged at his lips as his image was safely shielded from the camera by his sister's bulk.

The zombie, it seemed, had just arisen.

Paul started tapping her finger against the paper. She did it almost silently, but slowly and methodically. At first Sean couldn't understand what she was doing. But then it finally hit him.

She's communicating with him via Morse code.

And then another noise arose. Sean glanced down. Roy was tapping against his leg. He was answering her. She tapped her response back.

Edgar Roy's gaze returned to the spot on the ceiling.

Paul crumpled the paper, put it in her mouth, and swallowed it. As they walked out Sean whispered to Paul, "What was that about?"

"I gave him details and asked him to analyze them."

"What did he code back to you?"

"He wanted to know if I had told Bergin about the E-Program. I told him I hadn't."

"What do we do now?"

"Now we go on the attack," replied Paul.

"How?"

"I'll tell you exactly how, because you and Michelle will be the tip of the spear."

"Is Bunting behind all this?"

"We're going to find out."

Roy was returned to his cell. Once there he immediately turned away from the camera so he could at least close his eyes. He was tired, but the visit had lifted his spirits considerably.

His sister had come. He had always thought that she would. Her message had made it clear that she understood his situation. And she had told him quite a bit more using Morse code. She'd taught him the code when he was a child.

He opened his eyes and stared at the blank block wall across from him. It was painted yellow for some reason. Perhaps they thought the color soothing to the inmates here, as if a mere color could overcome what being here clearly meant.

Ted Bergin, Hilary Cunningham, Carla Dukes, Brandon Murdock, all dead. Think about a pattern there.

That was what his sister had asked him to do.

And so he did, dutifully. He turned over every possible combination in his mind.

Bergin and Dukes up close with a handgun. Cunningham killed and her body moved to Bergin's place. Murdock from a long distance with a rifle. Who had motive? Who had opportunity?

Roy's mind powered through the possibilities at a pace that would have been astonishing to anyone who could have somehow witnessed the execution of his thought process, the speed with which he considered and then rejected possibilities that ordinary people would have muddled over for months.

His mind slowed down, his factual base exhausted. He had not been given much to work with, but for him it had been enough. He had not detected a *single* pattern.

He had detected four. But he had no way to let his sister know this. He might never see her again.

53

Led by an armed escort, Bunting walked down the halls of the new DHS headquarters in D.C. It was a sprawling complex whose true price tag had never been revealed because it was classified. That essentially meant one had a license to print money, Bunting knew.

He was ushered into the room, and the door was closed and automatically locked behind him. He looked around the empty room and wondered if he'd been shown into the wrong space. He stopped wondering when Mason Quantrell and Ellen Foster stepped through from an adjoining room.

"Sit, Peter, this shouldn't take long," said Foster.

She opened a laptop that rested in front of the chair she took while Quantrell sat beside her. He smiled at Bunting. "How goes it, Pete?"

Bunting ignored him and said to Foster, "Secretary Foster. Again, I have to tell you that I'm extremely uncomfortable with having my chief competitor in the room during a confidential discussion."

She said demurely, "Peter, we have no secrets from each other, do we?"

"Actually we do. I employ a large number of people who perform very specialized work using procedures, protocols, proprietary soft- and hardware, algorithms, and the like that I have spent years and a great deal of money creating." He glanced at Quantrell, who continued to stare at him with what appeared to be an amused expression, making Bunting want to reach across the table and strangle him.

Quantrell said, "Well, Pete, under the current structure with the E-Program, all of *your* competitors have to send off their data collections for your use. I spent a lot of money putting my business together, too. But I share."

On the contrary, Bunting knew that Quantrell had made only a pretense of doing this over the years and was still collecting his government check. He had simply been waiting for any chance to take Bunting down. And it was clear he thought he had one now.

"Well, Mason, I'm sure if you'd been the one to come up with the E-Program you'd be smart enough to know it's far better than the way we all used to operate in the Dark Ages. That was when you were top dog on the private-sector side and everybody was going in a hundred different directions at once. You know, when 9/11 happened?"

Quantrell's patronizing smile faded and he snarled, "You have no idea who you're dealing with, you little prick."

"Okay, boys, we don't have time for schoolyard posturing," Foster admonished.

Bunting sat across from them and waited expectantly.

Foster entered her password and tapped some computer keys, read the information revealed on the screen, and showed it to Quantrell. He glanced over at Bunting and nodded.

If they were trying to intimidate him, thought Bunting, they were doing a spectacular job of it. But his face remained unreadable. He could play this game, too.

"Do we have an agenda?" he asked. "For the meeting?"

Foster motioned for him to wait just a moment while it appeared she was sending an e-mail. She closed the laptop and looked up at him.

"I do appreciate your meeting on such short notice, Peter."

"Certainly, whatever I can do," replied Bunting grudgingly.

She placed her elbows on the table. "I have one pertinent question and I'd like an honest reply."

Bunting gazed blankly at her. "I hope that you believe I am always honest with you."

"As it turns out, the question isn't that difficult, but the answer may well be." She paused. "Did you have Edgar Roy's lawyer, Ted Bergin; his secretary, Hilary Cunningham; the director of Cutter's Rock, Carla

Dukes; and FBI Special Agent Brandon Murdock murdered?"

Bunting's brain momentarily shut down. Then he literally shouted, "Of course I didn't! I can't believe you'd even ask the question."

"Please calm down. Now do you know who did kill them? If so, we really need to know."

"I don't have people murdered. I have no idea who did it."

"Bluster won't work. Do you know who killed them?" she asked again.

Bunting eyed Quantrell. "Why is he here?"

"Because I asked him to be here. In fact, he's been quite helpful in piecing some things together for DHS."

Bunting put a hand on the table to steady himself. "What sort of things?"

"Let's just say that Mr. Quantrell's people have done some digging and uncovered some interesting facts."

"Such as?" demanded Bunting.

"Not prepared to discuss them with you right now."

"If you're making accusations, I think I have every right to know what they're based on." He shot a furious glance at Quantrell. "Particularly if this guy is involved. He'd kill his own mother to win back the business I took from him because I was smarter than he was."

Quantrell rose and looked as though he was about to leap over the table at Bunting.

Foster put a restraining hand on his arm and eyed Bunting with contempt. "One more remark like that, Peter, and you'll force me to take action I don't really want to take right now."

"I want the record to reflect that anything this man has told you about me is tainted by the fact that he wants to destroy the E-Program."

"Willing to take a lie detector test?" inquired Foster.

"I'm not a suspect in the investigation."

"So that's a no?" asked Quantrell.

"Yes, that's a no," Bunting snapped.

Quantrell smiled and glanced at Foster and shook his head.

She said, "Peter, I hope you realize the serious trouble that you're in."

"I have no idea what you're talking about, Madame Secretary, I really don't."

If they had had a heart monitor on Bunting right now, they probably would have rushed him to the emergency room. But then again, he thought, these two assholes might just let him die right on the floor.

"Last chance, Bunting," advised Quantrell.

"Last chance for what? To sit here and confess to crimes I didn't commit?" he snapped. "And you, Mason, have no right to demand anything of me, so stop acting like you're the FBI. It's pathetic."

Foster said, "That's actually not true."

"Excuse me?" said Bunting warily.

"You know that the private- and public-sector lines have become increasingly blurred over time. Mr. Quantrell's company has been tasked with uncovering corruption and illegalities in the intelligence arena. For that purpose certain governmental authority has been given to him and his people."

Bunting stared at Quantrell in disbelief. "Is this like the idiot mercenaries in the Middle East who shot first and asked questions later? That was a stunning triumph for America's global reputation."

"It is what it is," said Foster. "And who else would have had a motive to kill those people? Is it that they had found out about the E-Program?"

"*Your* program," amended Quantrell. "The one you keep throwing in the rest of our faces."

"Where exactly is all of this coming from?" asked Bunting.

Foster said, "I'll tell you. It's *exactly* coming from the FBI director. He asked me questions, Peter, questions I was duty-bound to answer. As a result, I'm afraid that you are now a suspect."

"I see," said Bunting coldly. "What exactly did you tell the director?"

"I'm sorry. I really can't say."

"So I'm a suspect but you can't tell me why?"

"It's really out of my hands. I actually tried to protect you."

Like hell you did. "There's no proof that I've done anything wrong," said Bunting.

"Well, I'm sure the FBI is working on that right now," replied Foster.

Bunting digested all of this and said, "Is that all?"

"I suppose it is," said Foster.

Bunting rose. "Then I better get back to doing my job."

"While you can," said Quantrell.

Bunting said, "Six bodies in the barn. Interesting number."

Quantrell and Foster stared back at him impassively.

"Six bodies. The E-Six Program? If I didn't know better I'd think someone was playing a sick joke on me."

As Bunting turned to go, Foster said, "Peter, if by some miracle you are innocent I hope you make it through this in one piece."

He turned to face her. "I wish the same for you, Madame Secretary," he said.

54

Bunting spent the short plane ride on his G550 staring out at a large bank of lazy clouds. He barely noticed the plane had landed until the flight attendant handed him his coat and told him his car was waiting. The drive to the city took longer than the flight had. The maid greeted Bunting at the door of his Fifth Avenue brownstone.

"Is my wife in?" he asked the woman, who was petite and Latina.

"She is in her office, Mr. Bunting."

He found her going over details for another social benefit. He didn't even know what it was for, she was involved in so many. All good causes, he knew, that also allowed her and her friends to dress up, go to chic places, eat good food, and feel wonderful about themselves and what they did for the people who did not live in twenty-million-dollar brownstones on Fifth Avenue. But that was unfair. His wife had gone to hospitals with no photographers in tow and held AIDS and crack babies for hours because she wanted to help, because she felt compassion for them. She volunteered at soup kitchens and as a reading tutor at a homeless shelter, and she often brought their kids with her so they could see that life was not so wonderful for everyone. They had set up a foundation that funneled money and assistance to the poor and undereducated in the city.

And I do nothing when it comes to that.

But I keep the country safe. That was usually his easy answer to why he didn't share in his wife's philanthropic endeavors. But right now it didn't seem very convincing.

He kissed his wife, who looked up at him in surprise. He hadn't been home this early in years.

"Is everything okay at work?" she asked in a worried tone.

He smiled and sat down across from her in the exquisitely decorated office that alone had probably cost a quarter of a million dollars.

He wanted to talk to her about his problems, but she would have required the highest security clearances for that to happen. And she had none. Not a one, while he possessed the very highest of all. It was like living with someone from a different planet. He could never talk about work with the woman he loved. Never. So he simply smiled, even though he wanted to scream, and said, "Everything's fine. Just thought I'd come home, spend some time with you and the kids."

"Oh, well, I have to go out to a benefit at Lincoln

Center. It's so beautiful what they've done with the restoration. You need to go with me sometime."

"Right, I will," he said vaguely. "Sometime. And the kids?"

"They're at my sister's house. Remember? We talked about this. They'll be back tomorrow morning. We did talk about it," she added gently.

Bunting's smile faded. *I'm an idiot. I basically run the nation's intelligence grid to keep all Americans safe and I don't even know where my own kids are.*

He tried to laugh it off. "Right. I know. I've got some things to do in my study."

He went to his bedroom, dropped his two-thousand-dollar jacket on the floor, undid his three-hundred-dollar tie, poured himself a drink from the minibar in the adjacent sitting area, and gazed out the window at the darkening skies. Fall had settled in with cooler temperatures and fouler weather. It only added to his depression.

He looked around the confines of his bedroom, which had been personally designed by someone who went by only one name and was written up all the time in the sorts of magazines Bunting never read. Everything was elegant and in its place and spic-and-span clean. His entire home could be in a magazine. But it never would be because of what he did for a living. The country's spy heads expected their hired lackeys to tiptoe through life, not run screaming down the halls with money clutched in their fat fists.

He also had a library of handsomely bound leather books, many of them first editions of wonderful fiction penned by storied writers from the past. Or so he'd heard. The one-name designer and his wife had purchased them all in a single lot. He'd never actually read any of them. Didn't have the time. He wasn't much into fiction. Cold, hard facts ruled his entire existence.

He took one flight down to his study and spent about an hour working there. Then, when his concentration continued to wander, he clicked off his computer, rubbed his eyes, and went back upstairs, where his wife was finishing dressing for her night out.

"You can come with me," she said. "I'm on the board. I can certainly get you a seat."

"Thanks, maybe another time. I'm really beat."

She turned around, lifted up her hair, and pointed down to her zipper. "Can you help me, sweetie?"

Before he zipped her up he let his gaze wander down the inside of her dress, to the black thong she wore. He reached his hand down and squeezed her soft butt cheeks.

"I thought you said you were really beat," she chided him.

"That was before I saw you naked."

"God, your timing is incredibly poor."

"I know," he admitted.

After he zipped her up he moved his hand along her smooth back, which made her writhe a bit. She turned to him, smiled. "I shouldn't be too late tonight if you really want to fool around later. I bought some new lingerie."

"I'd like that," he said, momentarily forgetting that people were dropping all around him, and that he was facing professional doom or even an early and violent death. This thought coupled with the seeming domestic bliss of his life made him feel suddenly dizzy.

She kissed him and said, "I'm having Leon drive me over. He'll wait to bring me back. Or he can come directly back if you need the car."

"No, I don't plan on going out. See you later, honey."

He watched her leave. At forty-six his wife was still a stunner. They'd been married over seventeen years, and it felt like the first year over and over.

I'm a very lucky man. In some ways. Not so much in others.

Time passed and he wandered the house, a second glass of gin he'd poured dangling precariously in his hand. He finished it off, chewed the ice cubes down, sucking in every last drop of alcohol.

Foster and Quantrell were in this together and obviously had been for quite some time. Bunting had moles embedded everywhere, but they'd completely missed that little alliance. The E-Program, despite its proven worth, was going up in flames. And those two were poised to walk out of that fire with their kingdoms not only intact but far larger. And Bunting?

Either I'm dead or in prison. They've set me up nicely.

He had called James Harkes and gotten no answer back. It was clear to Bunting what that meant. Harkes was supposed to be his attack dog. But he had returned to his true master now, like Cerberus to Hades.

He rubbed his forehead. Harkes had been a plant. Either by Foster or Quantrell, or both. If he had killed those people? If the FBI thought that Bunting . . . Enough evidence to send him away forever, he was sure, was all neatly planted. Foster was nothing if not thorough.

He sat down on the edge of the bed. The comforter had been hand-sewn in Italy. It had cost more than Bunting's first year's college tuition. He had never much thought about this. And he didn't dwell on it now. He would buy a hundred such comforters if only he could put this all behind him.

He took a deep breath and smelled the alcohol coming out of his mouth. It tickled his nose, warmed him. He poured another gin, let it wash down his gullet, splash into his gut, and give him a cool burn, like diving into icy water naked.

His phone buzzed. Bunting lifted it from his pocket, gazed at it wearily when he saw who it was. He considered not answering it, then habit took over and he relented.

"Yes, Avery?"

"I just received a call from Sean King. He wants to meet."

Bunting didn't say anything. He felt a painful stitch in his chest.

"Mr. Bunting?"

"Yes?" He tried to keep his voice steady, but he heard it wobble.

"He wants to meet."

"I heard that. With you?"

"No, with you."

Bunting cleared his throat, tried to work some saliva into his mouth. "When?"

Avery didn't say anything.

"When!"

"He said he's standing outside your house right now."

55

Kelly Paul lowered her binoculars and studied the immediate landscape as afternoon fell away into evening in eastern Maine. She had a pad and pen. She made some notes: numbers, locations of things, degrees on the compass, obstacles, and possible advantages. She looked out to the ocean. The water was calm today. Cutter's Rock didn't seem nearly as intimidating from this heightened angle.

She lifted the binoculars once more as the van passed through security and arrived at the front doors to the facility. She adjusted the magnification and studied the writing on the side of the van. Cutter's must be having an issue with their power system, she concluded. And these gents were here to fix it. They were inside for nearly two hours and then did some work at a second, far smaller building behind the main facility. Later, they came out, put their equipment in the van, and drove away.

Paul lowered her optics when the van passed from sight.

The federal facility, she concluded, was an onion

with layers that needed to be peeled away. After Sean
had told her about it Paul had had Michelle tell her in
detail about the other pair of eyes she'd seen on
Cutter's. She had given Paul the approximate location
of these eyes. That was why she was here, to see it for
herself. It was a good observation point. She could
understand why they had chosen it.

She looked down at the facility plans in her hands.
They had been hard to come by. But she had built up
many favors over the years and could think of no better
reason to use them. She had also learned that Cutter's
Rock had gotten a new director to replace the
deceased Carla Dukes. She was certain that this new
person had been as carefully selected as the last one,
perhaps even more so. She wrote other things down
and then used her cell phone to make some calls. She
had suspected certain tactical actions were in the works,
and her observations today had confirmed that. She
needed help. With these phone calls she cashed in
more favors and got the assets she needed. It was proof
of the work that she had done in the field over the last
two decades that not a single person said no, or even
questioned why she wanted to do this.

She put the phone away, retraced her steps, and got
back in her rental. The drive back to Machias was
quick but it still gave her precious time to think. She
found Megan Riley in the front parlor at the inn.
Megan had her laptop, notepads, and legal documents
spread out in front of her on a wide, oval table that

Mrs. Burke had allowed her to use as a makeshift desk. She sat down across from her.

"Being productive?" she asked.

Megan bit on the end of her pen and looked up at the woman. "Depends on how you define *productive*."

"Making progress?"

"Marginally. It's not easy."

"Hard things in life are, de facto, never easy."

"Sean and Michelle are gone again."

"I know."

"Where?"

"I don't know."

"Or you won't tell me."

"Why do you think that?"

"Because you all think I'm a baby lawyer who will screw stuff up."

"You are and you might."

"Thanks. Thanks for all the support."

"You earn support."

"I'm doing the best that I can."

"Are you absolutely sure about that?"

"Are you always this rude?"

"You haven't yet seen me be rude. When I am it's unmistakable."

"I want to be in the loop on everything."

"Again, you have to earn that right."

Megan leaned back in her chair and studied the other woman. "Okay, why don't you tell me some things about your brother?"

"Why?"

Megan pointed to the documents. "I'm trying to draft motions to get him out of Cutter's. I have to have something to go on other than his insanity act."

"An act?"

"I saw what went on at Cutter's. You were communicating with him somehow."

"Maybe I was and maybe I wasn't. Sean said that the forensics don't add up. Different dirt on the bodies. That's something you can use."

"But it's just a point of evidence, something for the jury to decide. It's not going to get the charges thrown out."

"Getting the charges thrown out isn't necessarily the goal. We need to put pressure on certain people. We need for them to know that there is a lot at stake. More than my brother being executed for crimes he didn't commit."

"Well, drafting stupid motions won't do that."

"They can, if we execute the plan precisely."

"And how do we get to these certain people?"

"I believe Sean and Michelle are attempting to do that right now."

"And who are these certain people?"

Paul remained silent.

Megan pursed her lips and folded her arms over her chest. "I am the one who'll be arguing this case to save your brother's ass."

"It's a company in the intelligence field."

"Does this company have a name? It could have direct bearing on the case."

"I'm not inclined to disclose that information right now."

"So you do know?"

"Perhaps."

"You're not making this easy."

"It's not supposed to be easy."

She got up and walked away, leaving Megan to frown after her.

56

Bunting put down the phone and hurried over to the window overlooking the street. It was completely dark outside now, except for car lights and streetlamps. He checked his watch. It was nearly ten. He scanned the area outside of his house. For a moment he had a spark of hope that it was all just a bluff. But then he saw the tall man directly across the street, on the park side, under a streetlamp and near a tree.

Apparently, Sean King had glimpsed him, too, at the window. He raised his cell phone.

Bunting moved away from the window and debated what to do. Ordinarily he would have called Harkes to come and take care of this. But that was no longer an option.

I have to handle this one myself. And maybe it's about time.

He slipped on his jacket and headed downstairs. He passed the maid, who nodded respectfully to him. He passed the cook, who did the same. He attempted a smile, while his heart was slamming against his breastbone. When one of his security personnel stationed at the front door looked at him inquiringly, Bunting said, "Just going out for a quick walk. You can stay here."

"But, sir—"

"Just stay here, Kramer, I'll be fine. Just a walk."

The man stepped back and opened the door for his boss.

Bunting gripped hold of his nerves, squared his shoulders, and headed out, all alone.

Sean waited until the man crossed the street before coming over to him.

"Mr. Bunting, I appreciate your meeting with me."

"I'm not quite sure how you know who I am," Bunting said coldly.

Sean glanced around at the few people walking along the street. "Maybe someplace a little more private."

"I'd like to know what you want first."

Sean's features hardened. "We can waste time if you want. We waste too much time and then things get out of control. Everyone's control."

Instead of answering, Bunting turned and walked off. Sean followed. Minutes later they were at the back of an empty café staring at each other as a waitress poured them cups of coffee.

"What do you want?" asked Bunting after the woman had left them.

"Edgar Roy?"

Bunting said nothing.

"You know him."

"That didn't sound like a question."

"It's a fact."

"Again, what do you want?"

"Roy is being charged with murder. He's currently sitting in a cell at Cutter's Rock. You know all this. You've been to visit him."

"You have inside sources?"

Sean sat back, drank some of his coffee. It was fresh and hot and warmed bones that had grown chilly waiting outside of the fabulous brownstone. "A lot of people have died. My friend Ted Bergin. His secretary. Your person, Carla Dukes. An FBI agent. Not to mention the six bodies in Edgar Roy's barn."

Bunting spooned some sugar into his coffee. "Do you have any idea what you're involved in?"

"You're in a lot of trouble, Mr. Bunting. You could lose it all."

"Thank you for your assessment of my future. I think I've listened to enough." He started to rise, but Sean clamped a hand on his wrist.

"By all accounts you are a very smart man. Your work makes America safer. If I thought you were a bad guy I wouldn't be here. I'd let you sink in your own slime."

Bunting sat back down. "You can't know I'm not a 'bad guy.'" He peered closely at Sean. "So is this a test? And if so how am I doing?"

"You are meeting with me. And ask yourself why." Sean paused to let this sink in. "Because you know things are out of control. You know that your personal freedom is at risk. You know that if they can kill an FBI agent, who's to say they won't kill the CEO of an intelligence contractor and make it look like an accident." He paused again. "You have three kids."

"Leave my kids out of it," snapped Bunting.

"I would never do anything to your family. I'm one of the good guys. But do you think the people you're working with believe them to be off-limits?"

Bunting looked away, the answer to that question easily read in his desperate features.

"You're in with the sharks, Mr. Bunting. Sharks will attack anyone or anything. They're predators. Pure and simple."

"You think I don't know that?" he said in a hollow tone. "I had nothing to do with any of those people dying. What happened to them sickens me."

"I actually believe you."

Bunting looked surprised. "Why?"

"You stepped out of your palace back there and had the courage to meet with me, alone. That says a lot."

"It's not nearly as easy as you think it is, King. The people involved. There are almost no limits to what they can do."

"Edgar Roy is the key. If his innocence is established and he's released from Cutter's?"

"That's a big if."

Sean leaned forward. "I think you have to ask yourself a question, Mr. Bunting."

"What's that?"

"Do you want to stay in the water with the sharks or try to reach dry land? If you stay in the water, I only see one conclusion for you. Do you disagree?"

"No, I don't," said Bunting frankly. "I'll let you know." He paused. "And I appreciate what you're trying to do. Especially with Edgar. He doesn't deserve any of this. He's a good, kind person with a truly unique brain. He's just caught between forces he knows nothing about."

When he rose, Sean put a hand on his arm. "I know you need to think about this, but keep in mind that we don't have much time."

Bunting almost smiled. "Believe me, that one I know. But let me tell you something else. Even if we prove Edgar is innocent, this may not end."

"Why?"

"Because that's just not how the game is played."

"It's not a damn game," retorted Sean.

Bunting gave a weary smile. "You're right, it's not. But some people still think it is. And they play it for all it's worth."

57

Sean quickened his pace. There were only a few people on the street as the weather had deteriorated; rain was now falling and the wind was gusting.

A voice came into his right ear through the bud he'd placed there.

Michelle's voice was tense. "Sean, there's a black Escalade, tinted windows, out-of-state plates coming on your six."

"Doesn't have to be connected to me."

"It's moving fast and cutting through traffic for no apparent reason."

"Did Bunting call anyone?"

"Not that I saw, no. He's still walking back to his place, hands in pockets. But they might have followed him and waited till you two split up to go after you."

"Okay, what's the best move?"

"Go into the park at the next entrance. Pick up your pace. Now."

Sean started to walk as fast as possible without actually breaking into a sprint and drawing unnecessary attention. His hand moved to his coat pocket and curled around the pistol Kelly Paul had given him earlier. He chanced a glance behind. He saw the vehicle. Black Escalade, tinted windows, probably phony plates. It had a sinister look.

He cut to his right and entered the park.

Michelle's voice came on again. "Keep to your left, down the path. There are a few people there."

"Witnesses won't stop these guys, Michelle. They'll flash their real or real-enough-looking badges and haul my ass away."

"Then turn right at the next path and run. It'll give me time to figure something out."

"Where are you?"

"Right now, up a tree where I can see everything. Go."

Sean did exactly as she said. He knew she was good, one of the best at stuff like this, but he also knew the other side was bringing its best. And there certainly would be more of them.

He picked up his pace, turning right as instructed. There was a couple up ahead strolling along with their children. He passed by as quickly as possible. The last thing he wanted was a shoot-out in the middle of a bunch of kids.

"Turn left now," Michelle said into his ear.

He hung a left and found himself next to a large boulder with some dying flowers planted around it.

"Around the rock and up the path," Michelle said. "Go. Go!"

Sean King went.

There were five men after Sean. They were all armed, all had quasi-federal credentials and all had one mission.

Get the man.

Their leader split them up and they branched out across the park, about forty yards behind where they had last seen their quarry. Two other men were patrolling the exits to the park where Sean might come out onto Central Park South.

One man rounded a curve in the path. He had his hand in his pocket, curled around his gun. That meant he only had one hand free to defend himself.

It wasn't nearly enough.

The boot hit him squarely in the jaw, breaking it. He went into a crouch and his gun came out of his pocket. The second kick shattered his forearm and the gun nosed muzzle first into the ground. The third blow creased the back of his neck an inch below his medulla, and he would awake in a few hours with an enormous headache in addition to his broken bones.

Like a wisp of wind Michelle moved on to the next target.

Two of the other men had hooked back up, studied the topography, and then divided up once more. The first man headed north and west and the other in the opposite direction. In the growing darkness the second man didn't realize the person just passing by him— wearing a long black coat and a baseball cap tugged low—looked familiar until it was too late. The fist dug into his kidney. He bent over in tremendous pain and was felled by a thunderous kick to his jaw. He dropped to the ground unconscious, his shattered face already swelling.

Michelle kept moving.

"Sean," she said into her wrist mic, "where are you?"

"Coming up on Central Park South by the horse carriages."

"Nix that. They'll have it covered. Head on toward Columbus Circle, but stay in the park."

"What's your status?"

"Two down, a few more to go."

Michelle moved, but not quite fast enough. The blow glanced across her forehead and dug into her ear. She twisted sideways, found purchase on the asphalt path, pivoted, setting her weight on her right foot, and launched a kick to her attacker's left knee.

Michelle Maxwell loved attacking knees. It was the largest joint in the body where four bones—the patella, the femur, the fibula, and the tibia—all came together like a highway interchange and were held together by an array of ligaments, muscles, and tendons. It is one of the most intricate parts of the body and critical for mobility.

Michelle destroyed it.

She pushed through the grouping of bones, ripping muscle and tendons and ligaments, which unraveled like sprung springs, cracked the patella, and torqued the femur and fibula backward to angles they were never intended to go. The man screamed and crumpled to the ground, holding his ruined leg.

When you took out the knee, you took out the fight. Men, even trained ones Michelle knew, often aimed for the head, believing their superior strength would make it a knockout blow. But the head was problematic. The skull was thick, and even if you broke someone's jaw or nose they would not necessarily be incapacitated. Not so with the knee. No one could fight effectively on one leg, and no one could fight at all when in that much pain.

Michelle used her elbow, cocked at a forty-five-degree angle where it was at its strongest position, to deliver the putdown blow to the man's head. She dug out the man's cred pack and earbud and jerked the power pack running to the bud from his belt. Last, she ripped open his shirt. All she saw was white skin. No body armor. That was good to know.

She put the bud in her free ear and listened to the stream of chatter as she kept moving forward. It was clear they were on to her presence. Reinforcements had been called in. She heard some names go back and forth, none of which she recognized. And no one identified what agency, if any, they were with. She looked at the ID card and the badge she'd taken from the man. They seemed official but it was an organization she'd never heard of. There were so many now, and when you introduced the staggering number of private contractors into the equation, things got very confusing very fast.

She turned off the power box and spoke into her own mic. "Sean, three down, but they've called in reinforcements. What's your status?"

"Coming up on Columbus Circle. Where are you?"

"Somewhere behind you. Once you get to the circle, get in a cab and go."

"And you?"

"I'll meet you at the train station like we planned."

"Michelle, I'm not leaving you out here—"

"Sean, don't play the gentleman. We don't have time. See you in twenty."

Then she heard the click of the hammer on the gun being pulled back. And then another. One at four o'clock, the other at seven. One foot away, max. They had screwed up with their tactical positioning. Too close to her. Way too close.

Michelle closed her eyes, framed it out in her head.

Four o'clock target was to her right, her natural path of movement. Pivot on left foot, bend her torso downward in the same direction, as her right leg delivered a side kick to the man's right knee, effectively crushing it. Then reverse her pivot, duck, roll, while the man is going down, flailing, screaming over his ruined limb and unwittingly providing cover for her against the other shooter. Gun out, one-handed shot, pistol held sideways, aiming between the gap of her human shield at the other man, who would have instinctively moved to his left as his partner crumpled in the same direction from Michelle's strike. No body armor, so torso shot to incapacitate, then one to the head for the kill. Elbow to the neck of four o'clock, who would get to live, and she'd sprint on to Columbus Circle.

It was all doable. Fifty-fifty, maybe sixty-forty her way if she hit all her marks at the exact right moment.

Calculation was complete, except for one variable. Sean would be safe by now. Had to be. Safer than she was in any event. She opened her eyes.

Before she could move, however, the pistols fired.

58

Sean heard the shots and turned back toward the park and away from the cabstand at Columbus Circle. Panicked, he spoke into his mic. "Michelle? Michelle, are you okay?"

No answer.

"Michelle!"

Silence.

Sean turned to run back into Central Park.

People seized him.

"What the—" He grabbed his gun.

There were two men.

"Move, move," one said into his ear.

"Who the hell are—"

"Kelly Paul," the second man hissed into his ear. "Now move."

"But my partner—"

"No time. Move."

They hustled him back into the park through another entrance.

A minute later he was pushed under a blanket on

the floor of one of the horse carriages that was making a slow meander through the park. The two men disappeared and the driver, wearing a shabby, old-fashioned top hat and long black rain slicker, flicked his whip and the horse increased its pace.

When Sean started to pull the blanket down, the driver said, "Keep it on, mate. Not out of the woods yet."

That was when Sean felt a body next to him. He gripped a leg and then a hand and then what felt like a breast.

"Wow, your timing really sucks."

"Michelle?"

He maneuvered the blanket around until he could just make her out in the dark.

"What the hell happened back there?" he asked.

"Tight spot. Probably wasn't going to make it, but turns out we had some reinforcements in Central Park too."

"It's Kelly Paul."

"Figured, yeah."

The horse clip-clopped through the park and back out onto the street.

"So much for a fast getaway," said Michelle.

The driver heard this and said, "Sometimes slow is best. The other side just hightailed it after a decoy we sent out. You can come up for air now."

They both slid up in the seat and pulled the blanket down at the same time.

The driver turned sideways and looked at them. "Cut it close."

"Yes we did," Sean agreed. "So you know Kelly Paul? How?"

"Not going there."

"That's a big favor you just did us."

"You're lucky she's on your side."

"What about the guys in the park? The shots?"

"Your friend here disabled three of them. Bones busted, all out cold. The shots you heard were the pistols of two others going off right when we hit them. Apparently they had orders to take your lady out. Their shots missed, obviously, though not by much. Our equipment didn't. They'll live. The scene will be cleansed. The police report will never be filed. Never happened. Officially."

"Lot of weight behind them," said Michelle.

"Obviously." The man turned back around.

Sean said, "So Kelly had planned for this?"

"She plans for everything. She said you two were the tip of the spear. But a spear also has a handle." He tipped his hat. "We're the handle."

"Thanks," said Michelle. "We owe you."

Over his shoulder the driver said, "You two ever took the full carriage ride?"

"No," said Sean. "And I don't think we have time to do it now."

"We'll take a rain check, though," said Michelle quickly, snatching a glance at Sean.

The driver slowed the carriage near an intersection.

"Straight down that street. There's a car waiting, red four-door Toyota. Bloke at the wheel is named Charlie."

Michelle shook his hand. "Thanks again. I'd be dead right now if it weren't for you guys."

"We'd all be dead if it weren't for some guys," said the driver. "Just stay alive so we didn't waste the effort."

They stepped down from the carriage, walked off in the gloomy rain, found the car, and were soon on their way to Penn Station.

They retrieved Michelle's Land Cruiser from a nearby garage, gassed it up, and were on their way north before midnight. Michelle had changed the license plates on her SUV, replacing them with a pair of sterilized ones, just in case.

As they left Manhattan behind them, Sean reached out his hand and gripped Michelle's arm. "Like the guy said, we cut it close. Way too close."

"But we're alive. That's what counts."

"Does it?"

She glanced at him as she changed lanes and accelerated. "What do you mean?"

"Can we both really keep doing this until it comes to the point where way too close instead becomes, 'If she'd just not gone through that other doorway'?"

"We both take risks. It could be you too."

"You take far more risks than I do."

"Okay, so what?"

He removed his hand, looked away, and watched the wink of big-city lights in the side mirror until they disappeared from view.

"Okay, so what?" she said again.

"I don't know where I'm going with this."

"I think you do know."

"Okay. If it were just the two of us, you'd be dead."

"You did the best you could. And the alternative was what? Do nothing?"

"Maybe that would've been the smart thing to do."

"Smart for our safety maybe, not so good for trying to solve the case, which happens to be our job."

When Sean didn't say anything she added, "We're in a dangerous business. I thought we both understood that. It's like playing in the NFL. Every Sunday you know you're going to get your ass kicked but you do it anyway."

"Well, players retire too, before it's too late."

"Not many do. At least voluntarily."

"Well, maybe we should think about it. Seriously think about it."

"Then what would we do?"

"There's more to life than this, Michelle."

"Is this because we slept together?"

"Probably, yes," he conceded.

"So now we have something to lose?"

"Us, we have us to lose. Maybe you could . . . you could do something else."

"Oh, I get it. I'm the girl. Let the big strong guy do the heavy lifting, play the hero while I stay home in pumps and pearls and bake the cookies and pop out the babies."

"I didn't say that."

"In case you missed it, slick, I can take care of myself."

"I'm not denying that."

"So if you're really gung ho on this domestication thing why don't *you* stay home and play house, and I'll kick down the doors and shoot the guns?"

"I can't live my life that way. Always worried that you wouldn't come home."

She pulled off at an exit, drove the truck onto the shoulder, slammed the gear shift into park, and faced him.

"Well, how do you think I'd feel if *I* were the one waiting at home?"

"The same as me," he said quietly.

She nodded. "That's right. The same as you. At least if we're out here together, we have each other. We can rely on each other to get us both home every night."

"And if we both take it in the end? Like what almost happened tonight?"

"I can't think of any other way I'd want to go out. How about you?"

After a long moment of silence he tapped the steering wheel. "Put it in gear. We've got a job to do."

"So we're on the same page now?"

"Actually I'm pretty sure we always were."

59

The SUV had screeched to a halt on Fifth Avenue, the door had opened, two burly men had jumped out, lifted Peter Bunting completely off the pavement, and thrown him into the vehicle before he knew what was happening. The truck had raced off and he'd found himself squished between his two captors. They said nothing in response to his questions. They never even looked at him.

The place they took him to was belowground and heavily secured. It was a location New Yorkers would walk over millions of times a day and never know was even there. The room was dark. Bunting stared up at the man in fear.

James Harkes looked different than he had in past meetings. He was dressed the same; black suit that could barely restrain his muscular physique. But his demeanor was different. It was crystal clear that Bunting was no longer in charge.

If I ever was.

Harkes was. Or rather whomever Harkes was

reporting to, and Bunting now had a solid idea of who that was.

"Let's go over your debrief one more time, Bunting."

There was no more Mr. Bunting.

"We've been over it three times. I've told you everything."

"We'll go over it until I'm satisfied."

When Bunting finished Harkes said, "Why did you meet with Sean King?"

"Are you keeping my calendar now?"

Harkes didn't answer him. He was texting something on his BlackBerry. He looked up when he was finished. "There are certain people, all of whom would be familiar to you, that are not happy about your recent performance."

"I was already aware of that," Bunting shot back. "If that's all you wanted to tell me, I'd like to go now."

Harkes rose, went to the wall, and flicked a switch. The wall suddenly became transparent. As Bunting looked closer he saw that it was a one-way mirror. Seated in the brightly lit room was Avery. Bunting could see that he was strapped to a gurney. There was one intravenous cannula going to each of his arms. The young man was convulsed with fear. His head was turned and he seemed to be staring directly at Bunting, but it was apparent he couldn't see him. With the special glass and the bright lights he would only be able to see his own terrified countenance reflected back. A heart monitor on a stand was next to the gurney with a line running to Avery's neck.

Bunting shouted, "What the hell is going on?"

"Avery screwed up. King tracked you through him. And you were aware of it but didn't bother to tell me."

"I don't answer to you."

Harkes moved with astonishing speed. The blow hit Bunting right above the left eye. Harkes's hand felt like a block of cement. The blood pouring from a gash on his forehead, Bunting fell forward in his chair, feeling sick to his stomach from the violence of the strike.

He struggled to catch his breath. "Look, you bastard, Foster and Quantrell aren't the only game in town—"

Harkes hammered a fist into Bunting's right kidney, doubling him over and dropping him to the floor. This time he did throw up. An instant after the vomit left his mouth he was yanked up and thrown back in the chair with such force that he nearly toppled over backward. When his breath returned Bunting said, "What the hell do you want from me?"

Harkes handed him a remote control device. "Hit the red button."

Bunting looked down at the instrument in his right hand. "Why?"

"Because I said to."

"What will happen if I do?"

Harkes looked through the mirror at Avery. "You're a smart man. What do *you* think will happen?"

"What is that stuff hooked up to Avery?"

"Two IV lines and a heart monitor."

"Why?"

"When you push the red button you will put a series of steps in motion. Saline solution will begin flowing through both lines."

"Saline?"

"To ensure the lines aren't blocked so the chemicals that will be flowing through them next will not become mixed and possibly occlude the needles. If that happens the drugs don't reach the body."

"What drugs? Some sort of truth serum?"

An amused look eased across Harkes's normally serious features. "The first one through is sodium thiopental. That'll knock a lightweight like Avery out in three seconds. The next drug is pancuronium; it causes paralysis of the skeletal and respiratory muscles. The final drug through is potassium chloride."

Bunting paled. "Potassium chloride? But that stops the heart. That'll kill him."

"That's sort of the point. What do you think we've been talking about here, Bunting? A slap on the wrist?"

"I'm not pushing the button."

"I would reconsider if I were you."

"I'm not going to kill Avery."

Harkes eased a .44 Magnum pistol from his shoulder

holster and rested the muzzle against Bunting's fore-head. "I can hardly describe what the load chambered in this gun will do to your brain."

Bunting started breathing fast and closed his eyes. "I don't want to kill Avery."

"That's progress. You've gone from 'I'm not going to kill Avery' to 'I don't *want* to kill Avery.'" Harkes thumbed the hammer back on the Magnum. "One pull and most of your impressive gray matter will be on the back wall over there. Is that what you want?" He brushed the steel against Bunting's cheek. "Think about it. You're rich. Beautiful homes, your own jet. A sexy little wife who thinks you're hot shit. Three kids who'll grow up and make you proud. You've got a lot to live for. Avery, on the other hand, is a completely replaceable nerd. A loser. A nothing."

"If I push the button you'll just kill me too."

Harkes said, "Fair enough." He holstered his gun, took an envelope out of his pocket and took out four photos, lining them up on the table. "Change of tactics." He indicated the photos. "Tell me where you want me to start."

Bunting looked down at the photos and his heart skipped a beat.

His wife and three children were all lined up in a neat little row.

When Bunting said nothing Harkes added, "I'll give you a choice. We kill her, the kids get to live."

Bunting's grabbed the photos and held them against

his chest, as though that simple action would protect them. "You will not hurt my family!"

"We either kill the lady or all three kids. It's up to you. As a suggestion, if we nail the kids you and the missus can always adopt."

"You bastard. You heartless, sick bastard!"

"If I don't get an answer in five seconds, they'll be dead in five minutes. All of them. We know the kids are sleeping over at your sister-in-law's in Jersey. We have people there to do the termination right now. And please don't think we won't."

Bunting picked up the remote and pushed the red button. He wouldn't look in the direction of Avery. He couldn't. He held the button down, closed his eyes.

Three minutes passed in silence.

"You can look now."

"No."

"I said look." The slap across his face made Bunting's eyes pop open. An iron grip around the base of his neck made him look at the mirrored wall. What he saw stunned him.

Avery was still there, alive. As Bunting continued to watch, men came in and unstrapped the lines from Avery and then freed the restraints on the gurney. He sat up, rubbed his wrists, and looked around in both bewilderment and relief.

Bunting tilted his head upward to look at Harkes, who relaxed his grip.

"Why are you doing this?"

"Get out," said Harkes. As Bunting slowly rose Harkes ripped the pictures out of his grasp. "But keep in mind that anytime I want they're dead. So if you're thinking about talking to King again, or maybe the FBI, I would think real hard before you do."

"So this is a warning?" Bunting said shakily.

"It's more than a warning. It's inevitable."

Ten minutes later Bunting was in a car heading back to his house. His face hurt, his heart ached, tears soaked the collar of his shirt. He made six calls, all to people high up in the government. These numbers were for his use only, so there would be no doubt as to who was calling. They were monitored 24/7. Bunting rarely called them, but when he did they were always answered.

Six calls. And not one of them picked up.

60

Sean and Michelle finally reached Portsmouth, where they stopped at a pancake house and ate a quick breakfast, paying in cash. Then, exhausted, they slept in the truck in the parking lot for one hour. When Michelle's cell phone alarm went off they awoke and looked groggily at each other.

Sean checked his watch. "Six more hours to go. Be there by lunchtime."

Michelle said, "After this is over I am never, ever, driving to Maine again."

"I never even want to get in a car again."

"We can't go back to the inn."

"I know. That's why I'm calling Kelly Paul right now."

"What if they can trace your phone?"

"I swapped out the SIM card for another one I got while we were in New York. I texted her with the new info."

"How'd you leave it with Bunting?"

"He said he'd think about it. I left him my new contact info too."

"Think we'll hear from him?"

"I hope to God we do."

"And what about the guys in the park? They were definitely set on killing us. If Bunting was involved with them?"

"I looked the guy in the eye, Michelle. He's scared. And not just for himself. He's terrified for his family. My gut tells me he had nothing to do with the attack against us."

"You think he might be dead?"

"What do you mean?"

"They obviously knew you two met. They might have taken it out on him."

"I don't know. If he is dead we'll know soon enough."

They reached Machias by one thirty. After receiving Sean's call, Kelly Paul had arranged another place for them to stay. She'd moved their things there and given them directions to it.

When they pulled up in front of the rustic cottage that was set near an isolated stretch of coast about five miles from Martha's Inn, Kelly Paul came outside to greet them.

"Thanks for the help down south," said Michelle, as she stretched and did a couple of deep knee bends to work the road kinks out.

"I never send people on a mission without backup. It's an essential part of the equation."

Sean said, "Well, it would have been nice to know about it. I almost shot one of your guys."

"I tend to keep things close to the vest. Maybe too close," she admitted.

"But you did save our lives."

"After risking them by having you make contact with Bunting."

"Well, without risk there is no reward," said Michelle.

"Where's Megan?" asked Sean.

"Still at Martha's Inn."

"By herself?"

"No, she's got police protection there."

"How did that happen?"

"I made a few phone calls and the people I called made a few phone calls. It's the best we can do right now. You two are obviously marked. How did it go with Bunting?"

"He's stuck right in the middle and growing desperate. He said he had nothing to do with the murders, and I believe him. We're afraid he might be dead."

Michelle said, "Did you know all along Bunting wasn't behind this?"

"Not for certain, no. But the picture is getting clearer by the minute. And your meeting with him served one important purpose."

"What was that?" asked Sean.

"James Harkes will now be turned loose to clip his wings."

"So you *do* think he might already be dead?" said Michelle.

"No, at least not yet. When they went after you, I'm sure they also sent a very direct message to Bunting: 'Talk about this again to anyone and you will suffer.' They probably threatened his family too."

"And that's good for us why?" asked Michelle.

"Because now Bunting can be convinced to work with us."

"But according to you they just told him if he tried anything he was dead," said Sean.

"One thing you have to understand about Peter Bunting is that he is very smart and very resourceful. He is no doubt feeling cornered now. Maybe even beaten. But then he will start to think about it. He hates to lose. That's why he makes such a brilliant watchdog for this country. And on top of it, he's truly patriotic. His father was in the military. He bleeds red, white, and blue. He will defend his country to the last."

"You seem to know a lot about him," said Michelle.

"I almost went to work for him. I make a point of knowing as much as I can about such people."

"How do we get to him?" asked Sean.

"Actually, I believe he'll get to us," replied Paul.

61

Bunting's wife *was* wearing the new sexy lingerie when he got home at three a.m. She had long since fallen asleep, and he had chosen not to wake her. With Harkes's permission he had earlier texted her so she wouldn't be worried and call the police. He passed through the bedroom where she slept and into the bathroom, where he cleaned up his face. He looked at himself in the mirror and saw the reflection of a man who had fallen a long way in a short time.

He took some ice from the minibar and held it against the nasty bruise on his head while he sat fully dressed in his walk-in closet. His phone would ring from time to time. He would glance at the screen. Three times it was Avery. He never answered it.

What would he say?

Sorry, Avery, I chickened out and sacrificed you and it's only by the grace of God and the unfathomable tactics of the assholes I'm involved with that you're not dead.

He had stood in the doorways of each of his kids' bedrooms. They were lavish spaces, far beyond what any child, no matter how affluent, needed or probably

417

even cared for. He was thrilled his kids were in New Jersey. But realistically they wouldn't be any safer there. Harkes could reach them anywhere.

He walked back to his closet, sat in the chair there, and thought about it. Foster and Quantrell had him cornered right now. But what was the endgame here? Edgar Roy was still sitting in that prison; the E-Program was still operating, albeit at a slower pace. If Edgar were proved innocent, all would be right with Bunting's world. But Foster and certainly Quantrell didn't want that. They wanted to scrap the E-Program. Bunting understood now that there was only one way to guarantee that would happen.

He slipped off his tie and his jacket, kicked off his shoes, pulled off his socks. He trudged into the bedroom and stood next to the sleigh bed. It had been imported from France and was made of some kind of unique leather and antique wood. He couldn't remember the names. It had such a huge footprint that he and his wife almost needed a GPS to find one another within its confines. He watched the rise and fall of her chest. No trophy wife was she. His kids were her kids. They had so much. They had it good. No, they had it great.

But I've really got nothing because it can all be taken away. I can be taken away. Which means she has nothing. Which means my kids have nothing.

He kept imagining James Harkes coming through

the door with knife and gun in hand and his wife and kids defenseless against him.

Bunting spent another hour wandering his New York City mansion. He passed the maid's room, the chef's quarters. The driver didn't live on the premises. A second maid did. They had a nanny, too. She was asleep. Like all normal people, she would be at this hour.

Bunting was awake because he wasn't normal. Harkes was awake because he was abnormal. And Ellen Foster was probably at her executive desk right now plotting with Mason Quantrell to utterly destroy Bunting.

His phone rang again. It was Avery again. This time he answered it.

Before the other man could speak, Bunting said, "I'm glad you're okay."

"What? How did you know?"

"They didn't tell you?"

"Tell me what?"

"It's complicated, Avery, very complicated."

"Mr. Bunting, I think they were going to kill me."

"There was no thinking about it, they were."

"But why?"

"Edgar Roy. Carla Dukes. Mistakes, Avery, mistakes."

"So why didn't they do it then, kill me?"

Bunting leaned against a wall of his mansion. "Proving a point."

"To who? Me?"

"Realistically speaking, Avery, you mean nothing to them. They were making the point to me."

"To *you*? Were you there?"

"I was in the next room."

"My God. Could you see what was happening to me?"

Bunting debated whether to lie or not. "No, I couldn't. I only heard about it later." *I'm so weak I can't even tell him what I did.*

"Things are really getting out of hand."

"They've been out of hand for a while, Avery."

"What can we do? Can you call somebody?"

"I've tried. They're not listening, apparently."

"But you're Peter Bunting, for God's sake."

"I'm sorry to inform you, but that means jack shit to these folks."

"If they come and get me, next time I don't think I'll be as lucky."

"Neither will I."

"They wouldn't harm you, sir."

Bunting felt like laughing. He felt like sliding down the gilded banister in the two-story foyer of his insanely expensive home screaming at the top of his lungs. Instead he quietly said, "You think?"

"Is it that bad?"

"I'm afraid so."

He heard the other man sigh. "I can't believe we have no one to turn to."

The Sixth Man

The man's words perked up something in Bunting's tired mind. "Sir, did you hear me?"

Bunting said, "I'll call you back. Get some sleep. And keep your head down."

He clicked off and looked at his phone.

Did he have someone to turn to?

Did he dare?

Hell, did he have a choice?

He went to his bedroom and lay down next to his wife. He put an arm protectively across her. He had made up his mind.

I'm not going down without a fight.

62

"What are you two doing here?"

Eric Dobkin was dressed in jeans, thick socks, and a cotton sweater as he stood in the doorway of his house.

Sean and Michelle looked back at him.

Sean said, "We need to talk."

When Dobkin made no move to open the door farther Michelle said, "Can we come in, or do we do the powwow out in the cold?"

"It's not that cold."

"I grew up in Tennessee, Eric. *This* is like Antarctica to me."

He motioned them in and then glanced behind the pair as he closed the door.

Michelle noted this observation. "We made sure we weren't followed."

"You guys are putting me in a pretty awkward situation," said Dobkin sourly.

"Everyone's in an awkward situation," retorted Sean.

"And I thought you wanted to be in the loop with us," added Michelle.

"In a limited way."

"Doesn't work that way," said Sean.

"In for a dime, in for a dollar," added Michelle.

"What do you want?"

Sean and Michelle sat on the couch in the front room. Dobkin remained standing.

Michelle asked, "Where're your wife and the kids?"

"Out. I had today off, just catching up on a few things."

"Well, we have a few things to catch up on too."

"Like what?"

Sean said, "Just to confirm, the same gun killed both Bergin and Dukes?"

Dobkin sat down across from them and nodded. ".32 ACP."

"Anything else new on the case?" asked Sean.

"MSP is just pulling support, like I said. FBI is running the show. And Megan Riley is getting some police protection."

"We know," said Michelle.

"You two could probably use some protection too. The shooter who killed Murdock was firing at you too, Michelle."

"Trust me, I know. But protection would really cramp my style."

"Who cares about your style if you're dead?"

"Eric, if you help us break the case it'll do great things for your career," said Michelle.

"And if I stick my nose in and mess things up, it'll mean the *end* of my career," retorted Dobkin.

"I thought you Maine guys were made of hardy stuff," she said.

"We're also born with brains!"

"Then why don't you start using yours?" she snapped.

He rose. "Look, I don't have to listen to this crap. I covered your butt when Murdock went down. I emptied my clip at where those shots came from. And I gave you info I didn't have to. So lay off me."

Sean sat forward. "Okay, okay, you know what, you're right." He fell silent, letting Dobkin calm down and retake his seat. "For a change of pace, would you like us to fill you in?"

"I don't know," Dobkin said warily. "How bad is it?"

"So you *have* been thinking about the case?" Sean said.

"If I weren't thinking about it I don't deserve to be a cop."

"Before we tell you what we know, what do you think is going on?" asked Michelle.

Dobkin rubbed his chin. "If I had to guess, and that's all it would be, I'd say Roy must have some sort of government connection beyond the IRS. I mean why else would the FBI be all over this?"

Sean said, "Without confirming or denying that, I can tell you that it has a lot to do with national security. And that Roy is on America's side. And that those six bodies came along awfully conveniently."

"You saying he was set up?"

"Yeah, I am."

"Can you prove it?"

"Working on it. But there are some heavy hitters on this. Real heavy. We encountered them down in New York and almost didn't make it back to Maine."

"What happened in New York?" asked Dobkin.

"Let's just say we have seen the enemy and they play for keeps." Michelle added, "And they carry creds that would get them into just about any secure location in this country."

Dobkin stared at her with an incredulous look. "Wait a minute. Are you saying the bad guys are *our* guys?"

"Well," said Michelle, "it's always been my philosophy that if they're bad guys they can't be our guys."

Dobkin sat back and rubbed his thighs. "Look, I'm just a state trooper. I don't know anything about stuff like this. I don't know how the federal side works."

"Or doesn't work," said Sean.

"So what do you want from me?" Dobkin said abruptly.

"We need to make sure if we need another gun you'll be there."

"Like you were for me the night Murdock was killed," said Michelle.

"I don't mind helping folks out. But the bottom line is I'm a cop. I can't run around being a vigilante. They'd throw me out of the MSP."

Sean said, "We're not asking you to do anything like that. I'm just asking you to step up to the plate in case enemies of this country come to town looking to hurt America."

"But you said our guys basically are the enemy. And you still haven't given me any proof of that."

"Like I said, we're working on that. But we have limited resources and the other side has no such problem. So we're here to ask for your help if we need it. And I promise not to ask for it unless we really need it because from what we've seen so far, it's dangerous as hell."

Dobkin studied the floor. When he looked up he said, "I'm not going to let anybody screw with my country without a fight."

"That's all I wanted to hear," said Sean.

"Thanks, Eric," added Michelle. "It means a lot."

"So do you think you can really pull this off?"

"With a little luck and a little help from some friends," said Sean.

63

Ellen Foster walked down the hall as though she owned the place, nodding and smiling to people she knew. They all smiled back, for she was a Cabinet secretary and thus was owed substantial deference. While it was true that a person had never gone from being secretary of Homeland Security to the office of the president, there was something in Foster's demeanor that hinted the woman believed she could be the first.

The Secret Service agent respectfully nodded to her and opened the door. She was not in the Oval Office that was used primarily for ceremonial purposes. She was instead in the president's working chambers in the West Wing. This was where the real action took place.

The man himself rose to greet her. The only other person in the room was the president's national security advisor, a bulky man with a perpetual scowl and a twenty-year-old comb-over. They all sat and engaged in some perfunctory pleasantries that none of them gave a damn about. Then they settled down to business. This was a hastily arranged meeting crammed between two others, so Foster knew her time was limited. She got to the point as soon as the president sat back, the cue for her to present her agenda.

"Mr. President. I hoped to be bringing you better news, but I'm sorry to have to inform you that the E-Program matter has become untenable."

The president slid off his glasses and put them on the desk. He aimed a glance at his national security advisor, whose expression could hardly become any more melancholy. The notepad he was holding quivered slightly in his hands. He put it down on the table next to him and capped his pen. No notes of this.

"Give me the essential details, Ellen," said the president.

When she finished, the president leaned back in his chair. "This is truly unbelievable."

"I concur, sir," said Foster smoothly. "It's one reason that I kept requesting more control over the E-Program. Because of its *limited* success, Peter Bunting really has been given a free hand to operate. Oversight measures that would routinely be in place weren't. It's far more due to the relevant congressional bodies, Mr. President, than the executive side. But the situation has become fraught with risk for *everyone*."

The president's face flushed. "It's a nightmare enough that our top analyst is sitting in Cutter's Rock accused of six murders. I talked to Bunting directly about this. He assured me the situation was under control. That whatever happened with Edgar Roy would not affect the program's ongoing viability."

"I can't speak for Mr. Bunting, of course, sir, but from what I've seen the situation could not be more out of control."

"And now you're telling me that you suspect Bunting of orchestrating a series of killings, including that of an FBI agent. My God." He aimed another glance at his advisor, who sat with his hands in his lap but chose not to speak.

"I know it comes as a shock, sir," said Foster. "As it did to me when I learned about it barely an hour ago. That's why I requested this meeting. And to make matters even worse, we actually suspect him of involvement in a fifth death."

Both men stared at her, waiting for an elaboration.

"There was an E-Program recruit named Sohan Sharma. He made it all the way to the Wall. He failed that test miserably and was supposedly discharged through the normal protocols."

"But you suspect otherwise?" asked the president.

"Shortly after he failed the Wall, Sohan Sharma was killed in a car accident. I've seen the autopsy report. His neck was broken. But the ME suspects that Sharma was already dead when the accident occurred."

"Meaning Bunting had him killed? Why?" asked the president.

"My sources tell me that Sharma was his last hope to find a suitable replacement for the outgoing Analyst.

When Sharma failed, I believe that Bunting simply snapped and had him killed. Bunting is under enormous pressure with the E-Program, sir. Another of its drawbacks. I really don't think the man is stable."

"Unbelievable," said the president, shaking his head. "What a damn debacle. And on my watch."

The advisor coughed and said, "Your being on top of this is appreciated, Ellen."

Foster flashed him an appreciative look. This had not occurred by happenstance. She had spoken at length with the man about this exactly sixty minutes ago. She did so because his support was critical for her goals.

The president looked back at Foster. "You have to stay in the loop on this, Ellen. I know you've been hamstrung on this to an unconscionable degree, but I really want you on this."

"I will have no higher priority."

"I'm assuming the CIA is up to speed?"

"Yes. I've personally filled in the director. Now, I do think it imperative, after we successfully handle the E-Program matter, that fundamental structural changes be put into place."

"I would welcome your input," said the advisor, and the president nodded in agreement.

Foster said grimly, "For far too long we've put all of our eggs in one basket. And while there are those who still complain about interagency cooperation being a problem, that really is simply not true. And the key is redundancy. I've been preaching that ever since I took over at DHS. With responsibility and intelligence analysis spread over multiple platforms, this current situation never would have happened. I don't think we could put too high a value on avoiding that in the future."

"Completely agree with that assessment," said the president. "It's spot-on. I've never been comfortable with the E-Program arrangement, despite, as you say, its limited successes."

"I knew that, sir. Your instincts have always been rock-solid."

Actually, this president had lauded the results of the E-Program's clandestine work at every available opportunity, chiefly because its widespread successes had lifted his approval rating to new highs. But the three people in this room also knew that facts were never allowed to get in the way of political survival.

"And what of Bunting?" asked the president.

"I'm working with the FBI to build the case against him. It can be handled discreetly. The media will never know the full story, nor should they. National security cannot be compromised simply because a megalomaniac somehow got to the top of the food chain in his field."

"And Edgar Roy?" asked the advisor.

"A different problem," admitted Foster.

"Do you think he's guilty?" asked the president. "Of murdering the six men?"

Foster tapped one of her fingernails on the desk. "Roy is a strange man. I've met him a few times. I could easily see him having a dark side. Whether he indeed did kill those men is not something I can answer definitively. But I can tell you that even if he is eventually tried and acquitted, it will be a long and messy road. There will be requests filed by his attorneys that could reveal much. Far too much."

The advisor stirred. "Things we do not want revealed. Things we *can't* reveal."

"Precisely," said Foster. "And the same holds true for Bunting. If he's really involved in the deaths of these people, it will be a media circus the likes of which we have never seen. And from what I know of Bunting, he will use every resource he has to escape punishment for his crimes."

"You mean even revealing classified material?" said the president with a startled look. "But we would never allow that."

"There is only one person Peter Bunting looks out for and that is Peter Bunting. You can trust me on that. He can sell a bill of goods to anybody, but that's all it is."

The president nodded thoughtfully. "Yes, I can certainly see that now."

Foster added, "And look at the WikiLeaks debacle. Who would have thought that possible? I think we have to assume the worst."

The president sighed and eyed his advisor. "Thoughts?"

Choosing his words with care, the man said, "There are ways. There are always means, Mr. President. To avoid a trial, messy disclosures, and the like."

Foster studied the president carefully to see how he would react to this suggestion. Some chief executives were squeamish about this sort of thing. Others had large backbones and small consciences and never thought twice about it.

"I suppose we should start evaluating some of them," said the president.

Foster gave him a look filled with sympathetic pride. "These decisions are hard, sir, but also easy in a way. When the impact on the country is so clear."

"I'm not putting any of this in writing. In fact this meeting officially never happened," said the president. "But I want my options before any action is taken."

"There may be one caveat to that, Mr. President," said Foster. This was the moment of truth, she knew. This was what she had rehearsed over and over again in the mirror in her private bathroom back at DHS.

The president's gaze was piercing with a flash of anger lurking behind it ready to be unleashed. "Caveat?" Presidents did not like caveats to their decisions.

"Only based on one factor that we don't have control over," she said.

"What is that?"

"We don't know what Bunting may be plotting."

"Well, let's pick the man up and make sure he's not plotting anything."

"We have to tread cautiously there, sir," said Foster, who really didn't want to "pick the man up." "He's smart and resourceful. I'd rather let him play his hand out." She paused and looked at the advisor.

On cue he said, "You mean give him rope to hang himself."

Foster nodded. "You read my mind. Exactly, give him enough rope to hang himself."

"And then we act?" said the president.

"And then we can act in the manner that is most advantageous to us," amended Foster. "And there's one more thing, sir."

The president smiled in an irritated manner. "You're just full of surprises today."

She hurried on, sensing his patience was running out. "Edgar Roy's sister."

"His sister?"

"Half sister, technically. Her name is Kelly Paul." She glanced at the advisor.

"She was one of our very best field agents, Mr. President. Put the woman into any situation, any hot spot around the world, and she would fix the problem, whatever it might be."

"And she's Roy's sister," said the president. "Why am I just hearing about this now?"

"You have many things on your plate, sir," said Foster. "And it really didn't matter until now." She paused. "We think she's now working for the other side."

"Good God! Are you serious?"

The advisor said, "Officially she retired. However, there is some indication that she's back on the job. Only it's not working for us. That we know."

"What could she be after?" said the president.

"In the right situation Edgar Roy would be very valuable to enemies of this country."

The advisor added, "The amount of knowledge the man has about our national security and our tactical and strategic goals is staggering."

"But using her own brother?" said the president dubiously.

"They aren't close," lied Foster. "And Kelly Paul has the reputation, the well-earned reputation, of not allowing anything, not even family, to get in the way of a mission. So if she manages to somehow extract her brother from Cutter's—"

"That's not possible," interrupted the president. "Is it?"

"The facility is very secure, but Paul is very good," replied Foster.

"So we definitely know that she's involved in this?" asked the president.

"Yes. In fact we have information that Paul actually went to visit Roy at Cutter's Rock."

"If that's true, why didn't we arrest her then and there?"

"We have no proof of wrongdoing yet, sir," said Foster. "We didn't even have enough to pull her in for questioning."

"Why would she go there if she's not close to her brother?" the president wanted to know.

Foster hesitated but the advisor came to her rescue.

"Maybe she was there for another purpose, sir. She might have been casing the place."

The president's eyes widened slightly. "Do you really think they are seriously going to try and break him out?"

"No place is escape-proof if you have the right people trying to do the extraction," said the advisor. He eyed Foster. "Are you prepared for such an attempt?"

"Yes, but there are still no guarantees." She looked at the president. "So it may behoove us to really think long and hard about implementing some type of pre-emptive action along the lines we've already discussed."

"With respect to Roy and Bunting?" said the president. Foster nodded and said, "And also Kelly Paul."

He slowly nodded. "I'll give the matter some serious thought."

This wasn't exactly the response Foster had wanted, but her expression didn't show it and she had gotten most of what she wanted.

"Well, it looks like you have the matter well in hand, Ellen," the president said.

It was clear he wanted to move on to other things. While the E-Program was a critical matter for the country, it was only one of a hundred critical matters this chief executive was currently trying to juggle.

She rose and said, "Thank you for meeting with me, sir."

The president shook her hand. "Hell of a job on this, Ellen. Hell of a job."

As Foster walked down the hall to her waiting motorcade, she looked around the White House, as though in her mind she was measuring the windows for new drapes.

Right now, anything felt possible.

64

Sean stared out the window while Michelle cleaned both their guns on the kitchen table. He'd called Megan Riley, who was upset that she had once more been relegated to an afterthought.

"I'm resigning as counsel," she told Sean.

"Megan, please don't do that. We need you."

"What you need, Sean, is a kick in the ass."

"You're part of the team."

"I don't feel like I'm part of anything. Now I don't even get to stay in the same place as you two, so what's the point? I'll leave the court documents at the inn. You can come and get them. I'm heading back to Virginia."

"Megan, just give it a couple of days, please. We really do need you."

"Words, Sean. How about some action?"

"I promise you that your time will come."

There was a long silence. "You've got two days, Sean, and then I'll be back in Virginia."

He'd told Michelle what Megan had said.

"I can't really blame her," said Michelle. "And if

she does jump ship, we'll just have to find another lawyer or you'll just have to do it."

"But she knows a lot. She' could be in danger."

"True, but I'm just not sure what we can do about it."

Sean put his hand in his pocket and pulled out his phone. A message had just come through. "Damn!"

Michelle looked up from her work. "What is it?"

"Someone left a message. I must've been on the phone with Megan."

He listened to the voice mail.

"Who was it?"

"Peter Bunting."

"What did he say?" asked Michelle.

"He wants to talk."

"Kelly Paul was right. He did come to us."

Sean called the man back. He answered on the second ring.

"Hello?"

"It's Sean King."

"Thank you for calling me."

"I'm surprised to hear from you after our last meeting. My partner and I are lucky to still be breathing."

"I don't know what happened after I left you," said Bunting. "But I apologize if you were put in any danger. That was not my intent. For what it's worth the rest of the evening was far from pleasant for me either."

"Okay."

"You don't believe me, do you?"

"Actually, I do."

"I want to meet with you."

"That's what you said on the message. Why?"

"I have a proposition."

"Change of heart?"

"You could say that."

"They've come down hard on you, haven't they?"

"I need to know one thing. Is Kelly Paul working with you?"

"Who?"

"We don't have time for that," Bunting said irritably. "Is she?"

Sean hesitated. "Yes."

There was silence.

"Bunting?" Sean said sharply.

"We really need to meet."

"How can you get away from them? You know they're watching you. In fact they're probably listening to our conversation right now."

"Impossible," said Bunting.

"Why?"

"Because I'm using better scrambling technology than the president of the United States uses for his calls. Not even the NSA can touch it. And as soon as you picked up on your line, my technology pipeline was extended to your phone as well."

"But that still doesn't answer my question of how you can physically get away from them."

"Leave it to me. I didn't build a billion-dollar business in the intelligence arena by being a moron."

"And your family?"

"Let me worry about that. I'm assuming you're somewhere near Edgar Roy. How about we rendezvous halfway? Say Portland, Maine?"

"When?"

"Tomorrow night."

Sean said, "Where in Portland?"

"There's a restaurant down by the waterfront. Clancy's. They're open until midnight. My wife and I used to go there when we were dating."

"If you're trying to set us up—"

"My family is in danger, Mr. King, and I need to make this right."

Sean let the silence linger. He listened to the other man's tight breathing.

"See you in Portland," said Sean.

65

The next night the Bunting family left their brownstone and walked down the street, their two private security men a few yards behind them. The weather had stayed cold, and the Bunting family was bundled up, hats, gloves, and mufflers. Mrs. Bunting walked hand in hand with her youngest child. Not once did the man beside her check his cell phone for messages.

Twenty minutes before they had left, a furniture delivery was made to their residence. Three large boxes. This was not unusual as deliveries often came to the Bunting residence. Mrs. Bunting was an avid shopper.

The men watching from across the street saw the three large boxes carried in and three empty boxes carried out. Only one of them wasn't empty. The truck rattled off down the road and Bunting lay in that box, praying that his subterfuge had worked. After the truck had gone two miles without being stopped, he lifted the top of the wooden box, clambered out, and sat on one of the curved metal bump-outs over the wheel wells.

His thoughts were not on his predicament. Or on

Edgar Roy. Or the E-Program. He was thinking about his wife and children. He was thinking about their next step in his plan. And he bitterly chastised himself for having to put them through this. And of course he prayed that it actually worked.

It has to.

The Buntings' walk lasted about an hour and then they returned to their home. The children raced upstairs to their rooms. Julie Bunting took off her coat and hung it up in the closet. She turned to the man behind her as he also took off his hat, coat, and muffler. He had entered the house hidden in the same box that Peter Bunting had exited from it.

"Peter said you knew what to do," Mrs. Bunting said to the man, who was the same height and build as her husband. With the other man's clothes on he was a perfect decoy.

"I do, Mrs. Bunting. I'll be with you every step of the way."

A minute later Julie Bunting sat down in a chair in the foyer, her hands kneading her thighs. When her husband had come to her, told her what she needed to do, it had collapsed her perfect little world. She was a bright, educated woman. She loved being a wife and mother, but she was no wallflower. She had questioned him at length about what was going on. The little he had told her had frozen the woman's blood.

She had never wanted to know exactly what he did. She knew it was in the government arena, something to do with protecting the country, but that was all. The security team that he employed she had assumed was for this reason and also because the Buntings were wealthy and such people needed security. On the other hand she had her hemisphere of existence: her family, her charities, the wonderful social life of a New Yorker with money to burn. It was really all that she could have wanted in life.

But a colder reality had just settled into her bones. And she had felt guilt for wanting to remain oblivious to his world all these years, especially when it had provided her with such a wonderful existence.

She had asked him, "Are you in danger?"

She loved her husband. They had married before he had had money. She cared about him. Wanted him to be safe.

He would not answer her, which was an answer in itself. "What can I do to help?" she'd asked him.

And the plan had been hatched.

Now it was time for part two of that plan. This segment her husband had insisted on. And she understood quite clearly why. He had taken her through the paces time and again until she felt she could perform it flawlessly. The children had been prepared; the staff the same. She had tried to make it seem like a game to her youngest child, but the older kids knew something was very wrong.

Their father had sat with each of them before heading out in the box. He had told them that he knew they would be brave. He'd told them that he loved them all very much. He told them that he would see them soon. Julie Bunting could tell that it was only this last statement that her husband didn't quite believe.

She had gone to her luxurious spa-like bathroom, cried her tears, washed her face, and emerged ready to do what she needed to do. She headed up the stairs, where her children were huddled in her oldest child's room. They sat on the bed staring at her. She looked back, tried to give them an encouraging smile.

"Are you ready?" she asked.

Each of them nodded.

Her youngest said, "Is Daddy coming back?"

Julie Bunting managed to say, "Yes, sweetie, he is."

She went downstairs and opened the pillbox her husband had given her. She took three of them. They would make her very sick, but that was all. They would mimic medically all the symptoms she wanted to have happen to her. She next picked up the phone and made the call. She told the dispatcher she had taken the pills and needed help. She gave her address.

Then she collapsed to the floor.

The men watching from across the street heard the sirens long before they saw their source. The cop cars, ambulance, and fire engine pulled up in front of the

Bunting brownstone five minutes after Julie Bunting put down the phone. The emergency personnel rushed into the house with their equipment along with two uniformed police officers. Two more police cruisers showed up and the men in them set up a perimeter outside the house.

One man across the street called this development in to their superiors and asked for instructions. They were told to sit tight. They did.

Fifteen minutes later the stretcher came out with a haggard and pale Julie Bunting lying on it; an IV was running into her arm. Moments later the Bunting children came out, all looking terrified and the youngest one crying real tears. The man impersonating Peter Bunting held this child in his arms. All bundled up because of the cold and surrounded by EMTs, the fake Bunting was well obscured from the surveillance going on across the street. They all climbed in the ambulance with Julie Bunting and it headed off, with one cop car in front and one behind.

The same man from across the street called this in.

"Looks like the wife is really sick. The whole family went with them to the hospital, including Bunting."

He listened, nodded. "Right. Got it."

Most of his men stayed at their current location while he sent two of his people after the ambulance.

66

The private wings touched down, the stairs were lowered, and Peter Bunting stepped off into the chilly air flowing into Portland, Maine, from the ocean. He had not used the company jet; that was too easily followed. He'd flown in on a rental jet hired by one of his companies. During the flight he'd gotten a text from the man impersonating him.

It said simply, *GTG*, which was their code for "good to go." If Bunting had gotten any other message he would have known they were compromised.

He walked quickly to the car. There was no driver. No security detail. The wheels were just waiting for him. He climbed in and drove off. As both a New Yorker and a pampered CEO he hadn't driven a car by himself in years. It actually felt good.

Sean edged his head around a corner of the building. Clancy's Restaurant was just across the main street. There were few people about because of the lateness of the hour and the cold weather. Sean huddled in his coat and glanced down the road to his left. Somewhere out there was Michelle, holding a sniper rifle chambering 7.62 175-grain NATO rounds that had an overabundance of knockdown power. She had brought the weapon back with her from Virginia. She had carried the rifle and her sniper stand, disassembled in a black nylon bag, off into the darkness. But Sean was in communication with her through his earbud and power pack. He had lived with a communications bud in his ear for years while standing post as a Secret Service agent. Back then it was his job to look for threats against the president and sacrifice his life for the man if it came to it. Now the threats he would be looking for would be aimed directly at him.

Before leaving for Portland they had arranged for Megan to be brought to the cottage. The local police could manage only a single deputy to guard her at Martha's Inn, and he was nearing retirement. On meeting him Sean had not been impressed with either his skill or his enthusiasm.

Sean had called Eric Dobkin and asked him to watch over Megan while they were gone. He had come immediately. Sean had told him some more of what was going on.

"Real heavy hitters," Dobkin had said. "You sure you don't want me to come with you?"

"We need you here with Megan," said Sean. "No one knows we're here, but then again, there are no guarantees they won't find out."

"I'll do my best, Sean."

"That's all I can ask. And I really appreciate it."

Megan had once more complained bitterly about not being kept in the loop, and while Sean was sympathetic to this plea, he was in no mood to discuss it.

Finally he'd said testily, "The less you know about it, Megan, the safer you'll be. If anything happens you do exactly what Officer Dobkin tells you to do, understood?"

Megan had stood in the middle of the cottage, a defiant look on her face. "Fine, but just so *you* understand, when you get back, I'm out of here."

"You ready?" Sean now said into his wrist mic, as his gaze swept the street.

"Affirmative." Michelle's voice floated into his ear.

"Location?"

"High ground, a hundred yards west of you. I can see everything from here. Perfect sight line to Clancy's."

"How'd you get high ground?"

"Empty building, pathetic back door lock. Everything in place?"

"Affirmative."

"Good, stand by. Let me know when you see him."

"Roger that."

Sean did another turkey peek around the corner. He counted off the minutes in his head and then looked at his watch. One minute to ten. They'd gotten here early in case either Bunting was thinking of setting up an ambush or he hadn't been able to get away from the people watching him and they had come in his place.

The car moved down the street, slowed, and then came to a stop. It turned into a parking spot and the tall man got out.

Sean stiffened.

Michelle's voice came to him. "That's him."

"I see. Do a sweep and report back."

Thirty seconds went by.

"Clear," said Michelle. "No tail."

Sean stepped out onto the sidewalk, his gaze on the tall man across the street. Instead of taking a straight-line path to him, Sean skirted down the sidewalk, keeping close to the storefronts until he was fifty feet past Bunting and behind him.

Sean watched as Bunting stood in front of Clancy's looking around for him. Once he checked his watch.

"Hello, Mr. Bunting. Good to see you again."

Bunting whirled around.

"You startled me. Didn't hear you coming."

"That's the point," said Sean.

"Where's your partner, Maxwell?"

"Around."

"No one followed me."

"Good to know."

Bunting looked at the door to Clancy's. "I think they're still serving. You want to go in?"

"Let's do it."

67

The restaurant appeared empty. No one came to greet them, so Sean led Bunting around a corner and into a smaller room set off the main one. There was only one person in the dining area.

Bunting gasped and stopped when he saw her sitting there.

Kelly Paul looked at him from where she sat at a table with her back against the wall.

"Hello, Peter, it's been a long time," she said quietly.

Bunting shot a glance at Sean. "I didn't know she was going to be here."

"Problem with that?"

"No, I'm actually thrilled to see her."

Bunting sat across from Paul while Sean settled down next to her, his hand in his pocket clenching his pistol.

Bunting said, "I presume you're both armed."

Sean picked up his menu with his free hand. "Why? Make you feel safer?"

"Yes."

She studied Bunting. "Your family?"

"I took certain steps. They're safe, for now. I got confirmation. Thanks for asking."

"I have family in danger too, Peter."

"Yes, I know," he said, looking guilty.

"Is it as bad as I think it is?"

"Probably worse—" Bunting paused because the waitress came over to take their orders. She was wide of hip and weary of face, and her calves were red and puffy, probably from being on her feet for ten hours carrying large platters of seafood and mugs of beer. They ordered coffees and she departed, looking relieved that that was all they desired.

Bunting put down his menu and took off his glasses.

"Tell us," said Paul simply.

"They want to shut down the E-Program. They want to destroy me. They want to do the same to your brother."

"In fact they want things the way they were, you mean," said Paul.

"Yes."

"You had to know this day would come."

"Knowing and doing something about it are two very different things. And I guess I had hoped, however naïvely, that the climate had changed for the better. I was wrong, obviously."

She said, "Who's playing the black chess pieces?"

Sean said, "Hold on, here comes our coffee."

The waitress set down the mugs, creamer, and sugar

and said, "Will you all want anything else? The kitchen is getting ready to close up."

"No, thanks," said Bunting. He handed the woman a hundred-dollar bill and told her to keep the change.

She walked off beaming, and Bunting turned back to Paul.

"The black pieces, Peter?" she said again. "I think I know but I want confirmation."

Bunting pulled out two photos from his jacket. He laid them next to each other on the checkered table-cloth. "Just so we're absolutely clear on the point."

Paul nodded and said, "Thanks for the confirmation."

"So you suspected?" he asked.

"Of course. She was the most logical choice."

"Do you know who they are?" Bunting asked Sean.

Sean couldn't seem to pull his gaze from the photos. "The lady is Ellen Foster from DHS. I don't recognize the man."

"Mason Quantrell, CEO of the Mercury Group."

"They're a big player in the intelligence field, right?" asked Sean.

"One of the biggest. And my chief competitor. Ever since the E-Program came on-line and supplanted what he was doing for the government, he's been mostly relegated to low-hanging and far less valuable fruit. Though he still makes truckloads of money."

"And that didn't sit well with Mr. Quantrell, did it?" asked Paul.

"You know him?"

"Of him. He has a reputation for underperforming and overbilling. In most sectors that would lead to disaster. In the defense and intelligence-gathering world it simply gets you more of what you don't deserve."

"It's not just about the money, it's about the prestige. He doesn't like playing second fiddle, getting my leftovers. He's been after me ever since," said Bunting. "His way is to throw a lot of expensive shit against the wall and see what sticks. No integration. No thought. God forbid any sharing of resources or results. With that philosophy it's a wonder we only had one 9/11."

Paul tapped the photo of Foster. "I knew Ellen Foster before she was Madame Secretary. You would be hard-pressed to find someone more ruthlessly ambitious. With the brains to match."

Sean said, "But DHS? I thought it would be more likely CIA or NSA playing dirty games like this. DHS is homeland security. Are they that big on intelligence now?"

"They want to be the dominant player," answered Bunting. "And they have the budget and manpower to accomplish that. Especially with someone like Foster at the helm. She's a member of the Cabinet. The CIA director does the daily presidential briefings, but he's not Cabinet level. Foster has figured out that she is in a prime position to take over the throne and run America's intelligence empire. And she's making a hard run to do just that. But the E-Program is based on integration among agencies and cooperation. That model does not fit into Foster's plans."

"And Quantrell?" asked Sean.

"Extremely capable and equally adept at playing all sides. He's apparently riding Foster's coattails on this one." She gazed at Bunting. "The bodies in the barn?"

"I believe so, yes. Strongly believe, in fact."

"Six bodies. Eddie was the first E-Six."

Bunting grimaced. "Occurred to me too. Sick bastards' idea of a joke."

"The bodies were never identified," noted Sean.

Bunting shrugged. "Easy enough to do. You wouldn't believe the number of unidentifiable bodies floating around. Foster and Quantrell could get what they needed from multiple sources. Quantrell has assets all over Latin America, the Middle East, and Eastern Europe. Bodies are a dime a dozen in those places. You just ship them back."

"But there was different dirt on the bodies," said King. "That's a red flag."

"In an ordinary legal case, perhaps," said Bunting impatiently. "This is not an ordinary legal case. I don't envision any scenario where Edgar Roy goes on trial. They simply won't let it happen. The dirt is irrelevant. Foster knows that."

"And Eddie knows far too much," added Paul. "Which begs the question of why my brother has been allowed to live this long."

Sean looked at her in surprise at the unemotional way she was discussing her brother's potential murder.

She noted his surprise and said, "If I had time to play the role of the ordinary sister, I would, Sean. I don't." She turned back to Bunting. "Why is he still alive?"

"My theory is that Foster is orchestrating this like some insane symphony. Every piece in its place. She wants to discredit the E-Program and destroy me. Your brother is an integral part of that, so he has to go too. But he has to go down in a way that will satisfy both Foster and the people she has to answer to."

"Like the president?" commented Paul.

"Exactly. They framed him with the bodies in the barn to get him pulled off the E-Program. And I'm certain they've been feeding a pack of lies about me to the people who matter. Merely killing your brother is not enough. Now I have no doubt they plan to murder Edgar, I just don't know when or how. Hell, they'll probably try to blame that on me too, somehow. Bottom line is, I'll be gone, the E-Program will be over, and a concept like that will never be revisited again. Then it's business as usual. That's their plan. And it's actually a damn good one."

"How long have you suspected their involvement?" asked Paul.

"I suspect everyone. But I didn't seriously suspect them until recently. Frankly, though I know anything is possible in the intelligence field, even I didn't think they'd go that far. I was wrong."

"Foster needs political cover on this," noted Paul.

"She's been working that for some time. She's managed to cut off all my critical sources of support. I know she also made a very recent trip to the White House. She probably painted me as the second coming of Attila the Hun. And I can almost guarantee that the discussion involved your brother."

"And me, do you think?" Paul asked him.

"That I don't know," replied Bunting. "They know of your connection, obviously. And they may suspect that you wouldn't just idly stand by while your brother is in such danger."

Sean said, "And you visited your brother at Cutter's. They have to know that."

"I'm quite sure that Ellen Foster has built her political cover at the very highest level," said Bunting. "She excels at stabbing people in the back. And chances are very good she'll come out smelling like the proverbial rose."

Sean said, "I worked on the federal side a long time. I know how dysfunctional it can be, but do you really think a Cabinet secretary is capable of something like this?"

Paul smiled wryly. "You were Secret Service, Sean. You were with the Mr. Cleans of the federal government. Peter and I play in a different neighborhood."

Bunting nodded in agreement. "The intelligence side hoards its toys and scores the occasional triumph at the expense of a competing agency. They try to one-up each other every minute of every day. At least that's how it's worked ever since World War II."

"And until you designed the E-Program and got them to sign off on it," pointed out Paul.

Sean shook his head. "And Foster says to hell with the safety of the American people? Like you alluded to—what about another 9/11 happening?"

Bunting said, "Cost of doing business in their eyes, Sean. And blame can be deflected. You don't reach for such lofty positions in life and not expect the power to come along with it. Believe me, I've met with both Foster and Quantrell recently. Their intentions could not have been clearer. And they've backed me right into a corner."

"So we know the players," said Paul. "We know their strategy. They dealt the hand and they're blaming you for the result. What do we do about it?"

Bunting said, "She's poisoned the well against me. I have no allies left on the government side. I'm a pariah."

"You said she visited the president?" asked Paul.

"Yes. It was an off-schedule meeting, so it must have been important because the president squeezed the time in."

"Who else was there?"

"National security advisor."

"Is he in Foster's pocket too?"

"I believe they have an understanding," replied Bunting. "One of mutual assured cooperation."

"You don't do an off-schedule with the president for anything less than the most critical reasons."

Bunting said, "That's right. What's your best guess?"

Paul said, "She needed authorization for something. Something highly out of the ordinary that she was unwilling to stick her neck out for in the ordinary course of business."

Bunting nodded. "I think you're right."

Sean said, "She's DHS Secretary. According to you she's already had four people killed, including an FBI agent. Hell, isn't that out of the ordinary enough?"

"That was window dressing, Sean," said Paul. "And don't think I'm being callous. I know there are four people dead who shouldn't be. But the blame for those deaths will be placed elsewhere, so in her mind they don't even count. What Foster was probably going to the president for was *explicit* authorization for her to take extraordinary action on her own."

Bunting added, "In other words, she asked for permission to terminate certain people."

Sean looked incredulous. "Terminate certain people? Who?"

Paul said, "Eddie, Peter, and probably me."

"Three American citizens?" said Sean. "You really think the president of the United States would ever authorize that?"

"Mr. Clean again," said Paul. This time she didn't smile.

"Bullshit. Okay, I know the government has people killed. Terrorists, known enemies of the country, the occasional rogue dictator."

"We're a problem for the country, Sean," said Paul. "A serious problem. Eddie will never go to trial. Not with what he knows. If the president has bought the lie that Peter has had people killed, it's not a stretch to believe he would lean toward termination. He wouldn't want a murder trial where certain facts come to light which would be disastrous for America's security. The president is the commander in chief. He has to wear many hats, but that's the most important one. His number one priority is to keep America safe from her enemies. Wherever they might be."

"So let's assume that's the case," said Bunting. "Foster will get her answer. Let's also assume it's a go. She'll waste no time executing the plan. What does she do first?"

"There's little question in my mind about that," said Paul.

"What then?" asked Sean.

"Eddie will not be at Cutter's Rock much longer."

Sean snapped, "You can't possibly be thinking of breaking him out?"

"Oh, *I* won't be the one doing the breaking."

68

Mason Quantrell's aide unlocked the door to the warehouse and Quantrell stepped through. Automatic lights came on and Quantrell blinked to adjust his pupils. The Mercury Group owned this facility, but the chain of ownership was buried so deep that not even an army of lawyers and accountants would be able to dig through to the truth. Every substantial private contractor to the government, particularly those operating in the defense and intelligence fields, had such complex business structures in place. It was a necessity. Prying eyes were everywhere, and all contractors had secrets they didn't want either the government or their competitors to know about.

He eyed the column of black SUVs parked in the middle of the warehouse. He walked past them, evaluating each detail and coming away satisfied. In a corner of the facility a last planning meeting was taking place. All the men seated around the table stood when Quantrell approached.

The look in these men's eyes was clear. They both feared and respected Quantrell, perhaps more fear than respect. Quantrell had never worn the uniform, never fired a gun on behalf of his country, but he knew how to make money supplying those who did. His main business model was hardware sales to the Pentagon. He didn't build the planes, tanks, or ships, but he provided many of the overpriced accessories for them, like ammo, special fuel, missiles, guns, and surveillance and security gear. But he had determined long ago that the real money was in the soft side of war, namely intelligence. The profit margins there were huge, far larger than he had plying the traditional corridors of supporting the defense effort. And the world wasn't always at war, not anymore. But they were always spying on each other, always.

He'd made billions off the soft side by following the old-school models. Lots of analysts, lots of reports that no one had time to read, feeding the competition among agencies that desperately wanted to score a victory at the expense of their sister agencies, even if it meant the actual goal of keeping the country safe was lost. Yes, he'd made a fortune, but it still wasn't enough. And then Peter Bunting had arrived on the scene with a revolutionary model that would soon turn the intelligence-gathering world on its head.

Quantrell's soft business had dwindled, and his anger and frustration had grown.

But now that was all about to change.

"Prepped and ready?" he said to the leader of the team.

The man replied, "Yes, sir, Mr. Quantrell."

The team was comprised of elite foreign mercenaries who would do anything for money. They would never talk about what they'd done because that would kill their livelihood.

Quantrell asked the man some questions to judge whether they were indeed ready. He knew the plan better than anyone but came away satisfied at their level of preparation.

He left the warehouse, got back in his SUV, and was driven off. An hour-long plane ride later he was in D.C.

Though it was late he had another meeting. In his world those that relaxed simply were run over.

Ellen Foster was in her office at DHS. She was working late too. She often worked late. But now she was done. She was driven home surrounded by her security team. The pecking order in D.C. was often delineated by the size of one's motorcade. The president was at the top, followed by the vice president. After that it was a far drop to the rest of the pack. But Ellen Foster was right there.

A man was waiting for her at her elegant home in upper-bracket northwest D.C. Around her lived prominent members of the Washington elite, both in the public and private sectors. He helped her off with her coat when she walked through the door.

"Give me a minute," she told him.

She went upstairs and came back down a few minutes later. She had on the same clothes but had shed her hose and shoes. And she'd let her hair down.

They walked together into the old-fashioned drawing room of the nineteenth-century dwelling. She reclined on the sofa. She motioned for him to sit.

James Harkes sat.

Black suit, white shirt, black tie with nary a wrinkle. His face was impassive as he stared back at her.

"Would you like something to drink, Harkes?"

He shook his head. "No thank you."

"Then can you make me a vodka tonic?" She pointed to the sideboard. "It's all over there."

He dutifully made the drink, handed it to her.

"Thank you." She took a sip, nodded approvingly. "Very good."

"You're welcome." His gaze went toward the window. "You've got a first-rate security detail. They've set their perimeter with a lot of thought. Your alarm system is top-notch, your door locks the best."

She smiled. "Do you know what the best security is?"

He looked at her expectantly.

She rose, went to an antique secretary against one wall, and pushed against a piece of wood facing, and a small door was revealed. She reached in and pulled out a Glock 9mm.

She held it up for him to see. "The best security is

yourself. I wasn't always sitting behind a desk. One of these often came in handy."

Harkes said nothing. She put the gun back and sat down.

"Things are going well," she said.

"Things usually go well until they stop going well."

She lowered her glass. "You have doubts? Issues? You know something I don't?"

He shook his head again. "None of the above. I'm just a cautious man."

"Nothing wrong with that, but you need balance too. Invoke your wild side from time to time."

"Four people dead, five if you count Sohan Sharma. That's wild enough for me."

She said coolly, "Not losing your nerve, are you?"

"Considering I didn't kill any of them, no. But one was an FBI agent. That is particularly troubling."

"There is always collateral damage in situations like this, Harkes. It's unavoidable. You fought in Iraq and Afghanistan. You know that all too well."

"That was war."

"*This* is war, too. You need to understand that right now. Perhaps an even bigger war. This is for the heart and soul of American intelligence."

"And you want to run it?"

"I *should* be the one running it. The agency's name is Homeland Security, after all."

"The CIA—," began Harkes.

"Langley is a joke. The Pentagon listens to no one.

The intelligence czar has no power, and don't even get me started on NSA. It's all very pathetic."

"But the E-Program had merit."

"Stop drinking the Kool-Aid. That was Peter Bunting's world. He owned the space."

"And you didn't."

"Now you're getting with the program. Bunting's an idealistic fool. Can you imagine putting the whole of this country's security on the back of *one* analyst?"

"But that's not really the case, is it? There are still plenty of analysts out there doing what they do. The American intelligence agencies continue to hum along. And Bunting's company does a lot more than the E-Program. They have their fingers in lots of intelligence pies. But Bunting's person was tasked with seeing the big picture, connecting the dots. That's always been lacking across the intelligence spectrum."

She shook her head. "That is a very dangerous philosophy to have."

"What, quality over quantity?"

"We give them our hard-earned work and they get the credit for it. How is that fair?"

"I didn't think fairness was an issue when we're talking about the nation's security."

"I don't want to discuss this with you anymore," she said sharply.

"All right. I was just playing devil's advocate. It's part of my job."

"You can be devilish, can't you, Harkes? You have that reputation."

"I do what needs to be done."

"Bunting's wife attempted suicide. Did you know that?"

"I heard."

"Bunting must be frantic. I can't stand the man professionally, but I have to admit, he does care for his family." Her tone was gleeful.

"And it also helps you," he said.

"Exactly. It takes him off his game. He's not thinking about Edgar Roy. Or anything else. He knows we've set him up to take the blame. But he can't do anything about it. All the people who matter have been dealt with."

"It was a good plan."

She eyed him thoughtfully. "You know, you can relax a bit. You look like you're about to attack someone."

Harkes let his rock-hard body ease just a fraction.

"You've done excellent work, Harkes. I've been impressed by you from day one. I plan on using you a lot in the future."

She crossed her legs and let her dress slip back liberally on her bare thighs as she sat back farther against the cushions.

"I appreciate that, Secretary Foster."

"We're off the clock, Harkes. You can call me Ellen."

Harkes said nothing to this.

"You've had an interesting life, James," she said. "That was one reason I selected you."

"I chose the path less traveled," Harkes said simply.

"Combat hero, field agent with a list of successes. You can shoot straight and go toe-to-toe intellectually with a Cabinet member," she added. "As I can certainly attest."

Harkes said nothing.

She smiled demurely. "Am I making you uncomfortable?"

"Should I be?"

"I guess that all depends on how you want the evening to play out."

"Do you think that wise, ma'am?"

"I'm not old enough to be a ma'am."

"Sorry."

"The staff is off until tomorrow. Security detail is outside and will stay there unless I tell them otherwise. I'm a big girl. You're a big boy."

She stretched out one bare foot and touched his leg. "At least I *hope* you are."

Harkes sat in silence.

"Have you ever done it with a Cabinet member?" she asked.

"No. And since most of the Cabinet are male my options are limited."

"Well, then this is your lucky night."

Foster rose and went to him. She bent down and

kissed him on the lips. "I hope you're impressed. I don't do this for just anybody." She took one more sip of her drink and then put it down. She said casually, "I'm also in the market for a new chief of my personal security detail. I think you may like the fringe benefits offered."

"I don't think so."

"What?" she said, startled.

Harkes rose. "I don't mix business with anything else. Now if there's nothing else you need, I'll be going."

"Harkes!"

"You have a good night, Madame Secretary."

Harkes walked out the front door.

69

Bunting and Paul followed Sean and Michelle back to Machias. On the way Sean filled Michelle in on all that had been discussed at the restaurant. Hours later they pulled their vehicles up to the darkened cottage in the woods and cut their lights. Sean was first to notice something wrong. The door to the cottage was partially open. It was nearly four in the morning and still dark. Michelle noted the open door, too. She slipped out her gun.

Bunting, who had fallen asleep in the other car, awoke and said groggily, "Are we here?"

"Keep quiet," warned Paul, who was driving his rental. "Something's not right."

When Bunting saw that all three had their weapons out he sat upright, fully awake now. "What is it?" he hissed.

"Stay here," ordered Michelle, as she came up next to their vehicle. "And keep down."

Paul said, "I'll stay with Peter."

Bunting instantly crouched down in the floorboard

while Paul's gaze swept the house and the surrounding woods.

Michelle entered through the back door and Sean the front, and they met in the middle of the one-story house. Michelle picked up the overturned chair while Sean looked at the smashed glass cabinet that had sat against a wall, and the upside-down table. Megan Riley's legal documents were scattered across the floor.

But that was all secondary.

"Damn," said Sean in a low voice.

Eric Dobkin lay sprawled on the floor next to the table. He was dressed in civilian clothes because he was doing them a favor. His last favor.

Michelle knelt down next to him. "Looks to be a single GSW to the chest," she said, examining the bloody hole in the man's shirt. She edged him over. "Slug's still in him. No exit wound." Michelle laid the body back down, rose, and stepped back. "I can't believe this happened."

"Front door's been kicked in," noted Sean. "And Megan is obviously not here."

That's when he saw it over behind the couch. Sean picked it up. It was Megan's sweater, with blood all over it. He poked a finger through a hole in the garment. "Not a bullet. Looks like maybe a knife."

"If she's dead why take her body?" said Michelle.

"I don't know. But we have to call the cops."

"Wait."

They looked up to see Kelly Paul and Bunting standing in the front doorway.

"We can't wait, Kelly," said Sean. "This guy is a state trooper. He was doing us a favor. And now he's dead. He's got a wife and three little kids. This is a nightmare."

Michelle said, "And Megan has been taken too." She looked at Sean and added bitterly, "Some guardian angels we were."

They contacted the police. Sean and Michelle waited for them to arrive while Bunting and Paul left. It would have been far too complicated to explain the latter two's involvement. They arranged to rendezvous later.

Before she'd departed Paul had said, "It will be coming soon."

"How are they going to do it?" asked Sean.

"The only way they really can," replied Paul.

"And our response will be?" asked Sean.

"Unpredictable," answered Paul.

"And after that?" said Michelle.

"The real work begins," she said cryptically.

A moment later she and Bunting were gone.

Twenty minutes after that, two state trooper cruisers slid to a stop outside the cottage. Sean and Michelle heard running feet. A few seconds later two troopers appeared in the doorway. Their gazes swung around the room before settling on Sean and Michelle and then, inevitably, on Dobkin's body. They moved forward slowly. Sean recognized them from the Bergin crime scene. He assumed they were good friends of Eric Dobkin. The troopers in this area were probably all close friends.

Another car pulled up outside and a moment later Colonel Mayhew and another trooper came inside.

They all stood around Dobkin's body, staring down at it.

Mayhew finally eyed Sean and Michelle.

"What the hell happened?" he said, his voice low but full of raw emotion.

They both took turns explaining, leaving out the details concerning Peter Bunting and Kelly Paul.

Sean concluded, "Bottom line was we asked Eric to watch Megan Riley for us. We were worried about her after what happened to Bergin."

"And where were you two when all of this happened?" asked Mayhew.

"Portland, running down a lead," answered Michelle.

Mayhew drew a deep breath and said sharply, "Eric is a state trooper. *Was* a state trooper. You shouldn't have been asking him to perform bodyguard services for you. That was not his job."

"You're right," agreed Sean. "We never intended for this to happen."

"You certainly should have known it might happen," retorted Mayhew. "If you thought Riley was in danger then you had to assume that someone might try and harm her. Which would put Eric in danger."

"We feel as bad as anyone about this," said Sean.

"I doubt that," barked Mayhew. "You certainly won't feel as bad as Sally Dobkin when she finds out she's a widow."

Sean looked down.

Michelle said, "Colonel Mayhew, we needed help. Eric was a first-rate man. That's why we asked him for assistance. But we didn't force him to do it. He wanted to help us. He wanted to get to the truth too."

Mayhew didn't look satisfied by this but he broke off gazing at her and looked around. "Any idea who did this?"

Sean and Michelle exchanged a quick glance. They had discussed and decided how they were going to answer this question.

"We don't have the person's identity, but we have to assume it's the same person who killed Bergin," said Sean.

Mayhew looked at the bloody sweater. "And your call to the dispatcher said that Megan Riley is missing?"

"She must've been the target."

Mayhew said absently, "The forensic team is on its way."

"Okay," said Sean. "We're prepared to help in any way we can."

"It's been a long time since we lost anyone," said Mayhew. "And never under my watch."

"We understand," said Michelle.

"I have to go tell Sally," Mayhew said, his voice hoarse.

"Would you like me to go with you?" asked Michelle.

"No, no, that's my job," said Mayhew firmly.

He gazed once more at Dobkin's body. "I recruited Eric. Watched him grow into a fine officer."

"I'm sure," said Sean quietly.

"Did you find the truth?" asked Mayhew.

"What?" said Sean.

"Down in Portland? Did you find the truth?"

"I think we're getting there."

"This is a lot more complicated than it appeared initially to be, isn't it?" said Mayhew shrewdly. "Bergin, Dukes, Agent Murdock. Edgar Roy is smack in the middle of all this, and I seriously doubt he is who we've been told he is."

"I couldn't disagree with any of your conclusions, sir," said Sean diplomatically.

"Could you do me a favor?" asked Mayhew.

"Certainly."

"When you do find who did this to Eric, I want to personally arrest them and see that they're tried here for murder."

"I'll do my best, Colonel Mayhew. I'll certainly do my best."

"Thank you." Mayhew turned and left.

He had to go and deliver the tragic news to a young woman with three kids and a fourth on the way.

70

Two nights later Edgar Roy could feel it coming, almost like how animals react so early to an approaching storm. He hunched down in the darkness, his face pressed against the flimsy mattress that he slept on each night. He heard footsteps. Routine guard patrols. Ordinary chatter. But he still knew.

The lights flickered, went out, and then came back on.

He scrunched down further into his bed, his feet hanging off one end of it. He didn't care if the camera saw him moving now. It didn't matter. The lights flickered again, like there was a storm outside and Mother Nature was playing games with Cutter's electrical supply. Then the lights went back out and stayed out a long time.

He heard cries from the guards. He heard calls from some of the prisoners.

Feet were running.

Doors clanged open and then shut with a crash of steel on steel.

A siren started up.

Then the lights came back on. From somewhere there was an enormous rush of noise, like a jet plane powering up for takeoff.

The backup generator. Roy had heard it come on once before, only then it was a test. It had the power to run the entire facility, even the electrified fence. It was huge, contained in its own structure just outside the main building. It ran on fuel. They had enough fuel here for the generator to run the facility for an entire week. He had heard this, too, from conversations among the guards. They never expected anyone was listening or caring about this. But Roy listened and cared about everything. And he remembered it all. The generator was the fail-safe. After that there was nothing else.

The rush of power ceased. The instant it did the lights went back out. It was so black inside here that Roy could not even see his own hands. He looked out between the bars of his cell. Guards were hustling around with emergency lights. With no heat the poured concrete building quickly cooled. Roy started to shiver. He covered himself with the blanket. He tried to burrow down into the bed. But there was no hiding. Not really.

The caravan of black SUVs with government plates stormed the causeway and roared toward the entrance at Cutter's. Six men jumped out and approached the first layer of guards. Behind them Cutter's lay black and nearly invisible. The darkness was interrupted only by the weak moonlight and stabs of narrow beams as guards with flashlights raced around trying to secure the perimeter. Battery-powered sirens shrieked.

One of the men held up his badge. "FBI. We're here for Edgar Roy. Now."

"What?" said a bewildered guard.

The man shoved his creds and badge into the uniform's face. "FBI. You have a total security melt-down. Roy is a Level One Federal Prisoner. That was part of the paperwork when he was remanded here. His security is the jurisdiction of the Bureau in the event of a crisis at Cutter's Rock. Now open the gates or we'll arrest your ass right now."

The guards seemed paralyzed as they stared out at the flood of armed men wearing FBI windbreakers and body armor.

The guards turned and manually pushed open the gates and the SUVs raced through the gap.

When they reached the main entrance, the new director who had replaced Carla Dukes was there to greet them. He ordered the guards to open the last set of doors and to immediately release Edgar Roy into the custody of the FBI.

Edgar Roy heard the doors opening and closing. He heard the sounds of heavy boots racing through the facility. He didn't look up when the sounds stopped at his cell. He didn't turn his head when the cell door was manually opened. He let his body go limp when the strong hands reached for him.

He was yanked upward, his head banging on the combat helmet of one of the men who had come for him. They half-carried him down the hall.

One man said into his ear, "Move your feet, asshole, or I'll put a round right in your skull."

Edgar Roy started to move, his weakened legs scissoring in painful little hops.

The darkness raced past them. Sounds, voices, sirens. He wanted to cover his ears, but the men had death grips on his arms.

He saw faces as they reached the front entrance. The new director stared at Roy, barely concealing his triumphant smile. The massive front doors stood open.

For the first time in months, Edgar Roy was outside. He could smell the ocean; he could see the moon.

He had no time to enjoy this small taste of freedom, particularly because he knew he wasn't free at all. He was thrown into the rear seat of one of the SUVs, and men crammed in after him. Turbo engines started, wheels gripped asphalt. Roy was thrown backward in his seat as the SUV whipped around, hit sixty a few seconds later, and catapulted toward the exit.

They crossed the causeway. The truck turned left and slowed. The two trucks behind them did the same. Ten minutes later they followed a road that was their natural way out of the area. It was isolated, dark, nothing around except a long ribbon of asphalt and trees.

Their natural way out.

Roy felt a bump as the truck hit something in the road. There was an explosion, though Roy felt no concussive force. The truck wasn't lifted into the air, but it was suddenly engulfed in a wall of fog.

Someone yelled. Roy felt the SUV lurch to the right and then the left. Men around him gagged. Something tugged at his arm. He felt a metal barrel against his cheek. He thought he heard a click, like a gun hammer being pulled back.

The smoke poured through crevices in the vehicle. Roy could see nothing. It was like they were in an open-cockpit plane and had just flown into a cloud. He heard the other trucks whipping and sliding around behind them. Men screamed, cursed, choked.

He jerked as the shot was fired. Glass exploded next to his head. Some of the shards hit him, cutting his face.

He took one deep breath, and that was the last thing he remembered doing.

71

Slight movement.

Slight nausea.

He saw his sister pivot in the old family kitchen. Then the memory shifted to something far more recent.

He saw the face in the dirt staring up at him from the barn floor.

Back to his sister pivoting.

Then his father's face.

Then the face in the dirt.

It seemed all connected, though it couldn't be.

His mind was a mishmash.

It had never been that before. Never.

Edgar Roy opened his eyes once and then quickly closed them as a pain tugged at his brain. He opened them once more. Something pulled at him. He slid upward, as though being yanked from deep water. Everything around him felt slick, wet.

"Eddie?"

His eyes closed once more.

"Eddie?"

He forced his eyes open. He felt slow, stupid, drunk. Feelings he had never before had in his life.

"Eddie? Can you sit up by yourself?"

With an effort he righted himself and looked at her.

Kelly Paul sat next to him in the rear seat of a van that had tinted windows. There were other people with him and his sister. The van was not moving.

The tall man was in the front passenger seat. The skeptical dark-haired woman was in the driver's seat.

Peter Bunting sat on the other side of Paul.

Bunting said, "Edgar, are you all right? You were bleeding when they got to you."

Roy touched the side of his head and felt the bandage there.

He mumbled, "Shot. Missed. Glass."

His sister said, "It's okay, Eddie. Close call, but it's okay."

"K-el?" he said, the name coming out thick and disjointed.

"Just take it easy, Eddie. You breathed in some nasty stuff. No lasting effects, but it takes a while to run its course. Once it's out of your system you'll feel much better."

"You did that?"

"I'm afraid it was unavoidable."

He felt something at his ankle. Well, more accurately, he didn't feel something at his shin. He looked down. His restraint anklet was gone.

Paul said, "I didn't think you'd want that on any longer."

Roy looked at the dark-haired woman.

Michelle stared back at him in the rearview mirror. She wore a shoulder holster and an anxious expression. Sean was next to her, looking equally concerned.

Sean said to Paul, "Let's just hope that really wasn't the FBI who came to get your brother."

Roy rubbed his face and willed his mind to clear itself of all the smoke, the rubbish, and the inefficiencies.

"It wasn't the FBI," he said.

"How do you know that?" asked Sean.

"Because one of the men said to me, 'Move your feet, asshole, or I'll put a round right in your skull.'"

This came out more like a playback of a recording and both Michelle and Sean looked relieved.

"Okay," Sean said. "Definitely not the Bureau."

Michelle said to Paul, "How did you work out that was going to happen?"

"The men watching the facility? That was the first clue. Then a maintenance crew went in recently to do some routine work. Only that work had been done less than a month ago and wasn't due to be done again for another three months. They spent a long time with the backup generator."

"Then why did they even let them in the building?" asked Sean.

"Because the man who replaced Carla Dukes as director at Cutter's authorized it. And he was being paid off."

"And that work was really to sabotage the electrical systems and the backup generator," said Michelle.

"And as we saw, they were successful in doing so," replied Paul.

"So you called some . . . friends?" prompted Sean.

"Acquaintances," she corrected. "They came, they saw, and they kicked ass."

"They were going to do what, kill him?" said Michelle, eyeing Roy.

"Eventually, yes, and blame it on Peter or me or some other convenient target."

She turned to her brother. "When I visited you at Cutter's I asked you to think about some things. Have you?"

Roy nodded. He adjusted his glasses and said, "You asked me about patterns. I detected four different ones but all were connected to some degree. What we've learned recently has given me new information which I've now plugged into these scenarios."

Roy's speech now was firm, straightforward, more machinelike than human.

"Four patterns?" said Michelle.

He nodded. "First, Agent Murdock was killed because he'd discovered the existence of the E-Program. That's not a deduction. He actually told me that when he came to see me at Cutter's. He said something was definitely wrong and that he needed my help to get to the people responsible. Carla Dukes was eliminated because she wouldn't go along with the extraction plan, whereas we know now that the new director had no such compunction. I saw him looking at me as we left Cutter's. He has a terrible poker face; his guilt couldn't have been plainer."

Paul said, "He obviously didn't believe you'd be in a position to tell anyone."

"Right. Next, Hilary Cunningham was killed to incriminate Ms. Maxwell and distract you and Mr. King from the case."

"And Bergin?" asked Sean.

"Obviously by someone he knew."

"Why do you say that?" asked Sean.

"The window being rolled down and then back up by the killer." He glanced at his sister. "She told me about that in the Morse code."

"And Sean told me that," said Paul.

"I guess great minds think alike," noted Michelle.

"But I don't know who killed him," admitted Roy. "Not enough data to go on. The likely scenario was to remove him from the case so it wouldn't move forward. They were buying time." He paused. "But that doesn't really make sense."

"Why?" asked Michelle.

Sean answered. "Because the case wasn't moving forward anyway, not with Edgar sitting at Cutter's."

"That's exactly right," said Roy.

"But at least Foster and Quantrell must be throwing fits," said Bunting with a grim smile. "That's a positive for our side."

"But that means they're also going to come after us," added Paul.

"And do we sit back and wait for that?" asked Sean.

"Of course not," she answered. "Now we go on the offensive."

"How?" asked Sean.

"I know exactly how," said Paul. "In some ways, I think I've been waiting my whole life to do this." She looked at Bunting. "What about you, Peter?"

"Oh, I feel the exact same way."

72

They drove to a safe house arranged by Kelly Paul.

"Everyone will be looking for my brother," said Paul. "This place is far enough away from the action, but we still have to take maximum precautions. If they recapture Eddie, our plan won't work."

As he looked around the new space Sean said, "We're all felons now. Aiding and abetting. That's not really something we signed on for. And it sure as hell isn't something we're comfortable with."

Paul turned to face him. "I understand. If you have a problem with that, you and Michelle can leave right now. No one knows you were involved in any of this. I would ask that you not turn Eddie in. If you do then it's really over for him."

"You think he can't get a fair trial?" asked Sean.

"He'll never make it to court, Sean. They'll never let him. They broke him out of Cutter's to kill him. If he goes back they'll find him in his cell dead from some unknown cause. That's just the way it's going to happen."

Sean glanced at Michelle.

She said, "Rock and a hard place."

"Yeah," he replied.

"Other things being equal, we've come too far on this to let it go now, Sean," she said. "And we still don't know who killed Bergin. I know that's important to you."

Sean eyed Paul, who was watching him intently.

"Okay, we'll stay in. But we will not use force against federal agents or state law enforcement."

"Bona fide federal agents," said Michelle. "I already laid out a few bogus ones in Central Park and in a diner in Charlottesville."

Sean kept staring at Paul. "Do we have an understanding?"

She nodded. "We do."

Bunting gripped Sean by the shoulder. "Thank you."

"Don't thank me yet. We've got a long way to go."

After the others retired to their rooms to get some sleep, it was just Paul and her brother left in the room.

"It's so good to see you, Eddie," she said. "I've missed you." She paused. "I just wish it were under different circumstances."

"I've missed you too, Kel. A lot."

She looked down. "I should have come to see you a long time ago. Before all this . . ."

"I know you've been busy."

"Not that busy." She looked up. "I'm the reason

you're with the E-Program. I recommended you for it."

"I can't say I'm surprised."

"Analyzed the situation, did you?" she said with a weak smile.

"I'm pretty good at it."

"Bunting's done nothing but rave about you."

"But it's . . . it's not easy being . . ."

"God?"

"You understand then. It's not a role humans, no matter how smart, are designed to play. We have doubts. We have prejudices. We make mistakes."

"You keep a lot of people safe, Eddie."

"I also kill a lot of people."

"Not directly you don't."

"That's simply splitting hairs."

"What you do is try to make the world better and safer and more just. Yes, your decisions result in people dying, but only so that many, many more people can live. What's wrong with that? What does your amazing mind tell you about that?"

"Logically, there's nothing wrong with that. It's a no-brainer. But it's also not that easy."

She sat back. "I know it's not." She gazed at him. "Do you want to continue doing it?"

"I don't know. I need to see whether I survive this or not first."

"Whether *we* survive it. You and me."

"You and me," he said quietly, though it was obvious her words had pleased him.

"I got you into this and it's my job to get you out," she said.

"My protector," he said almost in a whisper.

"Can I ask you something?"

"Yes."

"Why did you choose to continue to live at the farm after Mom died? You could have sold it and moved somewhere else."

"It's my home."

"That's not a good enough reason, Eddie. We both know that." She paused. "I visited the place. Before you became the Analyst."

"Where was I?"

"At work at the IRS."

"Why did you come when I wasn't there?"

"I don't know. Maybe I was afraid."

His face fell. "Afraid? To see me?"

"No, of course not. To see you in that place, I guess."

"It was a long time ago, Kel."

"Not long enough. Not for me. Or you."

"You came back for me."

She put up a hand. "I never should have left you there in the first place. I knew. I . . . knew. That man. That animal."

"But he's dead now. It's over."

"It's never over, Eddie. Not for you. Not for me.

We both know that. Those scars run deep. I've never married. Never even thought of it. Never had kids. Never wanted them. You want to know why?"

He nodded.

"Because I didn't think I could protect them. Easy way out, really. I was a coward, Eddie, plain and simple. A coward."

"Kel, it wasn't your fault."

Paul rose and paced in small circles in front of him. "Of course it was, Eddie. I abandoned you. I've spent my whole life making penance for it by doing very dangerous things. And it just occurred to me recently that while I was making my penance I forgot one important thing." This all came out like a blast of pent-up air finally released.

"What was that?"

"You." She knelt in front of him, took his hand, and squeezed it. "I forgot you, Eddie."

"You never forgot me. You wrote. You came to see me sometimes."

"It's not the same. You know that." She sat back and put a hand up to her eyes.

"Please don't, Kel. Don't be sad."

She rose abruptly. "I will get you out of this, Eddie. That I promise. Even if I die in the process."

Kelly Paul turned and walked unsteadily from the room, leaving her younger brother alone with thoughts not even his unique mind was really equipped to deal with.

73

Ellen Foster was seated in a chair in an underground bunker she reserved for the most private of meetings. No notes, no recordings, no surveillance of any kind.

She sat there looking at the man who stared back at her.

"Can you even comprehend how furious I am about all this?" she said.

Mason Quantrell said nothing. He nervously tapped his fingers on the wooden tabletop and simply eyed her with caution.

She continued. "It was the neatest package I could possibly provide. It was perfect. All you had to do was your job. And now?" She slapped her hand against the table. "And now?"

Quantrell's face darkened and caution was thrown aside. "We were set up, Ellen. You have a spy in your operation, obviously. It wasn't my fault. We hit all of our cues right on the mark."

"Oh, don't be ridiculous. They just played you. They outsmarted you."

"They outsmarted *us*," he corrected in a high tone. "You and me. In this together."

Foster's angry look was slowly replaced with something far subtler: apprehension.

"I don't like your tone, or your words," she said.

"This is not the time to fight with each other," Quantrell said in a calmer tone. "They took one round from us, that's all. We've been victorious in every other one."

"They have Roy. That's a pretty big round to lose. That may be the knockout, in fact."

The other man in the room cleared his throat.

James Harkes said, "I believe Mr. Quantrell is right, Secretary Foster."

She turned to him and her face hardened even more. His rejection of her from the other night was still stark in her features. He would not have even been here except that with the recent disaster she needed him.

"And how do you figure that?" asked Foster icily.

"The plan was always to extract Roy and then blame it on Bunting and his allies. Well, now they actually have him. We don't have to fabricate the blame. It's a fact."

Quantrell said, "That's right."

Foster was already shaking her head. "You've forgotten one significant detail. The FBI convoy that took Roy from Cutter's was fake. It was Quantrell's people. His *idiot* people."

"That doesn't really matter," said Harkes. "Fake or

not, Mr. Quantrell's backup team was on the scene fifteen minutes after the attack on the convoy. They weren't in time to stop them from taking Roy, obviously, but the scene was sterilized before anyone else arrived there. So as far as the world is concerned a fake FBI team lifted Edgar Roy from Cutter's. And Roy is now in the hands of Peter Bunting. Ergo he must have been behind it."

"And Kelly Paul," snapped Foster. "She has to be in the middle of all this. It's her brother, after all."

"And now we know Bunting was never at the hospital with his wife," added Quantrell. "It was all a charade to draw us off."

"And his family has gone into hiding," said Harkes. "It was neatly done."

Foster's features hardened even more at this remark. "Neatly done? Why don't you start applauding, Harkes, if you think so much of them?"

"Underestimating the opponent is the single most important error one can make, Secretary Foster. They are good. We have to acknowledge that. We simply have to be better."

"So they have Roy," said Quantrell. "What will they do with him? He knows nothing that can connect us to anything."

"And since he's an escaped prisoner," added Harkes, "I'm not sure how Bunting intends to use him. He can't exactly put him back into the E-Program."

"And if we can find him, and them . . ." said Foster, her anger fading as she refocused on the problem.

"And tie it all together," added Quantrell, "then we can still accomplish every goal we had. Roy will be dead, Bunting blamed for it all. The E-Program over and never to return."

Foster rose and paced the room. "And with this latest development I received something this morning that might make our job easier."

"What's that?" asked Quantrell.

"Explicit approval from the president to take whatever means necessary to rectify this situation."

"Any means?" asked Harkes sharply. "From the president?"

She looked at him. "Any. So I think you have your work cut out for you, Harkes."

He looked at Quantrell and then returned his gaze to Foster. "Then I'm to be given the lead on this?"

"Are you not up to the task?" she snapped.

"I just want verification that we will do things my way."

Quantrell said, "I have no problem with that. My men screwed up, obviously. But your reputation precedes you, Harkes."

Harkes said, "Are you okay with that, Madame Secretary?"

"I want you to take care of it, Harkes, that's all. Using whatever means you choose."

"And who do you want standing at the end?" he asked.

Foster looked surprised. "I'm not sure I want any of them standing at the end. Why would I?"

"Again, I just like to be as explicit as possible in situations like this."

She drew closer to him and leaned in. "Then here are your explicit instructions, Harkes. Edgar Roy, dead. Peter Bunting, dead. Kelly Paul, dead. Michelle Maxwell, dead. Sean King, dead. Is that precise enough for you?"

"Yes."

She straightened and looked at Quantrell. "If that's all, Mason, I'd like a private moment with Harkes. We have some unfinished business on an unrelated matter."

After Quantrell left, Foster perched on the edge of the table next to Harkes.

"The other night did not please me. Your behavior was beyond ridiculous."

"I can tell you believe that," he said.

"What's that supposed to mean?"

"I could say that your behavior was actually the ridiculous one, but I doubt it would make an impression on you."

"I'm not used to rejection at any level."

"I can tell that too."

"I can make your life a living hell."

"Yes you can."

"And on the other hand I can make it the exact opposite of a living hell."

"I'm not a whore, Madame Secretary."

"You are what I want you to be," she corrected him. "So how do you want this to play out?"

"I have a mission. I will carry it out."

"And after that?"

"After what?"

She slid one long nail across his hand. "I want you, Harkes. And I get what I want. It's just that simple."

He looked up at her. "Why?"

"Why what?"

"You could have an ambassador. A senator. A rich Wall Street asshole. Anybody, really. So why me? What am I to you?"

"I've had all those types. It's like ice cream. Now I crave something different."

She leaned in closer. "So when this is over you will continue to work for me in any way I choose. Is that understood?"

"Understood."

She ran a hand along his cheek. "Wonderful. Now go do what needs to be done."

"I will," he said.

74

"Sir, it's him. On the phone!"

Mason Quantrell's secretary was standing in front of him in his office suite in northern Virginia.

Quantrell looked up from his work. "Who?"

"Peter Bunting."

Quantrell forgot all about what he was doing. "Bunting? Calling me?"

"Line one."

"Notify security and tell them to trace the call."

"Yes, sir." She hurried out.

Quantrell paused, staring down at the blinking light. Then he snatched it up. "Hello?"

Bunting said pleasantly, "Hello, Mason. I know your tech guys are trying to trace this. You can let them go through the motions if you want. You never could break my pipeline, mainly because your hardware is cheap crap that you sell to the Pentagon for fifty times what it's worth, but I'll still keep it brief."

"Where is Edgar Roy, Bunting?"

"Funny you should ask, Mason. I know that was

quite a curve we threw you when your boys got ambushed."

"Don't know what the hell you're talking about."

"Right, right, just in case I'm sitting at the Hoover Building and they're recording this call."

"I doubt you'd get anywhere near Hoover without being arrested. You're in serious trouble, my friend."

"You think so? Well, not nearly as serious as you are."

"You never did lie well, Pete."

"It was a blunder, you know."

"What was?"

"The team you used to extract Roy. How in the hell did you forget about the surveillance cameras at Cutter's?"

Quantrell felt his gut tighten just a notch. "I have no idea what you're talking about."

"Surveillance cameras, Mason. You get the concept, right? They *see* things."

"I . . . I understood from the news reports that the power was knocked out as part of the escape plan." He added in a loud voice, "A plan that *you* hatched."

"But Cutter's is a very special federal facility. And Maine is a very green state."

"What the hell is that supposed to mean?"

"Didn't you ever notice the solar panels, Mason?"

Quantrell remained silent.

"Or have you never personally been to Cutter's? Maybe you just let your lackeys do all the recon. Well, they have the diesel backup generator but they also have solar backup. It's not all that powerful. Can't run the facility. Can't even power the fence. But it can run the cameras for up to twenty-four hours."

"Solar backup?" Quantrell said slowly.

"So they got really good pictures of all of your guys. Really good ones. Even in their fake FBI gear the images were very revealing."

"You're not going to spin this, Bunting," said Quantrell, but his voice was weak.

"What I'm trying to do, Mason, is give you an out."

Quantrell had to laugh. "Not that I need an out, but why the hell would you do that?"

"Two of the guys caught on the cameras were identified as having worked for you in the past, Mason. The recent past. Were you that hard up for hired help that you couldn't send in sterilized personnel? I mean, I know you have the director in your pocket, but it's the little details that are the most important. So you blew it on two fronts: camera oversight and using traceable goons."

"I don't believe a word of what you're telling me."

"I don't blame you, actually."

Quantrell looked up as a man appeared in his office doorway. It was his head of security. He was shaking his head, his features edged with failure.

Quantrell dismissed him with a sharp wave of his hand.

"Mason, are you still with me? Did your security guy just report back failure to you?"

Quantrell almost knocked his chair over as he jumped up and looked wildly around his office for a set of eyes, electronic or human, peering at him from somewhere.

"Calm down, Mason. Just calm down. I can't see you. I just know you. I know you very well. You're predictable with a capital P."

"What the hell game are you playing, Bunting?" Quantrell yelled into the phone.

"No game, Mason. But it's obvious you have no interest in what I have to say. Now when Foster's men come to arrest you, what are you going to do?"

Quantrell's gut clenched so hard this time, he nearly doubled over. "Foster?"

"Did you really think you were going to walk away on equal terms with her? She's way too smart for that."

Quantrell slumped in his chair. "What are you getting at?"

"It was your guys who did all the heavy lifting, am I right? Planted the six bodies in Edgar's barn. Killed Murdock, Dukes—"

"Now wait just a minute."

"She played you, Mason. And now it's unraveling, so she's activated her survival plan. She's going to wipe the floor with you. Poor, trusting Cabinet secretary and sleazy defense contractor. Don't feel bad. It's not that original. It's the same trap you laid for me. At least

I was nimble enough to get the hell out of town. You, on the other hand, are sitting in your big, fancy office with a bull's-eye on your head."

"You . . . there is no proof. I can . . . I have friends. Allies."

"Yeah, I thought I had them, too. That is, before Foster turned them all against me. Which is what she's probably doing to you right now. And you know how persuasive the lady can be. I wonder if she's met with the president yet to update him on your treachery?"

"What treachery?" Quantrell snapped.

"Oh, didn't I tell you? The memory cards from the surveillance cameras were delivered to her this morning along with a detailed report of what they represent. You see, I had a secret asset still at Cutter's who came through for me in the clutch. Just call it a nice present from me. It'll be more than enough for an indictment. Your business will be disqualified from performing any more government work, and since that's all you do, you have no more business. But you won't care. You'll be in a federal cage where big, tough guys with time on their hands will want to get to know you very well."

"But I can take that bitch Foster down. I can—I know things—"

"She's too smart for that, Mason. He said, she said. And she's a Cabinet secretary, and your reputation precedes you. And it's not a good one. Why do you think she chose you to work with, you moron?"

The blood slowly drained from Quantrell's face as this all sank in. He licked his lips and said slowly, "You spoke about an out."

"Yeah, I did. Want to hear it?"

Quantrell coughed, trying to clear his suddenly dry throat. He croaked, "Yes, I do."

"Good. Sit tight and I'll get back to you."

Quantrell screamed into the phone, but Bunting had already clicked off.

75

It was a fund-raising gala at Lincoln Center. The stars were out from both coasts. Peter Bunting's wife was on the Lincoln board and had helped spearhead the event. She was not here tonight because of her recent illness, but she had found someone who could use her comp ticket.

Kelly Paul, tall and regal, and wearing a long gown with her hair tucked up except for a few dangling strands, walked along one of the corridors of the Center, a glass of Bordeaux in hand. People stared and commented on her, though they didn't know who she was.

Paul was here for only one reason. And she had finally spotted it.

Or, more accurately, spotted *her*.

Ellen Foster did not look very comfortable. It was not just the problem of Edgar Roy weighing on her mind. It was a matter of being at an event where she was far from the center of attention. Her public fame was limited, though she had more public power than anyone in the building. But that didn't seem to matter when a gaggle of guests nearly ran over you in their quest to corner the latest Hollywood or singing sensation.

Foster walked along with a glass of champagne in hand, stealthily looking for anyone who might recognize her so she could do a bit of preening. Failing to find anyone interested in her, Foster decided to visit the ladies' room.

Inside the ladies' room, while she was reapplying her lipstick, Foster heard a voice.

"Hello, Ellen."

She froze but only for an instant. She glanced in the mirror, saw no one.

"I locked the door. We won't be disturbed."

Foster slowly turned. "I'm armed."

"No, you're not."

Kelly Paul emerged from the shadows and faced her. Even in her three-inch heels Foster was dwarfed by the other woman.

"Kelly Paul?" Foster shook her head. "You have unbelievable balls to be doing this."

"Doing what? Taking a pee? Don't they allow that at Lincoln Center anymore?"

Foster rested her rump on the granite sink and folded her arms across her chest.

"I could have you arrested right now."

"For what?"

"Any number of things."

"You'll have to be more specific."

"Where's your brother?"

"I was going to ask you the same thing."

"I really don't have time for this."

"Peter Bunting?" said Paul.

"What about him?"

"You set him up nicely."

"On the contrary, he dug his own grave."

Paul held up her hands. "Check me for a wire if you want. You can be frank."

Foster looked at her like she had lost her mind. "I need to get back to the party. And just in case you're looking to get away, my men have all the exits locked down. I'll look forward to seeing how many charges are filed against you."

Foster started to walk out.

"It's interesting about Mason Quantrell, isn't it?"

Foster paused, her hand on the doorknob.

"Who?" she said.

"The Mercury Group? Mason Quantrell. Your partner in crime?"

"It's appalling to see how far you've fallen. You used to be somewhat special. This performance is about as amateur and pathetic as I've ever seen."

"Bunting is a very smart man. He outfoxed Quantrell," said Paul. "He connected the dots and found the proof. Quantrell knows he's going down for it. But he's also looking to work a deal with the FBI. Care to guess what they'll want in return?"

Foster just stood there, staring at her.

"Is this still an amateur production, Ellen?"

"I'm listening, if only for my own amusement." However, the woman's confidence was clearly diminished.

"The story won't take long. Quantrell is about to rat you out."

Foster managed a smile. "About what?"

Paul ticked them off on her left hand. "The six bodies in the barn. A dead lawyer and his secretary. A dead director of Cutter's. A dead Maine state trooper. And most of all a dead FBI agent. The boys at Hoover really get pissed when you take out one of their own. And you didn't have to, Ellen. So what if he found out about the E-Program? Did you really need to do that? He had three kids."

"This is the biggest load of crap I have ever heard."

"And yet you're still here."

"Why are you telling me this?"

"Because I want my brother back, safe and sound. And I need you to do that."

For the first time uncertainty crept into Foster's eyes. "Your brother was broken out of Cutter's Rock by people impersonating FBI agents. By *you*, in other words."

"That was Quantrell's people and you know it."

"But—"

"But what? Did he feed you some bullshit that the plan didn't go off? That he lost my brother?" Paul drew closer to the other woman. "I want Eddie back,

Ellen. And one way or another I will get him back."
She paused and a look of incredulity came over her
features as she studied the vacuous look on the other
woman's face. "Did Quantrell play you, too? Did he
tell you that he would snatch Roy and then kill him?
Blame Bunting? Hell, Bunting's ass is already fried.
The E-Program is over. You didn't need Eddie for
that. That's just piling it on. My brother could just rot
in that prison; it would make no difference to you.
You already won. Didn't you *get* that?"

She drew closer still, so she was looking right down
at Foster. "Eddie is innocent. I couldn't care less about
the E-Program, but I'll be damned if my brother is
going to lose his life so you can score a useless victory
over Peter Bunting. By now you must know the guy
tricked you with his wife attempting suicide. He's
already gone somewhere that doesn't extradite here."

"I don't know where your brother is, that's the
truth," Foster said slowly.

Paul took a step back. "Then my coming to see you
was a waste of time."

"I don't know what you mean," Foster answered in
a hushed voice.

Paul said, "You're the head of DHS, for God's sake.
You're supposed to think this shit through, Ellen. And
aligning yourself with Quantrell? Where did that brilliant idea come from? You knew that Bunting kicked
his ass with the E-Program. So you had to know he
wasn't in the same league with Bunting brainwise. Did

you think Bunting would just roll over and give up? He could eat Quantrell's lunch any day of the week. You really picked your ally very poorly. Who the hell advised you to do that?"

Foster was clearly now in full retreat mode. "I didn't . . . I mean—We can get Bunting—"

Paul didn't let her finish. "Good God, haven't you been listening to me? Your people lost track of Bunting. They have no idea where he is. The man is gone!"

Foster said nothing to this. Her mouth was moving but no words came out.

"You backed Bunting into a corner, but the man always has an out. And Quantrell was stupid enough to deliver it to him. But Quantrell was also smart enough to obviously recognize something you apparently didn't."

"What are you—"

"Edgar Roy? A true E-Six? Only one on the planet? Do you know what he would be worth to this country's enemies? Do you know how much Quantrell could sell him for?"

"He would never work for another country."

"Who, my brother or Quantrell?"

"Either."

"Did you know that when Quantrell was first starting out he was almost banned from government contracting work because he sold restricted weapons parts to China? He only got out of it through his fancy lawyers and blaming it on a subordinate. He'd sell his own mother to Kim Jong-Il if he thought he could make money. And while it's true my brother would never knowingly work against his country, don't you think the Russians or the North Koreans or the Syrians couldn't find a way to persuade him? Their torture techniques are old-school but they're still highly effective. Trust me, I know."

"So you're saying Quantrell—"

"Of course he double-crossed you. That's how he's wired. And now that Bunting kicked his ass and saved himself, Quantrell's going to throw you under the bus to save his ass. It's called dominos for adults. Which leaves my brother in total limbo right now. Which is not good. He's a loose end, and they don't have long life expectancies."

Foster was now tottering a bit in her three-inch heels.

Paul took the woman's hand off the doorknob and unlocked it. "But since it's now quite apparent that you were too stupid to see any of this coming and you possess absolutely nothing that can help me, I'll just have to look elsewhere for what I need. Besides, what can you do from a jail cell, anyway?"

She pointed at a corner of Foster's mouth. "You went outside the lines a bit there. Might want to fix that for your mug shot."

Paul closed the door behind her.

76

Michelle was driving.

Sean was shotgun.

Edgar Roy was in the backseat of the van.

The drive had been long and they had stopped only twice, for bathroom breaks. When they pulled down the country lane, Michelle slowed the van.

"I know Bunting told us we were off grid when we came here before to meet Kelly Paul, but this case has given me a large case of paranoia."

Sean nodded as his gaze swept the area. It was the perfect place for an ambush.

"But other things being equal it's better than checking into a motel."

"Only if we don't end up getting killed," Roy said.

Sean looked at him in surprise. Roy had spent most of the trip in silence.

"A brilliant observation," said Michelle sarcastically. She put the van in park and glanced sideways at Sean. "Plan?"

"I can always sneak up there, and if someone is waiting for us, they can kill me and you can get away."

"Sounds good to me."

"I was kidding."

"I know. I'll go."

"I'm not letting you do that, Michelle."

"I don't remember asking for permission, sire."

"Do you two always talk this way?" asked Roy.

They both stared at him.

"What way?" barked Michelle, her gaze boring into him.

"Uh, never mind," said Roy. He looked down at his hands.

Sean said, "We can drive past, see if anyone comes after us."

"Or we can set up a recon point on that hill over there, hunker down, and watch the place," replied Michelle.

"Or we can just do it the old-fashioned way," said Sean.

"What does that mean?" asked Roy.

"Wait in the van," said Michelle. "And don't open the door to strangers."

They approached the house from back and front. It took them all of ten minutes to clear it. The farmhouse was empty and looked just like it had when they had been there previously. Michelle drove the van into the barn behind the house, and she and Roy got out and walked toward the house after Michelle closed the barn doors.

"This is my sister's place?" said Roy, gazing around.

"For now, I guess. I assume she doesn't stay in one place for long periods of time?"

"No, she doesn't."

"But you two have obviously stayed close. She's risked a lot to help."

"She's always protected me."

Sean came onto the front porch and overheard this. "Have you needed protection a lot?"

"Yes, I guess I have."

"Let's get inside," said Michelle, looking around. "I'm not too keen about the surroundings. Sniper heaven."

Inside, they found a pantry full of food, wood for the fireplaces, warm coats and boots, flannel shirts, pajamas, and clean sheets on the beds.

Michelle lifted up one of the coats. "I think I'll put this on right now. It's freezing outside and it's not much better in here."

"I'll get a fire started," said Sean.

"I can cook if you want," said Roy.

Michelle shot him a glance. "You can cook?"

"Yes, but if you'd rather do it, that's fine."

"She'd rather not," said Sean quickly, ignoring a dirty look from Michelle.

After a meal of pork chops, vegetables, biscuits, and a slice each of a store bought apple pie that Roy had found in the freezer, they settled in front of a blazing fire.

"Any word from Kelly or Bunting?" asked Michelle.

Sean said, "Just got a text. They each made contact

with their respective targets. And each was apparently very successful."

Roy nodded, his eyes on the fire. "They're playing Quantrell and Foster against each other."

Sean said, "Did your sister tell you that was the plan?"

"No, it's just the most obvious one. I met Foster twice. She's clearly a megalomaniac. Mason Quantrell is just greedy and jealous. A lethal combination."

Sean put another log on the fire and drew closer to the flames. "Tell me about the bodies in the barn."

Roy turned to him. "Why?"

"We're investigators. Ted Bergin hired us to help you. That's what we're trying to do. In order to do that we need information. And this is the first real chance we've had with you."

Roy took a moment to rub his glasses lenses clean on his shirt. He settled them back on and said, "I was taking a walk before dinner. I usually did that. I hadn't been in the barn in a long time. It was just a whim I decided to go in. Everything looked the same until I spotted the disturbed dirt on one side. I grabbed a shovel and started digging, to see what was there. That's when I saw the face. I was about to call the police when I heard the sirens. They arrested me. I can't blame them, really. I had the shovel in my hand and the bodies were there. It must've looked like I was just burying them instead of trying to dig them up."

"And that's when you went into . . . ?"

Roy looked embarrassed. "That's when I retreated into my head, yes."

"But you remember everything that went on?" asked Michelle.

"I never forget anything. I remember the first jail they put me in. Mr. Bergin coming to represent me. He tried very hard. There were times when I thought about talking to him, but I was just scared." He paused. "I'm very sorry he's dead. It was because of me, of course."

"So Foster and Quantrell put the bodies there in order to frame you."

Roy said, "I appreciate the presumption of innocence."

"I never presume anything," replied Sean. "But the timing of everything was too neat, too tidy. If I had to bet I'd say you were being watched, and as soon as you went in that barn, the cops got the call."

Michelle added, "And what we know of you, you're a little too smart to get caught red-handed by the local cops."

Sean looked at Roy. "Okay, Quantrell and Foster framed you. They thought they were home free. Now they've been turned against each other. What will they do next?"

Roy didn't hesitate. "Foster has no history of wrongdoing, while Quantrell's reputation is far sketchier on that score. Other things being equal, Quantrell will react more calmly to the situation than Foster."

"In other words, he's used to stepping over the line," said Michelle.

"Exactly. His innate reaction will be to survive this and perhaps even continue his business. Foster may very well lash out and let the chips fall. Or she might withdraw from the field and do nothing, hoping it goes away."

"That option I doubt," said Michelle. "You don't get to be the head of DHS by being a wallflower, particularly a woman."

"I agree with you," said Roy. "Which means she will probably be very aggressive in trying to turn the situation around."

"So she goes to her allies again, trying to shore up support," said Sean. "And blacken the well against Quantrell?"

Roy nodded. "She has the advantage there. She can get a meeting with the president or the FBI director if she needs to. Quantrell can't. He obviously knows this and will play to his strengths."

"Which are?" asked Sean.

"Operations in the field. Foster never would have used DHS personnel for the murders or my extraction. But private mercenaries are far less picky. They pledge allegiance to whoever's paying them."

"So Quantrell will use his men to do what?" asked Michelle.

"Find me, kill Bunting and my sister. And if the need arises he may very well hit Foster."

"Taking down the DHS head, pretty gutsy," said Sean.

"When you have nothing to lose, it doesn't take that much guts," replied Roy. "And it doesn't take a genius to figure that one out."

77

Ellen Foster sat at her chair in the bunker underneath DHS headquarters. Above her thousands of public servants went about their tasks of keeping the country safe from all attacks. Normally, Foster would be intimately involved in the strategy that went into this everyday battle. She lived and breathed it, thought of little else outside of it.

Right now she couldn't have cared less about it.

James Harkes stood across from her at semi-attention.

She had confided in him what Kelly Paul had told her in that bathroom at Lincoln Center. He had asked a few relevant questions but remained mostly silent. She gazed up at him with the look of a person assessing her last, best hope.

"This changes everything. What can we do?" she asked.

"What do you want to achieve?"

"I want to survive, Harkes—isn't that rather obvious?" she snapped.

"But there are many ways to survive, Madame

Secretary. I just need to know which one you want to pursue."

She blinked and saw what he meant. "I want to survive with my career intact, as though nothing had happened. That's as plain as I can state it."

He nodded slowly. "That will be very hard to do," he said frankly.

Foster gave a little shiver and wrapped her arms around herself. "But not impossible?"

"No, not impossible."

"Quantrell is trying to work a deal, rat me out, Kelly Paul said."

"I wouldn't doubt that, knowing what sort of person he is. But he has limited access to the people who matter. You don't."

"But the problem is I've already been to the president and built the case against Bunting. The president told me to take care of it. He gave me explicit authority to do whatever was necessary."

"And to go back to him now with a new story about Quantrell would really make you lose credibility in the president's eyes?"

"Exactly. I'll be like the little boy who cried wolf once too often."

"You may have answered your problem with what you've already said."

She glanced sharply at him. "What do you mean?"

"The president gave you explicit authority to do what was necessary."

"But Quantrell?"

"Collateral damage. And it's not as difficult as it sounds. With Quantrell out of the way, your problems are solved. You have left nothing incriminating on the table. He goes, the road ahead is clear."

Foster sat there thinking about this. "It might work. But how will the collateral damage thing work?'

"We've blamed everything else on Bunting, why not this too? It's natural enough. They're bitter rivals. Everyone knows that. The evidence of Bunting's obsession with Quantrell will be easy enough to produce."

"So we take out Quantrell and frame Bunting for it?"

"Yes."

"But Kelly Paul said he was long gone."

"You actually believed everything she told you?"

"Well . . . I mean." She stopped, looked embarrassed. "I'm losing a bit of control here, aren't I?" she said sheepishly.

"You're under a lot of stress. But you need to push through it, Secretary Foster, if you really want to survive this."

"Please sit down, James. You look uncomfortable standing there."

Harkes sat.

"How do we go about doing it?" she asked earnestly.

Harkes said, "Here's how the playing field shakes out, at least as I see it. Bunting must still be around."

"Why?"

"He's not the sort to walk away with his tail between his legs. For all we know he's actually working with Kelly Paul and her crew."

"Paul? But why?"

"Bunting met with Sean King. After that I sat him down and threatened him and his family if he did it again. Then he concocts the fake suicide attempt by his wife and does a bunk. If he were going to flee he would've taken his family with him. Even you admitted that he really cares about them."

"I guess that does make sense," conceded Foster.

"And think about the fact that he'd met with King and then planned this whole subterfuge with his family shortly thereafter."

"Not a coincidence?" said Foster.

"Not even close. The other salient points line up nicely. King and Maxwell are working to help Edgar Roy. They actually visited Cutter's Rock with Kelly Paul. They're obviously in this together. And Bunting is in it with them."

"And his motivation?"

"Bluntly put, Madame Secretary, he's innocent. He knows it and he's probably convinced them that he is, too. And King and Maxwell now likely know that Roy didn't kill anybody. Bunting has few options left.

Paul and probably King and Maxwell must've offered him a way out. What that is I don't know yet."

"I wish we had confirmation of your theory that they're all working together."

"Paul coming to New York was really confirmation of that."

"What do you mean?" she said sharply.

"She used Mrs. Bunting's ticket to get into the fund-raiser. We knew Paul and King and Maxwell had teamed up and now we have a direct connect between Paul and Bunting: the ticket."

"Oh, shit. I can't believe I didn't think of that."

"That's why you have me," Harkes said.

She smiled and touched his hand. "Yes, yes it is."

"If we had some bait to draw them out. Something that they value. It would go a long way to helping me put this together in the right way." He looked at her expectantly.

"I think I might have just what we need," she said.

She powered on the electronic tablet in front of her, hit a few keys, and spun the screen around for Harkes to see. It was an image of a room with someone in it.

"My ace in the hole," she said.

The floors and walls were concrete. There was one bunk bed and a toilet in the corner. The person sat on the bed.

Megan Riley hardly looked herself.

78

Outside the farmhouse the sun had dropped low, throwing shadows through the windows. It would be fully dark soon. Sean put some more wood on the fire and stoked it. When he sat down Roy said, "Kel told you about the E-Program, obviously."

"Yes," said Sean.

"How about the Wall?"

"Not really."

"The Wall is all the data delivered in one fell swoop. I sit in front of a giant screen for twelve hours a day taking it all in."

"When you say all the data, exactly what does that mean?" asked Michelle.

"It literally means everything collected by US intelligence operations and various allies overseas who share intel with us."

"Isn't that a lot of information?" asked Sean.

"More than you can imagine, really."

"And you look at it and do what?" asked Michelle.

"I analyze it and then put the pertinent pieces together and give my report. They vet my conclusions, and then it becomes part of the action plan of the United States on all relevant fronts. In fact the actions taken are pretty immediate."

"You have a photographic memory," Sean said. "An eidetic?"

"Something more than that," said Roy modestly.

"How can it be more than photographic?" Michelle commented.

"True photographic memories are extremely rare. A lot of people can remember many things they've seen but not everything. And even for many eidetics the memory eventually fades as others replace it. I can never forget anything."

"Never?" Sean said, looking at him skeptically.

"Unfortunately, people don't realize that a lot of memories are ones you want to forget."

"I can understand that," said Michelle, drawing a sympathetic glance from Sean.

Sean said, "Mind if I test you?"

"I'm used to being tested."

"What was the name of the police officer who arrested you in the barn?"

"Which one? There were five," replied Roy.

"The first one to speak to you."

"His nameplate said Gilbert," replied Roy.

"Badge number?

"Eight-six-nine-three-four. His weapon was a Sig Sauer 9mm with a twelve-round mag. He had an ingrown nail on his right pinky. I can give you the other officers' names and badge numbers if you want. And since this is a memory test, over the last two hundred and six miles of the trip we passed one hundred and sixty-eight vehicles. Would you like their license plate numbers starting from first to last? There were nineteen from New York, eleven from Tennessee, six from Kentucky, three from Ohio, seventeen from West Virginia, one each from Georgia, South Carolina, D.C., Maryland, Illinois, Alabama, Arkansas, Oklahoma, two from Florida, and the rest from Virginia. I can also tell you the number and descriptions of the occupants of each vehicle. I can break it down by state if you want."

Michelle gaped and said, "I can't even remember what I was doing last week. How do you keep all that in your head?"

"I can *see* it in my head. I just have to dial it up."

"Like index cards in your mind?"

"No, more like a DVD. I can see everything flowing. Then I can hit stop, pause, fast-forward, or reverse."

Sean still looked skeptical. "Okay, describe the outside of this house, the barn, and the land around it."

Roy swiftly did so, finishing with "There are one thousand six hundred and fourteen shingles on the east side of the barn's roof. The fourth shingle over in the second row from the top is missing, as is the sixteenth one on the ninth row counting from the front. And the hinge on the left front door of the barn is new.

There are forty-one trees in the field on the east side of the house. Six are dead and four more are dying; the largest of those is a Southern magnolia. My sister obviously is not into landscape maintenance."

"Last four presidents of Uzbekistan?"

"A trick question, obviously. There has only been one since the office was established in 1991 after the fall of the Soviet Union. Islam Karimov is the current officeholder." He gazed at Sean with a knowing look. "You picked Uzbekistan because it was the most obscure one you could think of at the moment?"

"Pretty much, yeah."

Roy said, "But it's not just about memorizing data. You have to do something with it."

"Give us an example," said Michelle.

"After analyzing the data on the Wall, I told our government to help the Afghans increase poppy production."

"Why would you do that? It's used to make opium, which is the main ingredient in heroin," said Sean.

"Afghanistan had a blight when I first came on board at the E-Program. It knocked poppy production down thirty percent."

"But isn't that a good thing?" asked Michelle.

"Not really. When you have a shortage of something, what happens?"

"The price of the commodity goes up," answered Sean.

"Right. The Taliban derive ninety-two percent of

their revenue from the opium poppy sales. Because of the blight their income went up nearly sixty percent. It gave them a lot more resources to hurt us. It was speculated in the media that NATO had intentionally introduced the blight in an effort to destroy the poppy production. I conjectured that it was the Taliban that actually did so to cause the prices to skyrocket."

"Why did you think that?" asked Sean.

"On the Wall was an article published in an obscure agricultural journal. It mentioned a scientist whom I recognized as a sympathizer for the Taliban. The article stated that this scientist had traveled to India where it's believed the blight originated about six months before it appeared in Helmand and Kandahar. He brought the source of the blight back and the Taliban caused the blight to jack up prices. So it was my recommendation for the US to stop the blight from happening again and to allow more land for poppy production. Now the Taliban's income is projected to fall by half next year. But I also have a little surprise planned for them."

"Which is?"

"We've introduced a hybrid seed into the poppy plant production in Afghanistan. The poppies turn out just fine. However, when you try to use those poppies to make heroin you end up with something far closer to aspirin. So the poppy becomes what it always was supposed to be, a pretty plant."

"And you proposed that?" asked Michelle. "How?"

"The Wall provides me with everything, but I

supplement it with things that I learn on my own. The hybrid at first glance didn't seem to be anything special when I read about it. It wasn't even being discussed in the context of poppy production and certainly not in the effort against the Taliban. But when I learned of it and saw that it could be extended to such an effort I proposed it as a tactical maneuver with potentially strategic implications."

"What do you mean?" asked Sean.

Roy readjusted his glasses. He looked like the absentminded professor addressing a class. "Because now it goes far beyond mere supply and demand and price points. If the criminal element knows it can't rely on the integrity of Afghan poppy production it won't buy from them under any circumstances. It also has the added benefit of the drug cartels being very angry with the Taliban for ruining a year's worth of heroin production. That's billions of dollars. The cartel will take its revenge with the result that many of the Taliban's higher-ups will end up dead. With poppy production out of play other crop possibilities become viable, none of which will yield nearly the same amount of money to terrorists fighting us. Farmers will still be able to make a decent living, and the cartel will have to search for another source of heroin ingredients. Win-win for us."

"Pretty impressive," said Michelle.

"I can see the forest and every tree in it. It's an ecosystem of sorts where everything impacts everything else. I can see how things connect to one another, no matter how unconnected they might seem."

Michelle sat back. "You would absolutely rock on *Jeopardy*."

Roy looked alarmed at the thought. "No, I'd be too nervous. I'd get tongue-tied."

"Nervous?" exclaimed Sean. "That's just a game show. You're deciding policy for the United States of America."

"But I'm not competing with anyone. It's just me. It's not the same."

"If you say so," replied Sean, who looked thoroughly unconvinced of this.

"We have satellites positioned all around the globe. Much of what I see on the Wall are real-time video of events in every country." He paused. "It's a little like being God peering down at his creations, seeing what they're up to, and then flinging down fire and brimstone to those who most deserve it. I don't really care for that part of it."

Michelle stared into the fire. "I bet. And it creeps me out that there are people watching everything you do from hundreds of miles up."

Sean said, "They're not watching everybody and everything, Michelle. With over six billion people on the planet that would be impossible."

She looked at Sean. "Oh yeah? Well, they can keep eyes on whoever they want to. Remember when we went out to Edgar's house? No one followed us. No one could have seen us from the ground. But those goons still showed up. They knew we were there somehow. I bet they have eyes in the sky on Edgar's home."

Roy looked at her and said, "Eyes in the sky on my house?"

She said, "Yep. As far as I can see it's the only way it could have worked."

In the firelight Roy's eyes seemed magnified behind the glasses. "Do you think the satellite was watching my house 24/7?"

Sean glanced at Michelle. He said, "Twenty-four/ seven? I don't know. Why?"

Roy just kept staring at the fire and didn't say anything.

Finally what he was getting at dawned on Sean. He said, "Hold on. If that's the case, how did the satellite not see the people planting the bodies in your barn?"

Roy stirred and turned to him. "There can only be one answer to that, of course. Someone ordered the satellite to look away at the precise time it was being done."

"That would leave a paper trail. And that would take some pretty heavy authorization," said Sean.

"Like the secretary of DHS," said Roy.

79

"Give me the status. Bad?"

Mason Quantrell sat in a deep leather seat of his luxurious private jet that was actually a Boeing 787 Dreamliner customized for its fortunate owner. It had a painting of the fleet-footed Mercury on its tail representing the symbol of Quantrell's company. The jet was far larger and more costly than Peter Bunting's Gulfstream G550. Yet as a billionaire Mason Quantrell could easily afford the most expensive toys on the market. And in truth Uncle Sam had footed a large part of its cost.

"Pretty bad," replied the only other person in the passenger cabin.

James Harkes sat back and sipped a glass of water while Quantrell was already working on his second bourbon and water. The CEO looked haggard, with quarter-moon bags under his eyes.

"She's going to come at you hard, Mr. Quantrell."

Quantrell spread his hands helplessly. "But after our last meeting things seemed fine. And then I got the call from Bunting. Right in my office, no less. The ballsy prick. He dared us to trace him."

"And you couldn't?"

"No," Quantrell said glumly. "The bastard was always good at the cloak-and-dagger stuff. Did you know I recruited him out of the PhD program at Stanford?"

"No, I didn't know that."

"He was in Oxford on a Rhodes scholarship before that. He did college in less than three years. Was already on people's radars for some white papers he'd published on the rising threat of global terrorism and how best to deal with it. The work was very specific. He very nearly predicted 9/11 twenty years before it happened."

"So he came to work for you?"

Quantrell nodded as the plane banked left and began its initial descent. "For three years. He did a great job, really turned things around for us. Hell, I was grooming him back then to run the whole damn company. But he had other ideas."

"The E-Program? Seems like you would have jumped on that."

"I would have but he never gave me the chance. He left, started his own business, and quickly moved up the pecking order of contractors. I have to admit his stuff was good. No, it was better than good. And then he took it up to a whole other level with the E-Program."

"Ecclesiastes," said Harkes. "The E-Program?"

"What? Oh, right. Didn't know the man had a

biblical side to him." Quantrell downed the rest of his drink. "And then he sold the concept to the folks that mattered in D.C. Now the rest of us have been eating his dust for years."

"Ever think of suing?"

"No grounds. He developed the stuff after he left me and he never violated the noncompete we had. Way too smart for that. No, I hate him because I don't like to lose. And with him around I've been losing. A lot." He put his empty glass down and buckled his seat belt as the plane hit some turbulence. "But Ellen Foster can hurt me a lot more. And I'm not talking just dollars and cents."

"Yes she can," agreed Harkes.

"President gave her carte blanche."

"Yes he did."

"Collateral damage? Meaning me?"

"Makes sense, doesn't it?"

"But she has to tie it into Bunting and the others. How does she plan to get to them?"

"She has an ace in the hole," noted Harkes.

"Who?"

"Megan Riley."

Quantrell sat forward, looking astonished. "The lawyer? She's one of Ellen's people?"

"No. She was kidnapped from Maine. Foster is holding her somewhere."

Quantrell rubbed his chin. "This really is extra-ordinary."

"Yes it is," agreed Harkes.

"She kept me out of the loop on that."

"Me too, until now."

"And Foster is planning to use her to get to Bunting and the others? How?"

"Playing on their guilt. And their conscience. Riley is an innocent victim in all this. If it's played right, we can use her to draw them out."

"And Foster wants to survive all this with her reputation and Cabinet position in place?"

"Yes she does. I told her it would be hard but not impossible."

"Does she require my termination as part of the plan?"

"Desires, but does not require," was Harkes's diplomatic reply.

"Then we have an opening."

"I think we do. A very advantageous one for you if we play it just right."

Quantrell said, "You know what they're doing, of course."

"They're playing each of you against the other. Bunting called you to turn you against Foster. And Paul corralled Foster in that ladies' room and did the same thing."

"Clever. Foster has clearly fallen hook, line, and sinker for it. I have to admit Bunting scared the crap out of me when he called."

"And Kelly Paul can be very persuasive."

"She's the most worrisome pawn on the board right now," said Quantrell.

"I would hardly call her a pawn, sir. We can't underestimate the woman."

"Had run-ins with her before?'

"A couple of times. And each time the result was not one that I desired."

"If she can beat you, Harkes, she scares the shit out of me."

"She has to know I'm involved in this because Bunting would have told her, but they don't know I'm working for you. No one knows that."

"*My* ace in the hole." Quantrell gave a satisfied smile. "How quickly can you deploy the Riley angle?"

"As soon as you say go, Mr. Quantrell."

"Go," replied the CEO with Mercury-like quickness.

80

"I can't believe I never thought of that," said Bunting.

He stared over at Kelly Paul as she sat in a chair and looked down at her phone. She had just gotten off a call with Sean King. She and Bunting were in her "shared" apartment in New York City, not that far from Bunting's brownstone. The mansion was empty, his family safe, for now.

"The satellite coverage," Paul said.

"Twenty-four/seven," Bunting added.

"Provided by DHS?"

"I suppose. Although if they did it, they didn't bother to tell me about it." He looked out the window, where the rain beat relentlessly down. "But moving those eyes is not done lightly," he said. "Edgar would've been a priority for them."

"It might very well require Foster's signature," agreed Paul. "That's a paper trail."

"Now if we can just prove the satellite was watching and that order was issued."

Paul didn't say anything.

"What are you thinking, Kelly?"

"What if it wasn't moved?"

Bunting looked away from the window. "What do you mean?"

"What if the satellite saw exactly what happened?"

"Are you alleging that your brother is indeed a serial killer?" Bunting said in a bewildered tone.

"No."

"Okay. So the only other conclusion is that they framed him. They planted the bodies in that barn. If that were the plan, why would they allow the eyes in the sky to watch? It would prove that your brother was innocent. It would have destroyed their plan. And more to the point, that fact would have come out by now."

"Not necessarily. You know as well as I do that satellite platforms vary greatly. And who is to say it was a government one?"

"You mean commercial?"

"Or essentially a private one."

"Why?" asked Bunting.

"If the sat was government-owned it would be harder to control the information, even for Foster. But if it were private eyes?"

"Which she might have agreed to since she was planning this whole campaign with Quantrell against me and the E-Program outside of DHS channels."

"Or it might be more complicated than that."

"How?"

"Mercury has a number of satellites, correct?"

"Sure. Quantrell was one of the first in the field."

"So let's say he has the bird on Eddie's property too. They pick a weekday when Eddie is in D.C. Foster orders her sat to look away. They take the bodies in and bury them in the barn in a way that will be easily discoverable later. They phone in a tip to the police, and my brother takes the fall."

"But why wouldn't Quantrell turn his bird off too?" asked Bunting. Before she could answer his question, he did. "In case things went to hell he'd have leverage with Foster."

"Exactly."

"So how do we confirm this?"

"There are ways. I'll get working on them."

"If we can get pictures of what actually happened, then Edgar goes scot free."

"But that doesn't get us out of the woods yet."

"No, it's only one piece, you're right."

Bunting's phone rang. He pulled it from his pocket. Paul eyed him. "Who is it?"

"Avery."

He answered and put it on speaker so Paul could hear, too. "Talk fast, Avery."

The other man's voice was strained. "Mr. Bunting, I received a call from someone."

"Who?"

"I don't know. They didn't leave their name. But they had a message they wanted me to convey to you."

"What was it?"

"They want to make an exchange."

"What sort of exchange?"

"A woman named Megan Riley in trade for Edgar Roy." He paused.

"Avery, is that all? Roy for Riley?"

"No, sir. They also want you."

Bunting drew a quick breath and looked toward the window, as though *they* might be lurking right outside.

Avery sounded near tears.

"Calm down, Avery, it'll be okay. Did they give you details?"

They heard him swallow a sob and he said, "The day after tomorrow at the Mall in Washington, D.C. Twelve o'clock in the afternoon. Across from the Air and Space Museum. They said if you tried any tricks, called the police or anything, they'd kill Ms. Riley and shoot up the place. Lots of people will die."

"Okay, Avery, okay. I appreciate the call. You did good. Now you need to get somewhere safe."

Bunting flinched when the other voice came over the phone. "Too late for that," said the voice. There was a single gunshot and they heard a body drop.

"Avery!" screamed Bunting, as he snatched up the phone.

The voice said, "If you and Roy are not at the Mall on the day after tomorrow in the requisite place at the requisite time, Riley is dead and so are a lot of other people. Do you understand?"

Bunting said nothing.

Paul took the phone from him and said, "We understand. We'll be there."

The line went silent.

Bunting stumbled over to the window and pressed his face against it.

Paul said, "I'm sorry, Peter."

Bunting didn't say anything for a while and Paul let the silence persist.

"He was just a kid."

"Yes he was," she conceded.

"He shouldn't be dead. He's not a field agent. He's an office geek."

"Lots of people shouldn't be dead. But they are. Now, we have to focus on the day after tomorrow."

"Our plan didn't work. We were turning them against each other but didn't factor this possibility in." He turned to look at her. "They have an army, Kelly. We've got what?"

"I could say we have right on our side, but it seems a bit trite under the circumstances. Yet we still have to try."

"I want to strangle Quantrell and Foster with my bare hands, I swear to God I do."

"They forced Avery to make that call and they did it to throw you off, Peter."

"Well, they did a damn good job," he blurted out.

"They will expect your thinking to be clouded. They will expect you to act less than rationally. They will expect you to just give in."

"I don't even know this Megan Riley. And they want me and your brother in return?"

"They killed Avery. They will kill her too. And they've sweetened the pot. Lots of other people on the Mall will die as well."

He sat back down, wiped his eyes and cheeks dry, and drew a long, replenishing breath. "Okay, the best I can do to avenge Avery is to think this all through. First, why the day after tomorrow? Why wait?"

"The Mall is a popular place, always people around."

"But the day after tomorrow. Will there be more people around?"

He performed a Web search on his phone. Paul looked at the screen.

"I have to hand it to them. Shows some style."

"They're going to do a hostage exchange in the middle of a peace rally," said Bunting grimly.

81

It was early in the morning, and Michelle had driven most of the night to get them to D.C. Sean was asleep in the seat next to her. Roy had nodded off in the backseat. The sky was overcast and promised more rain from a storm system that had been pounding the East Coast.

"Cold, wet, and dark. Sort of matches my mood."

Michelle glanced over to see that Sean was awake and staring out the window.

He looked at her and smiled resignedly. "Tomorrow will be a busy day."

They crossed over a bridge and hung a right, following the directions Paul had given them when she'd called about the latest development involving Megan Riley.

Michelle glanced over at a street corner. "I held a post on that street corner for twelve hours. It was the day after 9/11. Nobody knew what the hell was going on. I wasn't even working protection back then. I was assigned to a forgery case in Maryland. They pulled a bunch of us in to supplement the protection detail for the president and the VP. By the time I was relieved every muscle I had was in a knot. But you know what?"

"You didn't want to leave your post."

She nodded. "How'd you know?"

"When 9/11 happened I was practicing law, been out of the Service for a while. I watched it on TV along with every other American. I wanted to suit back up, come to D.C., and help out. That could never happen, of course." He grew silent and then added in a low voice, "But I really wanted to come back and help."

"Things have really gotten screwed up, haven't they?"

"Actually, they've been screwed up for a long time. Which means we all have to work a little harder to fix them."

"That's a good attitude to have." Roy sat up and swept a hand through his hair. He looked at them. "The world is complicated, so people seek complicated solutions. And there's nothing wrong with that because simple answers don't usually work. But sometimes the answers *are* simple and people still refuse to see them."

"Meaning?" asked Sean.

"Meaning the simpler approach in certain circumstances is better, if only because there're fewer things that can go wrong."

"You know what they want," said Michelle.

"Me and Peter Bunting, yes. For Megan Riley. And

of course their threat to kill many other innocent people."

"So what's the simple answer to that?" asked Sean.

"To give them what they want."

"Turn you and Bunting over to them? They'll kill you both."

"Maybe, maybe not."

"They will kill you," said Sean. "They have no other possible reason to do the exchange."

"One would think," said Roy somewhat vaguely.

"We're meeting your sister and Bunting. Be there in about ten minutes," said Michelle. "Do you think she'll have a simple answer?"

"I think she'll have an answer. Kel usually does. To everything."

"Her options may be limited."

"She knows that, I'm sure."

"She's not going to give you up, Edgar," said Michelle. "You're her brother. She's not going to do that."

"But then a lot of people will get hurt."

"We'll have to do something called damage containment," replied Sean.

"I'm familiar with the phrase. But that's usually reserved for cases where you have multiple assets on the ground. We don't have that luxury. Foster and by extension Quantrell have lots of resources."

"Do you think they're working together still? Even

after they were told one is trying to screw the other?" asked Michelle.

Roy said, "They're playing it on multiple fronts. They'll prepare for the worst but execute any plan that seems feasible. Riley being a valuable asset is one they held in reserve. They may have intended on playing this one all along. That doesn't mean they now trust each other. In fact, they probably don't."

"So what's the glue that's holding them together?"

"My sister talked to me about that. She thinks the glue is James Harkes. And I agree with her."

"Tell us about him," said Sean.

"Decorated veteran. Purple Heart. Bronze Star. Short-listed for the Silver. Been a field agent for the CIA and DIA. He's good."

"Is he smart enough to play this all the way?"

"You'll have to ask my sister. She knows more about him than I do."

"So they've worked together? She mentioned something like that, I think."

"I'm not so sure they worked together."

"What then?"

"I think they almost killed each other. And from the way she tells it she was lucky to walk away."

"If they're both American agents why would that have happened?" asked Michelle.

"It's complicated, apparently. But Harkes being on their side is not good for us."

Sean turned back around and sighed. "Great."

A few minutes later they turned down a quiet residential street. The garage door opened at their approach, and Michelle drove into it. The door closed behind them.

Kelly Paul was waiting at the door into the house.

"Do we have a plan for tomorrow?" asked Sean, as they passed through into the house.

"We have a plan," replied Paul. "There's just no guarantee that it will work."

82

The day set for the hostage exchange broke clear and cold. The masses on the Mall were in place by ten o'clock. There were speeches, demonstrations, songs, more speeches, portable toilets by the thousands, and lots of signs with the peace symbol on them.

The Air and Space Museum was one of the most popular of the Smithsonian's offerings. It was just down the street from the Smithsonian Castle.

The museum was ground zero.

Two hours to go.

The cold weather helped, because everyone was dressed in coats, hats, and scarves, and thus disguise was made far easier.

Sean and Michelle were on the Mall near the US Capitol. Edgar Roy, wearing a hoodie and with his face pointed downward, sat in a wheelchair that Sean was pushing. Sean used one hand to tug his coat tighter around him. It was a snug fit for a very good reason.

Michelle's gaze swept the area. She said, "Looks to be over a hundred thousand people out here at least."

"At least," agreed Sean.

"A hundred and sixty-nine thousand," corrected Roy.

Sean glanced down. "How do you know that? Don't tell me you counted everyone?"

"No. But I've seen enough grids of the Mall in my work with the E-Program. It's a top target of terrorists. You can determine the number of people by how many grids are full."

"Regardless, it's still a lot of people," said Michelle.

"And potentially a lot of casualties," added Sean in a worried tone.

James Harkes was standing in probably the best observation post on the Mall: at the top of the Washington Monument with a pair of stellar optics. He surveyed the people down below and then made a call.

Mason Quantrell was on his Boeing Dreamliner coming back from a meeting in California. He answered before the first ring had finished.

"Status?" he asked eagerly.

"The Mall is filling up. I have a prime post. All the players are in place or soon will be. When will you be on the ground?"

"Three hours and twenty minutes."

"I hope to have good news to welcome you with, sir."

"Not that you need a reminder, but you pull this off, there's fifty million dollars waiting for you, tax free. And I'll throw in another ten million as a bonus. You'll never have to work another day in your life."

"I appreciate that, Mr. Quantrell. More than you know."

"Good luck, Harkes."

As Harkes clicked off he thought, *None of this will be about luck.* He made another call.

This too was answered on the first ring.

Ellen Foster was at her home sitting on her bed. She was still in her nightgown, her hair unkempt and her gut full of acid. Today was Saturday. She had had an event planned for out of town but had her people reschedule it, citing illness. Which wasn't far from the truth. She felt quite sick.

"Harkes, how's it going?" Her voice was high-pitched, riddled by nerves barely held in check.

"Things are coming into place. But you need to take a few deep breaths and get yourself under control."

"Is it that obvious?"

"Unfortunately, yes."

He heard her following his advice. One-two-three deep breaths. When she came back on the line, her voice sounded almost normal.

"Have you spotted them yet?"

"No, but I wouldn't expect to. They have a while yet. And knowing them, they won't show themselves a second before it's necessary."

"How do you know that?"

"Because if it were me, I wouldn't either."

"You really think they'll come?"

"Frankly, I can't control what they do, Secretary Foster. All I can do is create an atmosphere where the probabilities are that they will do what we want them to do. And I think that we have."

"How do you see it going down?"

"They get Riley. We get Roy and Bunting."

"I disagree. Kelly Paul won't let it go that easily. When she trapped me in that bathroom at Lincoln Center she was very clear. She wanted her brother back. If she has him she won't let him go without a fight. It's just not possible."

"She lied to you," said Harkes. "She had her brother the entire time. She was trying to turn you against Quantrell. If she didn't have her brother, why would she have agreed to come to the exchange? We called their bluff and it worked."

"You're right, I'm still not thinking clearly."

"But I don't disagree with you about Kelly Paul's intentions. She'll try to offer up Bunting only on this exchange. They'll figure we won't retaliate if we get something in return for giving up Riley."

"But what about Roy?"

"I have a plan for that."

"You mean follow them back to where they're holding him?"

"Something even better. Look, I've got to go. Things are starting to heat up."

"James, I will be very appreciative when this is all over. I mean that."

"I understand . . . Ellen."

After she put down the phone, Foster gazed thoughtfully out the window of her bedroom. She had not told James Harkes the exact truth. She had kept something back.

Her fail-safe.

And she had done that for one simple reason. While she trusted Harkes, there was only one person in the world that Ellen Foster trusted fully.

And that was Ellen Foster.

Harkes looked down at the Mall teeming with people rallying to restore peace in the world. They were completely unaware that the potential for violence lay right in their tranquil midst. Down there were a dozen of Quantrell's paid mercenaries set up in precise tactical positions. They were armed and unafraid to use their weapons. They took orders from James Harkes. It was his job to make sure they were where they needed to be. Also down there somewhere was Kelly Paul.

Harkes walked briskly down the steps.

On the way he checked his watch.

One hour and twelve minutes to go.

83

Kelly Paul gazed up at the Washington Monument. If she were going to have an observation post here, that would have been the one she would choose. As she continued to watch, her surveillance seemed to pay off.

James Harkes exited the monument, turned left, and headed toward ground zero. She followed his path until he disappeared into the crowds.

Paul walked for a while longer before glancing at the man next to her.

Peter Bunting was dressed in faded jeans and a college sweatshirt. A ball cap was on his head and he was holding a sign that read, Make Babies, Not War.

"You blend in nicely at a peace rally, Peter, particularly for a defense contractor," she told him dryly.

Bunting did not smile at her little joke. "How many do you think they have here?"

"More than they need. Overwhelming force is not just a government prerogative."

"Do you think Quantrell or Foster are here?"

"Nowhere near the place. Leaders invariably let their minions fight it out."

"Do you think it will become violent?"

"I have no way to know. I hope not, but it's really out of my control."

He gazed at her with respect. "You don't seem nervous."

"On the contrary, I am very nervous."

"You hide it well."

"Yes I do. And you need to do the same."

The whole time she was talking she was watching everything going on around them.

"What do you think they did with Avery's body?"

"I don't know."

"I'd like to give him a proper burial."

"Fine, Peter. But for now let's focus on those still breathing."

She looked at her watch.

One hour to go.

Megan Riley was wedged between two large men who had guns under their parkas. Her hair was filthy, her face was unclean, and there was a deep bruise on her left cheek from a blow she had suffered. Her wrists were rubbed raw from handcuffs she'd worn. Her blouse underneath the jacket was smeared with blood. She had lost weight and her eyes seemed unfocused. She trudged along, her gaze downcast.

Up ahead was the Air and Space Museum. If she recognized it, Riley gave no reaction.

There was now only ten minutes to go.

James Harkes moved through the crowds at a measured pace. He knew exactly where each of his men was positioned. The timing had to be precise. He looked ahead and saw Riley and her two bodyguards heading toward the museum. Riley had been told that she would be killed if she made a sound.

He looked in the other direction. The woman was tall and wore a dark trench coat nearly down to her ankles. The man next to her was taller. He was dressed in jeans and a sweatshirt and held a sign. They were working their way toward ground zero.

On the north side of the Mall Harkes spotted the man in the wheelchair. He was being pushed along by his companion. The dark-haired woman marched beside them. Their destination seemed to be ground zero too.

Harkes picked up his pace and reached in his pocket. He had to assume that everyone would be armed. If they weren't they were fools. He said a few words that were picked up by a communication device in his ear.

He glanced at his watch.

Two minutes to go.

*

Sean and Michelle were almost there. He tapped Roy on the shoulder.

"One minute," he said softly.

Roy nodded and put his hands on his thighs, tensing his body.

Michelle said, "See any of them yet?"

"Not yet. But they're here."

She nudged him with her arm. "Megan between two goons at five o'clock."

Sean saw this. "She looks like shit."

"This is going to be tight. You know that."

"It's always tight. Do you see Paul and Bunting?"

She nodded slightly. "Nine o'clock."

Sean glanced that way. "Do you think she sees Megan?"

"I think the lady doesn't miss much."

"Get in Secret Service mode, Michelle. Assess threats from all angles."

"That's what I've been doing ever since we stepped foot on the Mall."

Kelly Paul gripped Bunting around the elbow. "Thirty seconds."

"I know," he said. "Do you see Riley?"

"Have for the last four minutes. Quantrell's boys on either side of her."

"How many more around?"

"At least ten, I would think. I don't know the exact number."

Bunting stiffened when he saw the man.

He was gliding along; his movements seemed effortless as he slipped through the crowd. This time he was not wearing a black suit, tie, and white shirt, though. The sunglasses hid his eyes, but Bunting was certain they were registering on everything.

"Harkes! Harkes is here."

"Of course he is," said Paul softly. "Where the hell do you think he'd be?"

"He scares the shit out of me."

"He should. We've got ten seconds."

Bunting started breathing fast. "Tell me this is going to be okay, Kelly."

She gripped his arm tighter. "Almost there, Peter. Keep it together. Almost there."

She looked at her watch, picked up her pace.

It was all dead ahead.

This was her world. This was Kelly Paul's version of the Wall.

Five . . . four . . . three . . . two . . .

84

They faced each other across a two-foot span of grass that in some ways seemed as wide as the Atlantic Ocean.

James Harkes stared at Kelly Paul and she stared right back at him.

Megan Riley, engulfed by her captors, stared dumbly at the ground. Next to Paul and Bunting were Sean and Michelle, with Roy in the wheelchair.

Roy sat up and let his hood fall away.

When Megan glanced up and saw Sean and Michelle her sense of relief was profound.

"Let's make this easy and simple," said Harkes quietly. "Send Bunting and Roy over here. And you get Riley."

"Doesn't seem fair, does it?" asked Paul. "You get two and we only get one."

"That was the deal," said Harkes.

"No, that was the proposal."

Harkes eyed her with interest. "Do you really want to renegotiate now? My men have ten prearranged targets to hit if I give them the signal. If you want to be responsible for innocent people going down it's up to you, I guess. But I would advise against it."

"I can see the logic, Harkes, I really can."

"But you still disagree?"

"Not necessarily."

"We don't have unlimited time here. I need an answer."

"Suppose we give you Bunting." She grabbed Bunting's arm and pushed him forward. He jerked free and scowled at her.

"So I'm the sacrificial lamb," he snapped. "Blood thicker than water?"

Harkes shook his head. "We need the package."

"He's my brother."

"Half brother."

"Still," she said calmly.

"Do you want a demonstration of my intent?" Harkes pointed to a little boy holding a cup of hot chocolate. "I raise my hand he gets a third eye."

"You'd do that? A kid?"

Harkes looked at her with a blank expression. "I can take out a granny if you'd prefer. The point would be the same."

"You're a real bastard, you know that?" she said.

"A remark which gets us nowhere. Shall I raise my hand?"

"You'll just kill my brother."

Harkes looked over at Roy, who sat there in the wheelchair. "What if I tell you that won't happen?"

"Why should I believe anything you say?"

"His brains are a gold mine. Who throws away gold?"

"You mean not for this country?"

"That would be problematic."

"I'm not a traitor," said Roy.

"You'd be alive," replied Harkes. "Your choice."

"You probably won't even let us out of here alive, even if we do give him up," said Paul.

"I give you my word that that won't be the case."

"I don't trust you."

"I don't blame you. I don't trust you either."

"I hope they're paying you enough to commit treason."

"Your words, not mine."

"When did you sell out, Harkes? Do you even remember?"

Harkes's features hardened for barely a second. "I'm going to raise my hand unless Edgar Roy gets out of the wheelchair and walks over here with Mr. Bunting. Right now. Do you want the kid to be able to finish his hot chocolate?"

Sean and Michelle eyed the little boy. Michelle tensed her body to leap.

Roy rose from his chair.

His sister said, "Eddie! No!"

"Enough people have died because of me, Kel. No more. Nobody else. Especially not a little boy."

"They told me you had a big brain, Roy," said

Harkes. "Just right over here, please. Bunting, you too."

They watched as Bunting and Roy stepped forward. On a nod from Harkes the men released Megan, who stumbled toward Sean and Michelle.

Sean's gaze had not stopped moving. He had gone grid by grid, reaching far away with his gaze and then pulling it back in, step-by-step, like casting a fishing line and slowly reeling it in, looking for threats. It was like he had never been away from the Secret Service. He had pulled post on the Mall many times while with the Service. What to look for and how had been drilled into his mind until there was no difference between conscious thought and instinct.

As soon as Megan joined them Sean saw it. A man who was paying them a little too much attention while trying very hard not to seem to be. His hand went to his pocket. An optics flare followed as he took aim.

Sean leaped, his body parallel to the ground.

The shot was fired.

The round hit Sean squarely in the chest. He grunted once, hit the grass hard, and slid.

"Sean!" screamed Michelle.

The men who had been on either side of Riley suddenly went down fast, before they could pull their guns, their bodies writhing in pain. Men swarmed them, held them down, the glint of gunmetal flashed in the sunlight.

"Where's the shooter?" one of them screamed.

In the face of the shot, the crowds on the Mall acted like a wave gathering strength. This stampede built speed and mass, and soon the wave was beyond control.

James Harkes was on the move. He dropped two men with his weapon. They fell to the grass out of the fight. Harkes kept going, his gaze darting in all directions. He didn't know who had fired the shot, but it had severely messed up his plans. His carefully arranged tactical positions were now being swept away.

But all he could do was keep going, keep striking.

Michelle knelt next to Sean.

"Sean!"

He struggled to his knees. "Go. Go. Finish the plan. I'm okay."

She looked at the rip in his body armor where the slug had hit. "Are you sure?"

He grimaced, one hand pressed against his chest. "Michelle, just get them out of here! Now!"

She squeezed his arm, leaped up, grabbed Megan and Roy by the wrist, and shouted, "With me, now."

They raced off across the Mall, fighting their way through the screaming crowd that was now running flat-out in all directions.

*

Harkes finally spotted her and tenaciously fought through the crowd to get to the woman.

Kelly Paul's broad back was to him. He was inches away.

"Paul!"

She turned, saw him, raised her gun, and fired.

The man behind Harkes grunted once as the rubber bullet hit him smack in the chest. He fell forward, and the gun he was about to fire at Harkes slipped from his hand.

Paul joined Harkes. He looked down at the fallen man as FBI agents ran up and cuffed the injured fellow.

"Thanks," Harkes said.

"I think he spotted you taking out Quantrell's boys and realized what you were really up to."

She pointed to her left. "I got two more of them. The FBI has them as well."

Harkes nodded and held up his Taser. "I got two. Plus the two with Riley. That's five more to go, then," he said. "We've got the Mall locked down. They can't get away."

"Where did that first shot come from?" she asked.

"No idea. But it didn't help us a damn bit. Your brother? Riley?"

"On schedule. Where's Bunting?"

He pointed across the street where two FBI agents had escorted the man to safety.

"Good job," she said.

"Been after these folks a long time. Things could have blown up at any point along the way."

"But they didn't."

"Good working with you again," said Harkes.

"Couldn't have managed it without you, Jim."

Michelle, with Megan and Roy in tow, pushed and clawed her way through the panicked crowds. She finally saw a sliver of daylight and pulled them through it.

Roy shouted, "Look out!"

It was an unnecessary warning. Michelle had already seen it coming. She let go of his arm, twisted her body in the air, and laid the attacker out flat on his back with a thunderous kick, breaking his jaw.

"My God," said Roy, staring down at the fallen man who weighed about two fifty. "How did you do that?"

"I've got brains in my feet," she barked. "Come on. Move, move!"

They sprinted across the Mall. A few seconds later, they reached the van. Michelle fired up the engine and slammed it into gear.

Edgar Roy looked back at the chaos on the Mall.

"Didn't go exactly according to plan," he said.

"Almost never does," replied Michelle as the van sped off. "But we're alive, that I'll take." She glanced in the rearview mirror. "Megan, are you okay?"

Megan sat up in the seat and pushed her ratty hair out of her eyes. "I am now. I didn't think I was going to make it." She rubbed at her swollen wrists. "They beat the crap out of me."

"I know. We found your sweater with blood on it."

Megan touched her shoulder. "Knife," she said simply.

"But you're okay?"

"They just needed some blood to leave behind to make sure you knew they were serious. And I got really toughened up over the last few days," she said quietly. "I'm sorry about Officer Dobkin." She drew a long breath. "It was pretty damn awful. They kicked in the door and just shot him. He never had a chance to pull his weapon."

"I know. But at least you're safe," said Michelle.

Megan looked at Roy. "I'm glad they got you out." She held out her hand. "Nice to finally meet you."

Roy shook her hand and said shyly, "You too. Sorry about before. Not communicating with you and all."

"Don't worry about it," said Megan. "All I want right now is a hot shower and some clean clothes."

"Got just the place and it's close by," said Michelle. "Be there in five minutes."

Megan looked behind them and said in a panicked tone, "Michelle, I think there's someone following us."

"There is. FBI. They'll provide perimeter security at the safe house. Later, when everything is over, we'll go to WFO. They'll need detailed statements from you, Megan."

"More than happy to give them." She smiled. "But can I have the shower first?"

"You got it."

They drove on. The black SUV tailing them sped up and drew closer.

85

Quantrell's twelve men were all subdued, cuffed, and hauled away in FBI transport vans. The participants in the peace rally probably thought the gunshot was from some jerk that didn't share their enthusiasm for a less violent world. The crowd had congregated at the far end of the Mall, away from the less than peaceful activity.

Sean, Kelly Paul, Bunting, and James Harkes met in the middle of the Mall. Sean was listing to one side.

"How bad?" said Paul, as she looked at the hole in his body armor.

"Bruised rib, but it's a lot better than being dead."

"You saved Eddie's life," she said, gripping his arm.

Harkes said, "They obviously didn't fill me in on the entire plan. Didn't know they were going to do that."

Paul said, "Might have just been someone looking to get a kill bonus."

"How'd you spot the shooter before anyone else did?" asked Harkes.

"Used to do it for a living," replied Sean.

"Status of the others?" asked Paul.

"Checked with Michelle," said Sean. "They're at the safe house. Megan is pretty beat up, but with some rest, clean clothes, and some food she should be okay. The wound on her shoulder was nasty, but Michelle cleaned it up. When she goes into WFO to make her statement they can check her out more thoroughly."

"Good," said Paul. She looked at Harkes. "Next move?"

"I get to visit a couple of my favorite people and tell them things that will literally change their lives in a way they hoped would never happen."

"Please give Ellen Foster and Mason Quantrell my best."

"They thought they were using Megan to get Bunting and Roy. I've got nothing against the lady lawyer, but we were really using that to get them to a face-to-face."

Paul added, "Only way it was going to work."

"Are you sure you have enough to put both of them away?" asked Bunting anxiously. "They're both very good at deflecting blame. I have vast personal experience of that."

Harkes said, "I know you do, Mr. Bunting. But we've had this sting going for some time now, and the prosecutors are pretty confident we've got what we need. And I'll make a star witness. If it wasn't just he-said-she-said legal issues, I could have arrested her before now. The cost for waiting was huge. A lot of people died. The hit on Agent Murdock will haunt me the rest of my life."

"He found out about the E-Program, my brother said."

Harkes nodded. "They had the prison cell tapped. They freaked and authorized the kill without talking to me about it. I found out Murdock was dead when everyone else did." He paused. "But now we've got the bastards."

"I hope so," said Bunting without much confidence in his voice.

Harkes picked up on this and said, "Just to reassure you, we also got a nice little bonus on the evidence front."

Bunting perked up. "What?"

"We checked out the satellite angle that you gave us," said Harkes. "It was better than we could have hoped. Foster signed off on the sat position change over Edgar Roy's home for a three-hour period on a Wednesday night a week before Roy was arrested."

"And that's when the bodies were put in the barn," said Sean.

"Right."

"But why was it better than we could have hoped?" asked Paul. "You just have the sat change. That's instructive but not necessarily incriminating. There could have been other reasons for the change, or at least she could argue that."

"No, she really can't."

"Why?" asked Bunting sharply.

"Because it turns out Mason Quantrell also had a pair of eyes on the barn the whole time from his private platform. It was like you said, he wanted some extra insurance in case Foster turned on him."

"So you're saying we have video feed of the bodies going in?" asked Sean.

"Yes we do. Nice and clear. And it turns out the guys who did the deed worked with Foster when she was stationed in the Far East. I guess she didn't trust Quantrell to do the job right. We've picked up these men, and let's just say they are being cooperative with the Bureau in building the necessary case."

"Couldn't have happened to two nicer people," said Bunting, who looked and sounded far more confident now.

Harkes patted him on the arm. "Sorry I had to keep you in the dark on everything. And for roughing you up and threatening your family. The people I was dealing with were very smart and they were watching me the whole time. I had to play it right next to the edge to get them to trust me."

Bunting said, "I have to admit, my suspicions about you were aroused after you let Avery live, even after I pushed the button." He paused. "But now he really is dead."

"No he isn't. He'll be waiting for you at the New York office on Monday."

Bunting's face collapsed. "What? But the phone call?"

"They wanted to kill him. But I convinced them we could always do it later. So we just did a little subterfuge on you instead. I wasn't going to let them kill the kid."

"Thank God for that."

"And your family is safe and sound under federal eyes."

"I know. I spoke to my wife." He hesitated. "I'm thinking about taking some time off. I believe the E-Program can survive without me for a bit."

"I think that would be a great idea," said Paul. "And quite frankly Eddie needs a break, too. And he and his big sister are going to start spending more time together, starting right now."

Harkes walked off to finish what he'd started a long time ago.

"A good guy to have on your side," said Paul, as she watched him go.

"I'm sure he said the same thing about you," replied Bunting.

"How did you two meet?" asked Sean.

"Let's just say it was a mutually beneficial arrangement."

Sean was about to respond when his phone buzzed. He looked down and recognized the caller's name.

It would be a call that would change absolutely everything for Sean King.

86

The Dreamliner 787 landed at Dulles Airport right on time, and the jumbo jet slowly came to a halt. The pilot taxied the plane to an open space on the outskirts of the airport property. There were two SUVs waiting at this spot. The jet door opened, a set of portable steps was wheeled into place, and Mason Quantrell walked down them. He was dressed in pressed jeans and a white shirt with a North Face parka over that. He had a briefcase in hand. He looked casual and happy.

He smiled and waved when the window of one of the SUVs rolled down and he saw Harkes sitting inside. He climbed in next to him.

"Good flight?" asked Harkes.

"Fine, fine. Got your message. We were just descending into Dulles. Sounds like it could not have gone better."

"No, it really couldn't have," replied Harkes.

"I can't wait to hear all about it. Why don't we drive to my home in Great Falls? My chef studied in Paris and my wine cellar is open for your inspection.

We can have something to eat and you can debrief me." He paused and added, "Does Foster know yet?"

Harkes smiled. "I was saving the best for last."

Quantrell laughed. "You've set it up beautifully. She will be beholden to me forever since we saved her tight little ass. I can get any budget increase I want through now."

"We need to make one little detour," said Harkes.

Quantrell looked at him. "What? Where?" Quantrell also noticed that the SUV had not started up. They weren't moving.

Harkes rolled his window down again and motioned with his hand.

"What are you doing, Harkes?"

Quantrell flinched when the truck door was ripped open and four men appeared there.

"FBI," said the lead agent. "Mason Quantrell, you're under arrest."

As the agent read Quantrell his rights, Harkes opened his car door, climbed out, closed the door behind him, and walked off.

He never looked back.

One down, one to go.

Ellen Foster had bathed, taken time over her hair, and dressed meticulously. She now sat in a chair in the front room of her beautiful home, in her fashionable neighborhood filled with highly accomplished people.

This was where she belonged, she was sure of that. She had overcome much to get to this point in her life. And now?

When the message had come it was an unexpected one. She had thought it would be Harkes informing her that everything was fine. That would have been the fair and just thing, Foster firmly believed. Only life was often neither fair nor just. This was one of those times, unfortunately.

Sitting in her bathroom in front of her mirror applying her makeup, she had thought a lot about the last few years of her life. They had been filled with many triumphs and a few unavoidable failures—like her marriage. Her husband was rich but not nearly as famous as his wife, and that had grated on him. A supremely insecure man despite his fortune, he had finally driven away all the feelings she once had for him.

The divorce had made some headlines and then died away. And her life had gone on. As it should have.

She sat with her hands neatly folded in her lap as she gazed around the perfectly appointed room. It really was a beautiful space; she'd been so content here. So happy. It was a perfect blend of seemingly blissful domestic life and professional superstardom. She touched her earrings. Extravagant gifts from her ex. The necklace she wore was worth fifty thousand dollars. The diamond and sapphire ring nearly twice that. She wanted to look perfect for this, her final act.

It was an act necessitated because Harkes had betrayed her.

Harkes had been working for others. He had not been loyal. Instead of helping her, he had succeeded in destroying her. The underling had turned on its mistress. She should have seen it coming. But it was too late for that now.

Life really was unfair. All she had done was try to keep the country safe. That was her job. And for that, this was her reward?

She heard the trucks screech to a halt in front of her home. She rose, went over to the secretary, and removed the gun from its hiding place. She wondered briefly how the papers would initially report it. Not that it mattered, really. Her ex-husband would be mildly surprised, she assumed, though he'd remarried a far younger woman and was starting on the family she had never wanted to have with him.

Foster did regret that she would have no one to mourn her. That was sad, she concluded.

The footsteps raced up the front porch.

Her security detail would be powerless to stop them.

That was all right. She didn't need them to be stopped.

They had a warrant, she was sure of that.

She shook her head, took a breath.

They were right at the door. They pounded on it.

"FBI," one deep voice said. "Secretary Foster, please open the door."

She lifted the Glock to her right temple, positioning herself such that she would fall onto the couch. She smiled. A soft landing. She deserved that. It was fortunate that she had taken two Valium. That made things far less stressful. Anyone contemplating killing herself, she thought, should take advantage of the product.

The FBI gave one last warning. She could envision the hydraulic ram being placed against her front door. It was hundred-year-old reclaimed wood. It would not yield easily. She had a few more seconds.

She wondered if Harkes would be with them. She wanted to look into his eyes one more time. She would beat him still. She wanted to see the triumphant look ripped right off his face as the bullet slammed into her head. But he probably wouldn't be.

The coward.

The powered ram head hit the door once. It splintered, nearly gave way. With the second pop it did.

The door burst open.

The men rushed in.

Ellen Foster smiled at them and pulled the trigger.

Only nothing happened. She pulled the trigger once more. Then again. And a fourth time.

James Harkes strolled in, walked past the FBI agents arrayed around the woman, and stopped in front of her. He took the gun from her.

"You don't get the easy way out," he said.

She tottered in her heels. "You son of a bitch!"

She slapped him.

He didn't flinch. He just stood there, staring at her with contempt. She finally looked away.

"These men have something they need to tell you."

He stepped aside as they came forward, read off her rights, and cuffed her.

As they led her away, Harkes called out, "One more thing."

She turned to look at him.

He held up the gun. "You should've checked to make sure someone hadn't taken out the firing pin, *Madame Secretary*."

87

Sean looked down at the number on his phone. "It's Colonel Mayhew, from the Maine State Police. I phoned him earlier but he didn't pick up. I left a message for him to call me back."

Sean answered and explained things to the colonel.

Mayhew was understandably happy with the results. "You tell those people down in D.C. to make sure those bastards never see the light of day."

"I will, sir," said Sean with a grin.

"Damndest thing," said Mayhew. "Can't figure it."

"What's that?"

"Finished the autopsy on poor Eric."

Sean's stomach slightly tensed. "Gunshot wound, right?"

"Absolutely. No doubt of it. Right to the chest."

Sean relaxed. "So what's the problem?"

"Well, it was a .32 slug. Same type that killed Dukes and your friend Ted Bergin. But the really strange thing is it was a contact wound. I just can't figure how Eric could have let them get so close to him without getting off one shot. I mean—"

But Sean was no longer listening. He was running.

He was running not for his life. But for the life of the person he cared for above all others.

"Feel better?" asked Michelle, as Megan came into the room dressed in fresh clothes.

"The shower felt great. I think I'm halfway human again. And thanks for having my clothes sent here."

"No problem. After we failed you up in Maine it was the least we could do."

Michelle glanced out the window. In an SUV parked out front sat three FBI agents. There were two more in the rear yard of the safe house. For the first time in a long time she felt reasonably safe.

"Where's Edgar?" asked Megan.

"In the kitchen cooking."

"*Can* he cook?" asked Megan.

"That would be a definite yes. I'm sure you're hungry. I guess they didn't feed you much."

"Proverbial bread and water. I still can't believe I got out of there alive."

"It was complicated."

"I'll go see if I can help him. My mother always told me if I really wanted to get married I needed to know my way around a kitchen."

"Don't believe that for a minute."

Megan walked into the kitchen while Michelle,

always restless when no action was called for, simply paced.

On her second sweep around the room, her phone rang. It was Sean.

She started to answer, but never got there.

Blood spurted from the slash in her arm. It would have been her neck, but she had seen the knife an instant before it struck and flung out her arm. The blade cut skin, muscle, and tendon.

She dropped the phone, fell back, looked up and saw Edgar Roy coming at her again.

But then she realized he wasn't coming at *her*. He was throwing himself in front of her. No, at something else. At *someone* else.

He crashed into Megan Riley as she attempted to strike at Michelle again with the large kitchen knife. They fell together on the floor, large man on top of petite woman. It should have been over at that point.

But Megan Riley was obviously no ordinary woman.

She was, in fact, the fail-safe.

Roy groaned and rolled off her when her knee slammed into his privates. She was up in an instant and caught him with two crushing kicks to the head that flopped him over flat on his back. He lay there semiconscious, with blood pouring down his face from a deep gash in his skin.

She raised her knife for the killing blow but never got a chance to land it.

Michelle hit her with a kick to the knee. Only it wasn't a clean shot because as she was about to land it, she slipped in her blood, which was pooling on the hardwood floor.

Megan grimaced, glanced down at her injured limb, and then exploded forward on her good leg and smashed an elbow to Michelle's head, whipsawed around her opponent, and kicked her legs out from under her. Michelle fell hard, her head banging off the floor. She moved an instant before Megan slashed again with the knife. The blade punched into her thigh instead of her gut. Megan twisted the hilt sideways, and Michelle screamed as the blade ripped her flesh. She kicked away at the other woman and scrambled to her feet. The two women squared off, each favoring their injured wheel.

"I'm going to kill you," said Megan.

"No, you're going to try," Michelle shot back.

"You should have seen Bergin's eyes right before I shot him in the head. He looked as surprised as Carla Dukes did when I killed her."

"I'm not an old man. Or a big, slow woman."

Megan smiled wickedly. "Yeah, but you're also bleeding to death."

Megan made a couple of slashing motions with the knife but could not get through Michelle's defenses. Michelle grabbed up a floor lamp and twirled it in front of her like a nunchaku. She advanced as Megan fell back, outmaneuvered for the moment. But when

Megan leaped toward Roy with her knife held high, Michelle had to throw the lamp at her to defend him.

The brass neck of the lamp struck Megan across the face, cutting a deep gash in her cheek. Blood poured down her face. She fell sideways over Roy, but was on her feet a moment later, the knife held in front of her.

It was an instant too late.

Michelle's shoulder hit Megan in the gut, and both women torpedoed over a table and into the wall, popping holes in the drywall with the force of the impact.

Michelle, unfortunately, hit a stud in the wall, cracking her collarbone.

Sensing this injury, Megan landed a blow right on the damaged bone and Michelle slid backward, holding her shoulder and breathing heavily.

Both women slowly stood, each with a damaged leg, but Michelle had blood pouring out of two large wounds. She could feel her heart pumping harder and harder with each clench of the muscle, throwing more and more of her blood onto the floor with nothing to replace the loss.

She drew a quick breath. She didn't have much time left. She feinted a charge, and Megan stepped back. Michelle launched, aiming at Megan's knife-wielding arm.

But in her weakened state she arrived a second too late.

Megan flipped the knife to her left hand a moment

before impact. As the women fell backward Megan slammed the knife deeply into the other woman's back.

They hit the floor and Megan kicked Michelle off, rolled, and stood on a single wobbly leg.

Michelle tried to rise but then fell back to her knees. The knife was still in her. The blood now poured from three wounds, the last one in her back being the most damaging. She was seeing fuzzy images in front of her, and her breaths were becoming increasingly labored.

I'm dying.

She reached behind her, and with her last bit of strength she pulled the blade free.

She eyed Megan, her breaths coming in quick gasps.

"You're dead," taunted Megan.

"So are you, *bitch*," snarled Michelle, blood pooling in her mouth and garbling her words.

She threw the knife.

It missed badly and hit the wall, falling harmlessly to the floor.

As Michelle sat there helplessly on her haunches, her life rapidly draining away, Megan lined up the kill shot: an elbow strike to the back of Michelle's neck that would shatter her medulla and instantly end her life.

She leaped to deliver this final shot.

And Edgar Roy pivoted.

In his one-of-a-kind brain it was suddenly thirty years ago and Edgar Roy, then only six years old and the object of his father's sexual assault, pivoted. And struck. The man fell. The eyes turned glassy. The breathing ceased. The man died. Right there in the farmhouse kitchen.

Then, like an old black-and-white TV suddenly transformed to an HD flatscreen, the old images vanished and Roy was squarely returned to the present.

The six-foot-eight Edgar Roy slammed the kitchen knife he'd snatched off the floor into Megan Riley's torso with such force that the petite woman was lifted a foot off the floor. A moment later the staggering velocity of Roy's thrust catapulted Megan Riley violently against the wall. She struck it hard and slid down to the floor. She looked dumbly at the knife buried to the hilt in her heaving chest; the other end had cut her heart nearly in two. She attempted to pull it free. Her hands were around it. They gave one tug and then stopped. The fingers slipped off the handle. Her arms fell to her sides. Her head leaned against her shoulder. She gave one last shuddering breath.

And then she died.

Edgar Roy stood there for a few moments.

I *pivoted. My sister did not pivot. I* buried the knife into *my father. My sister did not. I* pivoted. I *killed the beast. I killed my father.*

His long-lost memory, his only such one, was finally back with him.

He rushed to Michelle's side and checked her pulse.

He couldn't find one.

The door burst open.

He turned to see Sean and his sister standing there.

"Please, help her," cried out Roy.

Sean raced forward. They had phoned for an ambulance on the way over, just in case.

It had been a good call.

The EMTs flooded into the room seconds later and started feverishly working on Michelle. It did not look good. Too many pints of her blood already lay spilled on the floor. They rushed her out on a stretcher, and Sean climbed into the ambulance right before the doors clunked shut.

The FBI agents started assessing what had happened inside the *safe house* that had turned out to be anything but.

Roy sat slumped against one wall. His sister knelt down next to him. As an agent came up to them she said, "Give us a minute, will you?"

The Fed nodded and backed off.

Roy glanced at the bloodied Riley, who sat dead against the other wall, the knife still sticking out of her. She looked like a large, ghoulish doll on display.

"I killed her," he told his sister.

"I know."

"She was trying to kill Michelle."

"I know that too, Eddie. You saved her life. You did the right thing."

He shook his head stubbornly. "We don't know that. She might still die."

"She might. But you gave her a chance."

He looked down, seemed as though he might be sick.

He looked up at her again. "I killed Dad."

She sat down beside him, took his head, and leaned it against her chest.

He said, "All this time I couldn't remember. I . . . I just thought you had done it. You've . . . always protected me."

"That time, Eddie, you defended yourself. And you saved me. You did the right thing. You did nothing wrong. Do you understand that?"

He didn't say anything.

"Eddie, do you understand that? You did nothing wrong." She said this last part with urgency.

"I understand." He swallowed a sob. "They took away my St. Michael's medal."

"I know. I can get you another one."

He glanced over at dead Megan. "I don't think I need it. Not anymore."

"I don't think you do, either."

He started to cry and his sister held him.

The melancholy sounds of the ambulance carrying the horribly injured Michelle Maxwell dwindled away until there was only silence.

88

The hospital room was colder than any morgue Sean had been in. It was dark, too. Most of the lights came from little machines that were making weird noises, signaling life or heralding approaching death.

He sat hunched over in the chair, his hands clasping hers, his forehead resting on the bed rail.

Michelle Maxwell was covered by a web of IV lines filled with things Sean had never heard of flowing into her body and carrying other things away.

She had died three times. Once in the ambulance. Once on the operating table. And once right here in this bed. She'd actually flat-lined while he was holding her hand. The Code Blue was sent out and the crash team hurtled in and did their magic, pulling her back from the grave while Sean had watched helplessly from the doorway.

The doctor told Sean, "That knife did a lot of damage. She almost bled out. But she's young and in incredible physical shape, otherwise she never would have made it this far."

"Will that be enough?" he'd asked. "To bring her all the way back?"

"We can only hope," the surgeon had said. "But frankly one more episode like that and we'll be hard-pressed to hold her."

And with that comment most of Sean's hope had evaporated.

He lifted his head when he heard them come in.

Kelly Paul was with her brother.

Edgar Roy's face still carried the wounds from his encounter with Megan Riley, or whatever her real name was. She was dead, that was all Sean cared about.

Paul drew close and stared at Michelle before touching Sean on the shoulder. "I'm sorry. It should never have happened."

"Things happen," said Sean in a low voice. "They happen all the time. Shitty things, to people trying to do the right thing." He eyed her brother. "And she wouldn't be here if it weren't for you. I owe you everything, Edgar, I really do."

"I owe the same to you, Mr. King," Roy said quietly.

Paul asked, "How is she doing?"

"Day to day, hour to hour, minute to minute. They can't tell me if she'll ever wake up. But I'll be here when she does."

He straightened and turned to look at her. "Quantrell and Foster?"

"Taking turns selling each other out. Even if the

prosecutors didn't have enough evidence before, they do now."

"Where'd they get the six bodies to plant in the barn?"

"From all over. People they knew were totally off the grid."

Paul leaned forward and took Sean's hand. "It was my mission to bring these people down, not hers. I accomplished the mission but I failed her. I failed both of you."

"I came here to basically say the same thing."

They all turned to find James Harkes in the doorway. He wore his black suit, white shirt, and black tie. His body was rigid, his features just as tight as his body. He moved forward to join them. He looked down at Michelle and then quickly glanced away.

"I thought we had every base covered," he said apologetically. "But we didn't."

Paul added, "Her real name wasn't Megan Riley, of course. It's not important who she was. She was Foster's fail-safe, one that nobody else knew about."

"Was she even a lawyer?" asked Sean.

"Yes, among many other things. That's why she was selected by Foster to work with Bergin."

"And she killed him?"

"Undoubtedly. We always thought it was someone he knew or else he wouldn't have pulled off the road like that. We knew there had been a phone call from Riley to Bergin that day. We just assumed she was in

Virginia. How she explained to him her coming to Maine I don't know."

"So she took out Bergin so she could be lead counsel and spy on us?" Sean said.

"Right," said Harkes. "And she killed Dukes because they couldn't trust her to go along with the extraction scheme."

"And of course she shot Eric Dobkin. That way she could be brought back in later as a Trojan horse. And it worked," Paul added ruefully.

"I had a gut feeling that Foster wasn't telling me everything," admitted Harkes. "She said Riley was her ace in the hole. I thought she meant as an innocent hostage. She obviously wasn't innocent or a hostage. Foster really outflanked me on that one." He grimaced and shook his head.

"Don't beat yourself up over it, Harkes," said Sean. "You did a good job. No, you did a great job."

"Frankly, it wasn't good enough." He paused and looked around the room. "Uncle Sam is footing the bill for all of this. She'll get the best care in the world, Sean. And from what I've seen of the lady she'll be up and kicking in doors before we know it."

"Thanks for saying that," said Sean.

Harkes slipped something from his pocket. "This is for you. For both of you." He handed the envelope to Sean.

"What is it?"

"Peter Bunting and Uncle Sam felt strongly that a

reward was in order for both of you. They contributed equally to the amount on that wire transfer receipt. The funds are already in your accounts."

"But we were just doing our job."

"No, actually, you two did a lot of *our* job," said Paul.

Harkes explained. "We knew something was off about the E-Program after a guy named Sohan Sharma failed the Wall and ended up dead. At first we suspected Bunting, but when we started digging deeper, things got a lot more complicated. When the bodies showed up at Eddie's house we called in Kelly. We knew she'd have every incentive to clear her brother's name and get to the truth. But we would never have gotten there without your help. And that's the God's honest truth."

When Sean saw the dollar amount on the slip of paper he gasped. He looked up at Harkes in disbelief. "This is way too much, Harkes."

The man shot another glance at Michelle in the bed. "No, Sean, it's not nearly enough."

"I'd like some of this to go to Eric Dobkin's widow," said Sean.

"You can do whatever you want with it," said Harkes. "You earned it."

After the three of them left Sean continued to sit by the bed. He planned to sit here until Michelle woke up or . . . Well, whatever happened, he would be there.

He gazed around the room. They'd been through so much together. A maniac from his past who had blown up his house. A serial killer that had very nearly finished them both off. A CIA rogue agent who thought torturing fellow Americans was an entirely legitimate exercise. And political leaders who thought they were above the law. During these times the only person he had really counted on was Michelle. She had saved him countless times. She had always been there for him. Their bond was like a million diamonds strung together and then sheathed in titanium, nothing stronger.

He sat back and listened to the machines keeping Michelle alive. She was young. She was strong. She had survived so much. She shouldn't lose her life because a traitor had literally stabbed her in the back. She just shouldn't.

He put his head on the cool bed rail and gripped her fingers with his. He would stay here until one of them stopped breathing.

I hope it's me.

Night turned to day. And day turned to night.

And Michelle still lay there.

And Sean still sat there.

The machines made their funny little noises.

Sean waited for a miracle.

The nurses and doctors came and went. They would look at him, smile, say some encouraging words, check Michelle's vitals and charts, and then scurry away.

Yet he knew that each day she didn't wake up lessened her chances of ever waking up at all.

Fluids pumped in and fluids pumped out.

The clock ticked.

The machines hummed and hissed.

The doctors and nurses came and went.

Sean sat. His fingers intertwined with hers.

He had imagined her suddenly rising up from the bed and smiling at him. Or him coming back from the bathroom to find her sitting in a chair reading a book. Or more likely, knowing her, performing push-ups and eating power bars and sucking down G2 by the quart. Occasionally he would dream that he would find her bed empty because she had passed, but he had mostly willed that thought away.

He lifted his head and looked at her. He blinked to clear his eyes.

He looked down at her hand. He looked at his. He shook his head and laid it back down on the rail.

That was the only reason he didn't see Michelle open her eyes.

"Sean?" she said in a voice that was crusty and weak from long disuse.

He lifted his head once more. His gaze met hers.

The tears came.

From both of them.

"I'm here, Michelle. I'm right here."

He had his miracle.

ACKNOWLEDGMENTS

To Michelle, Novel # 21, ready, load, launch! We did it again.

To Mitch Hoffman, my "Sixth Man."

To Emi Battaglia, Jennifer Romanello, Tom Maciag, Martha Otis, Chris Barba, Karen Torres, Anthony Goff, Kim Hoffman, Bob Castillo, Michele McGonigle, and all at Grand Central Publishing, who support me in every way.

To Aaron and Arleen Priest, Lucy Childs Baker, Lisa Erbach Vance, Nicole James, Frances Jalet-Miller, and John Richmond, for helping with everything from A to Z.

To Maja Thomas, for realizing long ago that ebooks are definitely for real.

To Maria Rejt, Trisha Jackson, and Katie James at Pan Macmillan, for helping me to roll in the UK.

To Steven Maat at Bruna for taking me to the top in Holland.

To Grace McQuade and Lynn Goldberg, for superb publicity.

To Bob Schule, for your eagle eye.

To Kelly Paul, I made your character really tall, which you're not, and also really smart and cool, which you definitely are.

To Eric Dobkin and Brandon Murdock, I hope you enjoy your namesakes' roles, and the various charities certainly benefited.

To the Harkes Family, for the use of your name and for being great friends.

To Lynette and Natasha, and you know why.

And a special thanks and welcome to Kristen White, as the newest member of the team.

extracts reading groups
competitions books new
discounts extracts extracts
competitions events
books new discounts
new events books
events extracts reading groups
new this reading groups
interviews new
events extracts events
discounts books
new books events interviews new books extracts
events new events reading groups
discounts extracts discounts books
www.panmacmillan.com
extracts events reading groups books
competitions books extracts new